THIS SIDE OF *Beautiful*

USA *TODAY* BESTSELLING AUTHOR

TIYE

Copyright © 2025 by Honey Magnolia Media

"Weightless" © 2025 Keisha Mennefee. All rights reserved. Used by permission of the author.

Cover design by Qamber Designs
Print book interior design by Qamber Designs

Honey Blossom Press
www.honeyblossom.press
@honeyblossompress

ISBNs: 9798990781788 (trade paperback), 9798990781795 (ebook)
Printed in the United States of America

HONEY BLOSSOM PRESS

Dear Reader,

This is a story about strength, redemption, and discovering beauty in the broken pieces. The characters you're about to meet are unapologetically honest, imperfect, and deeply human, navigating truths that reflect the realities of pain, triumph, and love in its many forms.

At times, their journey — reflected in language and situations — is both unfiltered and emotionally raw, a reminder that growth is rarely neat, and healing isn't always linear, but both are always worth the fight.

And for those who may identify with the more complicated sides of the characters, I strongly encourage you to take care of yourself first. If that means you step away from the book, breathe, and reflect on all that's light and rise above the shadows, or reach out to a family member, friend, or mental health professional (using any resources provided in the back of the book, if needed), I recommend you do so.

My hope is that you'll find a little bit of yourself in their struggles, their victories, and the love they learn to give themselves and others. My hope is that you'll remember that even in the depths of despair, a phoenix rises, a rose breaks through the concrete, and the sun peeks through the gray clouds.

And like the characters you'll meet in this story, you'll feel seen and embraced exactly as you are.

Thank you for opening yourself to this story.

Always,
Tiye

CHAPTER ONE

janae

**HOUSTON
MARCH 7**

BREATHE. BREATHE. JUST FUCKING BREATHE.

I clenched my fists so tight my nails dug into my palms. The reflections of people walking past behind me and smiling, laughing, chatting it up with family, friends, and lovers on a Thursday night only emphasized my utter aloneness. Why was it so hard to return to the living?

Why is it so hard to step inside?

If I wanted my career back, this was part of it. Pushing through. Alone. Always alone. The drugs, the alcohol, the parties, the random sex, and worst of all, my nerves. They almost killed me. Almost. But for the grace of God, no diseases, no unwanted pregnancies. Just scars. Too many scars.

MILA wouldn't have hesitated. MILA didn't freeze.

I was born Janae Camille Warner, but MILA was the girl the world knew. I once wore the abbreviated play on my middle name, pronounced *MEE-lah*, like a crown, something powerful, untouchable. Now the double syllables felt like a demon whispering at the edges of my mind.

A demon I fought daily to rebuke.

I stepped back from the doors, my rhinestone-covered cowboy boots scraping against the pavement. Cars honked, headlights flashed, drivers cursed, and the city's rhythm roared around me. The noise matched the storm in my head, loud and relentless. I rubbed the engraved rose-gold coin I wore on a chain, letting its cool weight ground me. A tether before I floated away.

Maybe I could skip this. No one would care because no one even knew I was here. *Go back to the hotel, Janae. Order some room service. Watch something mindless.* Yeah.

No.

No, no, no.

The voice in my head was crueler now, laughing at my hesitation. *Coward. Loser. You're not MILA. You're not even Janae. You're nothing. Just go home, you crazy bitch. Just go.*

I didn't have to be here. No one was expecting me. No one would miss me. The cameras for my reality show wouldn't roll until tomorrow morning, marking the start of my comeback. Then I wouldn't be alone. My makeup artist, stylist, manager, and crew would orbit me all weekend, filling the empty spaces. Maybe this time, I'd build real friendships with the people in my corner. Maybe I could get through a performance without the crutch of a high. Maybe I could finally shake this loneliness that clung to me like a second skin. Maybe I could find love again.

Where did that thought come from? Love had never been on my side. No family. No friends. No man. Just me, *always me.* So why the hell did I keep hoping, wishing, and praying like some starry-eyed kid who should've known better?

I scanned the street, desperate for an escape. For any car to take me back to the hotel. Then I froze. An Uber had dropped me off, a reminder of where I stood now. No private driver, no entourage, just me, budgeting my own damn money for the weekend. Once, I'd been a hip-hop princess worth millions. Now, I was catching ride shares like anybody else.

What a fucking joke.

I hated my mind. The way it never shut up, never let me breathe. My thoughts ran wild, unraveling, all because I'd made the mistake of leaving the safety of my penthouse suite. At least there, no one could hurt me. At least there, I could sink into hours of meaningless distractions, let the glow of the screen numb me. But here? Here, I was at war with myself, my own worst enemy.

People strolled through those doors like it was nothing, dressed to impress, laughing, belonging. I couldn't even put one foot in front of the other.

Why had I done this to myself? A gala full of Black folks in my hometown, and I was showing up alone. It felt like prom all over again, except this time, I wasn't just the girl without a date. I was the girl without anyone.

Voices sounded nearby. More people walked past me, and I pulled my black Stetson down, covering my brows. I didn't want to be recognized yet, especially looking like a maniac, pacing in front of the convention center on a busy street in Houston.

The last thing I needed was more noise. More whispers, more assumptions that I was still that pill-popping, drunken mess I used to be. That I still was a lost cause. If I wanted people to see the real Janae Warner, I had to show up as myself.

But who was that?

Did I have to be *Janae Warner* to be seen at all? And if so, what did that even mean? A has-been? A ghost of the girl I used to be? Another artist chewed up and spit out by the industry before thirty, fading from the charts like I was never there at all?

"Ugh," I groaned aloud in frustration. "Just open the door and walk in. Show your face, pretend you're that girl everyone loved, and go back to the hotel and crash. Simple. No more than thirty minutes... an hour at the most. Make your rounds. Speak to Del. Take selfies with the entertainment and fans. Pretend like you have another event to hit before the night is over. It's the rodeo in Houston. There's always some party popping off somewhere. I can easily sell it."

"Did you say something?" a woman asked.

Not realizing I'd been talking aloud, I shrank farther inside myself and moved my shoulder to block my face. She walked past with her date, her gait suggesting she'd already indulged. Probably alcohol. For a flash, I envied her. And not for the fine-as-hell man on her arm who smiled flirtatiously at me. The longer I paced outside on this busy downtown street, the more I looked

3

even crazier than I felt. I checked my phone again. There was no word from Dr. K or *my ex.*

They'd lied and said they would be here for me when needed. Now, I needed their comforting guidance, and neither had answered their phone or responded to my frantic texts for help. I had to do something to settle myself as more people walked inside the doors wearing expectant smiles and cowboy hats.

Purpose. I had to have a reason for standing outside and talking to myself like the crazy person I felt most days. Okay. I couldn't keep calling myself crazy… maybe unbalanced was a better description.

Does that really sound better?

Or should I just call it what it is?

Except that wouldn't feel any better.

People don't know what it's like when your mind won't slow down for days, when you're wired at three a.m. with a million ideas that all feel like genius. Or when the world dulls overnight, and suddenly every step feels like moving through wet concrete.

When it's not just being up or down. It's being at war with yourself.

The air felt too thick, pressing down on me. My breaths came shallow and quick, my pulse pounding in my ears. I needed something. Someone. Anything.

Instead, I lifted my phone higher and turned on the camera.

Pretend. Pretend you're live. Pretend you're okay.

The oval face staring back at me wasn't wild or crazed, no matter what the voice in my head whispered. My honeyed brown skin was smooth, my lips glossed, my eyes dark and wide. Only I could see the storm brewing beneath. The deep burgundy barrel-curled waves of my wig framed my face, bold and defiant like armor.

I forced a smile. Wide. *Girl-next-door* wide. The kind that had disarmed teachers when I was a kid, softened angry producers when I was late, charmed interviewers when I was high. I'd had hits. Multi-platinum hits. I'd grown up in this city, not one known for music, yet it had produced Beyoncé, Meg Thee Stallion, Bobby "Blue" Bland, Paul Wall, ZZ Top, Bun B, and my personal fave, Geto Boys. H-Town both haunted and inspired me.

4

I used to *run* this town.

And I would again.

I lifted my chin. *Yep. I'm that queen.*

"You've got this," I whispered to my reflection. "You've got this."

I clicked record.

"I see you," I said to myself, my voice low and steady, even though my heart thundered. "You deserve this. All that noise in your head? That's just trolls. Trolls who never thought you'd make it. Trolls who don't matter. But you do. You're here. You're going to walk through those doors and show them exactly who you are. You can have it all. Being on top again is just around the bend."

I jabbed at my reflection like I was reaching through the screen, shaking myself awake.

"You *can* and you *will* walk into this party solo. No entourage. No crew. No man. And you will *not* fall apart. Three years sober. Three years of work. You're ready. *You* are Janae. The dopest baddie making a grand entrance. You don't need anyone but yourself."

That's all you've ever really had anyway.

I pushed out a slow exhale and drew in a deeper breath, steadying the thrum in my chest. The wildness in my eyes shrank into a glint, the fear settling just beneath the surface but no longer controlling me.

I clicked stop, slid my phone into my bag, and tilted my hat. Squaring my shoulders, I gripped one of the massive double doors of the convention center and pulled it open, ready to step inside. Clad in a vintage, all-black tailored pantsuit, I let my newfound confidence and just enough cleavage lead the way.

This wasn't about applause. Wasn't about cameras or fans or the industry.

This was about me.

I exhaled again, slower this time. My pulse still raced, but the storm inside me quieted just enough.

I could do this.

I had to.

My courage blew away a few seconds later when I stepped into the huge ballroom and observed the dimly lit banquet setup. I'd imagined more of a dark, crowded club scene with people dancing or milling around so that my solo appearance didn't seem so… well, lonely. Most of the denim- and diamond-clad guests sat at western-themed decorated tables that filled every corner of the room, sans a small dance area in front of a live band and DJ booth. Guests hugged, laughed, and greeted each other like they were at a family reunion. The waitstaff, dressed in black and white, smiled as they served guests hors d'oeuvres and champagne.

I checked my pulse on my laced-out smartwatch. One thirty-five was too high. I took long breaths, trying to decrease my heart rate. I closed my eyes briefly and murmured, "Just stay on the edge so if you have to run, you can."

As a waiter passed by, I grabbed some stuffed mushrooms on a small plate. I needed to keep my hands occupied as I scanned the crowd, hoping to see Del, my manager, or a familiar, friendly face from my past in the music business. I chomped on the tasty morsel as I strolled on the periphery of the ballroom. Del had said he would sit near the front at a table for the performers and guests if I decided to show up.

The guests radiated excitement, eager to attend one of the premier events for Houston's Black elite. Black cowboys and the rodeo had been a part of Texas history for generations. Enslaved Black men had been among the first wranglers called "cowboys," a term that had nothing to do with the rugged mythos of the Wild West and everything to do with their servitude. Not to be confused with "cowhands," they were the backbone of an industry that would later erase them from its narrative. After emancipation, many of these skilled Black men became some of the most respected and capable cowboys in the West, even as history tried to erase them.

As a Houston native, I understood the importance of celebrating our place in spaces that had once shut us out. This gala, the crown jewel of Black Heritage Night at the rodeo, was an annual tradition, an honor to attend. And tomorrow, I would take the stage as a surprise guest of headliner Cash Black.

The joy was palpable with smiles, laughter, and a sense of homecoming woven through the room. But as I stood on the periphery, all I felt was loneliness as their excitement evoked my sadness.

I'd never imagined that if I were ever asked to perform at the rodeo, a place I'd gone to countless times as a child, I'd be here alone. No mother or brother in the crowd, beaming with pride, shouting that I'd made it. No ex, no man on my arm, whispering how proud he was of me.

I'd pictured Adam Temple, the retired NFL player I'd spent four years loving, standing beside me, sharing in the moment. But I'd burned that bridge to the ground long ago.

Now, on the eve of what should've been a momentous night, the only person I had in my corner was my manager of six months. A man who had sought *me* out after I posted a video of myself singing Lauryn Hill's "*Ex-Factor*" on IG — my mother's favorite song. A moment of nostalgia that went viral. A moment that led to this.

Del saw something in me. Maybe something real, maybe something profitable. I wasn't sure yet.

Both my last manager and my record label had unceremoniously dumped me after my final scandal, an affair with a married music producer. His wife? A beloved singer with a fanbase ten times more loyal and rabid than mine. I had been the villain in that story, and the industry had washed its hands of me.

Now, I was here, clawing my way back, trying to be seen as something other than a mistake.

I needed to find Del. I fumbled in my purse for my phone, distracted, gripping the tiny saucer in my other hand when someone bumped into me.

Everything fell. My plate and my purse crashing to the floor. My hand shot out to grab something, anything, to steady myself, and landed on the edge of a nearby table. A glass of water tipped over, drenching the bodice of the woman seated there.

She gasped, pushing back her chair, eyes wide with irritation.

"Sorry… sorry," I stammered, struggling to regain my balance. But the room had started to spin.

Oh no. Not now. Not here.

I braced myself against the table, forcing deep breaths. *I can do this. I can do this.*

"Aren't you that rapper?" a voice piped up from the table.

I blinked, vision swimming. My heart thundered in my ears, drowning out the voices around me. My knees felt like liquid. *Find something to focus on. Find something.*

"Are you okay?" Another voice. I couldn't tell whom it belonged to.

A phone appeared in my face. A young man holding up his fingers in a peace sign, grinning at the screen, angling for a selfie.

I recoiled, my breath catching in my throat as I caught my reflection in his phone. Wild eyes, lips slightly parted, panic written all over my face.

I shook my head and backed away, mumbling, "Sorry."

The young man bent down, scooping up my purse. He held it out to me hesitantly. "Are you okay, MILA?"

Not my name.

That name was dead. That name had been my destruction.

Hearing it now only made my chest tighten further.

Coming here had been a mistake.

This night was for family. For friends. I had neither.

The walls felt like they were closing in, the music too loud, the lights too bright. I needed air. My breath was coming too fast, too shallow, my chest caving in.

Thump. Thump. Thump. My heart slowed, dragging me down with it.

"Sorry," the boy muttered, stepping back.

The woman in the soaked dress waved him off. "Leave her alone. She don't want to be bothered, whoever she is."

Whoever she is.

Didn't even recognize me.

Maybe that was better. Maybe it was worse.

Breathe. Breathe.

I can't. I can't.

Breathe.

I don't belong here. I don't belong anywhere. I have to go. Right. Now.

I turned, ready to run, but smacked into a hard chest.

Strong hands caught mine, grounding me.

I blinked up, stunned by the warmth of his grip before my vision settled on the striking face staring down at me.

Arresting hazel eyes. Smooth caramel skin with hints of toffee and features carrying the traces of a blended African and Asian heritage. Maybe Indigenous. Perhaps not his parents. Somewhere down the line, he carried his ancestor's defined cheekbones, Nubian nose, and lips that pouted naturally. His hat wasn't quite like the others at the gala, and even in my heels, he towered over me. His chambray shirt was loose, but the way he held me — firm and steady — told me he was strong.

For the first time in minutes, my mind slowed.

The noise in my head quieted.

I could breathe.

He was the object that settled me.

"Janae?" His deep voice held familiarity, curiosity, recognition.

This beautiful stranger *knew* me?

I searched my mind, desperate to place him.

His hands were still wrapped around mine, like he *knew* I was on the verge of falling apart.

Like he didn't want to let go.

And for some unexplainable reason, I didn't want him to either.

CHAPTER TWO
landon

ONE. TWO. *THREE*. FOUR. FIVE. *Six.* Se-ven. *Eight.*

I bopped my head and tapped my thigh to the constant rhythm of my mind while I leaned on our leased Range Rover, watching well-dressed people and musicians I'd seen around the circuits walk through the doors of the Brown Convention Center. Some we'd played for in the studio, some we'd backed up on the stage, and others we would never entertain. At least, that was what Cedrick, my co-founder of The Hollow Bones, boasted. He and I had started our band as teenagers, and we'd gone further than our wildest dreams. My tendency to get lost in the music made it easier for him to speak for the band and specifically for me in my bumbling moments, though I'd long been considered the leader. My quiet strength and impeccable skills on the guitar and the legacy of my musician parents deemed it so. Cedrick had been the first person who'd only noticed what I could do and not what kept me on the fringes when people gathered.

My observant gaze zeroed in on a maroon-haired woman, probably wearing a wig, standing outside the convention center with a black cowboy hat that matched her black fitted pantsuit. She was petite, and without the widening of her hips and round ass, she could've passed for a young girl. The glitter-heeled boots broke the monotonous black. I hated that I couldn't see her face or even her profile. She'd been standing near the doors, wringing her hands, and from the movement of her head, she seemed to be talking to herself for way too long. Was she frustratedly waiting for someone before going inside? She dipped her head in a move I recognized as embarrassment when a couple walked past her to enter the doors.

Curiously, I observed her, wondering if we were kindred souls and if it were even possible to find someone like me. Watching. Waiting. Always hoping that no one noticed me. Was she a musician or a singer? Or maybe she was an invited guest of committee members and their friends and families, like me. And she dreaded going inside, like me, though it was my job.

Then the woman pulled out her phone and started talking, probably for her socials. Even from there, I could see she'd relaxed, and the spell had been broken. We were not kindred souls. She would never understand why I preferred solitude over people. Unreasonably, a stab of disappointment struck me. I shifted my thoughts to the familiar and resumed tapping my thigh to the constant rhythm in my head.

Despite an affluent upbringing in Brooklyn Heights, at sixteen, already a high school graduate, I'd been on my own struggling to make small change from playing my guitar on the streets of New York City and YouTube showcase videos. Until Cedrick Thomas, a pianist, only a year older than I was, messaged me. The rest, as they say, is history.

Cedrick and the rest of the band, Brian, Santiago, and Charles, had been inside the gala for probably an hour. I would eventually show my face, supporting my chosen family, Hollow Bones. I hated those parties. All parties, to be frank. Being social took far more energy than my brain had the capacity for. I never felt more alone or overwhelmed than in a crowd. The need to escape kept me from ever attending a sporting event or a concert in a stadium. Hats and my guitar were to me like Linus's blanket was to him. When I couldn't carry my guitar on my back, I didn't know how to fit my square piece in the circle of normalcy.

Cedrick understood me, and as we'd carefully curated the rest of the band, musical genius by musical genius, he'd made sure they understood and accepted my eccentricities as well.

I tilted back my straw pork pie hat, my version of a cowboy hat, in honor of my first time performing at the rodeo and to fit the theme of tonight's Black Heritage Gala of Glitz and Hats.

I'd only passed through Houston for a gig or two and didn't know much about this city beyond oil fields, NASA, and Beyoncé. We'd been asked to perform two nights of the twenty-one-day-long event, and the band had decided to lease a home in the suburbs of Sugarland for a few days before to have the freedom to rehearse and practice for the show and our upcoming album. Our second album had vexed us creatively and artistically after our debut release three years ago broke records and amassed numerous awards, including two Grammys. More money and more fame followed. Yet we still glided underneath the radar as an unrecognizable band until we were together on stage.

Cedrick believed we were stunted out of fear of the sophomore jinx. I begged to differ. We were at a fork in the road and had to become a commercially successful or artistically grounded band. Unfortunately, rarely did the two meet, but when they did, those records were timeless. Think *The Miseducation of Lauryn Hill*, *Off the Wall*, or The Beatles' last album, *Abbey Road*.

Winning awards hadn't shifted the needle of my dreams as it had for Cedrick and the rest of the fellas. I'd never cared about fame or fortune. I didn't require much. A place to lay my head and food to sustain my energy. I didn't believe I'd ever marry or have a family, so more would be unnecessary. I couldn't imagine a woman putting up with my simplicity when I had the money for complicated. Or be patient with my habits and my need to control my immediate environment. Or my obsession with any and everything music. Besides, women were still strangely foreign creatures to me. Their hypocrisies and beauty confounded me, especially my Juilliard-trained mother, Annalise, whose love for music and image kept her tethered to my equally brilliant yet deeply flawed father, Brandon Barrett Hayes.

My cell buzzed. I slid it out of the pocket of my dark slacks.

Dude, where are you? Everyone's asking about you. No one cares about Hollow Bones without Landon Hayes.

I shook my head. Cedrick still believed gaslighting me worked. I replied,

Give me a few. Catching a vibe.

Of what? You're standing outside the convention center in Houston.

The beauty of being a proud, card-carrying member of the introvert club was my ability to observe the world around me unobtrusively. Despite my height, my quiet presence allowed me to fade into the background like I had the power of invisibility. Cedrick would never notice the small, vibrant, green-lawned park across from the convention center, partially blocked by public buses and the luxury cars of celebrities like myself parked in the VIP section. He wouldn't notice the faint sounds of the trumpet played by a street musician for his keep or for potential fame. The teenagers stretched out on blankets on the cool March evening. Some parents were on their cells while their children enjoyed playing after a day at school, or maybe it was already spring break here. Or the people strolling down the busy sidewalk heading to dinner at any of the surrounding chain and original restaurants, or maybe going back to their hotel. Some were gawking at the spectacle of gorgeous Black people in dressy Western attire, ranging from denim dresses and suits to more formal dresses and tuxes. All were rocking cowboy hats as they entered the convention center.

My cell rang.

"I'm coming," I answered, and hung up in the same second.

I looked both ways to cross the street and noticed the woman had gone inside.

When the cool, manufactured air hit me and the sounds of loud music and noisy chatter assailed my ears, the gnawing started, and I faltered. *Become invisible and move through the crowds until you get to your table near the front.*

I inhaled. My lungs expanded, and I slowly blew the air out like I held a sax to my lips. I moved through the entrance, intent on keeping the approaching anxiousness at bay. Until someone ran into me.

I grabbed her hands out of reflex and stared at the maroon-haired woman I'd only watched a few minutes ago. The axis shifted when her fearful eyes met mine.

"Janae?"

Recognition flickered in her widened eyes and then became questioning. She didn't remember me, though we'd worked together a handful of times before she dropped off the face of the Earth. She'd just signed a contract to do ten shows with Hollow Bones after much negotiation with Del, the manager we now shared. Cedrick and I didn't want the drama of a diva on our brief tour, only conceding after reviewing her near-incomparable talent during past performances. We didn't want the fiery mess that usually trailed behind MILA. Del had promised us she was a changed woman now, and only wanted to be known as Janae Warner.

As I stared down into her pixie-like face, it was clear I had left no impression on her. In contrast, my thoughts had been unwittingly consumed by her natural musicality and undeniable mocha beauty since she'd been reintroduced into my life.

"Yes." Her forehead puckered as she searched my face. "Excuse me, I didn't mean to bump into you. Good to see you again."

Wow. She didn't remember me at all. Disappointment replaced my initial concern for her wellbeing. Janae's hands were trembling, cold, and clammy. I'd thought she might have been anxious or scared. Now, I wondered if something else had caused her to bolt.

"Hollow Bones," I reminded her, and when she still seemed unsure of who I was, I tersely added, "You know, the band backing you and Cash Black tomorrow night. The band that's touring with you for ten more shows after tomorrow night. That Hollow Bones."

"I wondered if you were here." She nodded with a smile that brightened her face. The dusting of freckles across her nose and cheeks became apparent. "Where are you sitting?"

"Near the front." I was purposely vague as I dropped her hands. "We worked together on more than one occasion, remember?"

"Yep... we did." Her eyes darted from my face to her surroundings before she touched her hat and tilted her head. "Of course I remember you."

This woman is so full of shit. I folded my arms and raised a brow, daring her to know the answer. "What's my name?"

She giggled self-consciously while she toyed with my shirt. "I know who you are. It's just that I've greeted and met so many people tonight. The names are jumbled in my head."

I scanned the room before asking, "What people? You just walked in, and if I'm not mistaken, it looked like you were about to leave."

"Can you give me a break? I'm not quite myself," she muttered, no longer able to look at me.

Mad at myself for letting her invade my thoughts when I'd made no impression on her, I snapped, "No, I can't. At the bare minimum, you should remember my damn name. I had to give the final okay for you to perform with us tomorrow night."

"Cash Black did that." She lifted her head haughtily. "Don't change the narrative to prove a point. You don't have that kind of power."

"I have no reason to lie. *We* were the invited headliners, and Del and Cash Black asked for you. We didn't. We're not the inconsequential band that you can discard and drop on a whim like you did before." It took a lot to get a rise out of me. And the more she spoke, the more my pulse pounded. She thought she was better than us.

"Did you follow me to brag about Hollow Bones? Put me in my place?" She pointed her finger at me. "Very convenient that the moment I turn around, you're waiting to pounce."

I bit back my urge to raise my voice. "You weren't watching where you were going. I was actually concerned. I only got mad when you couldn't bother to learn my name." Her body trembled while I held her hands. "Are you high or something? You're all jittery."

"No. I'm not," Janae said firmly as she touched a coin that nestled on her chest. A coin I recognized as proof of sobriety. My father had one that he no longer carried.

We locked eyes, and I saw the earnestness in her almond-shaped ones. I relented. "Make sure it stays that way. Or I'll drop you from the tour."

"We don't have to do shit together," she retorted.

For some insane reason, her stubborn attitude appealed to me, or maybe it was her flowery scent. I wanted to grab and kiss her.

Instead, I shoved my hands in my pockets and hurled more words at her. "You're right, we don't. Thanks for reminding me why I didn't want to work with your flaky ass in the first place. You cost us money the last time we were foolish enough to work with you."

Janae's arched brows gathered so deeply that I braced for whatever insult she planned to spew. She had a mouth on her and had no problem using it. She could cut a person with her words. I'd witnessed her verbal abuse in the studio about four years ago, when she yelled at one of the background singers who started off in the wrong key. And I'd watched the videos of her going off at the media when they questioned her wild behavior with married and taken men.

A man brushed up against her on his way to a table, and I reached out to steady her without thought. The alluring scent of her perfume caressed my nose, and I quickly dropped my hands when she looked over her shoulders and then back at me. The scowl disappeared, and her shoulders drooped.

"Look at me." She unflinchingly stared, moving so close to me that I leaned away to see her face. "I'm not the same MILA. I'm just Janae."

The determination in her chin and the softness in her eyes unsettled me. I had to look away before I became entrapped in her web. Still doubtful I could trust her, I asked, "Are you sure? Not bothering to know the names of the people you'll be working and traveling with seems like MILA to me."

"The old Janae wouldn't explain shit to you." The unexpected feel of her hand on my arm scorched me, and I had to maintain my attention on the people behind her to focus on her words. "Everything happened so fast. Del reached out to me, telling me he believed in me and wanted to work with me six months ago. He told me about you and Hollow Bones and already had dates set before talking to me a couple of weeks ago. I needed the gigs, so I went with the flow. Hell, he could've told me I was going on tour with Elmo, and I would've jumped at the chance."

Her genuine humor slipped past my guarded heart, which was already becoming unhinged by her beauty and talent.

"But he offered me the opportunity of a lifetime because I love your music, and I want another chance. Can we start over?" She begged with those soulful, pretty eyes that could change between seductive and innocent with a blink.

I gazed down into her alluring face. "Say my name, and I'll think about it."

Janae's eyes darkened, and she seemed drawn to me the way I'd been since I'd caught her hands.

"Landon?" An unrecognizable woman's voice from my right side called my name, and Janae grinned victoriously.

I didn't look away from her, hoping the woman would get the hint that she'd interrupted something.

"I was beginning to think that Cedrick lied when he said you were here. I've been waiting for this moment for so long. I've been following Hollow Bones for years."

"Hey, Mr. Landon Hayes. Good to see you again." Janae gave me an impish smile, and I couldn't tell if she'd known my name all along or if she'd figured out the rest. She shimmied her shoulders. "I guess we're starting over."

I didn't want our conversation to end now that I knew she recognized me and was possibly attracted to me. Janae moved slightly from one foot to the other, watching me as I was pulled into an unwanted embrace by my fan, the chairwoman of the entertainment committee. She held tight like I was her favorite pillow, and I limply responded. I wasn't the hugging type at all, which this woman didn't get as she squeezed me. In my mind, I pleaded with a now-smirking Janae to rescue me.

As politely as I could, I pulled back and pushed down the chairwoman's arms. "You'll have to excuse me. We were discussing tomorrow's show. I was in the middle of talking to—"

"No… no… You go ahead… *Landon Hayes*." Janae started backing away as I shook my head. "*Landon Hayes*, we'll chop it up later. I see your hands are full, *Landon Hayes*." She gave me an exaggerated wink and added an extra sway to her hips as she turned around.

"Hey. We still need to talk about tomorrow." I hated that my voice squeaked as I called after her. "Janae?"

I only saw the back of her hand as she waved before she pulled down her jacket and tilted her hat. The arrogant, sexy woman I remembered flashed through my mind. She'd tricked me into believing she was different.

The floral scent of her perfume remained in my olfactory senses long after she walked away triumphantly, leaving me alone with a woman whom I would have to be nice and respectful to because of her position in choosing Hollow Bones to perform on the rodeo's biggest night.

I sipped crisp water in an iced tea glass, quietly observing her. She'd been standing most of the night, talking and flirting with people at the tables around us. Despite how her career had tanked because of her own recklessness, she still had fans. Smiling people surrounded her to take selfies and ask for autographs. Some of the entertainers even seemed fascinated by her. Janae glowed, and her brown skin shimmered in the changing lights from the nearby stage.

I noted that she only drank water and shook her head when offered wine, champagne, or a cocktail. Del had sworn she'd been clean and sober for three years, and so far, she did seem determined to maintain her sobriety. She touched that coin around her neck every so often, the same way I rubbed the guitar pick I kept in my pocket. *Is it for the same reason?*

"Stop staring, or I might believe you're crushing," Cedrick drawled before he eased down in the chair he'd vacated earlier to mingle. The other three members of Hollow Bones were wandering the room, greeting guests and talent.

"Curious… not crushing." Dragging my unwilling gaze from Janae, I glanced at my best friend, who easily drew women to him with his dark looks and swagger. "I've never seen her this chill. She was always so high-strung, feisty, and crass."

"*High* being the operative word. Let's hope she stays this way through our shows." He smirked as he downed another cognac. "I guess we should be relieved that people still like her so far. Sales have been rising since we added Janae to the shows. Del might be onto something, suggesting she be Cash's special guest tomorrow night. Can you imagine how lit the arena will be when she walks on stage after three years, in her hometown?"

"Yeah." I refocused on Janae, who now laughed and touched the chest of Cash Black, an Atlanta rapper who'd risen to the top fast with two back-to-back crossover hits. He was in his mid-twenties and had bravado, an edge, and fearlessness that women loved. A platinum grill covered his teeth, and his locs hung down past his shoulders. He possessively gripped the small of Janae's back, his pinky finger grazing her ass. My stomach unexpectedly burned, and I looked away.

Cedrick chuckled. "Now I know why Cash had no problem with MILA being his special guest. They must be smashing, or he's using this opportunity to shoot his shot."

"She's Janae now," I corrected him.

He shrugged before he wiped his mouth with a napkin.

I slumped back in my chair, inexplicably bothered by Cedrick's astute observation. "How much longer do we need to be here?"

"Eat and settle your brain. We need to be here another hour to show our gratitude for being invited." He pushed his barely touched plate of brisket and mac and cheese toward me. Cedrick had recently become a vegan and had been tempted by the Southern comfort food since we'd arrived two days ago. He had to remind himself that he'd given up meat for health reasons while the rest of us happily consumed Texas beef in all its forms.

"How much longer?" I repeated, ignoring the offered plate of food but not missing how the barbecue sauce bled into the cheese.

He briefly closed his eyes. "Just go. I'll cover for you if anyone else asks about you."

"Thanks." We pounded fists, and I maneuvered through the small crowd, waiting to see Cash and Janae, careful to keep my head down and not to catch anyone's eye. I had no more energy to hug, take a selfie, or smile.

"Y'all, that's the hugely talented Landon Hayes of The Hollow Bones." Janae's Southern twang rose above the din of the music and chatter. "Come here and take a pic with us."

"No. I'm good," I replied loudly, narrowing my eyes.

She pushed through the small space between us and grabbed my forearm, pulling me next to Cash, who dapped me and smiled. "I didn't know you were here. Where you been hiding?"

"He was sitting over there, staring." She grinned at me. Her eyes twinkled with devilish mischief. "Figured he may want front-row access, since it's Cash Black and The Hollow Bones hitting the stage tomorrow night."

The small crowd cheered. I nodded and didn't focus on any particular person. I didn't have my guitar or anything to hide behind in this space. Beads of sweat rolled down my back, and my chest wouldn't inflate. I weakly waved before shoving my trembling hands in my pants and looked back at Janae, whose smile slipped.

Her arm curved around my waist. "Landon hates all the attention. He's really shy."

Some of the people *aww*ed me.

"Take your pics quickly before this Black man curses me out, and I don't want no drama with him." Janae chuckled.

The crowd laughed, and I breathed through my nose for a few pictures while she gently rubbed my back, much like my mother used to do when my environment became too much.

"All right… all right. He's done." Janae pushed me slightly, and with relief, I walked away, giving people just enough eye contact to seem normal. I didn't breathe until I'd stepped back out into the spring air.

I lifted my head to the stars and beyond, inhaling the sky's vastness and exhaling the dust storm of emotions evoked by one Janae Warner.

And we were just getting started.

CHAPTER THREE

janae

MARCH 8

AFTER A SUCCESSFUL SHOWING AT the gala last night, I was feeling myself. I'd stayed until the event was almost over because fans wanted to talk, take selfies, and tell me they still loved and supported me. My decision to attend was the best I had made in a very long time. The most important part was that no one, except for the stage production crew, knew that I was slated to perform. The reception at the gala eased my nerves on what to expect tonight.

I'd slept in and had a fantastic breakfast with my new team and the two cameramen following me on my journey back to the top. Del was the executive producer of the reality series that would begin airing a month after my last show, which would be in L.A., where I'd lived for the past seven years.

We'd finally made it to the dressing room of the smaller arena where rehearsal would take place. Tonight, we would be at the much larger stadium. The cameras were on and would remain filming until I needed privacy to change or when I had any personal time with people who hadn't approved of being recorded.

GloRilla blasted while I readied for the rehearsal. Her similar brand of bravado and femininity always pumped me up.

"Thank God for a traveling glam squad." I smiled as Frankie, the hair and makeup artist, applied my face, and Jeri, my stylist, reviewed my attire for the day. Three very different fits. A cropped hoodie and camouflage cargo pants for the rehearsal. A sparkly red pantsuit that fit like a second skin with a pearl-white Stetson for the show. A flowy, thin, yellow-strapped dress that barely draped my thighs for the after-party. And I'd be rocking a long red wig for rehearsal and the performance. I would be more subdued and sexy, slicking my hair back for the after-party.

"Are you sure you don't want a variation on the red wig for the after-party? Maybe a short cut or a bob?" Frankie asked. She was a thirty-year-old, no-nonsense woman whom I'd clicked with during our interview via Zoom. She was professional yet friendly. I secretly hoped that we could be friends, too. Dr. K had told me I had to stop seeing women as the enemy if I wanted to develop stronger relationships with others. "I'll probably wear the hat again, which is hot enough without a wig." I checked my face in the mirror. "Girl, you're talented. I almost don't recognize myself."

Del rushed into the staging area, dressed in his customary tailored suit with a cell permanently attached to his ear. He constantly frowned as if he expected only trouble, though he usually believed in the best of his clients. "Janae, we have little time to do the rehearsal. You were supposed to be on stage an hour ago."

"Cash is the only guest for The Hollow Bones, and I don't come on until forty minutes into the show." I closed my eyes as Frankie added a gold, sparkly shadow. "They can't possibly be ready for me yet."

"Janae, they need you there for the entire rehearsal. I sent you the schedule. You've never rehearsed with Cash or The Hollow Bones." His worried gaze traveled up and down. "You're not even dressed?"

"I am literally on stage for ten minutes. I sing the hook for his latest hit, and then I go straight into 'A Lonely Woman.' Besides, no one told me I needed to be there the whole time."

"If you read your actual schedule, then you would know," he pointed out.

"Where did you send my schedule, Del? If it was my email, you know I never check it." I stared at him in the reflection of the mirror.

"I also texted it to you."

I shrugged. "I didn't see it."

My twenty-three-year-old stylist, Jeri, who already had one hundred thousand followers on IG, squealed as she passed me my first outfit. "You're singing 'A Lonely Woman'? That's my jam. It was my anthem after my boyfriend cheated on me. That song got me through it."

I dapped her hand. "Good way to kiss up to the boss."

Del warned me, "Five minutes, Janae. That's it."

I winked at the cameraman who observed unobtrusively in the back of the small room. "Did you get that? I guarantee I will walk out there and stand around for the next two hours waiting for my spot. These things always take much longer than they plan for."

I was so very wrong. When I approached the stage with Del and the cameraman, I heard raised, angry voices. I scanned the small area, and all the band members were in place, rehearsing. Landon held his electric guitar, Charles — I'd learned all their names after my unfortunate run-in with Landon the night before — played with the keys on his sax, Brian sat behind the drums, and Santiago tightened the strings on his acoustic guitar while everyone watched Cash and Cedrick argue.

Cedrick explained, "It's not that big of a deal that she's not here yet. Her part is so small and we need to practice after Janae leaves the stage anyway."

"Small? This is motherfucking MILA, the kind of artist who turns a stage into a damn spectacle."

Cedrick rubbed his temples. "Del swears this stripped-down set will work for her comeback. No dancers, no background vocals. Just her and the music."

"She's not even bringing background singers? Or dancers? This is a stadium show, not open mic night. She better hope her little comeback moment is enough." Cash pointed at Cedrick. "It's ridiculous that you can't keep her in line."

Cedrick slapped his hand. "It wasn't my idea to ask her to perform. This is what she does. That's all you and Del, bruh."

Cash took a step back. "I didn't think the bitch would be almost two hours late."

Cedrick's head jerked. "Wait…"

The camera captured their words and my reaction — hurt and embarrassment that quickly turned to anger. I stepped forward from the shadows. "Who the fuck you calling a bitch?"

Cash looked me up and down with disdain. "You."

"The fuck." I walked right up to him. "Don't call me that."

Cedrick growled. "Everyone chill. He shouldn't have called you out of your name, but we don't have time for your attitude when you're wrong. Can we please run through the show?"

I closed my eyes, rattled by all the heated emotions warring for control.

"Now," Cedrick said before he strode to the keyboard. Once upon a time, I'd had a crush on him. That faded when I heard through the media that he discarded women like trash.

"Cash needs to apologize first," I demanded. "I thought I had more time to get here. I didn't know I was expected to be here for the entire rundown of the show. My bad. I still don't deserve to be called out of my name."

Cash shook his head. "I don't apologize. You can get on with all that noise."

My face burned. All the misogyny that I'd experienced while trying to make it, and then *after* I'd made it, and I still had to deal with this sexist bullshit.

Del stepped forward. "Please, Cash. She's here now. Just apologize."

"No."

Del pleaded with me, "Can we just rehearse? You don't have to like each other."

"But I do deserve respect." I lifted my chin.

The shimmering sounds of a guitar filled the stage area, and we all looked at Landon, who had his pick in his hand, playing Cash's song leading into my intro. He looked at me with surprisingly kind eyes. "On you. We practice with or without his apology?"

"Fine. Let's go." I grabbed the mic off the stand.

Cash bellowed, "Thank you."

I stuck up my middle finger at him, and everyone laughed except Cash as I prepared to take the stage.

Unfortunately, the tension returned shortly after. I was more rattled by the confrontation than I'd realized. I couldn't find my groove. I missed my cue twice, and my voice cracked when I sang Cash's hook. I even forgot a few lyrics to my own song. "Off my game" was a serious understatement.

"Are you kidding me right now?" Cash asked. "You show up late and can't get your shit together."

"Sorry, I got it. I swear I do," I said, fighting hard not to show any tears. One thing I knew for sure was that these men, especially Cash, would not be moved by crying. They would see it as a sign of weakness, and I couldn't afford to seem vulnerable.

"I wanted you specifically, and you're not about to fuck up my show. This is my big moment." He walked up to my face. "I'm glad I didn't apologize."

Although stunned by the contempt, I nodded rapidly. I gripped the mic stand and took calming breaths to avoid lashing out from the deep hurt of being demeaned again. Maybe I deserved to be called out of my name after being so late and giving a weak performance.

"Naw, Cash. We don't roll like that. I should've stopped it earlier. If you don't apologize to her right now, we're not going on that stage together." An angry and frustrated Landon approached with balled fists. My stomach churned. Cedrick jumped in between the two men, trying to push Landon back.

Cash, a hulk of a man compared to Landon, scoffed, "I told you, I don't apologize."

"Don't touch me." Landon shoved away from Cedrick and took another step toward Cash. "I don't care what you do outside of here. Tell Janae you're sorry, or we're going on that stage without you."

"You know you need me."

"Wanna bet?" Landon said, turning to Del, who had been silent, standing next to the filming cameraman at the front of the stage. "Isn't there a clause in the contract that we can refuse to play for an artist who doesn't best rep The Hollow Bones?"

Del nodded.

Landon looked back at Cash. "That clause also says that we can replace the artist if we need to do so. We were invited to perform and chose you. We can easily say that Janae is replacing you tonight, and I don't think Houston, her birth city, will mind at all."

Cash cursed under his breath. When he looked at the rest of the band, they all stood behind Landon. Even Cedrick looked at Cash with folded arms, as if waiting for his apology.

As Cash stalked past me, he quietly said, "I'm sorry."

"Sorry for what?" I asked, because I knew he wasn't.

His shoulders drooped slightly. "Calling you a bitch. I was wrong."

"Apology accepted." I touched his forearm and softly promised, "And I will smash it tonight. I won't mess up the show. I know this is your moment."

Cash grudgingly said, "You better," then walked away.

I stepped toward Landon to thank him for defending me, but he only shook his head before returning to his stand and packing up. The rest of the band followed his lead without saying another word. I'd disappointed everyone in this room, especially myself. Nausea assailed me, and I clutched my stomach, trying to keep the contents at bay. I couldn't let them down tonight. I just couldn't.

Del placed his arm around my shoulders as we left the stage area and whispered, "You better come through tonight like I know you can."

I looked at the camera that followed me closely and bragged, "Watch me make all these men eat it tonight."

I fingered my sobriety coin as I walked with my head held high back to my dressing room despite the mental beating I'd just taken. My nerves had gotten the best of me, and I couldn't afford to mess up. I had to have something just in case I couldn't calm my mind. I would only use if it were *necessary*. If I couldn't walk out on that stage ready to kill it, then and only then would I break three years of a promise to myself. Three years. I'd spent three long years using prescribed instead of recreational drugs to control my moods until I stopped taking meds the day I signed on with Del. I believed I didn't need anything but my sheer will and talent. I had been good, *so* good at fighting the darkness. I could and would do it again, even if it wasn't tonight.

I clenched my hands. I wouldn't mess this up. I wouldn't be MILA again.

I paused at the door of my dressing room to put on my happy face, ignoring the weight of guilt that made holding my head up harder. I pretended the sadness that engulfed my heart was determination and grit as I greeted my glam squad with a wide smile. I had to be the best and do whatever I needed to do. My entire comeback depended on it.

CHAPTER FOUR

landon

UNDENIABLY, JANAE KILLED IT. STOMPED her performance into the ground. Her command of the stage stole the show from Cash. When she sauntered out, singing the hook for Cash Black's latest hit, "Players Play," the stadium came alive. Every last person jumped to their feet, clearly excited to see their hometown hip-hop princess, destined to be the queen of superstardom until scandal silenced her. The roar of the crowd initially covered the music and her voice. The audience probably couldn't believe that Janae was back and seemingly better than ever. Del had kept news of her comeback at the rodeo a secret for this very moment.

Confident, bold, and beautiful in her fitted red suit, Janae never broke her stride, her face serious and determined. She didn't acknowledge the crazy attention and mad energy from the sold-out crowd. She stalked across the stage back and forth, her clear, strong, and raspy voice sending chills down my arms as I played to her rhythm, slowing down the song, and The Hollow Bones followed. Even Cash bopped his head to her groove and changed the flow of his delivery. The song ended all too soon, much to the disappointment of the audience clamoring for more of Janae as she twirled to face the band. Her back was to the audience with her head bowed as if in prayer.

The venue lights shut off for a few seconds. Complete darkness filled the stadium. Cash hurried to the side of the stage to take a breather. I tucked my head to my chest, and the sole blue spotlight focused on my fingers as

I plucked the first sparkle of notes to her biggest hit, "A Lonely Woman," which damn near caused pandemonium.

Red lights hit Janae as she gripped the mic in her hand. She rapped at an almost inhuman pace while bouncing with every step without sounding out of breath. When she finally stopped and held her mic to the audience, they sang the chorus at the top of their lungs. She looked back at me and signaled for the music to cease, allowing the stadium of her fans to sing a cappella. Janae spread her arms wide, dropped her head back, and closed her eyes. Tears streamed from the corners of her eyes as thousands of people told her she was forgiven for her trespasses.

After the crowd finished singing, Janae lifted her head without wiping away her tears, and we resumed playing. She sang along with the crowd and hooked her arm around Cash Black's neck playfully as he returned to the stage. He lifted her in his arms to hug her tightly, much to the crowd's approval.

Cash planted her on her feet and announced, "Your hometown girl, the artist formerly known as MILA, Janae Warner."

She waved at the crowd and yelled into her mic. "Thank you, H-Town, always. I'm back and better than ever. Don't forget to follow me on all socials as Janae Warner, and be sure to check out me and The Hollow Bones on our limited-run tour."

Janae took a bow before blowing kisses at Cash as Cedrick began playing the intro to his next song. She danced suggestively to his music, much to the crowd's delight, on her way backstage. As she approached the curtain on stage, Janae stopped before me. Her eyes were shiny and bright from the thrill of performing.

She whispered, "Thank you for being my knight."

Then she kissed me. Her soft mouth was pressed to mine as if it were the most natural conclusion to her show. Although the noise level was deafening, it didn't match my heart beating through my chest. She teasingly tapped my nose and rushed off the stage.

Still lost in the feel and sweet taste of Janae's lips, I almost missed my cue to join in and quickly recovered. I had to reorient myself to my guitar, and I never lost focus when I played.

I'd also never seen a more dynamic performer.

The five members of The Hollow Bones walked into Porter House in the Galleria area of Houston for the after-party to loud applause. We were escorted to a section beside the golden-lit bar. The cool and elegantly smooth vibe of the restaurant was perfect for someone like me. It was not too big, and dark enough to allow me to duck off into some remote corner yet remain near the action if I needed to appear involved. Black Heritage Night had been a resounding success, from the sold-out show to the phenomenal performance of Cash Black, featuring The Hollow Bones and surprise guest Janae Warner. Champagne bottles popped and flowed freely throughout the area. I tapped my glass to the others, though I didn't drink the pink bubbly. Del had already asked for water, fried lobster tails, shrimp deviled eggs, king crab and avocado stacks, mac and cheese, and the fluffiest yeast rolls at our table.

In times like this, I could hide in plain sight, surrounded by my closest friends. Cedrick sat on one side of me and Brian on the other. Santiago and Charles buffered the ends of our booth. Cedrick kept holding up his phone to take selfies of us eating and drinking, celebrating our first successful run at the rodeo.

Cameras for the reality show were already stationed, waiting for Janae. When she entered the restaurant escorted by Cash Black and Del, her first hit song, "Premier," blasted through Porter House. She grinned to wild applause and waved her arms high in the air to her song, making her flowy yellow dress rise high on her thighs. She wore a white velvet cowboy hat, and her black hair was slicked into a low bun under it.

"Are you ready for the circus for the next two months?" Cedrick joked near my ear.

"Ten more shows. I'm counting by the shows and not the time span," I responded, unable to tear my gaze from Janae as she enjoyed being the darling. She seemed different tonight… still sexy and gorgeous, but mellower and eerily calm. Cash had a possessive hand on her lower back while they were escorted to the bar table in front of our booth. Cash sat down without holding the seat out for Janae, which Del did before joining them.

Brian commented, "Del is excited tonight. His jaws have to hurt from all that cheesing."

Cedrick added, "He should be. He put us together, and miracle of miracles, it worked."

Janae scanned the bar as if looking for someone, and her gaze found mine. She didn't smile, then she returned her attention to Cash and the small crowd around them. I picked up my glass and drank the cool water to hide my smile. I shouldn't have been pleased that she'd sought me out, except I couldn't stop the heat that had invaded me since she'd kissed me on stage. Maybe I was just starstruck because although we'd been in the studio together, I'd never seen her perform live. Sooner or later, Janae would remind me she was human and walked among us mere mortals.

The benefit of being sober while everyone around me became intoxicated was that I could observe people in their true form, with lowered inhibitions. My three bandmates laughed and cursed more than they otherwise did. Cedrick became irritable and moody, and I usually kept my distance when he drank too much. Tonight was no exception. Once he snapped at the waitress for trying to remove what she'd assumed was a dirty plate off the table, I knew my time at the party was ending.

I excused myself to go to the restroom. As I walked between our booth and the table where Janae, Del, and Cash sat, I noticed that Cash's hand squeezed Janae's upper thigh underneath the table, and she pushed against it. I glanced at her face, and she downed a cocktail and slammed it on the table next to two other glasses. Disappointment hit the pit of my stomach. The allure of Janae, the performer, didn't mesh with the reality of the flawed woman who would even speak to a man who had disrespected her in front of others, as Cash had done.

After I came out of the crowded restroom, Janae danced in front of her table to one of her songs. Cash stood behind her, groping her as she moved seductively. Her eyes were glazed over, and her gait was unsteady. Although her moves suggested that she didn't mind Cash's hands, I noticed her grimace and that she periodically would tap his hand. I looked around the restaurant at the merriment and the intoxicated people from all the free alcohol and pills that had been passed around. Besides the staff, I might have been the only one not under the influence. It was way past time for me to go.

The Janae from last night wasn't the one there tonight. She'd ended her sobriety at some point, probably before her show. She had been too much of a hit to need drugs at the after-party. Disappointment filled me that she hadn't been able to remain sober.

I walked back to the table. "I'm out."

Brian pushed back his shoulder-length locs. "Come on, the night's young."

"It's after one in the morning."

He grinned at me. His eyelids were almost closed. "Exactly."

I waved at the rest of the guys, and as I headed toward the door, Janae pulled against Cash, who firmly gripped her wrist. The cameramen were filming. I went to one of the men. "Has he been grabbing on her like that all night?"

The guy nodded. "She seems to like it."

The other man shrugged. "I'm not sure. She seems too out of it to fully comprehend what's happening."

I assessed the situation, and Janae couldn't even stand on her own two feet. She leaned heavily on Cash, who gripped her hips, leading her out of the restaurant. Normally, I avoided situations like these because it was often hard to tell whether it was consensual. And I hated confrontation. Getting involved in a fight with Cash during rehearsal had been so out of character for me that the rest of the band had kept staring at me as we packed up.

I eased past Cash and Janae to move in front of them as they walked toward the exit. Or should I say, he dragged Janae.

Donning a fake smile, I suggested, "I think we should take her to the hotel room and let her sleep it off."

"I got her."

I firmly shook my head. "No, you don't. She isn't up for whatever you think she is."

He frowned. "What? Are you her bodyguard now?"

The cameras were on us, and I gritted my teeth. I could have walked away, but my soul wouldn't rest. Janae still hadn't responded with her usual spunk.

I leaned closer to him. "The cameras are following her. It's not a good look to walk out of here with her like this."

He looked over his shoulder. "I didn't make her take anything. She wants to go home with me."

Too tired to argue with a man with ill intent, I took Janae's hand. "Hey, I'm going to take you back to your hotel."

She frowned and looked at Cash. "I thought we were going to your place."

Cash smiled, his grill flashing. "See?"

I held three fingers in front of her face. "Tell me how many fingers I'm holding up, and I'll leave you alone."

A small crowd behind us laughed when she proudly yelled, "Five."

I shook my head and grabbed her hand. "You can go play with Cash tomorrow when you're sober."

She tried to yank her hand free as Cash grabbed my arm. I swung and connected my fist to his jaw. *Oh shit.* Um… I hadn't meant to do that. His eyes rolled back before he fell against the wall.

The silence was deafening in the small hallway leading to the exit as I tossed a fighting Janae over my shoulders. "Don't worry, she's my friend, and I'm bringing her to her hotel to sleep it off."

When we made it outside, I hurried to my car, needing to get the hell out of Dodge. The fellas would have to find their way back to the house. I'd never had a fight in my life and didn't want to start today with a man almost twice my weight.

"Put me down, Landon," Janae yelled.

"Ooh, you remember my name. While you're yelling at me, tell me what hotel you're staying in." My adrenaline overrode her heaviness as I carried her like she weighed nothing. I ignored my discomfort of unexpectedly being surrounded by people.

"Nope." She still struggled against me, and I didn't place her down until I'd buckled her up in the passenger seat of the Range Rover. We sped off past the patrons coming out of the restaurant, including an angry Cash and a surprised Cedrick.

And this was only day two.

CHAPTER FIVE

janae

MARCH 9

THE AFTERMATH OF BEING UNDER the influence always hurt. My temples usually pounded viciously, my mouth was dry as cotton, and my body ached from head to toe. This morning had been no different. I'd been sober for three years. Over a thousand days of struggling not to take a sip, a puff, or a pill. Each day had been a challenge, and I'd thrown it all away because I didn't believe Janae Warner was enough. I had old connects here, and I'd called one for Xanax bars and ecstasy. He'd shown up to my suite with a wide grin as we exchanged money and product.

I'd thought I could perform clean. Five minutes before I stepped on the stage, my hands had trembled so badly that I'd dropped the bars twice before I placed them under my tongue. I'd cursed my weakness, my defective mind, and allowed the drug to take effect, and I didn't let anyone down except myself.

I squeezed my eyes shut trying to stem the tears before they could fall. What was wrong with me? All that therapy meant nothing when I was faced with the real world. I turned over and curled into a fetal position. Cool sheets brushed against my bare skin. Only lace panties hugged my hips. Which man did I sleep with last night? He must have slipped my panties to the side, though I felt no traces of the aftermath. At least he'd used a condom, whoever he was. Probably Cash. He'd found excuses to touch my ass and my hips, and I allowed it before my brain became foggy. "A Lonely Woman" was a song I'd written and my personal anthem for how I felt most of my life. After I'd killed the show, I didn't want to be alone at the pinnacle of my night, even if it meant being with an asshole.

I slowly opened my eyes, almost afraid to see whom I'd slept with. Only empty, rumpled white satin sheets greeted me. I scanned the large, exquisitely decorated blue-and-white suite that opened into an expansive balcony. This room didn't seem like Cash's style. The midmorning sun's brightness burned my eyes, and I squinted to decipher where and with whom I'd landed.

It wasn't the first time I'd woken up disoriented. I'd just hoped my last time, more than three years ago, had actually been my last time. God's grace had kept me for fourteen years of mostly reckless sexual behavior, and I didn't plan to test him again when my life was starting to line up.

Then, the shower, which had been incomprehensible background noise, suddenly became clear once the faucets were turned off. I pulled the sheets around me and pushed up against the cushioned headboard to see which lecherous man had used my lack of inhibitions to his advantage.

Landon walked out of the bathroom, bare-chested except for the large white towel wrapped around his waist. His dark caramel skin glistened from the shower's spray. His clothes, which were always a tad too large, had clearly hidden his natural, muscular frame. Landon even had a well-defined Adonis belt that led to his large manhood outlined underneath the white towel. This man with the thick, wild curls on top of his head that I longed to touch had transformed from an attractive nerd to a man I wanted to have. Possibly again.

"Wait… not you?" I said aloud before I realized it. Landon didn't seem the type to take advantage of a woman. "Did we have sex?"

Startled, Landon pulled out his earbuds. "Good morning." The rich timbre of his voice evoked chill bumps on my skin. "Sorry about walking out like this. Thought you'd sleep longer."

He hurried to the large walk-in closet and didn't reappear until he had donned a T-shirt and cargo shorts and held another pair of shorts and a tank in his hand.

Landon passed me the clothes from the side of the bed. "Elastic should hold up the shorts. I might be able to find a safety pin. The tank might dip lower than you prefer, but you've worn less in public."

"Where's my dress?" I pressed the clothes to my chest. He seemed to be evading the question of whether we'd had sex or not.

Landon looked away and grabbed his watch off the nightstand. "Got ripped."

"Ripped?" *Was the sex that wild?*

His gaze narrowed. "What do you remember?"

I shook my head. "Going inside Porter House."

"That's it? You don't remember my fighting with you and Cash, and trying to bring you back to your hotel?"

"No. You fought with Cash?" I looked around the suite that opened up to a large balcony with a lake and woods in the background. "How did I get here if you tried to get me back to my hotel?"

"I wasn't trying to *get* you. I was trying to protect you."

"From Cash? What happened?"

Landon sucked his teeth. "Such a waste."

"Fuck you." I hurriedly pulled the tank over my head, ignoring the pounding headache that returned with a vengeance now that he'd insulted me.

"Fuck me? What's wrong with you?" He backed up.

"Oh, you can have sex with me, but I'm a waste?"

Landon's hands went up. "Hold up. We didn't have sex. You ripped off your own dress because, according to you, it was too tight. You tried to come on to me right before you passed out. I covered you up and slept on top of the covers beside you. Nothing happened. I prefer my women fully conscious and able to consent."

Women? He had women? The geeky man who seemed to avoid conversation, always wore a hat, and was awkward in a crowd had *women*? Then again, Landon Hayes was an attractive, wealthy, musically gifted man, and judging from his recent nakedness, he was a hot one. A woman could do a whole lot worse. *I* had done a whole lot worse.

He studied his feet. "You're not a waste, though I question your decisions. I meant Cash. I hate men like him. He believes his half-assed talents mean he deserves whoever he wants, whether she wants him back or not. Brags about being disrespectful to women."

"Well, I've been dealing with men like him my entire career. I could tell you stories that'd make you blush."

"Why do you allow it? You're too strong and fierce for men's bullshit egos." He seemed only curious, not judgmental.

"Do I really have a choice? A flirt there, a little sex there, and I get closer to my goals."

Landon shook his head. "Isn't that how a prostitute thinks?"

And there's *the judgment.* "Stop insulting me. I get it. You don't respect me, and in two months, you'll never have to speak to me again." I tried to rise too quickly from bed and fell back from my throbbing temples. "Ouch… my head is killing me."

"I wasn't insulting you. I was stating a fact. Prostitutes flirt and have sex to make money. Money is always their goal. Sounds like it is for you, too. It really shouldn't be. You're far too talented to believe people will only see that if you're being sexual."

I wanted to snarl, but that would take too much energy. "I wouldn't expect you to understand. You can dress like you already do and barely speak, yet you are an acclaimed musician. If I'm quiet, I'm stuck-up. If I'm noisy, I'm too much. I want to be respected for my talent, just like you. Ain't no one checking for the ones who refuse to sell sex anymore." I rubbed my temples. "You have something for a headache?"

"We agree to disagree on that one." He pointed to a cup on the bedside table. "I made that for you. Thought you might wake up in pain."

I sniffed it, and it surprisingly smelled like lemon. "Please say this is a hot toddy. My cure is usually coffee laced with Amaretto."

"Janae." He picked up a black bandana from the bench at the end of the bed and covered his hair. The wrap emphasized his hazel bedroom eyes, the angular shape of his face, and his keen nose.

"Damn, Landon. When did you get all fine and sexy?" I gestured to his face and body. "I had no idea you were hiding all that under your hat and clothes."

He blushed. "I don't hide."

I clapped my hands. "So adorbs. You're actually red in the face."

Landon gestured to the cup sternly. "Drink it all down. I won't contribute to your destruction."

"So dramatic." I rolled my eyes and sipped on the lukewarm, bitter liquid. "I taste the turmeric and ginger. Not bad."

"There's pepper, too. It should ease your headache," he added, and held on to the corner of the bed as he slid his feet into loafers.

"Is this what you use the next day?" I asked, curious about whether he drank or used anything. Most people in this business did. The Hollow Bones had indulged at least in alcohol. In the past two days, I'd noticed that he only drank water.

He looked at me. "I don't drink."

"Ever?"

"I don't like the taste. Don't understand why people want to get wasted or trashed. At the gala, you were sober, weren't you? That's why you wear that coin around your neck." Landon's unblinking gaze forced me to look down.

"Yes." I held the cup with both hands and ingested more of his home remedy, unhappy at the reminder I no longer deserved to wear the coin that hung awkwardly around my neck, taunting me.

"And I'd never seen you more beautiful. I couldn't stop staring, as you so eloquently pointed out."

His soft-spoken compliment might have been the most arousing words I'd ever heard in my life, even more so because the intent was pure and honest. My stomach clenched painfully like it had at the gala, and the undercurrent of desire between us now danced as we looked at each other. All I had to do was lie back on this bed and wait for him to take me. Except Landon wasn't that aggressive male. Just because I'd noticed him sexually, that wouldn't suddenly change his personality.

"Why would you ever it again when so much ugliness comes from it? Please don't." It was a plea I'd heard many times over the years. Yet his quiet demand hit differently.

I crawled toward the end of the bed, and his chest heaved up and down as he watched me warily. I kneeled when I reached the edge. His tank hung loose around my breasts and barely covered my ass. The plush bench at the end of the bed became a barrier. "It was just a slide. One that I regret. Imagine having your first performance in over three years in front of that large hometown crowd. A place that doesn't have the best memories. Then I messed up the rehearsal because I couldn't control my emotions. I had to make sure I wouldn't screw up the show. It wasn't just me on the stage. I had a moment, it won't happen again, and now I'm good."

Landon's brows rose. "Good? Are you sure? We have ten more shows starting next month. The last one is in Los Angeles. That's your town, too, correct?"

"Yep." I tried to sound more upbeat than I felt. "They love me there."

He tapped the bench almost rhythmically before he spoke again. "They loved you at the gala and would've loved you last night if you gave it a chance. Yet you had to take something. It wasn't just alcohol, Janae."

"And I won't take anything else. Can we move on?" I raised the bottom of the tank over my hips. His eyes drifted down for a second too long, and he bit the corner of his bottom lip. The temperature shifted dangerously in the room when he dragged his gaze back to mine. I softly said, "I'm fully conscious now."

Landon's brow furrowed deeply. "I'm not interested."

Unperturbed by his blatant lie, I planted my hands on my hips and tilted my head. "No one has to know."

"I would know." He picked up his hat from the bench. "I don't blur the lines."

"Then why did you bring me to your bed instead of mine?"

"I didn't know where else to take you." He lifted up his shirt enough to show me four raggedy scratches on his taut side. "You fought me when I carried you out of the restaurant and then refused to tell me where you were staying once I managed to secure you in my car. You almost got my face, but I blocked you."

I covered my mouth briefly. "Oh, shit. Was all that caught on camera?"

Landon didn't blink.

"Why didn't Del cut?" I scrambled out of bed, searching for my phone, anxious to call my manager and curse him out for not protecting me.

"You know how this works. The messier, the better. Cash kept putting his hands on you at the restaurant, and you seemed uncomfortable. You even hit his hand when he tried to grope you. He grabbed your waist when you were completely wasted and prepared to go. I didn't want anything to happen to you. I stopped him by knocking him out and grabbing you over my shoulders like a caveman because you refused to leave the restaurant. I'm sure by now what happened went viral, so if I were Del, I wouldn't have cut either. Your bad behavior is a dream for reality TV."

I walked back to him. "Landon, I don't want them to see me like that."

"Then move differently," he said, as if that were the simplest thing to do when habits were hard to break and change near impossible.

I sank back on the bed. "What did Cedrick and the rest of the band say?"

He whistled. "Not good. I stayed in here with you so I wouldn't have to hear their complaints when they stumbled back in the wee hours of the morning. They don't want to work with you anymore."

"What did Del say?"

"I don't know. I haven't spoken to him. He's probably champing at the bit. You just increased our ticket sales." He placed his hat firmly on his head.

"Where are you going?" I already felt the sunlight dull. I didn't want him to leave, though it was just as clear he didn't want to stay.

"Need to play," he reluctantly replied.

"Are you going somewhere to rehearse?" I hated the needy squeakiness in my voice.

"The studio downstairs."

"What about me?"

He frowned. "What about you?"

"You're just going to leave me hanging?" I gestured to my body. "You know I can't come out of this room and not be gawked or glared at by them."

"They are the least of your worries."

"What do you mean?" I stepped closer, and this time, he stepped back.

"There are consequences for your behavior, Janae."

"Trust me, I know."

"Do you?" He raised the back of both his arms to show that I'd inflicted more scratches. "Three years away from all of this, and you apparently have learned nothing."

Mortified at my actions against my one-time protector, I spat, "You don't get to judge me. You don't know what I've been through."

"You're right, and I don't want or need to know. You make sure you show up and not out for the rest of these shows, or I'll fire you myself. And the next time you're in trouble and can't see it, I won't waste my time saving a woman who doesn't want to be saved," Landon said quietly before exiting the bedroom.

I grabbed the pillow, covered my mouth, and screamed until I was hoarse. I wanted to destroy the room, break every glass. I wanted to hurt someone. I wanted to hurt myself. *Needed* to hurt myself. The overwhelming desire to feel more pain swelled within, and I rushed into the bathroom, searching through the empty drawers of a rented home. Landon's leather toiletry case rested on the counter next to the sink. He had to have a razor, because he shaved. I rummaged through the toothpaste and mouthwash, a few condoms, and grabbed the silver razor.

I pushed the lid on the toilet and sat down. I spread my thighs, prepared to slice myself in places no one could see. My old scars had healed and were so faint that they appeared more like stretch marks. The visible scars on my left wrist and forearm were covered with butterfly tattoos.

I closed my eyes, waiting for the sweet release from the agony. Then, as if a light switch had been flipped, my subconscious released what had happened the night before. The discomfort and disgust I'd felt whenever Cash touched me. And because I was high and drunk, I'd been leaving with a man I had no attraction to, to do things I wouldn't have wanted to do but would've been too powerless to fight. Landon had calmly protected me from

THE SIDE OF BEAUTIFUL

myself despite the insults I'd inflicted. He still refused to allow anything to happen to me. And he'd been a gentleman this morning even though he wanted me. Landon hadn't let his body overrule his mind and heart.

Why would he be interested in a woman like me? A woman who had only demonstrated impulsivity and destruction. Cutting myself in his bathroom with his razor would further solidify his perception of me.

With a shaky hand, I placed the razor back in his bag. I washed my face and rinsed my mouth with his Listerine, then pulled on the too-big shorts that managed to grip my waist. I walked into the closet. His clothes were neatly folded in his open suitcase on the bench in the middle of the space, so I grabbed a discarded red Nike hoodie on the floor and pulled it over my head, smelling hints of Landon. He probably hadn't offered the hoodie because he'd worn it. I found my heels, torn dress, and purse with my cell tucked inside on one of the shelves, then sat on the bench and pulled out my phone.

A pic of Landon with me over his shoulder leaving Porter House had flooded the internet. We were portrayed as a couple, and the gossip sites were saying he'd fought with Cash Black over me. I didn't know how long I remained in his closet, sobbing over the fact that, two days back in the game, I'd already failed miserably.

When I tiptoed through the mansion on my way to the front door to catch an Uber under my pseudonym, a shirtless Cedrick walked down the hall toward me. Although more muscled and ripped than Landon's, his chest didn't affect me as Landon's had. I saw a man who barely tolerated me and, after last night, probably hated me.

His gaze traveled up and down my body, and he snorted. "Should have realized Landon brought you here. He has a weakness for helpless women. Or women who pretend to be helpless to get the attention of men like him. Which one are you?"

"I have a headache, and I need to go." I went to walk past him, though he partially blocked my path. "Move the hell out of my way."

"Stay away from him."

"Tell that to him."

"You heard me."

"And you heard *me*," I said loudly.

I resisted the urge to run from the negative, poisonous energy that bounced off Cedrick. I'd dealt with men like him most of my life. Arrogant, brilliant, controlling, selfish, and used to taking what they wanted no matter who was hurt. The type of man that Landon said he hated, yet he didn't recognize those traits in his best friend.

"One more misstep, and you're gone. I don't care what Del promised you."

"Tell me something I don't know." I glared at him. "Can I go now?"

When he didn't budge, I shoved him away, and soon, I was riding in the back seat of a Toyota Prius on my way to my hotel, praying that my antics from last night would blow over soon. I belonged on that stage, and nothing would ever stop me again. Not even myself.

Once I returned to the hotel, determined to ignore any contracts I'd signed and run back to Los Angeles to recuperate, I threw my clothes in my suitcases, ignoring the cameras outside my suite. Del banged on the door, insisting that I open it, and when I didn't, he convinced the hotel manager to let him in my room, citing his concern that I would hurt myself. The cameras followed as he stormed in, demanding answers.

"When I call you, you answer me," Del yelled.

"I thought you worked for me." I zipped my bag angrily.

He surveyed the room. "Where are you going? You're supposed to be here until Monday."

"Doing what? My show was last night."

"Supporting The Hollow Bones. Your schedule included being here for them. Their last show is tomorrow night, and after what happened last night, your fans want to see you and Landon."

"What exactly happened last night, Del? Huh?" Then I remembered the cameras. "I want them out of here. Now." They continued to record, and I placed my hands over the lens of the closest one. "Get the hell out of here."

Del waved his arms. "Go for now. I need to talk to her."

The producer, who was also one of the cameramen, shook his head. "Del, we signed a contract. We already can't follow Hollow Bones like you promised, and now this. We agreed to certain hours of recording and we can't just stop because she wants us to stop. That's not how this works, and you know that."

Del wiped his brow. "*Please*, give me a second."

I pointed to the door, and they reluctantly left. When the door closed, I whirled around on him. "Do they work for you or me?"

He placed his hands on his waist. "You're busting my balls. You asked for this. You wanted cameras to follow you, and these are the rules, especially for a fallen star trying to make a comeback. They can record whatever they want."

"I also asked for the discretion to determine what could be recorded if past scheduled hours. They recorded everything last night instead of looking out for me." I jabbed the air between us. "*You* didn't look out for me. Cash had ill intentions, I was out of it, and you knew it."

Del dropped his hands. "Janae, I was out of it too. It was a good night, and I indulged a little too much. You arrived at the party with Cash and flirted with him for most of the night. You half listen when you're sober, so you damn sure aren't going to listen when you're high. You practically beat up Landon as he hauled you out of the restaurant."

His reminder of how I'd treated Landon, who'd stood up for me, only embarrassed me more. "I can't do this. I can't handle the pressure of performing with The Hollow Bones. They don't want me here anyway." I stalked to the bathroom to grab my toiletry bag. "Sorry for getting you into this mess. I'll pay you back every dime for the shows you already booked and for the reality show. I'll sell the house in Austin. Whatever I need to do to pay off my debt to The Hollow Bones and to you. I can't be here anymore. This was a huge mistake. If I'm going to make my career happen again, it has to be me and only me."

Once I stalked back into the bedroom, Del grabbed my shoulders. "You just had an amazing show. For a last-minute set, no dancers, no fluff, just straight bars and presence? You pulled it off. You're trending. Your old albums, Janae, are rising up the charts after one performance. You wanted a comeback, and it's happening better than I imagined. People love drama and a love story. Your fans believe one is happening between you and Landon. Give them what they want, since there's chemistry between you. I've known him for years and have never seen him come out of his shell like he has for you."

Ignoring my swell of happiness at Del's observations, I shrugged. "There isn't anything between me and him. He was just the only one to care enough to remove me from a potentially dangerous situation. I'm never working with Cash again."

"You don't have to, and I don't want you to either. People aren't talking about him anyway. It's all you and Landon."

I folded my arms. "Me and Landon? Or my performance?"

"Both. You stole the show from Cash, and Landon stole you from him. You're like the next power couple. It's your fault for kissing him on the stage in the first place and then leaving with Landon in a crowded restaurant like you did. What did you think would happen? Come on, Janae. I know all of this is overwhelming, but it *is* what you want." I dipped my head, and he tilted it and studied my face. "Janae, don't run away from your destiny again."

Running my hand over my ponytail, I nodded.

Del smiled widely. "Listen, I'm going to smooth things with the band later, but I think you should cut a song with them to be released right before the ten-city tour starts."

I scoffed. "They'll never agree. They hate me."

"They love fame and fortune more than they hate you. You need a song with an award-winning and respected band like them," he reassured me. "You're letting your nerves get the best of you. You already proved you still got it, and the fans know it, too. At least do these ten cities and a record with them, and then we can take it from there. If you're done after that, we'll cut our losses and move on. At least you won't owe anyone."

I shook my head. "I can't use anymore. Three years wiped out just like that after one performance because it wasn't just me on that stage."

Del raised his hands. "That's on you."

I rolled my eyes. "It's not just on me. I need help, Del. You know my history."

"I do, but I can't hold your hand. If you need your therapist or sponsor to travel with you, then I can arrange it. I'll make sure the dressing rooms in each city are free of alcohol, weed, and other drugs. Other than that, it's about the choices *you* make." He picked up his phone. "Figure out whatever you need to do to stay clean, because you can't quit, or you'll be sued by everybody, including the insurance company I had to get before any venue would secure a date. You can't afford to lose any more money. Selling your home in Austin wouldn't begin to pay back who you would owe, including The Hollow Bones. They've already threatened me with lawsuits if you cancel on them again."

I flopped back on my bed.

He held his phone to his ear. "What do you want me to tell the film crew?"

"I'll talk to them."

"Good girl." He clapped. "I can't get over how amazing you were last night. I need you to remember it, too. This is your dream, one that most people will never get to experience."

I stared at the ceiling long after he left, rubbing the sobriety coin I'd worn proudly. I traced the Serenity Prayer engraved across it one last time before I snatched it from my neck.

CHAPTER SIX
landon

THE STING OF THE MARKS her nails left on me inspired my creative flow while I showered, and I couldn't wait to play my guitar. Janae had been aggressive and mean, and I'd remained calm through it all. Usually, the exuberant expression of any emotion drew me into a shell like a scared tortoise. Janae's wildness had incited my peace. The type of peace I experienced when I hit the perfect note. The constant gnawing inside me had vanished while I handled Cash and Janae.

How could that be? How could she erase years of anxiousness and discomfort by needing me, especially because she didn't *know* she needed me?

I wasn't the hero in anyone's story. I had no desire to be the center of attention. I was more drawn to the secondary characters in a story than the protagonist, and yet I'd been the main attraction.

In the makeshift music studio, the panoramic view of the man-made lake surrounded by woods provided the perfect backdrop for our practice space. I smiled at the brightness of the day as I strummed the guitar and jotted down a few notes under the title. The title could possibly change, but the bittersweet twang of each pluck would remain.

I sensed his presence before he complimented me.

"Love it already."

Without turning my head, I replied, "Yeah. No matter how we end up arranging it, the guitar will lead in on this one."

Cedrick walked over, resting his hands on the edge of his setup. "You write my part yet?"

"No. Trying to get the notes right with the guitar first. Figured you might write it once you hear it." I played a few more chords. "Might need to tighten it here."

"Title?"

I shrugged. "'Stuck Between.'"

Cedrick chuckled. "The way we are right now."

"Maybe. I hear you and Brian, I really do. We can do trendy music. I just don't want to lose the integrity of our music. Branford Marsalis thought a gig on *The Tonight Show* was the right exposure and choice. He left because the role of smiling sidekick didn't work for him."

"Ah… It seems to work for Jon Batiste on Colbert's show."

"You mean the show he no longer works for?" I reminded him.

Cedrick shook his head. "Beside the point, because those are not good examples. We're not some sidekick to a white man. We're creating our own music regardless of which direction we decide to go. It's still our music. Our sound."

I argued, "Are we pandering to what's hot, what's popular, or what feels intrinsically right? Backing up pop artists with music different from ours is one thing. Producing an album that doesn't accurately reflect who The Hollow Bones really is would be a travesty. We're a rhythmic soul band first, and we both know that soul isn't always what's hot on the radio."

"A travesty or a smart business move?" He played around with the keys. "Like it or not, what you did last night with Janae has just placed The Hollow Bones in the middle of possible controversy, or maybe it was the smartest move ever. Have you seen anything since it happened?"

"No." I tapped my guitar. "I don't have social media for a reason."

"You and Janae are the new 'it' couple, and people want more. New Orleans and Atlanta just sold out, thank you very much," Cedrick announced. "Somebody even captured the kiss that Janae planted on you before she left the stage last night. You are Instagram official unless you state otherwise."

"After one night?" I asked. "I figured that people might speculate that we were a couple who got into it, and sales would go up. Not all that."

"Your reputation as an award-winning musician and leader of The Hollow Bones, and coming from music royalty, precedes you. You've been in this industry for years, and the man who's never been seen with a woman is now fighting Cash Black in a classy restaurant over MILA after her surprise knockout return to the stage at the Rodeo. The headlines can't get no better than that." He snapped his fingers.

"She's Janae Warner now," I reminded him needlessly.

He rolled his eyes. "A name change doesn't automatically change reputation. Her fanbase is different from ours. She's from the top of the hip-hop and pop world, and our association with her means we're on that path, too. If you don't want the people to decide our music for us, then we need to get ahead of this."

"What do you suggest? Because I really don't have time for this." I clenched and unclenched my jaw. I needed to create and not spend time determining how to market our band best. I took off my guitar and moved to the window.

"You make it clear it's not a love match. You and Janae are friends only, and she had too much to drink. You and Cash Black had words about the show. He'll probably appreciate your saying something, or otherwise, the story will be he got his ass handed to him for trying to take advantage of a star." Cedrick chuckled. "I didn't know you had it in you. I've known you for fifteen years and never seen you fight."

"It wasn't a fight." I scowled. "And I'm not releasing a statement. I don't do public speaking,"

He walked up beside me and leaned against the window, facing me. "We go to our Hollow Bones IG page and do a Live. Our fans would love to hear you speak, especially about Janae. They would eat that shit up."

"You know I don't do that. Ever." The gnawing increased. Speaking to the public frightened me into that scared little boy I'd been during my childhood, and it didn't matter if there was no actual audience before me. "Get Del to do it."

"He won't. Del loves the narrative. His gamble on her is paying off. I could *hear* the dollar signs as he raved about pairing us with Janae for more shows."

I glanced at him and back at the serene lake. "We're not doing more shows than we already agreed to. She can't handle all this. The more shows we do, the more likely she will implode or explode sooner or later. Either one isn't good for her, or for us." I lifted my hat enough to scratch my head.

Cedrick pressed his hand against the window. "I guess you would know what's best for her. I saw her leaving your bedroom a while ago before she caught a ride. I thought you were taking her back to her hotel. Isn't that what you yelled loudly as you threw her over your shoulder?"

"She didn't want to tell me where she stayed, and then she said she didn't want to be alone." I closed my eyes and imagined physically fighting whatever gnawed at my stomach. "Nothing happened."

"Nothing? Janae *exudes* sex. She kissed you on stage in front of thousands. You were her hero last night, and you still didn't get any?" Cedrick laughed and squeezed my shoulder. "Bro, have I taught you *anything*?"

My eyes popped open, and I glared at him. "She wanted to last night and this morning. I didn't want to."

"What?" His head snapped back. "Why?"

"She was fucked up. I thought you knew I don't move like that." I looked at him pointedly. "I hope you don't either. The Hollow Bones don't need any sex scandal attached to us with so much riding on our future."

"If that's the case, you need to leave Janae alone and not just for the cameras." He strode back to his instrument and ran his hands across the keys like a child who didn't yet know how to play. "We both know she's trouble. We lost money the last time we worked with her, which we never recouped."

I grumbled, "Don't interrupt my flow with this bullshit. I came down here for peace and music."

Cedrick's hands went up. "Woah, we're only having a conversation. This won't be the last time she'll do something stupid. You'll want to protect her every time. You were ready to fight Cash at the rehearsal and hit him at the after-party. All because of Janae's actions."

I raised my voice. "I couldn't let him disrespect her, or worse, rape her."

"She's a grown-ass woman who can choose how she wants to move. You can't save her from herself. All that does is keep you hooked to a woman who's no good for you." He added in a quieter tone, "I know you, bro."

"No, you don't." I twisted my neck to release the tension building there. Cedrick and I didn't argue or fight. "As you so eloquently put it, I'm a grown-ass man who doesn't need any advice from you about Janae or any other woman." Although I had just told Janae I wouldn't save a woman who didn't want to be saved, I didn't want to admit that to Cedrick, whose smugness grated on my nerves.

His brows rose. "One night with her, and you have balls now?"

"I'm done talking about Janae. Play or leave."

Cedrick blew a raspberry and counted off. When I began strumming the first chord, he easily picked up the rhythm. The tension dissipated as the music permeated the studio. I disappeared into the melody, hoping we wouldn't continue fighting over Janae yet accepting that we probably would.

Later that night, I chilled alone by the pool, wearing only basketball shorts. My hands were propped behind my head as I studied the midnight-blue sky. Being outside was my way of unwinding. I'd loved astronomy since I received my first telescope when I was six. I loved whenever I had a moment to admire the universe. If I were ever brave enough to ink my skin, I would definitely have a crescent moon or some representation of the celestial.

Needing this solitude to recharge before our show tomorrow night, I stared up at the stars, the planets, and the large yellow moon, which was presenting tonight as a crescent — my favorite view of it. The moon fascinated me because it was always round, but we saw different versions depending on its orbit or rotation. Like me, I was always Landon, yet people saw a different version depending on my environment and mood.

The first time I recognized the beauty of a clear, dark sky full of sparkles was when I was about seven years old. Growing up in Brooklyn and currently living in Harlem seldom offered me an unobstructed, clear view of the night. Maybe I should have bought some property in the South, or somewhere else where I could enjoy God's beauty. The gnawing didn't exist in the presence of greatness.

"I guess you don't like answering your phone."

A clean-faced, ponytailed Janae, wearing my hoodie and a pair of black leggings, stood behind my lounger and smiled down at me.

"Not when I'm playing music or enjoying the galaxy," I answered.

She looked up at the sky. "That sounds like how I'm fascinated with butterflies. They seem so mystical. Reminds me that there's something so much greater than me."

"Truly beautiful." I admired her.

Janae smiled as she returned her attention to me.

"You look funny from this angle. Almost alien-like," I teased.

She giggled. "So do you."

"How did you get in? It's just me here. The others are running the streets."

"I texted Brian, looking for you. He gave me the code."

"Brian?" I raised a brow. I wasn't aware they had exchanged numbers. Then again, he'd been less vocal whenever we discussed Janae.

She shrugged. "He might be the only one besides you in the band who doesn't hate me."

"Quite possibly." I gazed at her before admitting, "I'm glad you're here. I didn't think I would see you again until New Orleans next month."

She glanced around the backyard and then back at me. "When I left here this morning, I didn't think I would ever see you again."

"Canceling on us?" I asked without any bite.

"I was. I don't handle rejection and failure well," she admitted. "I was about to give up on myself and my dreams, which is my prerogative. There's a reason I don't have friends. I can get stuck in my head and forget I don't operate in isolation. But this tour isn't just about me. This is your showcase, your journey too, and your opportunity to grow your fanbase and for those fans to see how mad talented you are. The pressure of disappointing myself and The Hollow Bones got the best of me, and I wanted to run."

"What changed?"

She smiled shyly. "I wanted to be the type of woman you would be interested in."

Our upside-down gazes locked as her words set my heart pounding.

"Come again?" I asked. "You didn't even know me two nights ago."

She sighed. "I knew you, Landon. I couldn't remember your becomes sometimes my memory gets foggy. I've been under the influence since I was fourteen and it's taken its toll on me. Add three years of mostly solitude on top of that. I have to learn how to be among the living again." She moved to the end of my lounger, tapping my bare foot so she could sit. "After you left your bedroom, I remembered everything that happened last night. I was awful to you, and you never lost your temper or deserted me. Didn't take advantage of me and even temporarily healed me with that God-awful drink. I scratched you and never once apologized or seemed grateful that you'd saved me from Cash. So, I'm telling you right now, to your face, that I'm sorry, and thank you."

I touched her back with my foot lightly. "You don't have to apologize *or* thank me."

"I do." She smiled sadly before staring out at the pool. "For three years, I've been afraid to step back on that stage, scared to be booed. Scared that I would ruin my performance. Scared that my talent was a fluke. Scared I would never feel what I felt again last night. I went from a superstar who owned the charts to the pariah of pop music. I know everything that happened was my fault. I messed with the wrong man and destroyed my career and my relationship because I didn't know how to handle fame… my greatness."

I quietly watched her confessing her flaws and mistakes without airs or attitude. She wanted to be honest with me, and I instinctively knew this wasn't easy for her.

"During the rehearsal, you were the only one who encouraged me and stood up for me. You defended me, though I'd already given you reasons not to. Then you did it again at the restaurant, even after I relapsed. You didn't just discard me or believe I wasn't worthy of being saved or cared for." Her eyes sparkled like the stars above. "I want this so bad. I want the career I should've had if I hadn't allowed my insecurities to run amok." Janae straightened her shoulders and met my eyes. "I want to perform the right way. Without alcohol or drugs."

"Have you ever performed sober?"

"When I was a kid." She looked down at the ground.

"Then be that little kid every time you perform." I tapped her back with my foot again. "Find that innocent girl who only knew her talent."

"Don't think I've ever been innocent." She squeezed my foot, and I tucked it under my leg. Her head jerked back. "Are you so upset that I can't touch you?"

"Don't really like people touching my feet." I averted my gaze to the pool. "I'm sensitive."

"I wasn't going to tickle you, but say less. I don't want to touch your crusty feet anyway." She believed I was embarrassed by my feet instead of realizing the truth, that I wasn't comfortable being touched. Period. "I'm not used to rejection from men. Lately, that's all I've been receiving, or at least it's what it feels like. I didn't blame you when you told me you weren't interested. Why would you want a woman who can't get on that stage without doing something? What would a decent man like you want with a wreck of a woman? Yet, for some reason, I like being around you, like that I can be myself, and I haven't had that in a long time. So, I figured you could be my guide. Like my moral compass while we're on this road together."

I shook my head. "I'm not anyone's guide. I'm just as uncomfortable as you on that stage. I'm only relaxed when that guitar is in my hand and when a hat is on my head. If it wasn't for Cedrick, I doubt we would be as big as we are. Maybe I could enjoy life more if I drank or took something."

"Why don't you?" She held her hand up. "Not *encouraging* you to, just noticed that the other guys have no problems using. Had a bad trip or something?"

"Naw. Don't want to start something that I can't stop. So, I live with this uneasiness and edge and do my best to keep it under control. My discomfort is kinda my comfort now," I admitted.

She quirked a brow. "You were about to have a panic attack at the gala when I called you over, weren't you? No judgment if you were. I was about to have one before I went inside."

I didn't tell her I'd observed her initial nervousness outside the convention center. "Yeah. I don't do well in crowds or being put on the spot."

Janae laughed heartily. "I was so determined to get you back for earlier that I called you out. I felt bad once I noticed your eyes and that you had trouble breathing. I'm sorry about that, too."

I frowned. "No, you're not. You're still smiling."

"What can I say? I'm Petty Patty," Janae teased.

"Perfect name." I chuckled.

She squeezed beside me, shifted to her side, and placed her leg across my waist. I stiffened, and she brushed her lips against the center of my chest. "Calm down. I'm not going to jump your bones."

"Janae," I warned, my body responding to her sensual touch.

"What?" She snuggled closer to me and kissed my neck. "You smell good. It must be oils instead of cologne."

"It is, and we can't," I protested, though I didn't move away from her warmth.

She kissed my goatee. "Can't do what?"

I sighed. "If I'm your moral compass, sex is off the table."

Janae's eyes twinkled in the dim light. "I'm not thinking about sex. Just wanted to be next to you. Something about you makes me feel good. Settles me."

"Then why do you keep kissing me like it's your right? It's distracting. Are you always so touchy-feely with a man you just met?" I was trying desperately to keep my lower half from reacting. Her knee was dangerously close to my manhood, and if she moved an inch lower, I wouldn't be able to control myself.

"Only the special ones." Janae grabbed my face and kissed the corner of my lips. "And because you're so damn cute."

I groaned. "I'm not a puppy, Janae."

She propped her chin on my chest and traced my lips with her fingertip. "I'm fully aware that you're all man, Landon Hayes. I do want you. I offered myself to you twice, remember? I agree we shouldn't have sex. It muddies everything, and I get very possessive. And I would be totally in stalkerish mode with you."

"So, Petty Patty and Caulky Stalky?" I chuckled. "If you really got to know me, I doubt you would get possessive with me. You think *you're* a lot…" I whistled.

Her eyes grew soft. "Then it's a good thing we have time to get to know each other, because I'm not going anywhere."

Janae laid her head on my chest like she'd always belonged there. Soon, her slow breathing lulled me into comfort, and I hesitantly placed my arms around her. Even in sleep, her body responded to my embrace, and she nestled against me. I kissed the top of her head, wondering why this complicated woman was so determined to get next to me and under my skin.

And why I liked it so much.

CHAPTER SEVEN

janae

MARCH 10

I WOKE UP NEXT TO Landon for the second morning in a row. I tried to talk to him about the single last night, but the time wasn't right. I needed to do it today to get my career back on track.

We were in his bed, and he slept soundly on his stomach. He faced the wall, so I could only study the curls on his head and his toned back. He didn't seem the gym type, yet he must have done something to define his chest and back.

At some point in the night, after we'd fallen asleep on the sun lounger, he'd nudged me awake, and I held on to his waist as he brought me back to his bedroom. I'd crashed into bed, and he jumped in the shower. When he rejoined me, his skin smelling like soap, I'd cuddled against his warm, strong body, and though he stiffened as he had outside, it didn't take him long to relax.

I could admit that I could be needy. I had no shame in my game. I needed a man, needed his strength and his warmth. My neediness had gotten me in trouble and kept me too attached for too long to a man who I'd known no longer wanted or loved me. I didn't trust women enough to have female friends, so my world had been men since I'd been a teen. And after two days back in the game, I needed someone on my side. I needed Landon. I would do my best not to screw him over with my tendency to be rash and impulsive. His calm would mellow my storm.

I lightly touched Landon's back, wanting him to turn over and fuck me. Yet I knew it would jeopardize our tenuous brewing friendship. I wanted to be different with him. I *had* to be different. The old Janae, who didn't care, had ruined her career. I had to control my impulses and mood. I couldn't run or self-destruct every time I became uncomfortable. I also couldn't have sex with Landon and not expect it to mean something.

"How did you sleep?" Landon's voice was rich and deep in the morning. Sexy without his even trying.

I squeezed my thighs together. I probably couldn't continue to sleep in his bed and expect to remain friends without benefits.

"Okay. Thinking about my life and why I've made so many mistakes so young. So many that I can't afford any more. I'm not even thirty and have been through way too much drama."

"One theory on why?" he asked sleepily.

"My mother." She popped into my head without thought. Ebony Tanner. One of the most beautiful women I'd ever seen. A woman I'd lived to please until I realized through therapy that she would never be satisfied.

"Ahh… That mother will do a number on you. More than those fathers will," Landon said sagely.

I continued touching his back before he moved or told me to stop. "Should I go see her and my brother, since they're only about twenty minutes from here?"

"I forgot that since you're from here, your family probably lives nearby." He flipped over to his side when I did, and we faced each other. "Did they come to the show?"

"No. I never invited them."

Landon nodded slowly.

"You don't want to know why?"

"Do you want to tell me?"

"Not yet."

"Then don't." He smiled slightly.

"Yeah." I looked down. "I should at least go check on them or something, right?"

"I guess." His eyes appeared green in this sunlight.

I raised my head. "You guess? You're supposed to tell me that the right thing to do is go visit your family when you're in the city."

"Told you I wouldn't be a good moral compass. Families are strange creatures. They created us, yet the moment we can, we flee. Some of us never return." He propped his head on his arm. "If you don't want to go, then don't."

"How can I heal if I don't deal with them?"

"Or maybe it's harder to heal when you *have* to deal with them," he argued. "I live forty minutes from my folks and usually see them only during the holidays because my mother insists. I love them, but they stress me."

"What? I pictured you as that pampered only child with loving parents." I stared into his eyes, unable to look away from the curious intensity there.

"Looks are deceiving. They never pampered me or ever really saw me," he replied matter-of-factly. "It doesn't bother me anymore… most days. But we're talking about your parents, not mine. You think you're going to visit?"

"I'm not ready to see them."

"Then you have your answer."

The ease with which we conversed pleased me. For a man of few words, he was rather talkative. "I love talking to you. Can we stay in bed all day and be lazy on a Sunday?"

He shook his head. "Yes."

I giggled at his silliness. "I didn't expect this."

"What?" He frowned slightly, and I resisted smoothing out his forehead. Touching him right now would be detrimental to my aching sex.

"Your playful side. You're always so serious."

"Because I am," Landon said. "Always have been."

I tsked. "Last night and this morning, you're not."

He shrugged. "I only amuse you because you're focused on me. When you get your confidence back, you won't think of me as that funny dude. We won't be friends, and I'll go back to the nerd you can't believe you ever thought was hot."

"Why do you think we won't be friends?" I tugged on his in-need-of-a-trim goatee.

"Because you're scared, Janae, and I'm your life jacket. You won't need me once you're ready to swim on your own again." His tone suggested finality, and I couldn't decide if he believed it because that was how he saw me or himself, or if that was how he wanted it to be.

"When was your last relationship? I don't think I've ever noticed you with a woman."

"Isn't that a question you ask if you're considering me as your potential man? I thought we established that's not us." He closed his eyes, and his fingers played a rhythm on the sheets between us.

"It's a simple question from one potential friend to another," I insisted.

"I'd rather not answer."

"Is there a woman waiting for you in New York? I need to know if there is," I said, my temper rising. I didn't have the right to be jealous or angry, but tell that to my irrational heart. Landon was starting to feel like mine, and I didn't want to share.

"I'm not getting married or having children," he answered defensively. His eyes remained closed, and his fingers continued to move. "If that's what you really want to know, it won't happen."

"Chill, Landon. I didn't ask about your future plans with a woman. I'm asking about your past and your present." When he remained silent, I probed gently. "I didn't mean to upset you. Can you at least tell me why you don't want to marry or have children?"

"I didn't say I didn't want to… said I *wasn't*. I don't want to discuss it with a woman who may not be here tomorrow." He opened his eyes, and his hand stopped moving. "Can you not talk to me like I'm in therapy?"

"Habit that I'll try to break." I studied our hands, which were almost touching. "I'll be here tomorrow. That's why I'm here with you today. I want to be a better woman and practice the results of processing every aspect of my life." I raised my hand. "I know… I know… I sound like my therapist. And I still fear that after all is said and done, I'm just as screwed up as I was three years ago."

His pinky hesitantly rubbed my hand. "We're all screwed up in some ways. At least you're trying to address it, even if it has taken years."

We locked eyes again, and his gaze drifted to my lips. He moved closer before abruptly turning on his back and covering his eyes with the back of his arm. "You need to leave."

His shift in mood hurt. "What did I do?"

"Nothing and everything." He flipped his legs over the bed and stood up. "Going to take a shower, and please don't follow me."

"Didn't you take a shower last night when we came inside from the pool?"

"I take more than one shower a day." He walked toward the bathroom without turning around. His basketball shorts hung low, emphasizing his toned back and taut ass.

I rose on my arms. "Are you hard?"

Landon looked over his shoulder. "Can you go visit your family or something?"

"You are." I clapped my hands. "Let me see."

"Bye, Janae." He touched the bathroom knob.

Before I lost my courage, I quickly said, "Can you write and produce a song with me? Maybe fly to Los Angeles and cut it in the studio. The song will be a smash, and we could perform it during our tour." At his hesitation, I continued, "The cameras won't record us if you don't want them to. And it was Del's idea, which I think is a good one."

"Janae, we fought amongst ourselves and Del to get this far. The band just decided how we wanted the album to flow, and asking them to create a song with you might be too much."

I countered, "It can be a single, and it doesn't have to go on your album."

"They won't agree."

"Then let me talk to them. I owe them an apology, too."

"I don't know." He tapped the wall next to the door.

"It's hard to talk to you with your back to me," I reminded him.

"We'll talk after I shower."

I hugged a pillow to my chest and smiled. "So, I don't have to leave?"

"No," he snapped, and shut the bathroom door behind him.

"I can help you with your little problem," I called after him.

"It's not little," he yelled back.

"No, it's not at all," I muttered before lying back down and smiling at the recessed lighting overhead. Whether he realized it or not, Landon had given me hope. And a possible hit record.

CHAPTER EIGHT
landon

I NEEDED THE COLD SHOWER. I didn't want to be affected by her. I didn't want to like her or enjoy her presence, and yet she made me feel normal in ways my guitar didn't. Janae had an infectious, playful energy that eased my usual discomfort with people I considered strangers. She'd slept in my bed twice, and I'd been able to relax enough to sleep. I'd become accustomed to sleeping alone, and having a woman who insisted on curving her body to mine had been unnerving, to say the very least. I was thirty-one years old, and my body still responded like a teenager's because a woman flirted with me in my bed. I believed in order and structure, and Janae welcomed chaos. Still, I was pleased she'd sought me out last night and hadn't wanted to leave.

The water raining over me and cooling off my heated skin helped bring logic, not emotion, back to the forefront. Women had always been challenging to navigate. On the surface, I understood why they were attracted to me outside of my success. As the only child of two well-known musicians, I'd had unwanted attention most of my young life. With my hazel eyes and features considered handsome, cameras loved me whenever I held the hand of either of my parents or played the trumpet or piano.

As I grew older, my discomfort became a nuisance and then an embarrassment to my parents, who finally decided to keep me from the public eye. When I re-emerged as a talented musician in my own right and as the leader of a soul band, not the classical, Juilliard-trained musician they'd raised me to

71

be, my tendency to shy away from interviews and perform with my head bowed only made me more of a mystery like a puzzle to solve. Except I was a simple man whose only complexity was processing the world differently than others.

When I first met Cedrick, I'd wished I were more like him. Charismatic and bold. He knew what to say or do in any situation without much thought. I envied his arrogance and assurance with women that extended beyond the bedroom. He would have had sex with Janae by now and not thought twice about it. Meanwhile, I stared at my reflection in the bathroom mirror, trying to build my inner confidence through the outer version of me. The outer me was a fit, virile man with intense eyes and an orthodontic-fixed smile that I'd been told transformed my face on the rare times others had noticed. The inner me warred for peace whenever I experienced discomfort around others, wondering if they could see the scared boy I'd been and, in some ways, still was.

"Everything okay?" Janae called.

I looked around the bathroom. I'd forgotten to bring another outfit in and didn't want to wear the shorts I'd slept in. "Grab me a T-shirt and shorts."

"You didn't say 'please.'" She giggled. "Get them yourself. I've seen your body."

I gripped the counter. "Janae. I'm serious."

A minute later, she knocked on the door. I hurriedly wrapped a towel around my waist and opened it wide enough to take the clothes from a smirking Janae, whose lusty gaze heated my chest and abs. I shut the door, donned the cargo shorts and red T-shirt, and prayed that a fully dressed Janae waited on the other side.

"Are you dressed yet? I need to rinse my mouth and wash my face. Is there an extra toothbrush?"

"No." I reluctantly opened the door, and a still-dressed Janae pushed past me.

She grabbed my toothpaste and moved to the left side of the double vanity. "Just use the other sink," she said.

"So… so distracting." Teasing flowed from my mouth without thought. The ease with which she shared my space soothed my nerves.

"Everything seems to distract you," Janae wryly commented, meeting my gaze in the mirror. She washed her hands before pressing the tube from the center.

I took it from her hand and moved the paste from the bottom. "You're messing up my toothpaste. There's a right way to do this."

"I see that you're particular about your things." She mocked me with a fake British accent as she held her index finger out for me to spread the Colgate on the tip.

"I'm sure you have a certain way you'd do things, too, if I were in your space."

She looked around the tidy bathroom. "Probably not. I'm pretty open. My place is a mess until the maid service cleans it. I bet you don't need a maid."

"I don't like strangers in my space."

She smiled. "You seem comfortable with my being here."

Electricity crackled between us as she looked at me with flirty eyes. I leaned my back against the other counter and pushed the travel-size mouthwash toward her. "What type of song do you want to do with The Hollow Bones? Our styles are not compatible."

Janae opened the mouthwash. "They don't have to be. Think eclectic, like 'Bohemian Rhapsody' and Meg's 'Mamushi.' We can combine our styles. I might rap, hop it up, or keep it soulful. Or a combination. I usually decide my flow in the moment while I listen to the bomb beats or the notes that you create. The best music comes out of a jam session."

My creative juices flooded with possibility, and I couldn't help my anticipatory grin. "You write most of your songs?"

She nodded. "I may not be able to play any instrument, but I have an ear for music. I usually collaborate on some of the riffs and hooks. The lyrics are mostly mine." Janae brushed the paste on her teeth with her finger and then used the mouthwash.

"We've never written and recorded an original song with another artist. We usually play in the background or create and collaborate with an artist if we want a singer. We could write and compose the song and let you sing it. They might go for it then."

Janae turned on the water to spit in the sink, and I passed her one of the hand towels stacked neatly on the marble counter. She wiped her mouth. "No. It has to be a true collaboration, or I'm not doing it."

I tilted my head. "If you want it to happen, you may not have a choice."

She shrugged. "Then I won't do it. My voice matters, too."

"You're coming to us, and now we're the bigger artist," I pointed out.

Janae frowned. "I'm fully aware that the power has shifted. I allowed my voice to be silenced in the industry, and I won't anymore. Take it or leave it."

"Then we leave it as a tour only. We are a band who makes our own music. Period. But I'm not and won't ever shut down your voice simply because you're a woman." I bristled. "I'm not that chauvinistic dude who can't see the talent in a woman outside her sex appeal. Do you know who my mother is?"

"Sorry." She grabbed my wrist, stopping me from leaving the bathroom. "I know we can make magic happen together. The way you play that guitar hits me in the pit of my soul. Those chords you struck for my song bolted through me like electricity and had the audience begging for more. Where did you learn to play like that?"

I bit back my prideful smile. "Natural gift, with some training. I have two musically inclined parents who pushed the piano, violin, and trumpet on me. The guitar pulled me despite their best intentions to make me a jazz or classical musician."

Her eyes widened. "You play all those instruments?"

"Once you learn the piano, skills generalize to the other ones." I jammed my hands in my pockets. "I need to talk to Cedrick and the guys."

She clasped her hands together. "Does this mean that you're on board?"

"Doesn't matter if the rest say no." My stomach grumbled its hunger. "I need to eat."

"Is that your way of asking me to breakfast?" She followed me out of the bathroom.

"Are you hungry?"

She grinned. "I can eat."

"*Antwone Fisher.*"

She smiled wider. "Yep. I loved that movie. I had to watch it during one of my therapy groups. Why did you watch it?"

"Same reason," I admitted quietly. "Come on, let's get something to eat."

"I can show you my city." Janae looked at me expectantly.

I shrugged. "By the time we eat, they'll be awake. You can grovel to the band and plead your case."

She studied my face before she pulled on the drawstring of my hoodie. "I need to go back to my suite at the Four Seasons and change first. I didn't plan to spend the night."

"As in penthouse suite? Is Del paying for you to stay in a penthouse?"

"No. I'm paying for this whole trip. Del had to work overtime to get me this gig." She averted her gaze over my shoulder. "I had to agree to do it for free."

"You performed at the rodeo for free? Can you afford to stay in a penthouse? You haven't made any music in over three years."

Janae had been a young starlet who rose and fell in a short period of time. Not long enough to have money stacked for the rest of her life unless she'd invested well, and I was highly doubtful that a twenty-something from the poorest part of Houston knew how to handle her money.

"I haven't stayed in a penthouse in a long time, and I couldn't return to Houston and stay in a basic hotel. Cameras are following me for a reality show. My comeback has to be big. I can afford this splurge."

"Those two ladies were your hire too?"

She stamped her foot lightly. "I needed a wardrobe and makeup team."

"For one show?" I shook my head and headed toward the door.

Janae blocked me. "How does it look to my fans if I'm doing my own makeup and styling myself before one of the biggest concerts in the very city that I'm from? Huh? It's hard enough that Del managed to convince me to perform without my dancers and background. I can't go down looking like that. Like I'm the loser everyone believes I am."

I turned the knob. "It makes you look real, Janae. You are a fallen star trying to soar again. Show them how hard it is in this industry, not this fake image. Then you know who really rides for you. But hey, if you prefer quantity over quality, that's on you."

"Stop judging me," she admonished me.

After I walked through the door, I said over my shoulder, "*You* made *me* your moral compass."

"Ten minutes, tops." Janae turned around to face me at the door to the suite. "The camera crew isn't back until tonight, so you can chill while I get ready."

My stomach growled again. "Or we can order room service, because nothing in me believes it will take you ten minutes. It already was a thirty-minute ride here."

Her beautiful eyes shone hopefully as she slowly kissed my cheek. "I want to be outside with you."

The heat rose between us again, and I stepped back before I succumbed to her allure. "Not happening, Janae."

"What's not happening?" She pouted prettily.

Drawing an impatient breath, I asked, "What's the code? I'm starving."

She punched in a code and waltzed inside.

I slowly entered her luxurious temporary living space as she hurried past the formal dining and comfy living areas to her bedroom. This would have cost her a pretty penny. If she spent money like this all the time for her image with the lawsuits and lack of recent hits plaguing her, how long would her money last? Maybe this was why she was so insistent on making a record, doing this tour, and destroying three years of sobriety like it meant nothing. She needed cash.

"If you want a snack or something, you can request anything, and the chef will prepare it. But you better not get full, Landon," she called from the bedroom before she turned on the shower. She peeked her head around the door, and her shoulders were bare. "I want to go to a nice restaurant and have virgin mimosas and eggs Benedict with crab."

The vision of a naked Janae invaded my mind as my cell buzzed.

WYA?

I responded to Brian's text. *With Janae.*

Brian sent an eggplant and a peach emoji, and I sent the middle finger emoji.

What time you getting back?

In a couple of hours, why?

Cedrick wants to meet. Del asked us to do a record with Janae. You probably already know that.

Yeah. You think it's a good idea?

I do. She smashed the stage and we're getting buzz. Cedrick, on the other hand, hates the idea. Thinks she will take the focus away from us.

I sank back into the sofa. I agreed with Cedrick. Janae had too much natural star power to *not* take the focus from The Hollow Bones. The difference was that I didn't care about attention, and Cedrick lived for it.

Janae wants to plead her case. I'll bring her back with me.

No women at meetings.

I made the rule, remember? We can meet to decide after she leaves.

Bet.

Bet.

Janae was still in the shower. I took a deep breath before I finally scrolled through social media for the first time in two days. The Friday night incident was trending even without my googling it, photos of Cash Black against the wall after I'd punched him and pics of me with Janae thrown over my shoulder like I were a caveman. The stories indicated that it had been a fight between me and Cash over Janae, not a concerned man protecting a woman from potential harm. Someone had even captured a video of us speeding away like Bonnie and Clyde leaving the bank after a heist.

I leaned forward, resting my elbows on my thighs as I perused the thousands of comments. Most were positive and supported us as a couple. Women expressed interest in discovering more about me, since I didn't have any social media accounts. Only a few reactions were negative, calling Janae a slut and a homewrecker. No one said anything negative about me, since I was the hero in this scenario, trying to rescue his woman. Before this trip, I would probably have judged Janae similarly if I wasn't the man in the photos. I would have believed she hadn't changed, was up to her old tricks, and thought no more of her. One thing I hated more than anything else was wasted talent.

Janae was wasting hers, though I'd pretended I meant Cash Black when she asked me. When she called me out on it, I'd lied, unable to say it to her face. For three years she'd been sober, and now she'd broken the promise to herself because she led her performance with her head instead of her heart. I'd judged her harshly and was downright mean in how I viewed her. Maybe I was wrong.

In the little time we'd spent together, I'd realized that I had perceptions about her that might have been true in the past but no longer seemed to fit. I'd witnessed the nervous, scared, and unsure Janae. The funny, sensitive, and honest Janae. I'd even seen her pissed. I'd also observed how vulnerable and alone she was in the world. To be in the city of your birth and have no one from your family attend your show or stay with you in a penthouse meant to be shared spoke volumes without her ever telling me anything about her people.

If she and I were going to be tour mates for the next two months, I wouldn't do anything to dispel the rumors that we were a couple. I would be there for her as a friend rather than a foe.

Or, at least, I'd try. The woman was so irresistibly sexy and frustrating. Janae would push my buttons in ways I wasn't ready for.

"It took me longer than I thought," she announced softly.

I slowly perused her body and stood up when she strolled out in a flowy, thin-strapped, long pink sundress and flat silver sandals. The shower had curled her loose hair around her face. I could hear my breath hitch, which meant she probably did, too. If this outfit was an attempt to downplay her allure, all it had done was enhance Janae's natural beauty. I could stare at this woman all day.

She arched her brow slightly. "Landon, you good?"

"Um… yeah. You look nice." *Shit.* I cleared my throat. "Change of plans. The guys want to meet now. We'll pick up something to eat on the way back."

Her smile faltered, and she moved to me, rubbing her stomach. "I don't have an appetite now."

I awkwardly grasped her shoulders. "Hey… hey… It's going to be fine. Our bark is worse than our bite."

"Barks hurt too. Should I even waste my time? You know them."

"It's only a waste of time if they nix the idea." The warmth of her bare skin underneath my hands aroused me, and my voice deepened of its own volition. "Are you sure you can handle all of this? This is only the start of your apology tour."

"Apology tour? I made a mistake, and now I'm moving forward." Her face wrinkled with distaste, zapping my growing desire. "Either people accept me, or they don't. I'm not begging The Hollow Bones or anyone to forgive me. I spent years in therapy to forgive myself."

I dropped my hands. "You really don't believe you owe anyone an apology? I thought you said you would apologize at the house."

She folded her arms. "Whoever I owed one already received one."

"You don't get it, do you?" I hit the back of one hand in my other. "You blew off a lot of people, canceled appearances and shows. People lost money. Hollow Bones lost money and opportunities. You can't just get back in the game like you didn't hurt people. You want a legit shot, then be ready to scoff down humble pie wherever you go."

Janae straightened her shoulders and lifted her chin. "Or let my talent speak for itself."

We stared at each other for a few seconds. Neither of us wavered on our stance. My stomach broke the standoff, and we both chuckled.

"Then shoot your shot and hope it's not your foot," I said.

She giggled. "I love the way you slide in an insult or a judgment. It's a good thing I have thick skin."

"Not trying to hurt your feelings. Sometimes I'm unsure how my actions or words may hurt someone." I placed my cell in my pocket and strode to the door. "Looks like we're trending as the new couple. The Hollow Bones gained thousands of followers since Friday night. Probably best we're getting food to go anyway."

"You don't want to be seen with me?" Janae couldn't quite hide the hurt in her teasing tone.

"I don't want to be seen, period." I pulled my hat down farther on my head. A part of me wanted the fellas to say no to recording a song together. I didn't want the attention she would bring, not quite ready to admit that the more time I spent with her, the more I wanted her. And my simple, foolish heart couldn't afford to fall for a complicated woman like Janae.

CHAPTER NINE

janae

ACID, AND NOT FROM HUNGER, burned holes in my stomach as we walked back into the house carrying containers of eggs, bacon, sausage, pancakes, waffles, biscuits, and grits. Men loved sex and food, and since the only man I wanted to sex in this group was already on my side, I'd settled for food. It had to work. I needed The Hollow Bones to agree to record a song with me. It was my best chance to get back in the game and win again. Landon had been cooperative and accommodating when I suggested buying everyone brunch, and had helped me order their favs. He'd eaten a plain biscuit with a side of sausage to feed his growling belly before we left this Black-owned breakfast spot, willing to accommodate my order quickly once they knew who we were.

Brian, who lounged in the large living area, jumped up when he saw the food. He smiled wide, displaying dimples I'd never noticed, and quickly pulled his locs into a man bun with the band around his wrist. "I was just about to order something. Please say I smell cheese grits. Nothing like Southern cooking."

I sighed internally. *One down. Three more to go.* "Yep. Got butter and cheesy." I opened the cabinets and found plates and platters. With the help of Brian and Landon, I soon converted the wide marble island into a buffet full of delicious food, complete with orange juice and mimosas chilling in champagne flutes.

I nudged Landon's side. "Can you tell everyone that food is here?"

Landon yelled, "Food."

I popped his arm. "I could have done that."

Brian snickered. "They might not have come if they heard your voice."

"They really hate me?" I ignored the urge to rub my stomach.

"Hate is relative. Hate you as a human being, hate that you lost us money, hate that we've been coerced to perform with you, or hate that you might be the one to get us through the gate? Several hates to choose from." He tossed a biscuit to Landon, who immediately chomped on it.

I groaned. "That's not a good answer."

"It's the most truthful one."

"Then answer this." I straightened the plates into a tighter stack.

Brian gripped the island, his expression expectant.

"Do you want to do a song with me?"

He tugged on his long beard. "It's not if *I* want to do it. It's up to the band. We don't make moves until we all agree."

"Still, I want to know how *you* feel."

"He told you already. We don't make moves until we all agree," Cedrick growled as he entered the kitchen. A young, pretty woman wearing last night's party dress followed him.

"You speak for Brian, too?" I said.

"What she mean by that?" Landon asked as he leaned on the counter near the refrigerator, holding a flute of orange juice.

Cedrick replied, "She accused me of speaking for you… like I have control over what you do." He addressed the woman draping her arms all over him. "You want something to eat before you go?"

"That's not what I meant," I replied.

Landon turned to me. "What did you mean?"

"Do you want to stay or go?" Cedrick again asked the woman, who seemed more interested in our conversation than in answering him.

"Of course she wants to stay as long as you let her," I answered impatiently as I picked up a plate. "What do you want to eat? Shit?"

"Don't forget to add some pancakes to that shit," Cedrick drawled.

"Peace… peace," Brian interjected. "I need peace with my breakfast."

Landon swallowed his juice, grabbed two slices of bacon, and left the kitchen before I could explain what had transpired between me and his best friend. His quiet exit blew louder than a bullhorn. I had to humble myself. I couldn't let Cedrick get under my skin. I'd fucked up. Not him. He had every right not to trust me.

Humble pie. "Peace while we eat. Got it." I smiled at Cedrick. "I don't mind getting you a plate. What would you like?"

"I can make his plate," the woman tersely said, and kissed him, marking her territory.

"Trust me, you can have him and his plate." I raised my hands before anyone said anything. "Sorry… sorry. Peace."

Cedrick only smirked while she busied herself, preparing his plate like she was prepping for a role as wifey. I'd been on this side of the music business and knew most of these musicians and entertainers played at love. They ran through women like a flash flood, and at one point, I'd gone through men the same way. Along the way, I lost a man who'd tried to be there for me, and with how Landon just left, I might have lost him before I'd ever had him. Who was I to judge Cedrick or anyone?

The internal burn coated my stomach and chest again. I closed my eyes briefly. *Breathe in good thoughts and push out any negativity.*

I grabbed a flute of orange juice and gulped it down before I plopped a large scoop of cheese grits on Brian's plate. "More?"

He nodded happily. "I want the whole container."

"Hey… I want some grits." Charles walked in, shirtless, his walnut-hued chest completely tatted, rubbing his bald head.

"Bruh, we have women in here. Put on some clothes." Brian threw a dishtowel at him.

Charles shrugged. "Janae and whoever this woman is have seen more than this. They'll survive."

"Mocha," Cedrick's random announced.

"That's your name or coffee flavor?" Charles's bland, unconcerned tone completely flew over her head.

"My name," she said proudly.

"No one gives a fuck… especially Cedrick," Brian said under his breath, and I pinched his forearm. "Quit it, Janae."

"You want more cheese grits or not?" I replied.

He held his hands up. "Okay… I'll stop."

Another woman sporting a club dress led Santiago by the hand into the kitchen. "Looks good, Janae. And you remembered salsa. Thanks." He rubbed his hands together with a huge grin.

"How do you know she did this?" Brian asked as if insulted.

Santiago only scoffed, picked up a plate, and asked the lady, "What do you want to eat?"

At least he had manners. Santiago could be another ally. Cedrick would be the hardest to convince. Yet he was a businessman first. I had to appeal to his practical side without invoking his obstinate one.

The men moved around the kitchen like brothers, eating, teasing, smiling, and talking. They were a family. These would be my tour mates for the next two months. Ten cities. And I would win them over by taking care of them like I used to take care of my brother. The Hollow Bones would become my family, too. They would love me like they loved each other.

"You not eating?" Charles asked.

"Wanted to make sure there was enough," I improvised. My appetite was long gone.

He passed me a plate with a waffle and sausage. "Eat."

I preferred the eggs and bacon, but no way was I going to refuse a plate from the most nonchalant member of The Hollow Bones. I gladly received the food. "Thank you."

Charles grunted as he pulled out a stool at the island so I could sit. He and Brian joined me, and we broke bread together.

Progress.

With clasped hands, I stood before the men in the living area, where they were all sprawled out on the large maroon sectional and coordinating chaise longue. The women were gone, and appetites had been satisfied.

"Hear me out," I began.

"What do you think we're doing when we should be practicing?" Cedrick asked, centering the sectional with his arms strewn across its back.

Landon, who'd disappeared until I texted him that I was starting the meeting, straddled the chaise nearest me. "She won't take long."

Grateful for his presence, I smiled at him, and his brows dipped until the ends touched. *Okay.* I was on my own. "Despite what happened Friday night, I'm not that same chick you knew from the past."

The men snickered. Even Landon smirked.

"Seriously, I wasn't being a diva. I didn't know I was expected to be at the rehearsal the whole time. Cash's words got the best of me and threw me off. I didn't want to mess up the show for you or him. I did use after being clean for three years. I was a nervous wreck, and I couldn't figure out how to calm down without taking anything. But it won't happen again. I'll see my therapist as soon as I get back to Los Angeles. I'm not craving or tempted to use again."

"It can't happen again," Cedrick said firmly. "No drunken, drugged-out moments like Friday. No diva behavior. Whenever we rehearse, you stay the entire time and be on time. In fact, be there fifteen minutes early. We only have ten shows, and we don't have time for your shit, Janae. Del begged us to take you and guaranteed us a nice paycheck. Without that, we would have passed on you."

Refusing to allow his words to penetrate the armor I'd used to rise as far as I had, I boasted with a smug smile, "And your paycheck will double, possibly triple. New Orleans, Atlanta, and now New York are sold out. The rest of the shows are almost sold out. Los Angeles is the biggest venue, and by the time we wrap up there, promoters will be begging us to add more dates. Just think how much attention and money we can make if we have a hit single. A single that shoots to the top within a matter of weeks." I placed my hands on my hips. "I wrote the lyrics to every single number-one smash I had. I'll do it again. This time backed by The Hollow Bones."

"It's not our music." Santiago checked his watch. "We want to maintain who we are. We've won Grammys based on who we are. Mainstream has a way of demanding we melt into the machine and lose our uniqueness and individuality."

I stepped closer to them. "I'm not asking you to do my music. I'm proposing *our* music."

"Naw… it's The Hollow Bones and then Janae. There is no 'our' in whatever we create," Cedrick retorted.

"She just meant for the single." Brian sounded exasperated. "Janae has a point. We would make serious loot while the iron is hot. This will bring more eyes on us while we still do what we do best. Our second LP can be a commercial and artistically sound success, remembered forever. Pop music isn't the devil."

Charles snorted. "Just the idea of changing our music to reflect what's popular has caused a rift in the band. Creating a song with you could further divide us. We can't fall like many bands before us. The only thing that's a fact is that past behavior predicts future behavior. Hence, Friday night. Yeah, you killed it, but you were high, and if Landon didn't intervene, you were headed to Cash's room. We're all men, and you're the only woman. I don't want to risk our solid brand or our rep as good guys."

The other men nodded while Landon hunched forward. The tension from his body bounced off him.

"You have every right not to trust me or believe I've changed. You've laid down the rules and made it clear that you won't tolerate my past behavior. I accept your rules. Now, I need the chance to prove that this tour and recording a song with me isn't a mistake. I'm not asking you to shift your style of music to mine or change anything for me. I'm proposing a meeting of two worlds. People love the familiar and what's trending. Who says we can't establish the trend and let them follow us? Lauryn Hill's versatility made The Fugees different from any hip-hop group."

"And that group disbanded after two albums," Cedrick reminded me. "Let's tour first, and if you don't fuck it up, then we might consider an original song with you. The spotlight is already on us, and our brand is everything."

The guys all nodded except Landon. He leaned forward as if to say something and then sat back, tightening his jaw.

I took it as a sign that he still thought like I did. That hopping on it now was a better move.

A new idea popped up. I bounced on my toes. "Where are your instruments?"

Brian said, "Why?"

Landon answered, "On the ground floor."

"I can show you better than I can tell you." I beckoned them as I practically skipped through the house and down the stairs.

The men reluctantly joined me in the makeshift band room.

"Everyone go to their spots." I clapped my hands.

"We're not kids," Charles grumbled as he picked up the saxophone.

Surprisingly, Cedrick went to the keyboards without complaint. Santiago stood behind his bass, and Brian picked up his sticks. Landon lifted his guitar and strummed a few chords. Santiago nodded and replicated what he'd just heard.

I closed my eyes, allowing the sounds to carry me away. I uttered, "You got a way, got a way, got a way… pulling me closer, again and again.."

A drumbeat followed the pattern set by Landon and Santiago, followed by the sexy, melodic sound of the sax.

"Shit, y'all can play," I said, eyes closed. Words raced through my head. "Our song is a celebration of music… a love ode, right? We're talking about the love of music, but people will think we're talking about intimacy and passion between two people. We can even add a trumpet somewhere. Maybe an acoustic guitar. I'm waiting for the keys." I teased, "Trying to figure out where you fit in, Ced?"

"Cedrick," he corrected me crossly, though a second later, he joined in.

I hummed and swayed to the smooth sounds of The Hollow Bones. After a few notes had passed, the lyrics sprang from me. "Never thought I would find someone like you… someone so true, so fly, who gets my blues…"

More flowed from me as I settled into the groove. Brian whistled his approval before he quickened the pace. "Think it should be a more up-tempo song so Janae can throw a few bars after she sings."

Santiago said, "Nah… we should keep the whole song mellow. No rap."

"But she's known for her lyrical skills, too. Our new song should have bars and a hook," Charles argued, and I hid the smile that threatened as the band continued playing.

"Let whatever happens happen," Brian suggested.

More lyrics poured out of me, and we jammed. Our love of music overrode any differences. Only good vibes infused the space, and what had been a good idea by our manager became the best one in a long time.

I left my eyes closed to keep my head in the moment. Watching the men perform would disrupt my creativity, and right then, we were all on a fantastic roll. I swayed my arms around, listening for each instrument, judging the clarity and the blend. "The sound is so clear, and we just made this up. Imagine a trumpet coming in right now. The instrumentation will be even more powerful in the studio and these small venues, reminding fans why a real band hits harder than synths. Reminding the world why The Hollow Bones is not only relevant but the best in the world."

The band continued, and I opened my eyes and pleaded, "Come on, we can do this. The first time around, I didn't know my worth and how much I lost before. Now, I do, and I'm in therapy. I won't let you down again."

I kept my arms by my sides, though I wanted so badly to cross them over my rapidly beating heart as I awaited their answer.

Cedrick addressed the guys. "The Hollow Bones will play strong and clear for the first thirty seconds. Santiago can add a trumpet twenty seconds in. Let Janae come in with her big voice, and then before the song ends, she'll rip a couple of bars, and we'll finish with the instrumental and her humming. I think we could mix our two styles without losing us."

My chest expanded as I searched for Landon's approval. He stared back, expressionless, yet to speak.

I planted my hands on my hips again. "It's only been a half-hour, and we've figured out the arrangement. So, do we want to wait until two months to complete and release the song?"

Everyone except Landon looked at Cedrick. Cedrick's nostrils flared as he grudgingly agreed. "Fine. We'll go into the studio once we go home to New York for our shows. That's four cities in, and we'll know if you're worth our brand to do a record by then."

I bounced slightly from foot to foot. "I wanted to cut it in Los Angeles before we started the tour… I thought the laid-back vibe would inspire us. If we do the record now, we can open or close with the song when we perform together."

Landon finally spoke. "New York after four cities. Del will handle the money and business side, and it will be The Hollow Bones featuring Janae Warner."

The room grew eerily silent, and I realized that as much as Cedrick appeared to be the voice, Landon was undoubtedly the one everyone listened to, including me.

"That works." I nodded.

Brian suddenly picked me up and spun me around.

I squealed with delight and tapped his back to put me down. "Stop it."

"We're about to be on top." He placed me back on my feet, and I returned his beaming smile.

"It's time for the band to meet alone. If you need to take the Rover back to the hotel, you can. One of us will retrieve it later," Landon drily commented as he re-tuned his guitar.

"I planned to support the band at tonight's show, so I can bring it back tonight or meet you at the venue," I offered, hating the timidity in my voice at Landon's blunt tone.

Brian returned to his drum set, and the others drifted to their instruments.

"No need. We can get a car to drive us tonight. If I don't see you later, catch you in New Orleans in a month," Landon said, pushing down his hat. He turned, facing his bandmates, effectively dismissing me.

Suddenly, my victory seemed hollow. No pun intended.

"Hey, Del. The guys went for it. They want to cut a record with me," I announced through the Rover's speaker once he answered the phone. "We started working on the song, and I just know it'll be a hit."

I'd decided to borrow the vehicle and drive around the city to process my feelings about Landon and why his dismissal mattered so much. Cedrick was a bit nicer, and the other guys seemed to accept me. I should have been happy, and all I could fret about was Landon's coolness toward me.

The longer I drove, the longer the burning feeling faded. I couldn't allow a man I didn't even really know three days ago to make me feel less than. I had to be different in every way from the old me, and being different required that I wouldn't rely on what a man thought of me to dictate my emotions. I had convinced an award-winning group of men who didn't trust me to work with me. I should and would be happy and proud of what I'd done today, regardless of Landon's hot-cold behavior.

"That's good news, and a good look for you and Hollow. We can hammer out the details tomorrow once we leave Houston and take it from there." He paused. "The film crew has been looking for you. You're back home, Janae. We could be getting good behind-the-scenes footage, like of your old house, the schools you went to, your favorite places, and memories, and you keep disappearing. This is your homecoming. People want to know your background."

"I'll be back in time for Hollow Bones' show. We can film me getting ready for that, our planning for the tour, and I can show you my schools and my old neighborhood tomorrow before we head to Los Angeles," I said matter-of-factly, though I bit back tears that I didn't have happy memories of favorite places in Houston. Bad things had happened to me there. I lived in L.A. now, but with everything that'd gone down with my career and my last relationship, I wasn't sure I had a home base anymore. No place brought me comfort.

"Where are you? The cameras should be with you now. It's a beautiful Sunday."

"I just left Hollow Bones' place, and they don't want to be filmed."

Del countered, "They agreed to be filmed if it's related to the music, and if you were negotiating with them about music, the cameras should have been there."

If the cameras had been there, we wouldn't have created the start of a beautiful song together, and I doubted they would've agreed to do a record with me. I kept those thoughts to myself.

"I call you with good news, and I'm getting a lecture about what I should be doing and asking about my whereabouts. You're my manager, not my father."

He cleared his throat. "As your manager and not your father, I spoke to your mother and brother on your behalf. They're willing to be filmed, and they want to see you. We can stay another day or two to record you reuniting with your family again."

"You did what?" I tried to temper my tone and language out of respect. "Please, say you didn't speak to my family without my permission. Del, you're overstepping."

"I'm not. Your mother contacted me through the local radio station Friday night because she doesn't have your phone number, asking why she wasn't invited to see you perform. I didn't get the message until this morning. I called her to apologize for the oversight and explained that you were an invited guest to the show. I told her that you were probably waiting to invite her to one of your shows on the road. I also told her we were filming a reality series, and she wanted to be a part of it."

"Del, if I wanted my mother to see my show Friday or any other show, I would've invited her."

"I know that, but she sounded so hurt, and I couldn't make her feel worse," he reasoned.

I pulled to the side of the street and stared out the windshield. "I don't want her to be a part of my reality series or to be reunited for the cameras. I'm not ready. Not sure if I'll ever be ready."

"Your mother seems to be trying, Janae, and as a father who isn't on the best terms with my children, I know that sometimes all we need is a push in the right direction. I wish someone would help me reconnect with my kids."

His tone was wistful. I hadn't known that he had problems with his children. He never talked about his family, and I guessed I'd never asked because he seemed content with his work and life. Still, he couldn't bring his personal issues into any decisions concerning me.

"Sounds like a 'you' problem," I replied.

"Do I need to remind you for the millionth time that it was your idea to do a reality series following you as you make your comeback? People want to see it all, Janae. Of course they want to see a glamorous world most will never know. But they also want to know if you're just like them. Even if you're not ready to talk to your family, I still want to give them a chance to speak. You can get final approval before we release their portion of the video. Then you can do a confessional about your feelings on whatever they decide to say or talk about."

"You don't get it. I haven't even spoken to my mother in four years. I've been to hell and back, and she refused my calls. She doesn't care about me, and my brother does whatever she says. I don't want people to know that sob story." I wiped the tears that I hated still fell whenever I thought about the people who were supposed to love me unconditionally.

"That's exactly why they should know. It's your truth, Janae. Maybe then people can see why you self-destructed like you did before. Maybe people can understand how a talented and vibrant twenty-eight-year-old has no friends or family. Isn't this show more than just about your comeback? I thought this was a chance to show people the real you so they can stop judging your mistakes so harshly. I wanted to work with you because of your honesty. I see your determination and can feel your heart. Let the world see and feel it, too."

"Ugh… I hate it when you're right." I chuckled through my tears. "I'm serious, Del. I need complete control on the final cut involving my family. I don't care what the producer says."

"I'll work it out."

"Then you have my permission to talk to my family, but there'll be no reunion on camera."

I hung up and watched from three houses down as my mother, in her Sunday best, carried two plastic bags of groceries from her black 4Runner into the four-bedroom home I'd bought her with my first big check. She looked the same yet different, her pretty, cinnamon-colored face softer than I remembered.

Maybe she'd changed like I had. Maybe Del had been right, and she was hurt that I didn't invite her to my first show in three years at the rodeo, a place she loved. A place where I'd envisioned I'd perform as a kid, to a packed house with my family in the stands beaming back at me.

In one of her nicer moods when I was a teenager, Mom had told me she'd dreamed of seeing me be a headliner for the rodeo. Maybe she'd realized the error of her ways when I didn't invite her to the one event where she would've loved to see me perform. Maybe she wanted to make amends for not being the mother she should've been to me. Maybe she wanted to love me like I'd always loved her.

I waved as if I wanted her to see me as she walked inside and shut the door. "Hey, Mommy. I finally did it. I made Houston proud. I hope you're proud of me, too."

I didn't know how long I wept in the car, too afraid to get out and see if my maybes were correct, too afraid to talk to the woman who'd brought me into the world, too afraid she would trigger me worse than anyone or anything when my sanity needed to be protected.

My phone rang, and it was Del again. Instead of answering, I wiped my eyes and running nose with the sleeves of my sweatshirt and pressed the ignition button.

CONFESSIONAL

janae

"**DID YOU SEE THAT? YOUR** girl is trending! I'm still the name in their mouths!" I grinned, leaning closer. "Okay, okay. I know how it looked Friday night... Wherever MILA goes, trouble follows. I had a little fun that went too far. Landon Hayes, of the amazing Hollow Bones, thought he had to rescue me. I was a regular damsel for just one night." I licked my lips. "Isn't he delicious? Like, look at him and the way he plays that guitar like he's caressing a woman. Yum."

I winked at the camera. "Believe me, when this tour is over, and you see us on the road with all the shenanigans, he's going to be hot boy number one. And no, he's not my man. Just my overprotective friend who I might be crushing on." I shrugged. "Can you blame me? He tossed me over his shoulder and ran away with me. I have my very own knight."

Out of sight of the camera, the producer asked, "How did you feel performing in front of your home crowd after three years?"

"Y'all, I was beyond nervous. I hadn't performed in three years, and then I got the chance to be in H-Town at the rodeo to debut my comeback. It's like a legit rodeo with cowboys wrangling bulls right before entertainers like myself hit the stage. I pushed through my nerves and had one of my best performances. It's already trending." I smiled at the camera. "It doesn't get better than that.

"Don't tell Cash," I whispered, then laughed. "Okay, he'll probably see this, and he's already salty because Landon knocked him on his ass, but I smashed. Not that Cash didn't understand the assignment. I just had the entire NRG Arena in the palm of my hand. I am thankful for the opportunity to perform at the rodeo and for this tour. Like, seriously. And I can't wait for this tour. Y'all gonna see that Janae Warner is still a force. I'm just a li'l nicer and a whole lot wiser. Wait… that actually rhymed. A li'l nicer and a whole lot wiser." I danced in my chair, doing a roll with my hips. "I can't wait for all the fun, all the music, and all the love."

The producer said, "Tell them why they should watch your show."

Pointing at the camera, I said, "I'm telling you this will be the best time you and I have ever had. Taking a quick break and then hitting the road on a tour bus for the next two months. First, can I say The Hollow Bones?" I winked at the camera. "You saw their show on Sunday with me. Pure magic. I hated that I was backstage watching instead of the front row witnessing five fine-ass men who are all single and hella talented. We're like Snow White, and they're the five… Okay, they're not dwarves, and there's no evil queen. Still, this tour is a fairytale. I'm so lucky that they're on the road with me. Secondly, we have some tricks up our sleeves as we hit these cities. We're starting with New Orleans, and y'all know a lot of foolishness is gonna go down in the Big Easy." I held up three fingers. "I got my girls and glam squad, Frankie and Jeri, who'll paint the town red with me. Lastly, I have you, my fans. I promise to clown with you when I see you. I also promise to be real with you."

I gave an exaggerated throat-cutting motion with a smirk. "Dead me on anything that's not fun, about my music, and on the up-and-up." I leaned forward until the camera almost touched my face. "This is my journey. Buckle up."

CHAPTER TEN

landon

**HARLEM
MARCH 11**

THE SUV PULLED UP BEFORE my renovated brownstone in an affluent neighborhood in Harlem near Columbia University. I jumped out and grabbed my guitar case, backpack, and my rolling bag. I was grateful for the solitude of my home after a week of partying and performing with the guys. My social battery had needed charging after the second day in Houston, and we'd been there for five.

Tours and shows out of the New York area were a necessary evil that we only did occasionally for my benefit. I was a creature of habit. The fast-paced and ever-changing environments, venues, and cities unhinged me. I needed my bubble of comfort everywhere I went. When I performed, I had my hat and guitar and stood on the right of the stage, out of the main spotlight. That was my bubble on stage. My guitar pick was a constant in my pocket. On the road, I had to sleep in rooms with bland colors like white or beige. Too much color overstimulated my mind. We usually leased a home instead of a hotel to meet my need for space so I could unpack mentally and we could play our instruments.

I walked into my multimillion-dollar brownstone. I'd paid handsomely for an interior designer to choose furniture and to decorate my four-story home entirely in white and black. Gray was the pop of color or accent. My house was sparsely furnished. Three bedrooms, including the primary bedroom, contained one king-size bed. The fourth bedroom was my office. It was rarely used and included a desk, two bookshelves, and two chairs. I'd soundproofed the whole house so I could play in any room that inspired me. Sometimes, I'd wake up in my bed, playing my guitar. Or, while cooking dinner, a thought would strike, and I'd have to play. My living area only held a couple of folding chairs, though I'd been there for two years. I didn't need a sofa when I didn't plan to have company.

My only TV was in one of the guest rooms, and I'd bought it to keep abreast of the news and the stock market. Numbers and investments fascinated me. Not even Cedrick knew that I'd made my first million three years ago and had earned another couple this year from studying numbers since I was a boy. I didn't care about the money and figured that the more I earned, the easier it would be to help out family and friends when they were in need. So far, no one I knew needed money.

My thoughts drifted to Janae and how I suspected she would need cash sooner or later if her comeback run didn't work, or worsened her financial situation.

I pulled off my hat and stretched out on the carpet instead of resting in my crisply made bed. I didn't want to shower yet, and I didn't want to contaminate my bed with germs from the flight from Houston. I propped my head on my hands and stared at the glass-paneled ceiling, admiring the reddish gold of a setting sun with thoughts of Janae.

Yesterday, she had waltzed backstage while we were preparing to go on and running through last minute changes with our road crew. She was dressed in a dark suit and wore a cowboy hat, followed by the two cameramen who documented her every step. She greeted The Hollow Bones like we were old friends. She looked good, and though she seemed fully alert, her eyes didn't have their usual light when she tapped my fist instead of offering me the hug she'd given everyone else, including Cedrick, who'd returned her hug and chatted it up with her.

Del and Janae took some pics commemorating our past and future work together. She smiled politely, and anyone who asked for a selfie and an autograph had their request graciously granted. Del had grabbed two chairs for them to sit on while we did our show. I felt her stare while we performed, but she didn't appear to look at me when my gaze searched for her.

When we were done, she congratulated us on a good show and told us she would see us in New Orleans. And as she left, her energy whisked away along with her. I was so deflated that she'd ignored me, and I couldn't express my feelings to anyone. I'd made it clear to the guys and her that she didn't mean anything when I turned my back on her and focused on the band. Janae had honored that. I should've been relieved and not sad that she'd been friendly, polite, and not flirty.

Except I felt horrible. I hadn't meant to treat her like that. Whenever my emotions overwhelmed me, I'd shut down or ignore them.

Maybe I needed a woman's attention to make it easier being around Janae. It'd been at least four months since I'd spent time with any. I had the numbers of a few women who were at my beck and call because they liked being with a musician. A musician who had money. They weren't necessarily groupies, because these women were intelligent, had good jobs, and weren't hanging on, hoping to become a girlfriend or wifey. These women wanted a good time and were content with the status quo.

I continued to gain peace and clarity as I stared up at the ceiling, watching the day slowly turn to night.

My cell rang, and I reluctantly answered my mother's call.

"Hello."

"Hello, son. How long have you been home?" Her perfect diction indicated that she hadn't called to chitchat.

"Maybe an hour." The night wasn't as clear as it had been in Houston, when Janae joined me in the backyard. I couldn't spot any stars or planets.

"I need you to stop over this evening."

The gnawing began as I closed my eyes. "I just got home after two shows and traveling. I'm exhausted."

"It's just for a little while. We're having a dinner party to celebrate a colleague's promotion, and everyone wants to meet the Grammy-winning guitarist of The Hollow Bones," she said proudly.

"The same people you worried wouldn't accept my music because it wasn't good enough? *Those* people?" I asked.

"Landon, forget about the past. These people can get you in the right rooms. One wants to ask you to be a guest lecturer or maybe invite you to the faculty at Juilliard."

"I didn't go to college. When did I ever want to speak in front of people? I thought teaching required public speaking." I sighed deeply. My mother still refused to see her son for who he was.

"Yes, it does. You can focus on playing more than talking. How you teach is at your discretion." Her tone suggested she was smiling. "Just imagine the prestige of teaching young, gifted people everything we taught you."

"Then why don't *you* try to secure a job at Juilliard? I'm sure they're dying to work with you, an alumnus. Or Dad, from Oberlin. It's not Juilliard, but hey. Or maybe you can teach together. It would be a kickass class," I retorted sarcastically.

"They don't want us. They want you."

"It's a Monday night. Who gives dinner parties on a Monday night? What if I wasn't home? Then what?" I shook my head. "I'm not in the mood to deal with strangers, Ma."

"Son, I'll give you until nine to make an appearance, and you can leave by ten." My father's stern voice startled me. "We're not taking no for an answer. You wouldn't even be in a band to travel if I hadn't taught you how to play."

"Yes, sir," the eight-year-old child in me replied meekly.

They hung up the phone, and I curled into a ball, wishing the gnawing would stop.

An hour later, I stood before my family brownstone in Brooklyn Heights, the home and neighborhood I'd grown up in. I'd worn dark cargo pants and a long-sleeved white polo, hoping people wouldn't touch me. At these kinds of intimate, pretentious parties, people liked to grip your hand, forearm, or shoulder as if their touch made sure you listened to whatever self-aggrandizing statement they wanted you to hear. I'd been seven before I allowed anyone but my mother to touch me. My parents knew of my debilitating discomfort around people but didn't seem to care when it involved their image. I was expected to push through and smile.

I opened the heavy door and was assailed with polite chatter, soft laughter, and music… jazz, probably Coltrane or someone new who imitated him. I couldn't quite discern yet. I jammed my right hand in my pocket to rub my pick and walked past the hallway that led to the stairs and into the large living area where the intimate party was held. I barely glanced at the three large portraits of us as a family over the years. One of me at five, then at ten, and lastly at fifteen that lined the hallway. In each one, my parents smiled while I looked straight ahead, hating that this was my family.

The gnawing in my stomach increased the closer I came to my parents' elite friends and musical scholars. My parents were virtuosos of their respective instruments and tenured NYU professors. My mother cherished the violin. My father could rival the greats with his horns. I completed the trio with my mastery of the guitar. We were considered special and blessed as a family.

If they only knew.

My mother's beautiful, serene hazel eyes watched me as I entered the party of ten or twelve guests. I was sure she'd trained her gaze on the door to spot me before I attempted to duck upstairs to my old bedroom. Her perpetually red lips curved into a smile meant to engender warmth from her only child, but all I could feel were unattainable expectations in her welcoming embrace.

"Here's the prodigal son, fresh off a performance down south at the rodeo, of all places." She chuckled as she hugged me. I held on to her soft body to prolong the time before I had to greet the guests waiting to pounce. I tucked my head into her neck and inhaled the familiar Chanel No. 22 perfume she'd always worn because my father loved the scent. "Aww… he must have missed his mother."

The small crowd oohed and aahed, and she pulled back. "I keep hoping I'll see your beautiful hair again."

I pulled down the brim. "My hat is my superpower."

Her forehead wrinkled prettily, and she turned me around to greet the guests. "My handsome son… One day he'll bring home a gifted woman like himself so he can give me some beautiful grandchildren to spoil like we did him."

After I nodded and made the tiniest of responses to three of the guests, my mother curved her arm to my waist and pushed me toward an older woman standing separately from the party, who I could only assume was from Juilliard. The woman with the cloying floral scent that made breathing challenging gripped my forearm, and I clenched my jaw as my mother excused herself. The woman smiled wide, and I focused on the gap in her front teeth.

"Dr. Sarah Howard, faculty at Juilliard. We've been following your career for some time. My area is the piano."

I replied, "I play the guitar."

Her smile faltered a bit. "Yes, but you're also a classically trained pianist."

I repeated, "I play the guitar."

She waved her manicured hand. "We love that you can play more than one instrument, and we think you would be an asset to our program. We can sit and discuss it more if you like."

I looked slightly over her shoulder at a painting of a violin on the wall behind her. "I'm about to tour and finish my second album. I don't see how I would have time to teach."

"We are willing to work around your schedule to have someone of your caliber." She smiled, and I refocused on the slight gap in her teeth. Or was it something else?

I scoffed. "My caliber? I've been a musician all my life, and no one has ever been interested in me until I won a Grammy. My ability to compose for any genre of music you place before me didn't just happen this year. Suddenly, I'm validated and worthy of attention from your so-called prestigious school?"

"So-called?" She reached for her pearls, or at least where I imagined they would be if she'd remembered to wear them. "We have worked with the best in the world, and our students are extremely successful."

"I know. Look around. My mother is a graduate." I gestured around the expensively decorated living room full of rich hues of red and brown. The paintings on the wall were worth at least ten grand apiece.

A strong hand squeezed my shoulder, and my gregarious father, holding a glass of his favorite bourbon, joined in the conversation. He chuckled as he warned me with his tight smile. "My son is bitter that he wasn't accepted when he applied to your program at sixteen. He ran away from home after he received the rejection letter to chart his own path… a very successful path, and I couldn't be prouder of the life he has now."

Dr. Howard's eyes widened. "Oh, I see. Then, Landon, you must look at this invite as a full-circle moment to show our school's grand mistake in not choosing you. Maybe you can join our selection committee and choose applicants like the young man you were."

"That's an excellent point to consider." I tightened my jaw, wanting to yell at the lie that my father had contrived to explain my rude behavior. They'd wanted me to attend Juilliard, and I'd purposely messed up the audition. I hated my parents' refusal to love, respect, and treat me like their son and not a prize to tout or shun, depending on my accomplishments.

I longed for the parents that Cedrick had, who only wanted to spend time with him, without ulterior motives. Mine always had an agenda whenever they summoned me here. I couldn't relax with them while grabbing home-cooked food and talking about my music or friends. They always wanted to convince me to perform somewhere alone or with them, chastise me about choosing music that wouldn't take me far in the classical and jazz world I'd never wanted to be a part of, and whether I'd met someone special because they wanted to continue their lineage. I couldn't even recall my parents telling me that they loved me.

The gnawing traveled through my body at my father's grip on my shoulder.

"My son would be a wonderful addition to your program. He's skilled on several instruments and can learn more," he boasted as if I were the last car on the lot, and he was worried it wouldn't sell.

"If you'll excuse me." I shrugged away from him.

She pushed her card in my hand. "Please reconsider working with us. You can operate your class and teach your students in the best way you see fit. Or join us as a guest lecturer to get a feel of the students and program."

I stuffed the card in my pocket. "By the way, you have spinach in your front teeth."

She gasped and covered her mouth. I headed to the kitchen to soothe the gnawing away from everyone else.

"Fuck." I gripped the sink and stared blindly out the window facing the street. I hadn't meant to embarrass Dr. Howard that way. When I was uncomfortable, sometimes I lashed out and then regretted it. She seemed decent enough, and if she'd discussed Juilliard anywhere but here at my family home, I might have considered it, especially if I could teach a small class of two or three.

"Why do you insist on being rude?" my father demanded once he entered the empty kitchen. "Those people in there can take you far."

I whirled around. "Farther than an award-winning band? I'm living my dream at this very minute. Where can those people take me when I'm already where I want to be?"

My father's nostrils flared as he replied, "No one will remember your band in five years. Get a damn clue."

"That might be true, but I'll never be a bitter drunk like you, wishing for a better life than the one I have. Trust me, none of those people can do anything for me." I winced from the pain in my gut.

"You'll see what I say is true. Your career isn't going to last forever. Go back out there and talk to those people," he ordered me.

I shook my head slowly as the ache in my stomach worsened. "I didn't want to be here. I just flew in from Houston, and I'm exhausted. You told me to be here, and I'm here. I already talked to the Juilliard person like Mom wanted, and I'm done."

My father stepped close to me, blocking my path. His light skin reddened from anger or the flush of intoxication. Old, painful memories emerged from his menacing nearness and the smell of the alcohol on his breath.

"Move," I said.

"Or what?" he sneered.

The gnawing hurt so much. I winced and clutched my stomach, holding my other hand up protectively as my mother rushed into the kitchen with worried eyes.

"Get away from him," she demanded. She looked over her shoulder at the closed door before she pulled my dad's arm. "Leave him alone."

"I'm not doing anything to him." He roughly jerked his arm away from her, causing her to fall against the counter. "You wanted him here, and now he's embarrassing us like he always does. Told you he needed to see a shrink when he was a kid. He wouldn't be messed up now."

I shoved his broad chest, and in his slightly inebriated state, he lost his balance, hit the table, and tumbled to the floor. My mother's hand flew to her mouth, and she kneeled to aid him.

Imaginary hands suddenly squeezed my lungs, and black spots appeared in my vision. I clasped my hands together as I backed away. "I'm sorry, so sorry. I have to go before I really embarrass you."

I hurried through the back door only to collapse against the side of the house, praying for the hands to stop pressing against my chest and lungs so I could breathe. I reached for my cell in my pocket, needing to call Cedrick, who knew how to reset my brain when the emotions became too much.

The text from Janae startled me.

I'm drowning. I need my life jacket.

My relieved laugh sounded more like a hiccup in the quiet of the night. The pressure on my body lessened with each ring as I waited for her to pick up.

"I'm drowning, too," I softly admitted when she answered the phone.

"Really?" She sniffed.

"I'm sitting on the ground against the back of my parents' home in the dark because I got into it with my father. I don't think it can get worse than that."

"Try sitting in the LAX bathroom stall, scared to walk back out because suddenly people remember me."

"That's pretty bad." I chuckled before I gripped my cell tighter. "I'm glad you called."

"Glad you answered. I didn't know if you would."

"Yeah, sorry about how I acted at the house yesterday. I'm not the best with my emotions."

"I didn't think you apologized."

"I don't unless I mean it."

"Is that a jab?" she asked.

I grinned. "Not at all." I checked my pulse on my neck, and it had slowed down.

"I really do need to leave the bathroom. My film crew are outside wondering what's happening."

"Then stay on the phone with me, pretend it's the most important call of your life, and wave at anyone trying to approach you."

She giggled. "That sounds like it might work."

"I do it all the time." Finally able to breathe normally, I pushed up against the wall and walked toward the front of the house.

Dr. Howard exited the brownstone as I headed to my car. She noticed me and quickly refocused on her blue sedan parked on the street. My heart softened at how she quickened her pace to avoid me. I'd hurt a woman because I was mad at my parents, and if it were not for the woman on the other line, who'd made me her moral compass, I might have pretended I didn't see Dr. Howard.

"Give me a sec," I told Janae.

I held the phone against my chest and walked to meet Dr. Howard on the street. "Doctor, I'm sorry for my behavior. I'm not the best around people. What happened in there had nothing to do with you."

She smiled. "I hate these parties too. Everyone is so self-important and phony. People probably had been staring at the food in my teeth the whole time. You actually had the sense to tell me."

I shrugged. "I didn't know not to tell you until you were embarrassed that I did."

"I see." Her expression sobered. "I only came tonight to meet you. Your parents always brag about you, and I wanted to see the talented young man you've grown up to be. I've watched your performances over the years." She pointed at me. "You're every bit of the puzzle people think you are. That makes you rare and unique. Don't ever change. Use my card if you ever consider teaching at Juilliard."

I opened her car door, and she gave me a motherly pat on my chest. This time, her touch didn't bother me. "You be safe, doctor."

"You too, Landon."

I closed her door and then strode to my gray electric ride. "I'm back. Are you still in the restroom?"

"Dude, did you just get asked to teach at Juilliard? I heard some of the conversation," Janae exclaimed.

"Something like that," I grumbled as I dropped down into my car.

"Wow, and wow. And yes, I'm strolling through the airport and waving as I talk to a future Juilliard professor." I could hear the pride in her voice. "That's a serious honor, Landon. My friend is so freaking talented that Juilliard comes looking for him. We need to celebrate or something in New Orleans."

"It wasn't an official offer, nor do I have time to teach if it was."

Janae replied, "It is still an honor even if it's not yet your road to travel."

"Yet?"

"You never know what the future holds. It's good to have options, especially ones like that."

I stared at my family home, hating that I couldn't see the good in the opportunities my parents and my name afforded me. I relented. "It really is an honor."

I started my car and began the forty-minute drive back to my sanctuary.

CHAPTER ELEVEN

janae

LOS ANGELES

NO ONE NOTICED ME WHEN I boarded the plane to Houston on Thursday morning. My oh my, what a change a performance, a fight, and trending on social media could bring. As I walked through the airport in Houston a few days later, people asked me for selfies and autographs. My crew had reverted to a small handheld camera to avoid drawing attention to the fact that I was being filmed. I smiled and chatted with old and new fans. Rays of sunshine pushed away the clouds that had covered me since yesterday while I'd been parked in front of my mother's home.

As I was sitting in first class, passengers stopped and took pics on their way to their seats. The flight attendant had to step in and urge people to sit down so the flight wouldn't be delayed. At the height of my fame, I'd flown private and chartered planes and never had to deal with fans trying to get my attention.

Pleased by all the positivity and love I'd received, I thought I could handle my fans until I stepped off the plane and walked through the gate. It was spring break in Los Angeles, and the airport bustled with teens and college students traveling. The airport was always noisy because of all the people traveling to and from there. I'd been here for seven years and mostly flew under the radar when I passed through this place.

This time, a group of UCLA students wearing their sorority colors and college gear spotted me. They began screaming and shouting and surrounded me, drawing an even bigger crowd. I realized too late that Del failed to arrange VIP services for me to help me bypass such a scene and I didn't have any security. My crew were the only people who could protect me, and they were busy capturing the madness. I smiled, waved, and hugged until faces started to blur and blend into one. Clenching my fists, I tried to push air through my lungs. I couldn't feel my face, so I didn't know if I continued to smile or if my expression reflected my blinding terror.

I squeezed through the mostly Black crowd apologetically and hurried into a nearby single occupant restroom for privacy. I hated that I couldn't place the lid on the toilet as I sat there, wondering how everything had blown up so fast that. A couple of years ago, I could walk through any airport without a second glance. No cameras. No whispers. No one checking for me.

I want this level of fame again, right?

My thoughts raced, and I couldn't settle my mind enough to breathe and relax. I needed something or someone to center me. I couldn't function. Immobilizing fear began to threaten my legs. If I had a Xanax, I would have popped it in my mouth and walked back out with my head held high, welcoming all the love.

"No," I said sharply, and then lowered my voice to a whisper. "Pills are not an option. You can do this."

My therapist hadn't reached out to me since I'd left Los Angeles, and Adam must have blocked me. The only person who might have answered my call of distress had been indifferent to me last night at the show. Maybe he was trying to maintain professionalism, or maybe he'd realized he didn't want to be my friend. None of that mattered right now. At this trying minute, I needed a lifeline. I needed Landon.

Tears sprang to my eyes when he answered almost immediately, saying he was in the same boat as me. Just hearing the light in his voice soothed me, and his admission energized me. I wasn't in this rocky boat alone.

Feeling victorious, I strolled out of the restroom with my head held high, smiling and waving at others as Landon discussed ideas he'd had about our song and the upcoming tour. I didn't process anything he said, still marveling that he cared enough to answer my call and was patient enough to stay on the phone until I reached the hired car Del had arranged for me.

I settled in the back seat while the crew headed to their rides, done with filming for the next month. My driver nodded before closing my door and hopping in the front seat.

"You're in the car?" Landon asked.

"Yeah. Don't want to get off the phone yet." I looked out the window as the car eased into the busy airport traffic.

"It's cool. I'm still driving."

"What city are you most excited about?"

"Probably New Orleans because of the rich musical culture, and New York because it's my home. You?" He asked.

"New Orleans and Chicago." I pulled my legs up and leaned against the door, loving his voice.

"Chicago? Really?"

"I'm low key into cold weather, deep dish pizzas, and museums. You should take a walk with me down Michigan Avenue. Then we can eat hot dogs and take selfies at the Bean at Millenium Park." I squealed. "I love that city."

Landon chuckled. "You sound like a tour guide. Didn't picture you as someone who remotely cared about anything not related to fashion or music."

I rolled my neck slightly. "You do know your words hurt."

He was silent.

"Landon?"

He quietly replied, "I'm here."

"What's up?" I shifted again to look out the window at the bright lights of the Los Angeles skyline in the twilight. For once, Los Angeles didn't trigger thoughts of my ex and his new woman.

"I'm not trying to come across as judgmental or mean. Sometimes I'm not aware of how my words affect others or when I'm coming off rude. If I'm your moral compass, then you have to let me know when my tongue stabs."

"Tongue stabs? You have a way with words." I giggled. "Trust, I won't have any problem checking you."

"Can I ask you something?"

"Anything," I said, and meant it. I wanted to be an open book as I learned how to make friends again.

"It's been three years. Don't you have regrets?"

"Not really. I needed to do it at the time, and I won't let what led to me using happen again," I said, not quite ready for this type of questioning.

"If we're going to be friends, and I at least believe we're heading that way, you have to be honest with me."

The aesthetically pleasing palm trees and mountains in the distance reminded me, as they always did, how far I had come from that little girl from the hood. I insisted, "I *am* being honest. I made a decision, and I have to live with the consequences. I can't dwell on it."

"Then where's your necklace? You haven't worn it since Saturday morning."

I touched my bare neck. "I don't deserve to wear it anymore."

"Do you still have it?

"Yeah."

"Then you should wear it again," he suggested.

"It doesn't work like that, Landon. I used. I lose my coin."

"Says who?"

I sighed. "My substance abuse counselors. My therapist."

"And even they're divided. Some say once you're a drunk, you're always a drunk, and others believe that a substance user doesn't have to look over their shoulders for that monkey for the rest of their lives. It doesn't seem fair that you don't get to wear the necklace anymore because you relapsed one day. It's like the other thousand-plus days you didn't use no longer matter. You already have fingers pointing at you, left and right. You don't need the necklace to do that too. Wear it to represent what you've already achieved and what you will do again. Wear it proudly because you believe you can beat your addiction."

"This might be the most I've ever heard you speak." I chuckled as the car turned onto my street. "But I hear you, and I appreciate it."

"No problem."

"Sounds like you're not driving."

"I'm sitting outside my house waiting to make sure you get inside yours safely, since you've been gone a few days."

"And I thought chivalry was dead." I smiled, pleased that I'd actually met a decent man who had no ulterior motives. A man who cared enough to make sure I got into my home safely, though he was thousands of miles away.

"Or I just don't want your death on my conscience."

I jerked my head slightly and gripped the phone tightly until I heard his soft chuckle. "If you were here, I would punch the mess out of your arm."

"I'm good on your hits. I have marks, remember?"

"Then you know I don't play," I teasingly warned.

The car slowed down, and the darkness of my condo reminded me of my current reality, which was that I was utterly alone. "Mind staying on the phone a little bit longer? After being around people the last few days, suddenly going into an empty place seems the hardest thing ever."

Landon simply replied, "I'm here."

For the second time that evening, I wiped my eyes.

MARCH 14

"What am I supposed to do when I need you?" I complained to Dr. K, otherwise known as Dr. Amanda Kelley, my psychologist. "That was a big night, and I didn't have anyone to call." I picked up my coffee cup and sipped while I waited for an answer.

"Is that decaf?" she asked with an amused smile while jotting down notes on her purple clipboard.

I rolled my eyes. "Doc, give me a break. I need something."

"You already had your break, Janae. And you keep glossing over whether you're taking your meds or not."

I tucked one leg underneath my other leg on the plush yellow sofa as I faced the woman who'd been in my life since I overdosed three years ago. "The meds take away my creativity, and I don't feel like myself."

Her forehead puckered as she pushed her glasses farther up on her nose. "When's the last time you took any meds?"

I shrugged, though I knew how long. Five months and ten days.

"Janae, we can't continue this back-and-forth. You make great strides, then lose it the minute there's strife. Life will always be hills and valleys, and you must learn to deal with challenges without falling apart. You're no different than anyone else."

Nursing my warm cup of java, I quipped, "You mean besides those of us who have bipolar? Or do you mean most people who look for an escape through alcohol, drugs, porn, violence, or whatever is the latest social media trend? You mean those people? I feel like I'm being punished for trying to get my life right. Can you give me credit for what I've achieved?" Landon's words about wearing the coin again rang true, and I rubbed it through my T-shirt.

"What's that smile for?" she asked.

"I didn't realize that I was." I lowered my gaze. Thoughts of Landon made me smile. We'd been talking on the phone every day for the past week.

"You didn't answer my question."

I blinked. "You haven't answered mine either. What am I supposed to do when I need you?"

She placed her purple notepad on the desk behind her. "I am your psychologist and not your friend. We have boundaries. We've been through this before. You know I care about you and want the best for you, but I can't and won't be at your beck and call. I gave you the numbers to call after hours if you're in crisis. You chose to pop pills. Not taking your meds leads to more poor choices and impulsivity."

"I don't want to have to explain my issues over again with some random person. I've only called you a couple of times after hours in the three years we've worked together. Don't act like I'm stalking you or something. I'm asking for something more. Advice or something tangible when my back is against the wall…" I held my hand up. "Besides meds. I'm less of a person on meds. I feel freer than I have in a long time since I stopped taking them. More vibrant. More alive."

"Or is it because of a man?" Dr. K raised a sharp brow. "Love is a beautiful thing, but it doesn't cure you. That smile is because of a man. Is it that musician who's in the news for getting into a fight with Cash Black and pulling you out of the restaurant?"

I knowingly smiled and hugged myself. "He saved me, Dr K."

"He wouldn't have had to save you if you weren't high that night. If you don't get that you crave drama, then you'll never heal."

I shook my head. "He's not like that. He's not drama at all. He doesn't drink or do drugs and prefers solitude."

"It doesn't matter what he's like. I'm talking about you. You grew up in chaos. It's your norm. For the past three years, you've been struggling with accepting that order and stability is the only way for you to manage your mental health." She tapped the arms of her leather chair.

"You mean being less than who I am," I argued. "Why can't I be me without meds? I mean, honestly, what's the difference between street drugs and prescription drugs? If I want to truly be clean, then I don't want to put anything in my body that alters my mind. I want to learn how to like myself. Me." I hit my chest. "I can brag about how much I love myself despite how everyone else hates me, but the reality is that I barely *like* myself. Instead of focusing on whether I took my meds or if a man is giving me false beliefs that I'm healed, help me get rid of these evil thoughts of demeaning and hurting myself. Help me control my raging moods." I took another sip of my warm coffee before I pulled out my coin. "I put this back on because my friend, which is all Landon is to me, suggested that I keep wearing it to remind me what I had accomplished for three years and that I would achieve again."

The ends of her lips curved downward as she settled back in her white leather swivel chair. "Does he know everything that you're dealing with?"

"He will in time." I met her concerned gaze. "I'm doing what you've been preaching to me all along. I need to trust. I need to be vulnerable without a motive. I need to have someone real in my life. You just told me I can't rely on you after hours, and my ex, who used to be there for me, stopped taking my calls. I have no friends, and you know my family ain't worth shit. Let me have this man, Dr. K. Please." I gripped my cup harder. "Am I attracted to Landon? Yes. Have we had sex? No. Do I want to be different with him? Yes. I want to be different with him because he's different than any man I've ever met. He's a legit good man, and I don't want to mess up. I *can't* mess up."

"Then you have to be mindful of your patterns with men, Janae," she advised me.

"Why do you insist on focusing on the negative? I haven't been with a man in a long time. Give me credit." I could feel my temper rising. I needed her to believe that I could have a normal life. That I could have love.

Dr. K leaned toward me. "My job is to be real. If you want a therapist who will lie to you, then go ahead. I've been with you in the trenches, Janae. I've seen you at your worst and how self-destructive you can be. Last Friday was just an example of how wrong it could have gone if Landon didn't intervene. Love is a powerful drug. You have to be sure you're not exchanging that urge to use with relying on a man to fulfill your every need. It's not fair to you *or* to him."

I planted my feet on the hardwood floor and stared at the petite woman, who'd been both gentle and firm in her treatment of me. "I respect and trust you, Dr. K, I really do, but I've been alone for three long years working on myself. I can't tell you when I last had sex since I stopped random hookups. Some of Friday night was my need to feel desired by a powerful man. The old Janae would have still found Cash and fucked his brains out once Landon had turned me down. I *chose* to seek out Landon, a man so unlike anyone I've ever dealt with. He represents stability and truth. I'm not afraid to say I want to be with him. I'm also good if we only end up as friends. He already gets me. Maybe that's all I need right now. I can't remain on an island of one anymore. I have to put myself back out there, win or lose. I can't be afraid to be me. I can't. I can't. I can't." I hit my thighs with my hands, forcing some of my coffee to slosh from the little hole at the top of the cup. "Sorry. I'm sorry. I'm just tired of feeling like I'm the problem and I don't have a right to love or to a good life."

Dr. K adjusted her glasses again and sighed. "No, I'm sorry. You're right, this is your safe space… your path to healing. I've been so focused on you losing your sobriety that I forgot that you have made great strides. Most people who relapse avoid therapy or being honest about using again. You admitted what happened with your head held high. You have been dedicated to overcoming your trauma and substance abuse. So, let's reset and begin again. We can choose to look at Friday night as a setback… or…"

"As a step in my winding path to healing."

We smiled at each other.

Feeling heard and seen, I eased back in my fluffy armchair, ready to receive whatever advice Dr. K had to offer.

CHAPTER TWELVE

landon

NEW ORLEANS
APRIL 14

I FELT A TAP ON my shoulder, and I opened my eyes sleepily. Cedrick's lazy grin greeted me. "We in New Orleans."

"I can't believe I slept the whole flight." Flying unnerved me, and usually, I had trouble relaxing. Talking to Janae until the wee hours of the morning, though we would see each other later today, had helped. My body was too exhausted to be anxious.

Brian leaned over the back of my seat. "Bruh, you were snoring and farting the whole time."

I laughed. "That would be the man sitting beside you."

Santiago's smiling brown face appeared next to Brian's. "Hey, leave me out of it. I never talk about how you can't dress worth shit and have never met a barber." He knocked my hat and bandana off my head in one big swoop. "See?"

Before I could react, Cedrick picked up my hat and gave it back to me. He glared at Santiago, who raised his hands.

"Hey… you good?" Brian asked, his expression full of concern.

They knew I was sensitive about touch and my hat and had never made fun of me. Grateful for my chosen family, I smiled. "Only my brother can do that and get away with it."

119

"In that case…" Cedrick pulled me into a headlock. "When are you going to do something with this hair?"

"Hey… hey." I playfully pushed off him. I slammed my hat back on my head and stuffed my bandana in my pocket. "Don't push it. I did punch the fuck out of Cash."

The men roared with laughter before we gathered our bags and took pics with the passengers in first and business class as we waited for the door to the plane to open. We were slowly becoming celebrities. I didn't believe we had the star power of Janae, but we were making a name for ourselves in the industry just being who we were. I had all I needed growing comfort in my own skin, fellow musicians who accepted me, and a woman who was becoming a confidante and a friend.

As we headed to the SUV that Del had arranged for us, soft hands covered my eyes. I froze at the unexpected contact until she whispered, "Relax. It's just me."

I moved her hands from my eyes to around my waist and looked over my shoulder at a radiant Janae. "Hey."

"Hey." She gazed up at me with those pretty eyes of hers, wearing a black Hollow Bones T-shirt and jeans that molded to her like a second skin, and I ached to kiss her.

Correction: I ached to claim her as mine until Cedrick cleared his throat. I looked up and belatedly realized that the guys in the band and a small group of people, including Janae's film crew, seemed amused by our happy greeting. We appeared to be the couple in love that the media said we were.

The heat of embarrassment coursed through me, and I started walking again, practically dragging Janae, who still held my waist. I hadn't made a statement or asked Del to denounce the reports of our relationship. A part of me believed the rumors would die down on their own, and the other part of me didn't want to hurt Janae's feelings. In the course of a month of conversations, I'd learned how sensitive and insecure she often felt regarding herself and her career. Still, I actively ran from the spotlight, and being linked publicly to Janae put me front and center in the public's eyes.

"Can you slow down?" She tugged on the back of my shirt.

"This isn't me," I said. "I don't want people to think we're more than what we are. I don't want to be a fake couple."

"We're friends who are happy to see each other, Landon. We're going to be in different cities, traveling together and staying in the same places. We will be photographed together. Let people think what they want as long as we know the truth." She struggled to keep up with my fast pace and much longer legs. Everyone else behind her did as well.

I saw a couple of flashes from phones while she trailed behind me. I'd never believed a woman should walk behind a man, so I slowed down until we were able to walk together. Janae looked hurt, though she beckoned Charles to walk on the other side of me, and the other three members flanked us, so she was the center of the group. Admittedly, it was the perfect picture as Janae and The Hollow Bones hit the first city of our limited-run tour.

I kept my distance as our luggage was loaded into two SUVs in a flurry of activity. Between the film crew, Janae's glam squad, and the guys trying to make sure the airline hadn't lost anything, it was a little chaotic. At least our equipment and tour gear were already taken care of, driven down ahead of us by part of our hired crew who handled that side of the show. In the midst of my grabbing my guitar case from one of the handlers, my cell buzzed.

Can we talk?

I looked around for Janae, sitting on the second row in one of the SUVs. She stared at me, and I could feel her deserved disappointment. The guys were still sorting out luggage, so I casually eased into the space next to her.

"Landon, we've spoken to each other every single day since we left Houston. If we're going to be friends in real life as well as on the phone, you can't treat me like you just did," she said calmly, though her hands were balled into fists and her chest heaved.

"You caught me off guard. I didn't expect to see you, and when I did…" I shook my head. "I honestly don't know how this is going to work. I like simple, and you and I are definitely not that." I glanced back at our group and caught Cedrick's disapproving glare.

121

Janae frowned. "No, Landon. You can't get scared now that we're here together and your friends are around. I admit that I *like* like you, but I need your friendship more. Don't you feel the same?"

"I do." I flopped my head back against the seat and admitted quietly, "This attention isn't easy for me."

"I know, but how lucky are we to do what we love and get to visit these amazing cities like the one we're in right now? If I have to stay sober, then you have to be more social. Live a little. Have some fun and get out of your head. Whenever it gets hard for either of us, we talk it out." She held out her hand. "Life jacket?"

I picked up the other still-clenched hand, straightened each finger, and held it to my heart. "Life jacket."

Janae's eyes softened again before she reached up to my hat. "What's going on with your hair sticking out? Did you forget to tie it down? Good thing your hair is curly, or it would look a hot mess on all these pics people took of us while going through the airport. I swear I'm going to do something with that wild bird's nest of yours," she threatened as she jumped back out of the SUV when one of her glam squad beckoned her.

Cedrick approached me as I stepped out too. "You're playing checkers with a woman who understands chess. She'll break your heart."

I quietly assessed the man who'd been my best friend since we were teenagers. Cedrick had his faults, and there were aspects of him I didn't like, but acceptance was a two-way street. He'd taken his role as my big brother seriously, and I understood his concerns regarding Janae because they were also mine.

Her joyful laughter while she spoke with her crew made me smile without looking her way. I genuinely liked her infectious energy and rapid way of speaking.

I. Liked. Janae.

I rubbed my guitar pick in my pocket and wondered how long before her interest in me flitted away like an elusive butterfly.

I shrugged helplessly. "You're probably right. But I hope we're both wrong."

Cedrick's jaw tightened, and he nodded before returning to the other SUV.

I jammed my hands in my cargo pants pockets and observed the determined, anticipatory, and happy expressions of The Hollow Bones, Janae, and her crew. We were about to embark on a new journey together, and we wouldn't be the same people once our time on the road ended. I was willing to bet my heart on that truth.

CHAPTER THIRTEEN

janae

"ARE WE REALLY STAYING HERE for the week?" Charles's eyes popped like an excited kid's.

"Wow." I looked out the window over his shoulder. He and my glam squad were riding with me while Landon rode with the rest of the guys in the other SUV to our lodgings for the next six days. "Del did us right with this house."

Charles narrowed his eyes at me. "It's not just any house."

I glanced back at the large, white, old structure, which appeared to have been designed by Spanish and French architects. "Okay, it's a historic mansion. Did someone famous live in it?"

He grabbed my shoulders. "This is where MTV's *The Real World* filmed the second time the show went to New Orleans. The first time was the Belfort, but this one is larger."

Jeri, my stylist, snickered from the back seat. "How old are you?"

"We're all millennials in this car." He huffed.

"Um… I'm Gen Z," Jeri corrected him.

I admired the home. "It doesn't matter who was here before. This house is fire. I love that the streetcar is right there." The clanging and screeching noise of one passing by punctuated my sentiment. "One of my favorite plays is *A Streetcar Named Desire*, which took place in this very city, and I've been dying to ride one. We are so catching it after we rehearse."

Charles chuckled. "How old are you?"

I punched his shoulder as we climbed out of the SUV after the other group had already approached the front door. Cedrick had the code to enter. Landon hung back, grabbing his case as the rest of us burst into the home like siblings fighting to be the first through the door. The cameras captured our playfulness as we ran through the elegant mansion and around the small pool in the backyard. The Hollow Bones' contract now allowed filming if it was related to music and their daily lives whenever I was with them, which would be often. We all would have some control over what could be released, since Del was the executive producer, and The Hollow Bones wouldn't proceed otherwise.

We'd decided to stay together in New Orleans, since we hadn't rehearsed the show yet. We planned to settle, unpack, and rehearse for the next four days. Our show was Friday night, and then on Saturday, we would load up on the tour bus and make the six-hour trek to Atlanta for a Sunday night show.

The men graciously allowed me the primary bedroom so I could have privacy. The band took the other five bedrooms, while the film crew, road crew, and my glam squad stayed at a quaint hotel within walking distance of the mansion. I laughed as the guys fought over every bedroom but the one farthest from all the others on the lower level. It appeared to be a given that it was for Landon.

Throughout our laughter and fun as a group, he walked around checking out each room. He smiled whenever we locked eyes, but he remained on the periphery as if looking at me through a window. His quiet didn't disrupt the loud, fun vibe in the air. Landon simply remained himself. Self-contained and observant. Seemingly content to watch our excitement.

After everyone had settled their belongings in their respective rooms and the ladies and camera crew had retired to their nearby hotel, The Hollow Bones and I congregated in the living area. I sat on the wooden coffee table in the middle of the room and held my phone up. "I'm going to order groceries because I'm going to cook for you tomorrow after rehearsal. I need to know if you have any dietary restrictions."

Santiago raised his hand. "Excuse me?"

126

Brian pushed his hand down. "Why your hand up?"

"Because Janae looks like the type I have to ask permission to speak…
She's bossy."

I shook my head as the guys laughed in agreement. "That's because
y'all loud as hell. My voice too light for you to hear me unless I yell." When
Santiago raised his hand again with an impish smile, I rolled my eyes. "What?"

"You cook?" He sounded skeptical.

"Yes, I love to cook. It's how I relax. Trust, you want me chill on this
tour." I opened up an empty note on my cell. "Tell me what you like to eat."

Charles added, "We have food. Del made sure the pantry and
refrigerator were stocked."

I waved my hand. "Snacks and alcohol. You need real food."

Landon leaned against the wall by the entrance of the living area.
"This is New Orleans, with some of the best food in the world. We can go
out or order in. Why do you want to bother with all that, especially after
rehearsing? You're going to be exhausted."

Cedrick scoffed. "No offense, but I don't eat everybody's cooking."

I crossed my arms. "Fine, when I prepare my gooey baked mac and
cheese, fried catfish, hush puppies, and green bean casserole with a pound
cake for dessert, don't ask for a crumb."

Brian raised his hand. "I never said I didn't want to eat your food."

"Then you and I will eat while the rest go find a restaurant," I told him.
"Would you like me to make sweet tea or lemonade to go with your dinner?"

"Can you make both?" He steepled his hands together.

"Yes." I had to choke back my laughter at the gaped mouths of the
other men as I looked down at my phone. "I'll make enough for me, Brian,
the ladies, and my crew."

"Now wait… wait," Charles said. "I never said I didn't want to eat your
food. That was Ced, Landon, and Santi. Add me to your list. You're from
Houston and live in Los Angeles. I'm not doubting your culinary skills."

Landon's hazel eyes sparkled green in this light. "And I was just trying
to look out for you. If you want to toil at a stove and cook us up some good
food, who am I to stop you?"

His words struck a chord in my chest. I wanted to cook, to show my appreciation and to keep my mind occupied. As long as I was busy, I could fight the darkness and my sleeplessness. Then I could hide my struggles from them. I worried that this level of closeness might show all of the chinks in my tough-girl armor and my ugliness when all I wanted them, especially Landon, to see was my beauty.

"Whatever you cook, I'm eating." Santiago hopped up and strode out of the room. "Got to make a call real quick. Need to let me fam know I'm here."

Cedrick scowled. "I'm a vegan and can't eat anything you're preparing anyway."

Brian nudged his shoulder. "Dude, you ate a burger at the airport."

"Which is why I can't eat anything else that's not vegan."

Everyone's arms went up in exasperation like we were characters in an old Spike Lee movie. Cedrick ducked his head to hide his teasing smile. Yeah. He and I would be good by the time we finished this tour. I was already having more fun with them than during the years I toured before everything fell apart.

APRIL 15

After a good first run of the show in the large family room that was easily converted into practice space the following day, we rode to Frenchmen Street, a strip full of music and food. Frankie and Jeri, who'd also watched our rehearsal, joined us. Frenchmen Street, not as famous as Bourbon Street, had more of a musician's vibe. Cameras recorded us walking and discussing music as we passed the historic French buildings that now housed bars, restaurants, and stores. We stopped at the Louisiana Music Factory, an eclectic record store, which drew us like a child drawn to a toy store.

We'd been moving as a group since we were in the house, and I hadn't had a moment alone with Landon. The guys were spread throughout the store. Frankie and Jeri were at the souvenir shop next door.

I sidled up beside him and started flipping past albums without looking at the covers. Landon's forehead puckered as he pored over the records and pulled out Jimi Hendrix's *Electric Ladyland* album. "He was a legit icon. Doing things with a guitar no one had ever heard before. He was rock and roll. He was blues… R&B."

Landon seemed so focused on the albums that I hadn't realized he'd noticed me until he started speaking.

I nudged his side. "He was also popular."

He looked at me. "Died at twenty-seven."

"Your point?"

"He hated performing in front of large audiences, and at the time of his death, he was the highest-paid rock star during an era in which Jim Crow had barely ended. My point is maybe the pressure of being a star took its toll on him. To be great young is an honor, but it's a hell of a lot of pressure."

I exhaled sharply. "Landon, he choked on his own vomit after taking sleeping pills. It was accidental."

He didn't blink. "Where's the line between coping and an accident?"

I hesitated, then shook my head. "Not everyone using something is trying to escape. Sometimes they're just trying to get through the night."

Landon's fingers flexed around the album. His expression barely shifted, but something flickered in his eyes. Doubt, frustration, maybe something deeper.

"That's what they all say, right up until it kills them." His voice was even, but I didn't miss the edge beneath it.

I folded my arms. "I can handle it. Can you? I'm not the only one who gets anxious."

For a second, I thought he might argue. His lips parted, then closed again like he was reconsidering whatever was on the tip of his tongue. Instead, he just gave a slow nod, gripping the album like it was something steady, something certain. Then he turned and walked away.

I blew out a breath and pulled the baseball cap to hide my identity further down on my head. I moved next to him again as he perused the jazz albums and whispered, "Are you going to remind me every chance you get that you think I'm an addict?"

He fingered the *Kind of Blue* album. "Miles Davis, once a heroin and cocaine user, who beat it. Or at least he appeared to beat it." He glanced at me as he added the album to the growing stack in his hand. "I don't think you're an addict. Just an observation that musicians and drugs go hand in hand. The pressures to create and perform even when we don't want to is insane. The Hollow Bones don't operate like that, and while you're with us, we won't put that type of pressure on you either."

Cedrick yelled, "Hey… the manager wants us to take a pic over on that wall. Bands perform here, too."

Landon mumbled, "And so it begins."

He followed me to where the rest of the group stood on a small stage with the Louisiana Music Factory logo behind us. I stood in the middle, and we took several pics, drawing interested gazes from customers and people walking past. A small group gathered outside while we finished taking photos and purchasing our items.

Landon grabbed my shoulders from behind when we prepared to leave the store and bent, speaking softly in my ear. "Think I'll hang back here, then return to the house. Go have fun. We'll talk later."

I closed my eyes involuntarily at the headiness of his nearness, and the air cooled around me when he moved away.

Frankie, who'd wandered back into the store alone, pulled me by my hand into the street before I could protest that I wanted to stay with Landon or at least be in his presence longer. I was scared that he and I were already losing the connection we'd established in Houston and over the phone during the last month. "The fellas want to go to the reggae club down the street." She smiled, and her eyes were lit.

I arched a brow. "Uh… oh, do you have your eye on any of them?"

"Cedrick." His name rolled off her tongue like she'd been waiting to tell me she liked him. "Is he married or has a woman?"

"I don't think so. All he wants is a good time," I warned as Jeri joined us and we headed to the club.

Frankie snickered. "And the problem with that…?"

I shrugged. "Do you."

Jeri slung her arm around my neck. "I love long hair on a man, and Brian is hilarious. Then I love Latino men, and Santiago is so pretty with that accent. But if Charles wants to holla, his tatts make up for his hair challenges."

Laughing, as Jeri had made it clear she was down for any of the men, I shook my head. Since time immemorial, men and women could not be in the same space for too long without something jumping off. "Do you, too."

"We already know that Landon is off-limits," Frankie said with a hint of a smile. "Y'all were so cute at the airport. I'm rooting for you."

I giggled, thinking of Landon's initial reaction to seeing me. He seemed so happy. Smitten. "Rooting?"

"Relationships are hard, especially in your shoes, and you just upgraded him to the hot-as-fuck man every woman wants."

I slowed my pace. "He's not that man who cares about women's attention."

"Maybe he didn't because he never had that type of attention before." Frankie waved her hand. "At the end of the day, he's still a man."

I shrugged. "Well, we're just friends anyway. The media made more of what happened than what it was. I was drunk, and Landon didn't want Cash to take advantage of me."

"So you and Landon *aren't* a thing?" she asked incredulously.

"No," I said, firmer than I believed. Then again, he'd been politely distant since we arrived at the house. During rehearsal, Landon had had his head down and been focused on his guitar almost the entire time. He didn't watch me and smile as the other men did. Landon didn't seem angry or annoyed. He seemed more interested in getting the music right than in my performance. Landon was… He was being a professional.

"Then he's an option for one of us," Jeri slyly said, and Frankie leaned closer.

"Hell no. He's off-limits to every woman." I tilted my head and threatened them, "I hope the three of us can become friends, but if you even look at him sideways…"

Frankie chuckled, her hands up. "We both know you're feeling him. He isn't checking for anyone but you, either. The rest of the band has checked me out at least twice, and he has barely looked at me. I hope we can become friends, too."

The men of The Hollow Bones and the film crew beckoned us at the entrance of the club as the island beats of Café Negril captured my ears.

Standing in the middle of my glam squad, I hooked my arms through the women's. "I don't make friends easily, and I want to try."

"Then let's go!" Jeri yelled.

I pushed thoughts of Landon to the side and decided to have a little fun, since a small crowd followed us. Some patrons sitting outside eating and enjoying their meals gasped and took pictures as I graciously greeted them. When I walked inside, the leader of the live band stopped playing and announced, "Guess who just walked in… MILA."

I smiled and waved as the restaurant cheered, feeling the acid burn my stomach at my old name. It was synonymous with strife and drama. I pushed out my breath slowly.

"Why don't you come on stage with us? Grace us with a song."

I shook my head and pointed to Cedrick and Santiago. "I rock with The Hollow Bones."

The dreadlocked singer smiled wider when he noticed them. "The Hollow Bones, a musician's dream." He gestured toward the clapping audience. "These are future legends. Mark my words. Is it okay if she rocks out with us?"

Brian shouted, "She's her own woman."

The leader laughed. "I got something for her." He covered the mic as he talked to his five-member band. Lights flashed around me in the dimly lit bar, and all eyes were on me as we waited to see what was up the singer's sleeve.

He smiled at me, and the band started playing "Lonely Woman." My nervousness faded as the restaurant came alive, with the patrons singing the first few lines. Pleased with the band's arrangement, I allowed Brian to escort me to the stage by hand, much to the delight of the patrons, who were getting a glimpse of the star trying to make a comeback.

I grooved and sang to the small audience of maybe sixty. It reminded me of when I first started performing at seventeen at Houston's local clubs and bars, hoping to be discovered. I moved sensually to the beat, dancing with abandon with the lead singer, letting the music soothe the lingering acid in my chest and releasing my inhibitions naturally. I floated above Café

Negril without meds dulling my senses and without street drugs blurring my senses. Tonight, it was simply me, and I loved every second of it.

I'd never felt more like the me I'd been trying to find than I did as I sang for this group.

When I finished to a standing ovation, I bowed and blew kisses at the band and acknowledged The Hollow Bones again. My eyes found Landon, who stood at the very back of the café. His expression was hidden in the shadows of the restaurant, and his hands were in his pockets while everyone clapped and shouted their approval. Had I been too much, too flirty, too sexual with the singer? Men were my comfort zone. I knew how to talk to and entice them. How to get and maintain their attention. My ways had worked in the past. For a reserved man like Landon, I had no clue if my style appealed or turned him off.

As we rode back to the house, Landon sat next to me in the back row of the SUV, and his pinky finger curved to mine. That simple, reassuring act made breathing challenging, and I laid my head on his strong shoulder, needing his calmness to stop the racing thoughts, a constant part of me that I had yet to share with him.

Maybe that was why I wanted him so badly. I wanted as much of him as I could have before he decided, like everyone else in my life had, that I was too much.

CHAPTER FOURTEEN

landon

AFTER WE RETURNED TO THE house, everyone went to their rooms. I opened the refrigerator to grab a water bottle.

"You hungry?" Janae asked from behind me.

"I thought you went upstairs," I commented, bracing myself against temptation before I closed the door. She'd changed into a white T-shirt and black shorts, and her hair was brushed back in a ponytail. She looked like the high school cheerleader she'd probably once been.

"I can cook you something quick," she offered.

"I don't eat this late or this early." I twisted off the top of my water, and she pushed up and sat on the kitchen island across from me. "You're not sleepy? You did a lot today."

"I get wired when I perform. Takes me a while to calm down. You don't seem sleepy either."

I shrugged. "Not comfortable yet in the house." I really wanted to say that it was hard for me to relax knowing that we were under the same roof.

"So, what do you suggest we do?" She smiled.

"Not that," I answered.

Janae giggled. "Ain't nobody checking for you."

I took a big gulp of water to avoid saying something that would probably get me slapped.

"I was surprised to see you at Café Negril." Her eyes were bright and expectant.

"You're meant to perform." I tilted my bottle toward her. "I couldn't look away."

The smile on her face was pure sunshine for those lucky enough to see her entertain. This was the way she'd told me she wanted to perform that night when we were under the stars. She held the small crowd captive, and we were all trapped in her seductive web.

"It was so freeing to get on that stage and know I could get a random group of people to sing with me. They didn't expect to see me, and I didn't know I would perform, yet tonight was perfect. Maybe I'm not as hated as I believed."

"You were clean and you still owned the stage. That was the best part." I finished my water and threw it in the trash. I belatedly realized that I should've kept the bottle to have something in my hand before I did something crazy, like grab her. I pulled my pick out of my pocket and held it like I planned to play my guitar.

She stuck her tongue out at me. "I don't know if I'm annoyed or not that you keep mentioning that."

"Do you want me to be your moral compass or not? I didn't ask for the role, remember?"

"I also thought we were becoming friends." She reached for my wrist and pulled me between her legs, firmly placing my arms around her waist. "It feels like you're still putting distance between us."

"Kinda have to so we can be friends. I can't afford to fall for you." My gaze drifted to her mouth.

Janae smiled wider. "Why?"

"You know why," I replied, dragging my attention back to her alluring brown eyes.

She slipped her hand under my shirt and touched my abs, and I subconsciously recoiled.

Her forehead wrinkled, and she removed it. "Sorry. Guess you really don't like me like that. Friends it is."

I'd hurt her, and that was the last thing I wanted to do. I entwined our hands without thought. "Sorry. I do like you. More than I want to, and you

136

THE SIDE OF BEAUTIFUL

know that. We wouldn't have spent hours on the phone this last month when I really hate talking if I didn't like you. I'm not used to sudden touches."

"Why? I noticed you flinched when I touched you the last time that we were together." She seemed more curious than bothered.

"More of a loner," I answered. The longer answer was that it'd been months since I'd had sex, and I had always felt some discomfort with people touching me.

She nodded as she opened my hand gently and touched my palm. "Your skin is rough."

"Hazard of being a guitar player. Callouses are a badge of honor."

Janae traced my palm with her finger. "Still, I bet if I oiled your hands every night, it would feel smoother."

The touch of her finger on my hand while her eyes flirted with me was so erotic that my pants tightened. "So damn distracting."

"That's the point." She lowered her head to press her lips slowly on my palm. "Did I tell you that the guitar is my favorite instrument, too? Maybe you can teach me how to play. Like stand behind me, with your arms around me, and guide me."

My words were caught in my throat at the brush of her lips. I shook my head. This woman would destroy me. Time seemed to stand still as lust darkened her eyes.

She kissed my hand again. "You have nice, long fingers. The way they glide across those strings." Janae's lips curved into a wicked smile. "Tell me, Landon, do you fuck as good as you look?"

We heard footsteps on the stairs before I could answer in the affirmative, my willpower gone. Grateful for the intrusion, I moved away from Janae. "I better go."

She hopped down. "Think I'll catch the trolley. I can't sleep."

I gripped her wrist. "Not alone and not wearing that. It's four in the morning."

"I haven't seen my father in forever, and you're not my man." She dared me with her pretty eyes and twisted her wrist from my hand. "Bye."

Brian walked into the kitchen. "Am I interrupting something?"

Janae didn't break her gaze from mine. "Nope. I can't sleep, so I'm catching the streetcar."

He rubbed his hands together. "I'm down. Let's go."

"See, Landon? I won't be alone. You can sleep peacefully knowing I'm with Brian." She wrapped her arm around Brian's. "I've been waiting to do this."

I watched them walk out the front door with smiles on their faces, my jaw tight. That could've been me and her. I punched the air. Why couldn't I just relax? If I fell for her, I fell.

I paced in the kitchen, trying to figure out what to do next. What if she became interested in Brian, who was friendly and… and… normal? Sleep wasn't going to happen until they came back home. I headed to my suite and grabbed my guitar.

When they returned about forty minutes later, laughing about some joke Brian had told, I played my acoustic guitar on the winding steps leading to the front door. Brian nodded at me as he walked inside the house, followed by Janae, who didn't look at me. When she passed me, I tugged on the end of her shirt. She removed my hand, but not before I saw her face.

Her pleased smile was enough to settle my soul.

APRIL 16

On Wednesday evening, we gathered around the long dining table. Delicious aromas tempted me from the late dinner Janae had prepared after a long day of rehearsing. Her glam squad, who'd been enjoying the city as tourists, joined us for dinner. Amazingly, Janae had whipped up this home-cooked meal within two hours. I wouldn't have believed she'd actually made it herself if I hadn't strummed my guitar at her request while she hummed and prepared the meal from scratch.

She'd pulled out the chair so I could sit at the head of the table, though my inclination was toward one of the other chairs.

"This is for you. Without you, I wouldn't be welcome here with the band." Janae chose the seat to my right, and her nervous energy shrouded me as everyone found a place at the table. I squeezed her shaky leg, and she smiled apologetically and stopped moving. "Before everyone digs in, I want to say grace. I don't know people's spiritual or religious beliefs, so I'll just call on God to thank him for bringing us all here together."

We all touched fists, adopting my style of connection as we bowed our heads and Janae led the prayer.

"Words can't describe my gratitude for being here with you all. I have been alone and lonely most of my life, and just being around you, even those who aren't sure they should trust me, still feels like I've found the best family. Thank you for allowing me space in your world. I won't take you for granted. Here's to more fun and creating timeless music that we are always proud of. Amen."

When I opened my eyes, hers were still closed, and I impulsively kissed the tear on her cheek. Her eyes popped open in surprise, and she grabbed my face and kissed me. She rubbed the lipstick off my mouth and chuckled through her tears. "Sorry… sorry. I forgot myself. Don't mean to make you uncomfortable."

Before I could reassure her that it was okay, Charles grabbed my face from the other side and pinched my cheek. "Isn't he so cute? I want to just pinch his cheeks *all* the time."

Laughing, I swiped his hand away. "I already told Janae I'm not a puppy. Now, I have to add 'a boy' to the list."

Cedrick, who sat at the other end of the table, hit the side of his glass with a fork. "I want to make a toast." He glanced around the room. "Make sure everyone has something in their glass."

Janae had made fresh lemonade and tea, though Cedrick and Santiago had added liquor to their drinks.

Once we all had our glasses full, Cedrick said, "If this year so far is any indication, we're about to go up yet another level. I am hard and tough on you, Janae, and will continue to do so because this business will eat you up and spit you out. Make you forget who you are." He narrowed his eyes at her. "I hope that the Janae we're seeing right now is the real you and not a façade to get into our good graces. Time will tell if this is truly you. If I'm wrong, I'll be the first to embrace you and treat you like my sister." He slanted his gaze to me and then back to Janae. "But I promise you, if you destroy my family, I will destroy you."

Janae stilled, and I picked up her hand and placed our entwined hands on the table. "And if you ever speak to her again the way you just did, you'll have to deal with me."

We glared at each other until Janae pulled my chin in her direction. "It's okay. I can't expect a couple of days and good food to fix what I did to others for years." She straightened her shoulders and addressed Cedrick. "You're going to have to get used to my being in Landon's life. I'm not going anywhere as long as he wants me to be there. I don't want to hurt him or any of you, including you, Cedrick. Most of all, I don't want to hurt myself anymore. Now, I made this dinner so we could laugh, joke, and eat some good food that's getting cold. Can you break bread with me and, for now, put away your reservations?"

Cedrick gripped the glass in his hand while staring at us.

Brian, who sat beside Cedrick, quietly said, "Peace while we eat."

Cedrick finally nodded.

Janae breathed a sigh of relief before she picked up a bowl of mac and cheese that was paler than the other, larger bowl. She passed it to Santiago. "This is a special vegan mac and cheese for Cedrick. I also made him a rice and bean dish down there next to the green beans."

Cedrick received the bowl and looked at the rice dish. Wordlessly, he spooned some of the mixture on his plate. The rest of us passed the rest of the plates back and forth, normalcy returning after a tense moment. Cameras had been rolling the whole time, and I would ask for the footage to be cut, though I was sure Cedrick and Del would want to keep it.

"Mm…" Cedrick said with a begrudging smile. "This might be the best vegan dish I ever had." He pointed to the other mac and cheese. "I have to try the real one if she can make fake cheese taste like that."

Brian shook his head vehemently. "She made that big bowl just for me. She made you your special bowl. Now enjoy."

Cedrick punched him in the arm, and the two kept hitting each other like the brothers they'd become until Brian passed him the large platter, and I was finally able to breathe.

Janae whispered, "Can we be alone later?"

My groin tightened at her suggestive tone, and I nodded as I gulped down her sweet lemonade. I wanted her like I'd never wanted another woman. Still, something inside of me knew she wasn't ready. Janae's fragility was hidden behind layers of tough walls she'd built over the years. She wanted my comfort to assuage what had just happened with Cedrick. She wanted to forget using her body. And if we were to have sex, I didn't want our first time to be anything but what it was meant to be.

Beautiful.

I sat on the fluffy rug at the end of the bed with my guitar, anticipating Janae's knock after she returned from a late night out with the group. I'd remained at the house, playing my music. I needed space and quiet to build up my resistance. One look from those pretty eyes and I was a goner.

Janae immediately fell into me when I opened the door, kissing my chin and cheeks. Before she could touch my lips, I pulled back, searching her face.

She frowned. "I'm sober, Landon."

"That's not what I'm looking for."

Her hand went under my shirt again, rubbing my abs, and this time, I welcomed her touch though I struggled for control. She whispered, "Why are you looking at me like that?"

"Do you want to have sex with me tonight because you want to be with me, or am I just someone to use because Cedrick hurt you?"

"What?" Her eyes widened. "I would never use you that way. I can't stop thinking about how you would feel inside of me. I do want to be with you. It has nothing to do with him."

"Well, if you want me now, you'll want me later." I gestured toward the back door. "Take a walk with me."

She groaned and looked down at the thick outline visible through my sweatpants that I couldn't prevent, no matter how I tried to distract myself. "Damn."

"You'll find out in time," I said smugly as I headed toward the back door, knowing she would follow.

"When?"

"Not yet. Impatient Iesha."

She laughed. "Stop while you're ahead."

The cool, crisp April air chilled my face. The clear, bright crescent moon and the sounds of the fountain trickling water into the dark blue pool soothed me.

Janae asked, "You want to look at the stars?"

"No. We're catching the streetcar." I opened the back gate, and we walked around the house and down the road. "I want to ride in silence with you."

She smiled. "I was hoping you would ask me. Why silence?"

"It's the world I prefer. I want to show you a little of my world. It's okay to be quiet, Janae."

"So, we don't talk?" she asked skeptically.

I chuckled. "We simply exist and observe using our senses." I kissed her neck gently at the frown on her face, inhaling her floral scent. "You smell good even after being out most of the night."

"Landon, are you trying to seduce me to get me to do what you want?"

I plastered on a frown. "Is that what I'm doing?"

As the streetcar approached, she studied my face and finally broke into a smile. "You know exactly what you're doing, and it's working."

She held on to the back of my shirt as I led the way onto the almost-empty streetcar. Two other passengers stared out their respective windows. I adjusted the moving seat so we faced each other, and each had a window seat. I reached down, took her heels off, and placed her feet on my thighs to rub them.

"I thought you had a thing about feet?"

"Sensitive about *my* feet. Don't mind touching yours. You've been on them all day. Look out the window or close your eyes and pay attention to your senses."

She shook her head slowly. "Kinda hard to look anywhere but at you."

"I'm trying to slow us down," I said. She'd made it so impossibly hard to ignore my body, which still warred with my mind.

"Massaging my feet isn't the way to slow us down. Taking care of me is so sexy and such a turn-on." Her breasts rose and fell as she stared at me.

"Should I stop touching your feet? Because how you're looking at me is so distracting."

She giggled and looked out the window before refocusing on me. "It's crazy how much I like you."

"I want to keep it that way."

"You really believe that I can't possibly be into you? One thing I know is men… and you are a good one, through and through. I want something real."

"And you need to be quiet. This is a silent ride, remember?" I squeezed her foot. I had no desire to be reminded about her history with other guys.

"But…"

I shook my head and pointed to the window. "Notice the sights. Listen to how the streetcar's noise ebbs and flows depending on the starts and stops."

As the streetcar traveled down historic St. Charles Avenue, she folded her arms and stared out the window. Soon, I watched the smile glide across her face before she drifted into the much-needed sleep she'd seemed hellbent on avoiding.

Then I finally became silent and observed the affluent homes and neighborhoods en route to the relatively busy downtown area. I soaked in the history, culture, and early dawn noises, building my armor against a woman whose brown eyes left me defenseless. She was already causing a shift in the band because she was causing a shift in me. I'd meant what I told Cedrick, because I also knew he'd meant every word he said to Janae.

I looked at the sleeping beauty. Was she worth risking The Hollow Bones, my brothers, my best friend?

Resting my head against the window's edge, I watched as the sky slowly changed from midnight navy to a pale blue, waiting for answers I knew wouldn't come.

CHAPTER FIFTEEN

janae

APRIL 17

MY PHONE'S SHRILL RINGING JOLTED me awake. I shot up, then flopped back onto the mattress, groaning. Sunlight stabbed through the window, burning my tired eyes. The heaviness pressed down, familiar, inevitable. The encroaching darkness of my thoughts and mood would soon follow. I cursed and let the phone ring. This was why I hadn't wanted to sleep. Landon couldn't see me like this. He couldn't know this side of me. *Shit. Shit.*

Tears sprang to my eyes, and I curled up into a tight ball. "No… no… no… not now."

I'd been doing so good since I'd stopped taking my meds, managing my nervousness, my incessant need to do something. I'd found cooking helped ease my mind. But this… this was horrible. No, I was a horrible person. Landon must have seen through me already. He wouldn't even kiss me, no matter how much I told him I wanted him. Landon knew. He knew and was too nice to tell me he didn't like me. And who'd want a messed-up woman who couldn't control her tears or her smile? I couldn't go out there like that.

I covered my face and started rocking. *No one loves you. No one even calls you unless it's about work. You think a man like him would ever give you the time of the day?*

I looked around the room. Tears fell fast and hard down my cheeks. But I needed something. I needed to clear my mind.

I grabbed my phone and called Dr. K, and still jumped at the sound of her voice greeting me.

"Dr. K?" My voice sounded extra scratchy. I cleared my throat and tried again. "Hello."

"Did I just wake you? I called about five minutes ago. We have our appointment."

I ran my hands through my mussed locks, regretting that I hadn't used a scarf to preserve my relaxed hair. "Yeah. What time is it?" I squinted to see my cell.

"It's after three. Is everything okay?" Dr. K and I had decided to have weekly phone sessions. We would have virtual sessions and practice meditation and breathing together if I needed more than a talk. She'd expressed concern that I wasn't on meds but would be there for me as much as she could.

"Yeah," I said dully.

"Honesty, Janae."

Tears welled. "You'll say I need my meds, and I don't want them. They make me like a zombie, and I want to feel even if it's bad. I have to get through this."

"What's happened?" she asked in that no-nonsense voice layered with concern.

"The darkness. I can feel it. It's just so hard when I feel this way. I don't know what to do or think. I just want the sadness to go away." I wiped my eyes. "I need to be clear and levelheaded… full of energy and life. That's the Janae everyone sees. If you can hear it over the phone, how can I pull it off in front of the guys?"

"What did I tell you to do when the darkness takes over your light?"

"Use the dark to reflect and rest, and the light will soon return. There's a purpose no matter how I feel," I recited.

"How many hours have you slept in the last week?"

I leaned against the wooden headboard and pulled my knees to my chest. "I couldn't settle my mind enough to rest until last night. I've been too afraid to sleep… scared I would wake up like I just did."

"What was different? Did you finally fall asleep because your body shut down? Or did you choose to sleep?"

"Landon forced me to relax… to be silent. It worked." My chest started to expand again. Some light returned to my brain. His hands had been strong and soothing as he'd caressed my feet, and the quiet of the night had lulled me into sleep. He hadn't woken me until we were two stops from the house. Noticing my lethargy as we stepped off the train, he'd scooped me into his arms and carried me inside. Landon had placed me in my bed, given me the sweetest forehead kiss, and left my room.

"Let's talk about him for a second. How's that going?"

"So frustrating." I chuckled through my tears. "He's making me wait."

"I thought you were content to be his friend anyway?"

"I am, but I do want to try him before we permanently place each other in the friend zone, which he seems determined to do. I can feel how much he wants me, but he doesn't trust me yet. And why would he? He knew me from the past, and I didn't even remember his name."

"Don't count yourself out with him. Let him take the lead on this. You've been the aggressor. Maybe it's time to sit back and allow him to woo you. You've only known him for a month. You have time."

"He said the same thing." I hugged my knees. "I swear, I hate that I feel like I'm on borrowed time. That I'll slip into a black hole again, and this time, I can't climb back out. Time seems to travel fast, and I'm helpless to stop it. This urgency burns inside of me to find love, to get my career back, to fight my demons, to find friends, to not screw up. My mind runs in circles, and I keep myself busy fighting my thoughts. Landon wants me to welcome silence, but I can't. Silence, for me, means darkness and despair. Maybe that's why I woke up feeling like I'd been swallowed by quicksand with no branch to save me, though nothing has changed in my life since yesterday."

"What happened when you became silent? Not what you believe will happen. What *actually* happened?" she asked gently.

I slid back under the covers. "We were on the streetcar, and I watched the passing scenery, and… I… felt peace, and then I fell into a deep sleep."

"You needed the quiet. Exhaustion also plays games with your mind. Stop running from your thoughts. Face them and challenge them. They might not be as bad you think. You do deserve real love… a healthy love, and he might be that person. You're no more on borrowed time than the rest of us. Enjoy him and enjoy this journey. But before we focus on your thoughts and this man, I want to know if you're ready for tomorrow night."

Tucking the cell against my ear as I curled into a ball, I admitted, "When I first woke up, I wasn't sure. But when you asked just now, my answer came without thinking." I grinned, relief coursing through me. "Unlike in Houston, the guys have been fair with me. They're giving me equal time on the show, and rehearsals have gone well. I've been recognized almost everywhere without the madness I experienced at LAX. Sung at this reggae joint and partied on Bourbon without craving a damn thing. Just clean fun. The New Orleans vibe is my jam."

"Your voice changed. That tells me that when you focus on the possibilities of love and performing, your mood lifts. Let go of any problems you're facing, at least while you're on stage. If your anxiety gets the best of you, ground yourself with your coin and remember how much clean, sober fun you've had for the past three days."

I sighed. "It feels like so much longer than three days, in a good way, you know?"

"Because you're among the living again, and truly living." She sounded pleased.

"Dr. K, your timing is everything," I said. "I needed your advice more than I realized."

"Like you needed sleep more than you realized," she teased. "I think I like this Landon."

"Well, I *know* I like him." I bit my lip.

"If Landon wants to take it slow, he's doing it for a reason."

The silence grew between us as I pushed off the comforter and stared at the ceiling.

"Janae?"

"I'm still here. Should I walk away from him before we go deeper?" Hurt added to the heaviness slowly creeping back into my body.

"Do you think you can walk away from him?"

"No," I answered.

"Then continue doing the work to have the type of relationship you hope to have and it'll take work. Open and honest communication."

"He's worth it."

"And never forget you are too," Dr. K added.

"Thank you. Sometimes, I get stuck in my head and only believe the negative, no matter how good I have it." I scanned the large bedroom with a balcony and bathroom bigger than the bedroom I grew up in. "Like the fact that I haven't worked in three years and still have a bank account that affords me more than what most people can buy. And more days than not, I'm sad and alone."

"Have you reconsidered Del's idea that you use the reality show to tell the world about your diagnosis or speak at that mental health fundraiser? Do you know how many people you could help? More importantly, it's going to help you."

I started rocking again. "I don't know if I'm ready for the backlash. No matter what I post, people have an opinion. They'll think it's just a cop-out for my bad behavior. No one believed Simone Biles when she said she couldn't perform and needed therapy. André 3000 barely performs anymore, and no one wants to hear he's protecting his mental health."

Dr. K countered, "They also had supporters, and the more that people who have a voice as big as yours use their platform to advocate for mental health, the more society will accept people who have bipolar, just like anyone who has high blood pressure or cancer."

"I don't know. I'm barely hanging on with Cedrick, and he might write me off as a liability if I start telling the world I have bipolar." I rubbed the burning in my chest. "And what if Landon can't accept it?"

"We don't know how anyone will handle any of this, but you wanted to be honest in everything that you do. It's a part of your healing. And hiding a big part of your struggles is a step backward."

"It's not fair. It's so un-fucking-fair." I raised my voice, and my hand holding the phone trembled. "I don't even remember what my father looks like, my mother hates me, and my brother is too caught up in his world to bother with me. Started using drugs young to escape the pain of having no one. And I get to spend the rest of my life dealing with shit most people never have to deal with. What man is going to love me when they know? Huh?"

"Shh… shh… Janae, please calm down. I didn't mean to upset you. Breathe in and breathe out. Come on, Janae. Breathe with me."

I closed my eyes and did as I was instructed repeatedly as I tried to hear Dr. K over my own negative mind.

"It's not your fault," she reminded me. "Bipolar disorder isn't just feeling good or bad. It's your brain pushing you too far in either direction. The goal isn't to erase emotions, but to keep them from running you into the ground.

She paused, giving me space to absorb that. "You are not alone in this. I'm here with you, and you are so much more than whatever those thoughts are telling you. You're beautiful, smart, strong, and capable of fighting whatever comes your way. Your career is moving faster than you believed. You haven't relapsed in over a month. This is only a slight valley. The hill is right there."

The heaviness started to lift as she reminded me of what I knew on my good days. But the dark… the dark. I couldn't win.

"Breathe, Janae. Relax your mind. We can complain about how life is unfair or focus on what is fair. Your choice. You made the decision to be sober and not take meds, so that means you have to push harder through those demons to see the light. You can't give up on yourself. You, and only you, have to keep fighting."

I sobbed. "I'm tired."

"Open your eyes. Look around the room. Tell me what you see."

I struggled to open my eyes, and I squinted in front of me. "A TV."

"Is it on?"

"No."

"Turn it on."

I searched for the remote, and it was on the marble table beside the bed. "I found it."

"Are you still breathing? Because if you're not, you're going to pass out any minute."

I chuckled. "Yes. You were changing my focus. Doc, you're good."

"I love that you're laughing. Even your laughter sounds like a song."

"I know you lying now." I laughed again, and my chest felt a little lighter.

"No, ask Landon. I bet he'll say it too. Can you do that, Janae?"

"Ask him if my laughter sounds like a song?"

"Can you push through this darkness to get to the other side?" she quietly asked. "You have a show tonight, and a promising future in music, and a man who may just get you. If you fall apart, you won't get to see if this comes true. Can you, Janae?"

"Yes." I wiped my eyes. "I don't really have a choice."

"You always have a choice, no matter what. You aren't that helpless, powerless girl anymore."

"I meant that I don't have a choice to push through because I don't want meds, and I want to see how far I go in my career. If it's meant for me with Landon, I want to see what happens, too." I sniffed. "Oh, God, with all this crying, I'm probably all puffy."

"Tell them it's allergy season if you don't want to tell the truth." Dr. K chuckled.

"I like that." I crisscrossed my legs, ready to fight again.

I took a gulp of air and stepped back into the world. The sounds of The Hollow Bones rehearsing drifted through the air as I walked down the stairs. When I stepped into the kitchen, my heart skipped at the sight of a hatless Landon leaning on the counter with a plate of pastries before him.

"You ever had a beignet?" He smiled wide, causing slight wrinkles in the corners of his eyes that would no doubt make him more distinguished as he aged.

"I heard a thing or two about them." I walked to him and tugged on his curls, which I hadn't seen since we were in Houston, and he wrapped his arms around me like it was the most natural thing for us to do. "You smell good."

"So do you." He tightened his embrace, and in his arms, I felt safe. Landon frowned when he studied my face. "How did you sleep? Your eyes are puffy."

"Good." I looked up at him, grateful that at least that part was true, though I saw the question in his eyes and how close our lips were to each other.

151

He seemed to notice, too, and backed away. I bit down my disappointment. *Let him take the lead and not see it as a sign of rejection.*

Landon pushed the plate of powdered-sugar-dusted fried dough toward me. "Try it. Might make you feel better."

"I'm good. Slept a little too long." I leaned over the plate to bite into the pastry and instantly adored the light, sweet taste of the doughnut. "Mm… oh my God. This is sooo good."

Landon smiled again. "I thought you might like it. When I'm alone, no one recognizes me. So I caught an Uber to Cafe du Monde."

"Why didn't you wake me up? I would've gone with you." I took another bite.

"I can tell you haven't been sleeping. You needed that more than hanging with me."

"Or maybe hanging with you is exactly what I needed." I grinned, allowing more and more light into my body. "Why do you cover that pretty hair of yours? It's your glory."

He dipped his head. "Now you're sounding like my mother."

"How could she not spoil you? You were probably the cutest baby with those gorgeous eyes and curly hair."

His grin faded. "Yeah." He looked past my shoulders. "I've been gone a while, so I'd better head back to rehearsal. I'll tell them you'll be down soon."

"What did I say? You just went cold on me. I don't care if you like to wear hats all the time." I dusted the sugar off my hands.

Landon didn't quite meet my eyes. "You didn't say anything. I waited for you to come downstairs. Now you're here, and I need to get back."

"How long have you been waiting?"

He tapped the counter and walked away. "I would've waited forever if I needed to."

I stared after him until his tall frame moved from my sight before dancing around like I'd won the lottery. I really liked that man.

APRIL 18

"It's standing room only." I peeked out of the curtain. It was Friday night and almost showtime at the House of Blues in New Orleans. The crowd was already thick, though we still had an hour until the show. "This energy is otherworldly."

"Once the seated tickets sold out, the promoter decided to sell general seating, and here we are with a maxed-out venue," Brian said as he peeked over my shoulder. "Glad we're starting off in a smaller space. They can really feel us in a place like this. We can experiment and see what works and what doesn't and then perfect it while we're in New York."

Clapping my hands, I danced in place. Dr. K had been right. As long as I kept my focus on the good, which was Landon and performing, my energy returned to ten. The happy feelings continued when we were greeted at the House of Blues with ready smiles and dressing rooms filled with our food and drink preferences earlier today. We flew through the sound check, and we sounded amazing.

I looked over my shoulder at Brian. "We're about to rock out tonight."

He embraced me from the back, and I patted his arms. When I stepped from his friendly embrace, I sensed someone's glare. I expected to find a scowling Cedrick, but a clenched-jawed Landon stood on the other end of the stage behind the curtains, holding his guitar. Brian walked away without noticing him, and when I beckoned Landon to meet me backstage, he shook his head.

The manager approached me as Landon strode off. "Your team is trying to get through the lines outside. You haven't answered your phone. You want to let them in?"

"Of course. Let them in. They work with me," I barked, heading to my dressing room.

As much as I wanted to talk to Landon, I needed to get ready. I twisted my neck as I walked, trying to erase the visual of his disapproving frown. When I touched the doorknob to my space, his hand covered mine, startling me.

I looked up into his fiery gaze and apologized. "It was just a hug."

He pushed the door open and followed me into my small dressing room. My suits were lined up on the wardrobe rack. Bags of popcorn, Reese's

Pieces, and grape sports drinks were spread on a nearby table, and a small TV stuck to the wall played a montage of past performers. The ladies would be here any minute, and we only had a little time.

I grabbed the collar of his button-up black shirt. "You have no reason to be jealous. I only want you."

Landon frowned. "I do have a reason. Just not the one you probably think."

I gestured at his displeased expression. "Then stop looking like I did something wrong and explain what you mean."

"Nothing to explain that we haven't already discussed. I'm a simple man with ways that may seem complicated to you. Once we get to New York and you see me in my element, I'm yours if you still want me. I can't fight what I feel anymore."

His eyes softened and appeared almost golden in this dull light. He pulled out a vibrant purple-and-pink flower from behind his back and tucked it into the side of my loose hair. "This is a tropical hibiscus. It's my favorite flower because it reminds me of a trumpet, and it symbolizes beauty and passion. Wear your hair like this for me, even if it clashes with your outfit. Whenever I look at pictures from this night, I'll know that once upon a time, Janae Warner only wanted me."

Entranced by the seriousness with which he gazed at me, I nodded.

He lowered his head, and his lips brushed my neck. "This might be my favorite part of you."

"You haven't seen every part of me," I said breathlessly, wanting to grab and kiss him so desperately.

The left corner of his pouty lips turned up. "I bet you have a favorite part of me and haven't seen everything."

"Your heart." I pressed my palm against his firm chest.

His brows dipped, and he curved his calloused hands to my face. My breath caught in my throat, and I licked my lips in anticipation of his kiss. Our first real kiss.

The knock on the door spoiled the moment, and he dropped his hands and opened it. Frankie and Jeri looked back and forth between the two of us with amused grins. Landon spoke briefly to the ladies and quietly left my dressing room. I swear it took everything in my power not to follow him.

While the ladies chatted and prepped my area, I eased down in the chair in front of the mirror, lost in my thoughts. Landon made me feel good, like the girl I should've been before I became a woman. I'd been in love before and had chemistry with plenty of men, and still, no one had made me feel like that giddy girl who couldn't wait to go to school so she could see her crush, even if he never spoke to her.

When Frankie attempted to pull the flower out of my hair, I snapped back into the present. "Leave my hair as it is, and I'll wear the black suit instead of the blue one."

Jeri tsked. "I have to change the accessories, too, if you're wearing your hair like that."

"Do what I'm paying you to do," I reminded her more coldly than I'd intended. I was too lost in Landon to correct myself.

Frankie quietly opened my shadow palette. "We can switch up the colors to match the flower. I can add more gel so your hair can have the wet look. You'll look even more fab."

I didn't answer, preferring the tense silence to their noisy chatter as I stared at my reflection. My eyes were hooded, and my mouth was slightly open as if I were still anticipating his kiss. I really had it bad for Landon, and I couldn't wait for New York.

CONFESSIONAL

janae

"HEY, Y'ALL. IT'S BEEN A little rough. Sometimes I have good and bad days. It's hard being in the spotlight, and I swear I'm not being the whiny, spoiled celebrity. I no more chose this life than the person who has a calling to be a teacher or a doctor. It's a feeling I can't exactly explain, but I'll try. I think it's like how light and free you feel on a sunny, clear, cool day, only doing something you like times ten. Every time I get on the stage, electricity flows through me. I'd forgotten that feeling after being away for three years. The downside is that I have to put my big-girl panties on, wear my thick skin, and deal with all the criticism. For every two people rooting for me, there's a troll determined to tear me down, ragging me about my hair and my clothes, calling me everything but the child of Satan, and if I search hard enough, I might find it." I scoffed.

"I know my attention should be on my fans and not my haters, but damn, some of y'all be ruthless. Some of y'all even hating on pics of me and Landon, like I can't move on, or I don't deserve love. It's been three years since I messed things up. I lost a lot. Not just my recording contract. I believe I've paid for my misdeeds in a world full of sinning folks. I'm not trying to go backward, so I'm not MILA anymore. Going by my government name represents my transformation." I held my tattooed wrist up. "Every time people want to pigeonhole me into the person I was, I stare at my butterflies. Guess I have to keep trucking, because no matter how the criticisms can weigh on my soul, this is the only life I want."

"What about tonight's show?" the producer asked.

Waving my hands in the air, I shouted, "We smashed it. They rocked with us, screaming our names long after we left the stage. House of Blues in New Orleans owes us nothing, okay?"

I laughed. "I'm in this room in the back of the house and I was so loud, I heard Cedrick tell me to shut up. Like they haven't been running around this big-ass house like boys this entire time or getting carried away and start swinging fake lightsabers whenever they put on *Star Wars*. I'd honestly be shocked if nothing is broken by now."

The producer asked, "How are you and Cedrick?"

Wiping my forehead, I teasingly replied, "Whew... dinner the other night was intense. I have to prove myself before he trusts me, and I get it. We go way back, and MILA burned The Hollow Bones... Janae is picking up the pieces. Cedrick and Landon have been boys since they were teenagers. They will always have each other's backs, and I won't ever interfere with that." I leaned closer to the camera. "But ain't no one scared of you, Ced."

I backed up. "I can't talk too long because they want to celebrate. This is our last night in the Big Easy, and this city is so my flavor."

The producer grinned. "What about the streetcar? Heard you had two different rides with two different men in the middle of the night."

I frowned. "What little bird told you that? Are you trying to get me in trouble? I'm not that girl anymore. Only one man on my mind." I drew my knees to my chest and smiled. I couldn't resist being truthful. I just hoped that by the time this aired, Landon and I would officially be a couple.

CHAPTER SIXTEEN

landon

APRIL 19

Checking on you. Haven't heard from you. Please let me know that you're okay. I worry when you disappear for too long.

MY CHEST SQUEEZED WHILE I read the text from my mother and placed my cell on the bedside table without responding.

To ease the inevitable tightness when dealing with my parents, I stared out the large window, breathing slowly in and out. The trees and shrubbery served a dual purpose, as shade from the sun and by preventing nosy neighbors from seeing in. Birds chirped loudly outside my window, alerting me that a new day had begun. My body began to settle as I admired the view and focused on our performance last night. We had officially smashed our first Hollow Bones and Janae show.

I'd loved the intimacy of the stage and that Janae was always within a few feet of me as she sang or danced beside me. She'd been a dynamic entertainer in the large arena in Houston. On the small stage, she'd been everyone's sister, embracing her audience with her genuine warmth, charisma, and talent. Janae had all of us captured in her enchanted web. My chest swelled with pride that she seemed at peace and in complete command of the stage without using anything, as she had in Houston.

TIYE

"Is it hard for you to perform every time?" she asked quietly from the other side. We were in my bed in New Orleans and would need to get up soon to travel to Atlanta on the tour bus.

The guys and the glam squad had decided to spend their last night partying in the French Quarter. Janae had insisted on returning to the mansion with me, and after we showered separately, she'd joined me in my bed, wearing a T-shirt and short shorts. She'd wrapped herself around me and promptly fallen asleep on my bare chest. Sleep for me was a long time coming, with such an alluring vixen clinging to me.

This morning, a clear-eyed Janae interlocked our hands as we rested on our backs. "I watched you last night, and you refused to look at the audience. You kept your head down the entire time, but your hands never trembled or shook until we exited the stage and had to take photos and sign autographs."

I asked with a slight smile, "How did you end up in my bed again, asking me difficult questions early in the morning?"

"I can't stay away, and I want to know more about you. That's the plain truth, like I expect from you. Now answer my question," she replied.

I stared at her, searching for any sign that she truly wanted my truth. She looked back at me, waiting for me to answer. I admitted, "I'm anxious and stressed from the moment I wake up the day of a performance until I hit the stage. Sometimes I need to isolate myself from everyone to get through my nerves that threaten to cripple me at any moment. Then, for some reason, once I'm on the stage, all I can see and feel is the music. Can't really explain how I can perform when everything in me wants to hide in the audience." I flipped on my side, still holding her hand. "Now, answer *me*. I've watched you perform flawlessly twice without taking anything, so why do you ever want to use?"

"How do you know I haven't?" She averted her gaze to our hands. "I could've popped a pill and gone on that stage."

"I know," I replied.

"How?" Her voice quivered.

Hesitantly, I reached out to touch her cheek. "I watch you, and I don't mean in a stalkerish way. I can't seem to look away anytime you're in my presence. That night at the gala, I saw you outside and how nervous you were.

160

You were so unsure and shaky, pacing, and I could tell you were talking to yourself. I recognized you because I saw me, or at least the part that's afraid I'm not enough. Then there's the part of you that's not like me. You're always moving. A chair doesn't know your name.

"You're flirty, charming, smiling, laughing, always talking fast, dancing to the smallest beat you hear, and so restless that sleep has to hunt you down. You used to keep me on the phone until the crack of dawn with the same energy in your voice as when you started." I dragged my finger softly under her eyes. "And when you think no one is looking, the sadness lurks, ready to show itself if you give it a sliver of a chance. When you use, the sadness may be gone, but there's nothing in its place. I noticed it in your old performances, too. That's how I know you didn't last night. It's all in your eyes."

Janae stared at me for what seemed like forever before she broke out into a loud sob and covered her face. "Sorry. Sorry."

My pulse raced as I pushed her hands down, trying to replay my words in my head again. "Did I go too far? I told you my mind doesn't always filter what I should say or not say."

She started rocking back and forth and wouldn't look at me. Her face was mottled red and scrunched up again. She fought to free her hands.

I wouldn't release them. "Please. Why are you crying?"

"No reason. You can let my hands go. I'm fine."

I dropped her hands, and Janae continued to rock in place, her hands scratching her arms like she itched. She blinked rapidly, and her voice shook. "Keep talking… so you only get nervous off the stage… dealing with the people?"

"Janae, that's not important right now." I shook my head, refusing to talk about me when she was clearly upset. "I'm being honest like you asked, and you won't tell me why you're crying. If it's something I said, please tell me. The last thing I want to do is hurt you when I can tell you've been hurt before."

Janae screamed, "Why can't you just leave it alone? Why can't you let me change the conversation when I asked you what's wrong with you first?" She shoved my chest. "Read the room, Landon. It's everything you said."

Janae's taunting words about the lack of social awareness I'd heard so often pricked my thin skin, and I punched the air between us. "You want to know what's wrong with me? I don't get women. I don't always know how to read the room, and I don't play the games that other men do. I only know how to say what I think and what I feel, if she even gives a damn about my opinion."

Her eyes were wild, and her hands curled into fists like she wanted to fight me.

"I try to stay away from you because you invade my every waking thought. I haven't been able to sleep knowing you are under the same roof as I am. It messes with me that all I have to do is knock on your door, and you'll let me have you. I also know you'll break my damn heart, and I don't know if I'll ever recover. That's my truth. Like right now, you're crying and pissed with me because I answered your question. I know you're not using because your eyes are not dead. If you can't handle my truth, don't ask."

Her face crumpled before she scrambled out of bed. "You're right. I can't handle it. And you don't have to worry about my breaking your heart. I finally know when to walk away from a man first."

"Janae," I said, and she shut the door firmly behind her.

I ran my hand down over my face. I'd messed up, and for the life of me, I had no idea what I'd said or done.

CHAPTER SEVENTEEN

janae

AFRAID I WOULD SEE ONE of the guys, I ran through the house and up the stairs as fast as I could. I couldn't take the throbbing pain. Landon had read me from head to toe. Everything I hated about myself, he noticed. I hated that restlessness had been my middle name since I was a child. My mother used to pinch and hit me to remain still at church and at the dinner table until she gave up. I was the disruptive girl in class who would talk too much or get up without asking permission, because to sit too long physically hurt. I would get into fights with boys and girls at school because I would react to the simplest comment instead of wondering if the other person truly meant to insult me. After a while, it became easier not to make any friends.

I'd wanted to yell until my lungs bled when Landon said he could tell I was sad. That my eyes were only two things… either dead or sad. Three years of being alone, working hard on myself, staying sober, and I was still depressed. Landon had called out the parts of me that I thought I'd hidden… that I thought no one noticed, like they were the most obvious thing about me. He had seen me. He saw me.

And what he saw, he didn't want. Or even if he did, sooner or later, he wouldn't.

How *dare* he tell me how consumed he was with me and that all my heart wanted to do was sing, only to chase his genuine feelings with how he believed I'd break his heart and that he'd never recover? The truth of the matter was that I'd never broken a man's heart. They always left me or never claimed me in the first place. I'd wanted to laugh in his face and tell him that he would wreck me long before I ever hurt him. I wanted to scream that he'd gotten it all wrong. No one had ever truly loved me. Even the man I'd thought loved me for four years looked at his new woman in a way he'd never looked at me.

Busting through my bedroom door and locking it behind me, I scoured my suitcases for any pills I might have forgotten about. I had to find peace. Every inch of my body throbbed and begged for release. *God, help me. God… please…* I couldn't… This was too much. *Why me? Why allow me to be this close to heaven, only to land in hell?*

Fuck. Fuck. Nothing.

I rushed to the bathroom and found my razor in my toiletry bag. I sank to the cold floor and pushed up my shorts to cut the top of my thigh. No man would see my inner thigh anyway. My ex had stopped sexing me a long time ago. The meds took away the things I hated, like my uncontrollable moods, dark thoughts, my impulsivity, and my restlessness, along with the parts of me I loved especially my creativity, my sexuality, and my carefree approach to life. How could I possibly win in this battle for my mind… for the battle of my heart and my soul?

I pressed the razor against my thigh, anticipating the rush of emotions and then the sweet, sweet release when the red line appeared against the brown of my skin. The sharp pain hurt more than I recalled, and the silver razor clanged when it hit the ceramic floor. I stared at my leg, and the cut began to clot, showing little blood because I didn't slice as deep as I had in the past. How could that be? In the past, I'd barely felt any pain. I'd always reveled in the blood that leaked from my self-inflicted wound.

I looked past the ceiling to the great beyond reminding myself that I *was* healing. My physical pain was greater than my emotional pain. I could push through the darkness. A sliver of light peeked behind the gray clouds.

Slowly pushing up from the floor, I stared at my reflection. My eyes were wounded, like I'd just lost everything that I'd ever loved. I brushed back my wild hair, studying my face. My high cheekbones, the soft hair that framed my oval, asymmetrical face. The diamond chip in my nose, so tiny that it went undetected unless the light hit it a certain way. My full, bow-shaped lips, perfect for pouting and any lip shade. Like my mother's, my skin was flawless, except for an occasional breakout because of makeup and improper cleaning. I could say without flinching that I was a beautiful woman. I could see what others saw and not the ugliness my mind often saw.

I kept looking at myself until my eyes only seemed sad and no longer desolate. Happiness would take time, and I would get there someday, I vowed to myself.

In the shower, I bowed my head and allowed the hot water to run over my hair and body. I couldn't keep being afraid of my moods, scared to sleep, and when I would be triggered. I was no longer locked away in my condo, watching TV, exercising, writing music, and journaling. I was out in the world with people who could hurt me, even if unintentionally, like Landon. The more I engaged with the public, the more the inevitable scrutiny of my past behavior and decisions that I'd made would resurface. I'd been warmly received thus far and still felt like breaking with the tiniest mark against myself. What would happen to my psyche when I was publicly ridiculed or criticized? The last time that happened, I'd tried to take my own life.

It was time I fully accepted my struggles. If a man who'd only known me for a short time could see me, it didn't make sense to hide anymore if I truly wanted to heal. I had to learn to be vulnerable with others and trust in me, my treatment team, and the process of living with this disorder.

Wrapping towels around my hair and body, I perched on the edge of the bed and called Del.

"I was just about to call you and the guys to congratulate you on your first show and tell you we have a lot to discuss now that your tour is trending. I'm on the way to Atlanta now, and we can all meet over dinner tonight. Proud of you."

"Then you're about to be prouder, because I want to use the reality show to talk about my struggles. Not just about how hard it is to be an entertainer but how much more challenging it is because I have bipolar." My shoulders sagged in exhaustion. I was tired of fighting in silence.

"Are you sure?" Del asked. "It might be harder than you think to be honest with the world."

"Everything in my life has been hard and I'm still standing, if barely." I chuckled. "Why should this be any different?"

"In that case, you should reconsider speaking at the fundraiser tonight in Atlanta. They would love for you to say a few words. It won't take long. Dip in and out. Raise some money for a good cause. You can say you're a supporter of mental health rights if you're not ready to share your diagnosis."

I sank back on the bed and stared at the recessed ceiling.

"Janae? You still there?"

"Set it up." I hung up.

The knock on the door startled me. I shot up, tightening the towel around me. Was I ready to see Landon and explain myself?

"The bus will be here in less than thirty, ahead of schedule. You ready?" Brian announced through the door.

"Yeah…" I cleared my throat of the lump of disappointment that swelled. "Yes. Thanks, Bri."

"No problem."

I closed my eyes and flopped back on the mattress, trying to console myself that I'd done the right thing by ending us now before deep feelings were involved.

Then why did my heart ache so badly?

CHAPTER EIGHTEEN

landon

ATLANTA

ON THE LONG RIDE TO Atlanta, Janae kept her distance on the tour bus, sitting with the ladies or clowning with Brian and Charles in the dining area. The familiar gnawing in my gut was replaced by lead pressing down on my chest, and my head pounded. The only remedy was Janae. She'd given up on me before we'd even started, as I'd predicted. I wished I could feel justified in believing she would lose interest, but all I felt was lost without her. She'd taken her sun from my moon. I'd grown used to her flattering attention like I was her world.

I sat alone on the sofa near the front of the bus and covered my face with my hat.

"Hey… I know you're not sleeping," Cedrick said.

"What do you want?" I kept the hat over my face.

"Del wants us to make an appearance at this bar and club in ATL tonight."

"And do what? Our show isn't until tomorrow. I'm not performing back to back." I folded my arms over my stomach, hoping to keep the gnawing at bay. I didn't like sudden changes or surprises in the schedule, and Cedrick and Del knew that.

"We are trending, bro. Our show has sold out and our fans want to see us. It's not a performance. Show our faces, and if the band on stage performing wants us to join them, we can. Like Janae did at Café Negril.

Someone recorded what happened there, and it has gone viral, like pretty much everything we post with her in it. Like it or not, she's gold."

I lifted my hat and glanced at him. "Now she's cool because she's bringing attention to the band?"

"I didn't say all that, but I'm man enough at least to admit that we made the right decision working with her. Last night was crazy. They were still chanting our name long after we left the stage." He slapped my thigh. "Come on, bro. You can do it. We walk in, show our faces, and take a few pics. Bring your guitar if it helps."

"If I do that, then you know they'll expect me to play, and are they paying us for that?"

Cedrick grinned. "That's the point. They're paying us mad money whether we perform or not. I was just trying to make it easier for you by telling you to bring the guitar. Bring it or don't bring it. You can leave after they take pics."

"Janae, too?" I asked, hoping my tone seemed neutral.

"Naw. Del has her going to her own thing. She's headed to some dinner or banquet. She's a surprise guest at a charity event. Del had been asking her to go, and this morning, she suddenly decided she wanted to show up."

"Oh." I looked out the window, hating that I'd already grown accustomed to her presence after six days. What would I be like at the end of the tour?

Cedrick glanced at Janae and then at me. "What happened between you two?"

"Decided to chill." I shrugged.

He chuckled under his breath. "Her idea."

I didn't respond.

"She feeling herself, and you're not good enough anymore?" Cedrick chided me.

I held back my sigh. "No. I said some shit that upset her."

"Like what?"

I didn't want to share something that personal, so I improvised. "You know how I do. Say things without thinking it hurts."

"Then apologize. It's never too late." Cedrick nudged my shoulder.

I shook my head. "Better this way anyway. Stop before either one of us is hurt."

"You sure?"

I lifted a brow. "Leave it."

"Forever done talking about her. But I am telling Del it's a go." He quickly rose and walked away before I could protest.

Once we arrived in Atlanta, all I wanted to do was crash in my hotel room. The last thing I wanted was to be social. I slapped my hat on my head and walked past everyone to rest in my bunk. I felt Janae's gaze as I eased into my space. I refused to look her way. I would get over her. I would just remember what I didn't like about her.

Except I'd gotten to know her enough over the past month to know she'd changed.

I groaned and turned over to try to sleep, since I wouldn't be getting any in Atlanta.

As usual, I was the last one to join the group for dinner at the hotel restaurant. The longer I lingered in my room, the less time I spent around others. We were meeting up with Del over a meal to discuss our appearance and other promotional stops between our concerts. We'd discovered during our recent fame over the past year or so that fans didn't bother us as much if we ate at whatever hotel we were staying at, especially the luxury ones.

I leaned against the elevator, grateful I was alone in such a confined space. The elevator opened on the tenth floor to a sensual Janae. I straightened up, and my hungry gaze devoured the beauty in a red strapless dress that hugged her curves. She wore a long, straight black wig that shaped her oval face. Her light makeup didn't cover the freckles across her pierced nose, elevating her allure. My resolve to leave her alone evaporated in the air.

She clutched her silver glitter handbag and said softly, "Um... I can catch the next one."

Wordlessly, I took her hand and pulled her inside with me. When the door closed, the fire between us blazed high. "Wow."

Janae blushed. "You can let go of my hand."

"Maybe I don't want to until you and I are good again. I'm sorry about what I said this morning."

Her forehead puckered briefly, and she looked down at her feet. "We're fine. Just realized you may be right, and we should only be friends."

My heart dipped, and I tugged her closer. "Maybe I was wrong."

She tilted her head, wearing a smile that didn't connect with the sadness in her eyes. "If I didn't know better, I would think Landon Hayes was flirting with me."

"Or being honest." I couldn't look away from her. "Damn."

"Stop gassing me up." She giggled. "It's a good thing we're doing different things tonight, or we might forget that we're better off as friends."

"Where are you going?" I asked. "Maybe I can pass through later."

Janae's gaze slipped from mine. "Doubt you want to go. It's a fundraiser at the Loews Hotel. Del been on me about going for a while now, and I decided to attend at the last minute. The ladies are waiting in the car for me. They want to meet up with the guys later. Think I'll come back here and finally get some rest."

"Same." I released her hand when the elevator dinged. "If you need me, I'm here."

"I think I'm good." She stepped off the elevator and entered the lobby. As she sauntered through the plush area, guests stopped in their tracks to gawk at the star who'd just graced their presence. Some took pics as she walked away from me for the second time today.

Melancholy assailed me. Cedrick had been wrong. Sometimes, it was too late to apologize.

CHAPTER NINETEEN

janae

ON THE SHORT RIDE TO Loews Hotel, I kept my hands in my lap and didn't speak while Frankie and Jeri made small talk. I looked at them and envied their normality. Two self-assured, gorgeous women around my age with full lives outside of their careers. Frankie had a close relationship with her two brothers and parents and had a friend circle. She talked to them throughout the day. Jeri, an only child, was in a sorority and was close to her mother, with whom she spoke to at least once a day. I was sure they believed that with my fame and fortune, I was lucky and blessed, when they were the blessed ones. They had friends and family who treasured them and didn't have to fight demons every day.

"You've been quiet for most of the drive," Frankie observed. "Nervous about the event?"

Jeri added, "Don't worry. We got your back, girl."

My eyes watered, and Jeri grabbed my hand. I squeezed her palm. "Sorry, I've been a mess all day. Got into it with Landon, and now we're done before we ever started. My fault more than his. And I guess I'm scared because I'm about to get in front of these people and announce for the first time that I've been diagnosed with bipolar." I chuckled. "I guess you're the first to know outside my doctors, my ex, and Del. I decided to use my platform to advocate for bipolar. It has been so hard to deal with this by myself. I might help someone else who suffers like I do. Maybe they won't feel alone." I wanted to add *like I do*, but I didn't want them to feel sorrier for me than they probably already did. "I don't know what people will say or if they'll think it's some PR stunt. I just know I want to take charge of my life for maybe the first time ever and do something constructive instead of beating myself up about having this."

Frankie picked up my other hand. "I already thought you were a badass. Now I know for sure. Do you know how brave you are? You're being honest about something that people keep a secret. And don't worry about Landon. It'll blow over. He's been mopier than he usually is. I'm sure he already misses you, and you'll make up. Even if you don't, do you know who you are? You are Janae 'MILA' Warner, baby. Breaking records and hearts as soon as you step on the scene."

I giggled through my tears and admitted, "Is it weird if I say I don't know who I am most days, even with my success?"

Frankie leaned on my shoulder. "Nope, not weird at all."

Jeri hugged me from the other side. "I thought I was the only one who felt that way. I have to take something for my depression."

I studied her pretty face as she nodded. "How long?"

"Since I was a teenager. It was bad back then. Much better now. I'm on a low dose."

I put the back of my hand against my mouth. "I was about to say something stupid and say you don't seem like you're depressed."

"You don't look like you have bipolar. Although I can tell you have a sharp tongue when you need it," Jeri said before her gaze plummeted to her nails.

"Difficult was my first name for a long time. I thought I had to be that way to be heard and respected." I firmly shook my head. "Not anymore. I apologize in advance for my mouth. My nerves get real bad sometimes, and the world seems to move slow while I'm already at the finish line. I'll do better, and if my tongue is sharp, I'm giving you permission to check me. We have so much fun ahead of us, and I don't want to ruin it with my ways."

Frankie admonished me, "Then don't put yourself down. At least not in front of me. We all got issues. At least you're addressing it when most of the world doesn't."

I lifted my head higher. "Thank you for that."

The car slowed, and my stomach roiled again.

Frankie squeezed my hand tightly. "Just be Janae."

"Yeah. Just be me." My breath rattled as I pushed air out of my lungs.

Fans and people crowded around the car as I got out and waved. A tall, redheaded woman with a high ponytail approached me through the growing crowd. She gushed as she gestured for us to follow her. "I'm Elaine Medow, program coordinator for Allies and Support for Mental Illness. I can't believe we were able to get you to speak. When your manager called and told us that you'd been a supporter of our organization for the last two years and wanted to say a few words, we couldn't have been more honored. I've been a fan for years."

"Thank you. Glad to be here." I gestured to Frankie and Jeri. "These are my friends who are here for support."

"Aren't you lucky you get to be friends with Ms. Warner?" Elaine smiled at both of them as we walked briskly inside the hotel. "I've been a fan for years."

"I'm the lucky one." I winked at Jeri.

People called my name as we rushed through the lobby. Two hotel security guards walked alongside us to keep people from getting too close. My fame was rising again. I prayed my decision to be open about my mental health wouldn't block that rise.

"Your production crew's already here and set up in the hall. They have consent forms for the recording and will do their best to keep the camera focused on you and edit if anyone doesn't want to be seen." She smiled. "You only need to speak for about five minutes. We know you're in the middle of a tour, and we appreciate your taking the time."

"So, when do I go on?"

"In about ten minutes. We'll walk you straight in, and you'll come forward once you're introduced and do your spiel raising money for a good cause. Then, afterward, we want to take pictures."

My stomach felt so queasy, and I kept my hands clasped to control the trembling. I nodded, telling myself that this would be done within an hour. I hadn't told Del that I planned to announce my diagnosis publicly.

Tonight would be my special announcement, because word would spread more quickly through social media than if I got word to the press myself.

The audience of about two hundred and fifty donors sitting at white linen-covered tables clapped and howled as I walked to the podium after the chair of the local chapter of Atlanta had so graciously introduced me. While I was waiting to speak, a ginger ale soothed the nausea, and breath control calmed my nerves. Standing before the diverse group, I reminded myself to just be me.

"Thank you, Linda, for that wonderful introduction." Turning back to the audience, I chuckled. "I was standing out there nervous, wishing I was sitting with you and watching someone else speak. I don't think I realized how intimidating it can be to speak in front of this many people when I've performed in front of thousands more. Maybe I need to sing my words to relax."

The audience laughed, and one person shouted, "Go ahead and sing."

"I want to make my time here with you short and to the point, and y'all know if I sing, we gonna be here all night. I know you're anxious to let loose and dance the rest of the evening. I hear the DJ is amazing."

A few more chuckles and nods encouraged me to confess before I lost the nerve, gaining more confidence from the attentive group.

"I am a relatively new supporter of the Allies and Support for Mental Illness. I was impressed by their advocacy work and all that they do for people with mental health diagnoses and the people who love them over the years. But I didn't even know of ASMI's existence until I was diagnosed with bipolar three years ago."

The room grew quiet.

"No one knew tonight that I was going to make this announcement, and most people don't know that I have bipolar. Now, I know that in ASMI's name is 'illness,' and I finally understand why we want to keep saying 'illness' so that society can take us as seriously as all physical diseases, like sickle cell anemia and high blood pressure. This organization has done so much in advocating for people like me to be heard, treated, and respected for their challenges." The more I spoke, the more the words tumbled freely.

"I woke up this morning feeling like I'd been hit by a ton of bricks, though I didn't have a hangover. I started crying uncontrollably while starting a fight with someone who cares about me. I've been fighting the blues for a long time. I believed I was sick, which is technically the definition of ill. Yet, somehow, claiming I have a mental illness is a struggle that doesn't feel right in my soul. Maybe it doesn't feel right because of how society views people like me, or because I want desperately to have control of my moods and thoughts."

Some nodded.

"This morning, I was in New Orleans with no idea that by the time my night ended, I would be in Atlanta speaking in front of you and announcing to the world for the first time that most of my struggles are because of a chemical imbalance." I scanned the room. "I'd rather call what I'm dealing with a challenge, if you will, to living my life. Now, I don't know your religious or spiritual beliefs, so I hope I'm not offending anyone as I tell you my testimony. Earlier today, I cried to God, asking him why I suffered with this affliction. Why is my life so unfair? Why do I have to go through so much sadness and pain, and it's not even my fault?" I gripped the podium.

More heads nodded, and tears glistened in some people's eyes.

"And the more the anger and despair churned in my head, the more I became determined to speak before you. Tonight, I only ask God to continue to give me the strength to persevere and embrace all that is me. To truly accept that there will be good and bad days. The sun and clouds. To help me believe that no matter how dark it gets, the light is on the way." My chest swelled with pride that I was on this stage, baring my soul and taking control of my diagnosis and my life.

The audience clapped their approval.

"This decision to be before you today could be considered impulsive, and at the basic level, it is. But it's definitely one of the best impulsive decisions I've made. Standing before you, telling you a private truth, is freeing in ways I can't possibly describe. I can walk out of this event tonight with my head held higher than it has been in a very long time, if ever.

"From this day forward, I will use my platform to advocate for people living with bipolar and other mental health challenges." I smiled. "I want to be the voice for people who don't have one or for those whose voices are constantly shut down. I want people to know that they no longer have to handle all that it means to live with a mental health challenge alone. I hope tonight you dig deep into those pockets and donate to the largest grassroots mental health organization so that they can continue providing resources and services to the nation. So that we can continue erasing this horrible stigma associated with mental health."

I scanned the audience and noticed a familiar hat, and my heart thudded painfully against my chest. Landon stood at the very back of the hall with his hands in his pockets, and he positively glowed when our eyes connected. He nodded approvingly, and the freedom I'd already experienced by speaking honestly with this group became an exhilarating high.

While grinning at him, I announced, "I'll start with a personal donation of twenty-five thousand, and I'll make sure my brothers in The Hollow Bones will match my donation."

Landon shook his head ruefully, although his smile never faltered.

I concluded, "Thank you all for being supporters, and I thank you for listening."

The crowd clapped loudly, and most stood up for me.

This was a new first on several levels. I'd received a standing ovation for talking in front of a room full of people about my diagnosis and had friends in the audience supporting me. I waved and walked off the stage with a newfound energy that I was finally starting to matter outside my talent.

The chapter president shook my hand as she walked back behind the podium to close out the program. People had already started gathering around me to take pics and request autographs. Frankie and Jeri congratulated and hugged me. I searched past the crowd of well-wishers for Landon, but he'd disappeared.

My happiness deflated like a recently released balloon. I'd thought he would stay around to congratulate me, and maybe we could've hung out. Then again, I'd told him I didn't want to be with him this morning, and maybe he was simply honoring my wishes. I hated allowing my negative emotions to overrule what I wanted, which was him.

Over the past month, Landon had become a constant in my life, and I missed him already. What if he agreed that only being friends was best?

I kept a smile on my face for the cameras, wondering if I could bear the next two months being in such close quarters with a man who'd seemed to accept my diagnosis and whom I wanted so much.

More than three hours later, with no texts or calls from Landon, I'd just settled in my room after dinner with the ladies, who'd decided to join The Hollow Bones at their club appearance. I probably could have gone with them and sought out Landon. I just didn't want to pursue him or any man anymore. It was exhausting, and I needed to focus on adjusting to my diagnosis while pursuing my career again anyway. I'd done something monumental tonight, and I'd diminished that accomplishment by focusing on a man. I'd spent most of the last three years alone and without a man. I could do it again and do my best to allow Landon to be the friend he'd originally wanted to be.

If he still wanted that role. Although from the way he couldn't stop gawking at me in the elevator, he definitely wanted me. *Ugh.* I hated that my thoughts or perceptions, even if they were inaccurate, *seemed* so real.

I stepped onto the balcony of my room overlooking Centennial Olympic Park. Landon would probably love this view. The stars and moon were visible in the sky above the Ferris wheel. *Would he ride a Ferris wheel? He seems the type to hold everyone's belongings so they can have fun. What does* he *do for fun?*

I laughed at myself and rubbed my chilled arms despite the warm April night. Obviously, he and I needed to talk again if I couldn't stop thinking about him. I would apologize, explain myself to him, and see what could happen between us. Try to take it slow, as he and Dr. K had suggested I should.

I walked back into my room, sat on the edge of my bed, and pulled off my shoes. Then I stood to unzip the back of my dress. I allowed the material to puddle around my feet, then stepped out of the dress and picked it up to place in a bag to be laundered. Sleep would be a long time coming. Maybe I should reach out to Landon tonight, since I was the one who'd botched things and made him feel as if he owed me an apology. I would grovel until he forgave me. We could wear hoodies and share a hot chocolate at the hotel bar. Or find the pool and sit and talk. We could go anywhere or do anything.

I wanted to see him and talk or not talk. Just wanted to be in his comforting presence on such an important night.

My cell buzzed in my purse on the bed, and my heart skipped. I quickly pulled out my phone.

Can we talk?

I held the phone to my chest and could feel my rapidly beating heart. He affected me too much. Landon couldn't afford to fall for me, and I couldn't afford the emotional roller coaster I already felt with him. It wasn't too late to talk reasonably and walk away from each other. Maybe this time, we could ignore this insane chemistry and legitimately be friends and leave sex off the table.

Who are you kidding? You want that man more than you've ever wanted another man.

I thought about everything that had transpired from this morning until now. I'd left him confused, and he deserved more than how we'd ended things, especially because he'd shown up for me when I least expected it. I wouldn't let my mind get in the way of my heart.

I replied,

Yes. Because I want to apologize for this morning and start over.

Are you in your room yet?

Yes, but I can come to yours or wherever you want to meet. You didn't do anything wrong. It was all me.

While I waited for his next text, I was startled by the knock on my door. I peeked through the hole, and Landon stood there with his hat cocked to the back, showing some of his curls. His hands were behind his back. Butterflies swarmed in my stomach as I slowly opened the door, deciding to do so wearing only a black lace strapless bra and matching panties.

His hazel eyes smoldered a trail of heat from my feet to my breasts to finally rest on my face. He held a purple hibiscus. "I had to see if I could still knock on your door."

"Ooh, I hate you," I muttered as I grabbed him by the lapels of his jacket and pulled him into the room. The door slammed behind him with finality.

CHAPTER TWENTY
landon

MY INSATIABLE DESIRE FOR JANAE emboldened me to knock on her door unannounced. I'd asked Jeri for her room number at the club, and she'd gladly given it to me. I texted on the elevator to her room, testing the waters. I couldn't say I would've left her alone if she'd ignored my text or told me she didn't want to talk. I needed her, and I knew she needed me, too. The wide smile that brightened her already luminous glow when she'd noticed me at the ASMI event spoke volumes. I'd made the right choice to skip dinner with Del and be there as she announced to the world that she had bipolar.

Knowing she struggled with mental illness didn't deter me from the allure of Janae. Her honesty and truth had only enhanced her beauty in my eyes. When she opened the door, boldly letting me know that I could have her, my already-aroused dick became rock hard at the inevitableness of the passion we would share.

Cradling her face between my calloused palms, I pressed my lips against hers and uttered, "I just want to be buried deep within you."

Her eyes lowered demurely from mine as she stepped back and unhooked her bra, releasing her full, pear-shaped breasts. I shook my head slowly at the goddess before me, feeling impossibly lucky that I would get even one taste of her. I closed a hand over one breast, cradling the soft flesh and stiffened tip. She licked her lips and reached for the buttons on my shirt.

I continued to roll her nipple in between my index finger and thumb as her sexy eyes darkened with temptation and sensuality. I lowered my head to suckle on the other breast, and Janae moaned loudly and could no longer unbutton my shirt. Her hands urgently pressed the back of my head into her.

She stood on tiptoes, clearly wanting my mouth to devour her breasts. I toyed with her rigid nipple with my fingers, using the same rhythm with my tongue. Her breath hitched, and her panting became frenzied. She cursed me. "I don't want to come yet."

Her plea only encouraged my focus on her breasts. I pushed them together with one hand and ran my tongue across both hard buds while running my other hand over her stomach and the diamond in her belly button to slip it under her lace panties, cupping her mound. She closed her eyes and gripped my forearms as I dipped my long finger inside her wetness. Janae shivered as I slowly moved in and out of her, stretching her and building her anticipation for my throbbing manhood. When she froze while scratching my arms, I increased the sucking of her nipples while fingering her.

I fisted my hand in her hair while my lips captured her orgasm in a fiery kiss. She gasped in my mouth, though her tongue eagerly joined and mated with mine. Janae tasted of chocolate and sweet, sweet sin. My finger continued to probe in and out until she succumbed to her climatic release within seconds of her first wave.

Janae stared up at me in exhausted wonder. "Damn, Landon."

I removed my hand from her panties and backed her to the bed. Before I laid her on the firm mattress, I trailed kisses between her breasts and down her writhing body, stopping to tongue her belly button. Her hands rested on my shoulders as I hooked the sides of her lace panties and eased the material off her ass and over her thighs. I kissed her intimately as I moved the lace from her feet.

I looked up at her hooded eyes, drunk on desire. I would cherish every inch of her body and this unexpected night of smoldering passion. I rose to my full height, and the heat from her naked breasts seeped through my shirt. I could no longer wait to feel the softness of her skin on mine.

She pushed the shirt off my shoulders and soon we were both naked. Janae's warm hands roamed my chest and stroked my erection as she sucked on my neck. She murmured, "I love your body. Why are you so incredibly sexy? I can't get enough of you."

Shuddering from her touch, I lifted her enough to place her on the bed and whispered near her ear, "I haven't been able to stop thinking of fucking you ever since you stepped on that elevator. I wanted to push you up on the wall, snatch up your dress, and lose myself inside of you until you screamed my name."

"Next time, do it." She shifted her head to kiss me, opening my mouth with her tongue. I indulged in her sweetness before licking and sucking on her neck.

"I think I will. Mmm… you taste so good." I spread open her legs and touched her engorged clit. "Probably not as good as this."

She coyly smiled. "Don't mess around and get addicted to my kitty kat."

"Oh, I'm already there." I gripped her thighs, and she winced slightly. A thin cut marred her skin. "What happened?"

Janae shook her head. "Nothing. Nothing. Um… being clumsy while shaving."

I gently stopped her from covering the mark and kissed the tiny wound. "Hope that makes it all better."

"It does." Her eyes glistened as she raised her sensual core to my mouth. "Your kiss right here will make it even better."

I dragged my tongue up and down her inner lips while nipping her pulsing button. Janae cursed me, though she pressed my head deeper into her. The loudness of her sensual sighs and her writhing, naked body against the white sheets propelled me to push past my usual reluctance when performing oral sex. I could feast on her all day. I was completely intoxicated by the taste, smell, and feel of her undulating femininity against my mouth.

When she tried to close her legs around my neck, no doubt from the building pressure, I spread her wider, wanting her to take all that I offered and then some. Her moans and purrs of pleasure grew intense, and her hips rocked against my lips and tongue.

Janae came loudly in my mouth, and I licked and sucked her until she collapsed on the bed. Her eyes were closed, and her breasts heaved up and down. Her arms and legs were sprawled across the sheets. I grabbed a condom from my pants before curving my arms around her waist and cuddling behind her. "Wake up. We're not done."

Janae turned over and melded her soft body to mine. "I'm exhausted, but I don't care if I can't move another part of my body, I'm getting fucked by you tonight." She reached down in between us, though her eyes were still closed. "You're so thick and ready to drill me."

"You're sure you ready for me?" I teased her entrance with my erection. "You did have a long day. I can always come back in the morning."

She looped one arm around my neck, tapped my ass with the other hand, and encircled my waist with her legs. "I swear I'll kill you if you leave me hanging tonight. I'm serious, Landon… like, kill you dead."

"I think there's only one outcome to being killed." I chuckled, enjoying that we were so comfortable with one another… that I could feel this relaxed with another human being as I tore off the condom wrapper and sheathed myself. "Open your eyes, Janae."

She slowly did as I said as I eased inside of her walls, which clenched as I pushed in inch by inch until our bodies were one. She curved her other arm around my neck, and I moved in and out, loving the way her inner walls stretched to accommodate my length and width. Loving how her gaze caressed my face while she bit her lip in ecstasy.

"I've waited for this moment ever since the night at the gala when you bumped into me," I admitted softly.

"Me too." She kissed me. "I didn't want you to let me go."

"And I didn't want to let you go."

"I know." She hugged me tighter to her and begged, "Please."

Her soft, urgent plea released the last of my restraint, and I began thrusting more forcefully, though maintaining the same pace. "Please, what?"

Janae's nails became claws on my back and ass as she urged me to move faster. I didn't quicken my speed once the pressure built within my body. I wasn't yet ready to come, wanting to savor our first time. If I picked up speed, I would explode in seconds.

She moaned and yelled with every pump and thrust, cursing me for delaying her body's incessant need for release. I kept moving in and out of her, feeling my desire spiral out of control. Janae started thrashing on the bed, and I caught her lips and tongued her, though she kept moving her head. She was beginning to climax, and I curved my hands to her face, kissing her wildly, madly as my body, almost of its own volition, bucked hard and fast. I roared as evidence of my passion emptied in the protective barrier between us. Her orgasmic yells followed mine within seconds. She received my spent body in her arms as I fell on top of her.

Her naked body was draped across my lap as I rested against the headboard, softly rubbing her hair while she slept. Despite my best intentions, I'd had to have her. I'd tried to talk myself out of following her to the Loews Hotel, but my heart wouldn't listen to reason. Janae enchanted me without even trying, and the sun finally shone on me when she did try.

"You seem to have trouble sleeping too," she said, voice raspy.

I shrugged. "I haven't been able to sleep since you came into my life."

She looked up at me. "That's not good."

"It's like I don't want to miss a moment of you." I kissed the butterfly tattoo on the inside of her wrist. She had eleven tattoos on various parts of her body, and I'd kissed every one.

Her eyes softened. "I feel the same way. I feel that way about my whole life. Like I'm on borrowed time, and I better do all I can to make the most of it."

"Is that why you decided to share that you have bipolar?"

"Partly, and partly because of what happened between me and you." She rose, kissed my lips, and then rested her back against my chest. "I'm sorry about yesterday."

"I've been trying to figure out what I said that hurt you."

She tilted back to see my face. "You still don't know after hearing that I have bipolar?"

"No, I don't."

"You pointed out everything I hated about myself. Parts of me I thought I hid, you noticed like it was the most obvious thing."

"I've been invisible for most of my life. I disappear and reappear whenever I choose. My superpower is observation. I kinda have to observe others because I don't always know the right thing to do in certain situations. I can probably say that no one noticed anything you didn't want them to see."

"I was afraid that if you truly saw me, you wouldn't want me."

I brushed my index finger over her freckles. "I love all the things I pointed out to you. The reason I hate that you feel the need to use, besides the obvious, is because it hides who you are. I like you as you are, even with the underlying sadness and constant need to move. It's like what you said tonight, there are sun and clouds. It's life. I don't care if you have bipolar, if you have to label what you have. Or if everything you are is just who you are. I was proud of you because you did something that made you happy. You looked so strong and confident and seemed so happy up there." I chuckled softly. "But I will have to donate that money on Hollow Bones' behalf. I don't want to hear Ced's response. Your pettiness knows no bounds."

Janae laughed. "I couldn't help it when I saw you."

"Remind me not to cross you." I hugged her tighter.

She kissed my cheek. "I want to stay with you in New York."

No one had ever been in my space for more than a few hours. I tensed, trying to figure out the words to explain the impossibility of her staying with me without hurting her.

"Is there someone else?" Her tone was no longer gentle.

"Why would you say that?"

"You just went all stiff on me. You disappear when we're all together. Maybe you're calling her and checking on her when you're not around me or the cameras. I've been with men with wives and girlfriends, and you're moving like them."

"Then maybe you should stay at the hotel if you believe I would handle you like they did." I bristled at her accusation. How could she still think I was like those other men? We'd spent hours on the phone for a month getting to know one another, and she'd spent nights in my bed. I thought she understood it took me a moment sometimes to respond. I thought she at least trusted me enough not to jump to the conclusion that I had a woman. Was she already pushing me away?

"I don't know what to think, Landon. I'm trying to follow your lead and take it slow. I want to be with you, and not just for sex. I think we have something potentially amazing, and you pull away every time I feel close to you. I've dealt with men—"

I cut her off. "I don't want to keep hearing about your other men. I *know* you've had men. Very powerful men. Men who command and want attention when they enter a room. The way you do. None of those men are like me."

Her eyes focused on mine. "I know that. I love that you're unlike any man I've ever been with."

"You're saying that now… See if you feel the same in a few weeks." I tapped the back of my head against the cushioned board, trying to find the right words to make her understand. "There is no other woman. I don't feel comfortable with people in my space. I just don't. My home is the only place where I can breathe. Where I can be me, and I don't have to hide in plain sight." I stared over her shoulders and out at the balcony, unable to look at her. I feared what I would see in her eyes or her expression. "The Hollow Bones is the only place I fit in besides my home. I never fit in with my parents or in school. Kids used to make fun of me because I never seemed to get it, you know? Catching on to the punch line too late. Not quite wearing the right clothes, or wearing the brand wrong. Fear taking my voice when I least expected it. No girlfriends and no friends."

Janae pressed the side of her face on my chest, and I resumed rubbing her hair.

"I was the kid who wore a hoodie even in the summer so I could cover my head and pretend no one could see me. I disappeared into my music and spent my lunch in the band room, learning how to play any instrument my teacher allowed me to touch. I was naturally drawn to the guitar. I could control how I wanted it to sound more than any other instrument. My guitar never made me feel bad or awkward that I didn't get the joke or that girls didn't pay any attention until I walked on that stage."

I sighed. "You know how you said you wanted to be the woman who would interest a man like me in Houston? I believe I fell for you right then because I never thought a woman like you would ever notice me. And I'm afraid out of my damn mind that I may be too much for you."

"Landon." Janae sounded sad. I didn't want her pity. She grabbed my chin to force me to look at her, and I refused to meet her eyes. My shame heated my face. "Baby, listen to me. For most of my life, I have been nothing. When your mother can't seem to love you and your father has been long gone, you can't help but feel unworthy. I did things to be seen… so I could feel worthy. The only thing that ever made me feel worthy was my talent. Until you. None of those men can hold a candle to you, even in the short time I've known you.

"You think I won't want to be with you anymore once I *see* you? Well, I have the same fear. That the more you're around me, the more you'll run screaming the other way. God help me, I want to *try*, even if we fail miserably." She curved her hands to my face, and my eyes slid back to hers. "I see how this life isn't easy for you like it isn't for me. You want the quiet, and I run from the quiet, and we both do it to hold on to our sanity and live out our dreams. We get each other in ways no one else does or probably ever will. We both could choose other careers, choices that don't play with our minds, yet we're on a tour tempting our mental fate. Why can't we be insane together?"

My heart swelled with impossible emotion as I gazed at the fire in her glistening eyes. I shook my head slowly, in awe that this beautiful, brilliant woman truly wanted to be with me.

Janae gripped my face harder. "You don't have to hide in plain sight anymore. Let me be there for you like you've already been there for me."

"Stay with me in New York."

She nodded rapidly with a relieved smile.

I used my thumbs to wipe her tears and pressed my lips to hers before murmuring, "My life jacket."

"Life jacket."

CHAPTER TWENTY-ONE

janae

APRIL 20

AFTER WE MADE LOVE AND talked most of the night, Landon finally returned to his room to prepare for our busy day. I slid deep under the covers. My thoughts were everywhere, though I was physically exhausted. He'd worn me out in a good way and had exceeded my expectations sexually. Landon had been tested, and I needed to get that done as well. I didn't want to always use condoms, since we were headed toward a relationship.

Although I knew it wouldn't change how I felt about him, Landon wanted me to spend time with him in New York at his place to decide if I wanted to pursue a relationship. I also knew the natural high I felt from the hope of new love wouldn't keep the darkness away. Even now, my mind still warred over whether I was good enough for him or capable of being in a healthy relationship. I hated that I'd accused him of having a woman when he'd been honest, almost brutally so, in our interactions. One of the reasons I adored him was how he moved differently than any man I'd known. He'd been a protector and a friend. I wanted him. I wanted *us*, and I couldn't allow my conflicted mind to overrule what I knew in my heart.

I curled into a fetal position, needing to settle my racing thoughts and relax to grab a couple of hours of sleep before preparing for tonight's show.

Del had other plans.

"Janae, you are hitting a home run," he greeted me when I answered his call a few seconds later. "Once again, you're trending. You got the world spinning, trying to figure out what'll happen next. New tour. New song. New man. Telling ASMI that you have bipolar. I can't keep up with all the calls and demands asking for you. We need to discuss these new opportunities tomorrow while you're traveling to Charlotte, when I have more details."

I smiled at the ceiling. "So, I did the right thing about the bipolar?"

"You did. I was already proud that you'd decided to speak, but I can't say how much prouder I am that you did such a brave thing."

"Thank you, Del. That means a lot to me." I pushed up from the bed and propped a pillow that still smelled like Landon behind me. "Now, what did you really call about?"

He chuckled. "I called about that, *and* I'm sending you what your brother said about you when he was interviewed for the show. I thought you should see it instead of waiting until after the tour. Please check your email."

"My brother?"

"Yes. Don't wait. I think you'll like what he says. Your mother isn't ready for her interview yet."

"Okay." I hung up, then scrolled through my email and clicked on the one from Del. I pulled my knees up. Rashad Warner was my older brother by a year. We'd been close when we were kids. Over time, we grew apart, and he seemed to always take our mother's side whenever there was a family disagreement. Eventually, we'd stopped talking.

My finger hovered over the button as I debated whether to watch it or not. My brother had never intentionally hurt me. He'd just seemed indifferent. Focused on running women and hanging with his friends, he didn't really have time for me. Now, he was a father of three, with two different mothers, and wasn't with either. I hadn't seen nor spoken to him or my nieces and nephew in four years.

If I wanted my familial wounds to heal, I had to confront the knife that cut me. I pressed play.

The video started with Rashad in the backyard of the house we grew up in. I smiled at the sight of my handsome brother. His huskiness as a child had firmed up over the years. He had a full, long beard now, and he wore his Dallas Cowboys hat as defiantly as he always had.

He touched the chains of the old rusty swing. "We used to spend hours outside, pushing each other fast and hard so we could fly as high as the sky. She has a small scar under her chin from when she fell off. My mother was so mad at me for letting anything happen to her, Honey-Nae."

I laughed because I remembered that day. I ran into the house with blood dripping from my chin and scared my mother to death. She yelled and popped my brother on his arm and then bandaged me up. I wiped my tears. At one point, my mother had loved me. So had my brother.

"And my sister used to sing all the time. Lauryn Hill, Jazmine Sullivan, Keyshia Cole. Any singer with a big voice, she sounded just like them. She would sing to me whenever I had a bad day at school, and we would have rap battles she won every single time. She could just flow from the top of her head."

The producer must have asked what had happened to our relationship over the years, because Rashad suddenly looked away. "Um… I don't know. Maybe we just grew apart because we live such different lives. When she came back to perform at the rodeo and didn't call, stop by, or invite us to her show, I realized that somewhere down the line, I'd done something to hurt my baby sister. I wasn't mad or blaming her for not reaching out. I understood why and was hurt." He stared into the camera. "Janae, whether they keep this part of the video or decide not to use it, I hope you see it and call me. I have the same number, and I want to apologize for not being the big brother you needed me to be. Love you."

The video stopped, and I hugged myself. Life was looking up in so many ways because I'd decided to step back into the world. I just had to remember that when the darkness took over, too.

I sent a text to my brother.

Just saw the video. I'm also sorry I wasn't the sister I needed to be to you. Promise to call you soon and catch up.

A few minutes later, I received a reply.

Can't wait.

For now, that was enough.

APRIL 22

After another electrifying show in Atlanta, Landon and I had spent the next two days holed up in my hotel room, lost in each other like we were on our honeymoon. We only left our private haven for a meeting with Del and the rest of the band. By Tuesday, we were back on the road for a performance in Charlotte on Wednesday. The film crew followed behind us in a van. Jeri, Santiago, and I were watching *Black-ish* on the bus, talking and laughing. We were into our second week of the tour, though it seemed like we'd been traveling together for much longer.

When my cell buzzed, I moved away from the group to sit near the front alone to talk to Dr. K. I hated that she hadn't returned my call until this very moment. I didn't have the privacy I wanted to really talk.

"Hey, I'm on the bus headed to Charlotte."

"My assistant said you called a couple of times over the weekend. Is everything okay?"

"Yes and no. Still sober. We smashed New Orleans and Atlanta. I spoke at an ASMI fundraiser and announced my bipolar diagnosis. Landon and I have decided to date, and I reached out to my brother."

"All sounds amazing, and when we have our regular session, I want to hear all the details. So, what's the emergency?"

"That's the point. My life is going well, yet the lows are too low. When I perform, I seem to be fine. It's when I'm not on the stage that I stress. A couple of days after you and I spoke when I was in New Orleans, I started a fight with Landon because I didn't like what he said about me, which was only the truth, and I cut my thigh." I looked toward the back of the tour bus to make sure no one could hear me. Santiago and Jeri were still watching TV. Cedrick was on the phone. Landon, Charles, and Brian were taking a nap. Frankie read a book. "The moment I did it, I remembered how wrong it was and came to the realization that I wanted to truly heal. First by being honest with everyone about my struggles, then I wanted to know if I can pay you more to be more accessible to me. Whatever you want to charge."

"We've already discussed this. I have other patients, and I have a life outside of work. No." She paused. "Maybe you need to reconsider meds, Janae. I'll get Dr. Brownson to follow up with you by tomorrow so you can find a lab somewhere and have the results sent to her. She'll give you the rest of the instructions." Dr. Brownson was the psychiatrist who was a part of my treatment team with Dr. K.

I groaned. "If I ever get back on meds, it won't be lithium. I hate needles." Lithium required that I get bloodwork done every three months because too much of the prescription med in my system could cause severe symptoms.

"I know. Maybe you can speak with Dr. Brownson about other options for your mood."

"I have already, which is why I need more sessions with you." I hated the whine in my voice. I'd tried other meds, and lithium, even with its faults, seemed to stabilize my moods the most, but it also dried out my mouth and hampered my sex drive.

"You sure this isn't an impulsive move on your part? You've been on meds before, and you weren't irritable or self-destructive. With all the pressure, it might be just too hard for your brain to handle. Maybe talk with Dr. Brownson about a lower dose and see how you feel."

The greenery and cars speeding past on the highway suddenly seemed blurry as I quietly admitted, "I've been wondering if this tour is too much, too soon. It's not just about the expectations to be great every performance or to be nice to the fans even when you don't give a fuck. It's also about navigating new relationships with others. I went from being alone most days for three years to a group of different personalities every day. For the most part, we get along. I'm trying to hide my moods, my irritability, and the fact that I can't sleep most nights. I'm exhausted. Then there's Landon, who picked up on everything I tried to hide. Don't get me wrong, he's crazy about me, already supportive, and accepts that I have bipolar."

"Is he why you don't want to get back on meds?"

"I've managed for six months without meds, and he likes me as I am." I gripped the phone.

A heavy silence anchored us.

I glanced behind me, but Landon was still sleeping in his bunk on the bus.

Dr. K cleared her throat. "You just met him. He doesn't know how bad it can get, Janae."

"Well, maybe it won't get that bad again, or if it does, he can be there for me," I insisted stubbornly. "He has his own issues, and he gets me more than any other person ever has."

"What issues does he have?"

I glanced over my shoulder again. "He has anxiety and probably OCD because he's kind of rigid and uncomfortable around everyone except the band and me. Of course, that's me diagnosing him. I don't know if he has a proper diagnosis or has been in treatment. He could be just stuck in his ways, since he's an only child and grew up with money."

"Janae, please be aware that you could be trauma bonding with him, and that type of relationship isn't healthy." Dr. K's sharp tone grated my nerves. "More importantly, don't forget that love can feel like a drug. You might be trading one addiction for another."

Blinking back frustrated and angry tears, I retorted, "Umm... I think I need to find another psychologist. One who doesn't judge me for simply wanting to be happy."

"Janae, that's not what I'm trying to—" she started.

"I appreciate everything you ever did for me. Goodbye." I hung up before my wayward tongue took over and lashed out at a woman I still respected.

Tucking one leg under the other, I shifted on the cushioned seat and allowed my head to fall against the window. Regret and indignation tied for first place. I needed a safe space, and Dr. K had offered me that for three years. But if she couldn't help guide me in my treatment without meds or give me support for the type of love I'd always wanted, then we had run our course as patient and doctor. Maybe it really was time for me to use what she had taught me over the years and strike out on my own.

When I looked toward the back of the bus, Landon was awake and had his guitar in his hand. I'd learned that whenever he pulled it out around us, it was always fun. He would play something, and we would have to guess the song. Landon smiled at me as he started strumming.

Maybe he would be my safe space, since he was already my life jacket.

I did a little twirl and danced to the back, doing what I'd done forever, feigning happiness. Sometimes I could trick my sad mood into having a good day, and other times I couldn't.

I grabbed a large plastic bag from the kitchenette area. "I have gourmet popcorn."

They all yelled their approval like big kids and held their hands out to catch the bags of popcorn I threw while we all gathered around Landon, whose smile grew when I winked at him.

Today would be a good day.

CONFESSIONAL

janae

RICHMOND
APRIL 27

I SAT CROSS-LEGGED IN THE green-screen space in the corner of my hotel bedroom in Richmond. "The calls and comments about my bipolar diagnosis have been so overwhelmingly supportive. I never thought I would ever feel comfortable enough to share this with you all. The speech at ASMI was from the heart. I impulsively made the decision to be honest after an argument with Landon. I can say that we are seriously contemplating a relationship. Whether he realized it or not, he made me own up to what I thought I was hiding. He could clearly see how much pain I was in and still wanted to be there for me. I can never thank him enough for being my biggest support during this new part of my ever-winding journey.

"I asked the producer not to be in here during this recording because I didn't want his presence to alter my thoughts in any way. To be in this place, where I'm admitting that I have the darkest days, I am allowing myself to be vulnerable. Something I don't believe I ever have been. I've got trust issues that stemmed from not knowing my father or having a good relationship with my mother, which makes being vulnerable with Landon or anyone hard." I paused and nodded to myself slowly. "The only reason I'm being this honest now is that maybe I can help someone who's been where I've been or where I'm currently at right now. Maybe you're feeling so down and heavy

hat you don't want to live anymore, just don't want to exist, and you have to
cut or hurt yourself in some way to know that you're real."

I stared at my arms and wrists. "I have eleven tattoos. Five on my arms
and wrists and two on my thighs to cover the scars of wanting to matter. If
my testimony can help, I don't want anyone else to believe that they have
to do this to themselves. It's not healthy, and it could lead to your wanting to
take your own life. Talk to someone you trust, even if it's not your parents.
A teacher, a therapist, or your neighbor. Just tell someone that you're tired of
the pain."

I glanced around my luxury hotel room from the king-sized bed with
the Egyptian sheets, the ornate light fixtures, the plush beige chaise longue
and the large balcony. "I know I'm more blessed than most, so maybe my so-
called charmed life may not resonate with some of you who are doing their
best to survive every day. All I can say is don't give up the fight, even when
everything in you is demanding that you do it."

Resting my head on my knees, I lamented, "There are some trolls who
have called me a liar and said that I'm hiding behind my mental health to
excuse my behavior. Those types of comments were what kept me from living
my truth. I had to accept that no matter how much I'm honest or whatever
advocacy I do for mental health, some may always believe it's a publicity
stunt. And I can no longer worry about those people.

"For too long, I walked around with this façade that I was okay. I might
have seemed strong and didn't give a fuck. I really did care. I played around
with love and got my heart handed to me by a man who wasn't perfect and
had his share of women but loved me the best he could. I thought I had to be
hard, and even when I started this whole journey back in Houston, I slipped
into being MILA instead of Janae. I don't want to be that lonely woman
anymore, and I believe I'm finally on that path.

"We are almost halfway through this tour, and I can't tell you how I feel.
So blessed." I wiped my eyes. "I'm already changing in ways I never imagined.
Spending every day with this phenomenal group of people is shaping me to
be a better person… the best person.

"I love Atlanta in so many ways besides peaches and the ten-minute
ovation." I winked, thinking of the hot sex I'd had. "Jammed in Charlotte

and Richmond chanted our name. New York is next with the Big Apple in April. Spring is in bloom. We'll be in Landon's and The Hollow Bones' hometown for almost three weeks. We may have a surprise or two up our sleeves, and I can't wait."

I waved at the camera. "Until next time."

CHAPTER TWENTY-TWO

landon

NEW YORK
APRIL 29

MY HEART SWELLED WITH PRIDE every time I returned home. The one thing my parents had done right was choose New York to raise me. I loved this city. The hustle and bustle of its inhabitants didn't bother me because I could disappear and reappear, take in a Broadway play on a whim, visit any of the museums, take a walk or a horse ride in Central Park, shop anywhere, and eat the best pizza and hot dogs the city could offer on a dime. Or take a stroll down the brilliantly lit Times Square. A car was an unnecessary expense with the massive train and bus system.

I tapped a beat on the window, smiling as the familiar, crooked skyline with the Freedom Tower touching the brightening sky appeared in the distance. Manhattan. In a city this large, invisibility was the norm unless you made an effort to be seen. I continued to tap a happy rhythm on the tour bus window as we drove in the wee hours of the morning. We would drive into Manhattan on a Tuesday morning as the April sun rose over the largest city in the United States.

The tour had been a certifiable hit. Every remaining show was sold out, and our names were everywhere. The Hollow Bones and Janae had become a trending topic, drawing the kind of attention we had once only imagined.

Festival invites poured in. Club appearance requests filled our schedule. Del was even negotiating a performance slot for us at Austin City Limits in October.

After being on the road for half a month, we would stop in New York for twenty days to perform for two shows, the completion of our second album, and our collaboration with Janae. The Hollow Bones were still independent, and Janae hadn't signed with a label since hers dropped her nearly three years ago. For now, we'd be producing the collaboration independently, releasing it as a standalone single.

When the rising sun greeted me as we rode onto the island, Janae snuggled deeper against my side in the primary bed on the tour bus. We had given her the largest area at the back of the bus, which definitely worked in my favor. Janae hadn't liked being separated from me after Atlanta, and though I didn't like being apart from her, I still needed solitude after being around so many people for most of the trip. In fact, Cedrick and Del had worked out the schedule so that we could spend a stretch in New York working on music, and so I could be in my own space and reset. It would also be the first time having someone stay with me in my home. My original reluctance had faded because I had grown used to sleeping beside Janae.

Her knee rose over my morning erection, and I didn't move it, wanting to feel the pressure of her body on mine. I brushed my lips on her forehead and hugged her to me. Janae was a naturally affectionate person, and I believed that sometimes she touched me unconsciously. I'd become accustomed to and welcomed the feel of her hands and her body in the weeks we'd spent together. Now that I was on my home turf, the urgent need to be with her again overcame me. I placed kisses on her face, her cheek, and her neck. My hand drifted to her bare stomach, where her T-shirt had risen during the night.

I traced the stud that peeked out of her belly button with my finger. She moved my hand under her shirt and guided it toward her naked breast. I rubbed her soft, full orb that fit my palm while my finger teased her nipple. She moaned and writhed as she slowly awakened. I raised her shirt to suck on her stiffened bud and my slid other hand inside her panties, dipping my finger between her legs. Janae was so wet for me and moved against my palm urgently.

She pulled on my head until I released her nipple. I looked up at her. She said, panting, "If you don't want to fuck me on this bus, you have to stop. And if you do decide to fuck me right now, I swear everyone on this bus will know."

I chuckled, removed my hand from her panties, kissed her nipple, and then rested my head on her breasts. "We can wait until we get to my place tonight."

We rode through the city in the quiet of dawn, her breasts my pillow as she caressed my hair. I inhaled her sugary vanilla scent, hoping she could accept me and that what we were beginning to have would never end. I closed my eyes, feeling so grateful for this moment with this beautiful woman. Suddenly, I couldn't wait to make love to her in my space.

I murmured against her breasts, "Naw… we're going to my house as soon as the bus stops."

She ran her fingers through my hair. "We can wait. We're here for a while."

"I don't feel like waiting. Once we get into the studio, we're not coming out until we've finished your song and our album. It's how The Hollow Bones operate. I don't want to be distracted by the thoughts of how much I want to have you in every room of my home when I'm supposed to be focused on the music."

Janae smiled wickedly. "Mmm… I hope you have a lot of rooms. I love the way you feel inside me."

I kissed her nipple. "Yep, my brownstone is four levels."

"Then I don't want to wait either."

I should've realized that my decision to ignore the schedule wouldn't go over well with Cedrick. One of the reasons we worked well together was that we both believed in making and keeping routines.

Once the tour bus stopped to unload us, everyone gathered their belongings. We had cars that would take us to our various destinations. The cameramen filmed us as we stepped off the bus to record our various emotions and feelings about being in New York. For The Hollow Bones, it was home. For Janae, it was an extended stay in a beautiful city. Del had also told us to be open to any opportunity and to always be ready. With that in mind, Janae had asked her glam squad to remain in New York for the full stretch of our stay. Originally, they had planned to rejoin us the night before our first show, but now, they were here for the long haul.

As Janae packed on the bus, I pulled Cedrick to the side. "I need to push the schedule back a day. We can get together earlier than we planned tomorrow if you think that'll work. Or we can chill today and hit the studio late for an all-nighter."

He pulled his bag from underneath the bus. "What? We need to work on Janae's song, and we have rehearsals and our own songs to record." He placed his duffel bag down. "We still have promotional stops while we're here. These days will fly by like that, and we won't be back in the city until after L.A."

"I know." I ran my hands over my head and realized I'd forgotten to wear my hat. "Come on, Ced, I've never asked to alter our schedule. Give me a break."

"So why are you now? Is something wrong? Are your parents okay?" His concerned eyes became annoyed when I didn't answer. He turned his back on me. "You can fuck her later. We have work to do. You can have your version of *Love & Hip Hop* on your own time."

"Don't do that." My blood started to boil. "Don't make fun of us."

He sucked his teeth and waved his hand. "I'm not changing the schedule for that bullshit."

Incensed that he could be so dismissive of her and me, I pushed him against the bus. Though Cedrick was stunned, his hands became fists, and he swung and missed. Brian jumped between us. "Hey... hey... we're in public. People see us. The cameras are on. Calm the hell down. Now."

I immediately dropped my fists. I didn't want to fight my best friend. "I never alter the schedule or ask to take a break. Never. All I want is today. Just a day. That's all I'm asking. We can still meet tonight if you want. I just want to go home. My idea. My decision. Not Janae's, before you start blaming her."

My breathing became shallow as Brian looked at me with worried eyes. I turned to him. "I want to push the schedule back a day. That's all."

He frowned as Charles, who'd grabbed his bag from under the bus, shrugged helplessly.

"You have never changed the schedule. Never. I warned you she was trouble," Cedrick spat.

"What trouble has she caused? In fact, she's brought nothing but good attention to us. When it's convenient for you, you can change the schedule, and I go along without any argument. When I say I want to change, it's a fucking big deal."

"Really? This is the *only* time? You missed out on a meeting with Del to go with Janae to her event in Atlanta," Cedrick replied.

"*One* meeting. But later that night, I was at the club I didn't want to go to and stayed longer than I wanted for the group." I shook my head. "I don't have to explain myself. Fifteen years of going along with the group, and you tripping on one day. I'll see you tomorrow."

The guys stared at me, and I backed away.

I hopped back on the bus. "Janae, let's go now."

She was stuffing a bag with some of her clothes. "I know I should've packed up last night…"

"Leave it. We can get it later or arrange for someone to bring our stuff to my house. I just want to go."

She finally looked at me, and her eyes widened. "Okay."

Frankie and Jeri were silent as she quickly searched for and found her purse and phone. She hugged them both, and I reached for my guitar and her hand as we exited the bus. The guys silently watched Janae and me head to the curb like they were holding their breath, uncertain of what might come next.

"I don't know what happened, but I'm sorry." Janae pressed her head into my shoulder, her arms wrapped around my waist as we walked to one of the cars waiting to take us home.

"Don't ever apologize to me about any choice I make," I muttered as I tried to ignore the curious gazes and photographers snapping pics. I refused to look back at the guys as the car slid into morning traffic.

Why did Cedrick have to make such a big deal of my taking a day off? I gripped Janae's hand tight throughout the silent, tense ride through the city.

He'd wrecked my good mood. I could feel her questioning gaze, but I wasn't ready to tell her what'd happened because it really was silly. I worked hard all the time, and I deserved a break.

I fumed. If I thought about all the times I'd been left alone at the studio working on music because they had women or family obligations, it would be absolutely laughable that any of them would dare be mad at me for changing the schedule for once.

We pulled into my neighborhood and then parked in front of my brownstone. I was proud of my home, especially because I had my own garage in a city where those were a luxury.

I assisted Janae out of the car and walked up the stairs. She stared at the house with her mouth gaped and wistfully remarked, "I already know I'll love it. This neighborhood is how I always envisioned the elite and rich live."

"You do know you're considered the elite and rich too?" I smiled as I punched in the code for my door. "You also have fame that my neighbors don't have."

Janae scanned the community of brownstones and neatly manicured trees that lined both sides of the street. She looked back at me. "I'm always going to be that girl from the Third Ward of Houston."

"That girl who probably has at least a million in her bank account," I reminded her. She glanced around again with a furrowed brow, as if she didn't belong in this neighborhood after being worth more than eight million when she was only twenty-four. Being stripped of her fame and most of her money had scarred her.

I asked as I opened my door, "You good?"

She nodded.

My phone chimed as we entered the cool air of my foyer and living area. I closed the door before I pulled my cell out of my pocket.

Charles had sent a text.

We're headed to the studio to work on the album if you want to stop by later.

The gnawing started again. "They decided to practice without me."

As she took my guitar out of my hand, Janae asked, "All these years and no one has ever missed practice?"

"They never practice without me." I stared at my phone and then at her. "I'm the only one who's never missed a session."

She caressed my face. "It's not too late to go, Landon. I'm not going anywhere. I can wait here for you or return to the hotel and wait for you. I can't come between you and them. They're your family."

She had just entered my home, and I already knew I didn't want her to leave.

I turned my head and kissed her palm. "What if I want you to be my family too?"

Her eyes softened as I swooped down to kiss her, capturing her tongue in my mouth as I lifted her enough for her to wrap her legs around me. I carried her up the stairs, wanting our first time in New York to be in my bed.

CHAPTER TWENTY-THREE

janae

I HELD ON TO ONE of the eight showerheads as I was getting head. Landon confessed he'd always been picky about what he put in his mouth and had barely tolerated oral sex until me. Now, his desire to give and receive seemed insatiable. We'd already had sex in his bed twice, and now we were supposed to be washing each other's bodies. The next thing I knew, he was telling me to hold on while he kneeled, with my leg over his shoulder, ravishing the most intimate part of me with pure delight.

After I came loudly in his mouth, he rose to kiss my lips with a huge grin and a resounding smack. "I can so get used to you here with me."

I hugged his waist as my legs became strong again. "Are you sure now? I can always stay in the hotel and let you have all this space to yourself."

He started lathering my breasts. "Ha… ha."

I snatched the loofah from him. "Nope, we'll never get out of the shower if you start this up again. You wash yourself, and I'll wash me. I want to see the rest of this gorgeous house."

Landon chuckled and grabbed another loofah off the copper caddy for himself.

After we showered, I toured his renovated four-story brownstone wearing one of his hoodies that barely covered my ass. He refused to allow me to walk around nude until he'd recovered from the three back-to-back sessions we'd had today on very little rest.

"I don't have visitors," Landon explained when I noted the two lonely, crushed-velvet armchairs in his living area.

"I don't need a disclaimer. Your house is your house. If you want to be the grumpy old man who lived in a shoe, I wouldn't stop you."

"Ha. Ha. Ha," he mocked, spreading the Chinese takeout we'd ordered on his kitchen table. He heaped shrimp lo mein and fried rice on one plate for me. For himself, he had ordered plain lo mein and a separate side of shrimp.

"Surprised you have a table when you can just eat on the floor," I teased as he pulled out the chair so I could sit. "Your house is beautiful. But why spend all that money on an interior decorator and not include a budget for a sofa?"

He swallowed noodles before saying, "Why waste money when I know I won't have company?"

"Yet you have beds in the bedrooms." I regarded him for a second and started laughing.

"Are you making fun of me?" His eyes were lit with humor, though his forehead was wrinkled.

"A little bit." I slipped onto his lap and straightened the lines on his forehead. "You're still like every man. You don't want women walking through those doors feeling this is home. 'Warm and cozy' gives women ideas of marriage. You have the extra beds in case you don't want to fall asleep with her after having sex, and you're too much of a gentleman to kick her out. You ain't slick, Landon."

He smiled. "I plead the fifth."

"You better call all your lady friends and tell them you're taken now. And I know just the sofa I want to buy as a housewarming gift."

"Santiago was right. You *are* bossy." He kissed my neck. "I've seen all of you, and this is still my favorite part."

I slid my hand down into his pants to touch his limp manhood and began urging it to come back to life. "I don't know. It's a tie between this and your heart."

He groaned. "You're trying to kill me." I shifted to ride him. He quickly picked me up and headed out of the kitchen. "Need a condom."

"You're not about to carry me up the stairs. We're exhausted."

"No." He brought me to the guest bedroom on the first floor and pulled a gold wrapper from underneath the pillows.

"Men are horrible." I chuckled.

"But at least I'm prepared." Landon smirked as he sheathed himself before thrusting deep inside.

APRIL 30

The following morning, I woke early in a slight fog. The fog didn't compare to the darkness, and I breathed a sigh of relief as I rested in bed beside him.

Take it day by day. Don't overthink it or stay stuck in negativity. I picked up the water bottle from the side table and sipped. *Maintain hydration. Breathe in and out. Sleep isn't the enemy. You can beat this.*

My cell alerted me that I had to be in the studio with The Hollow Bones in less than two hours. And I was ready to sing.

Landon slept nude, curled up on his side. Admiring his body, my kitty purred. *Focus. Focus.* We had way too much to do today to stay in bed. I kissed the back of his neck. "Good morning."

He mumbled.

I shook his shoulder. "Wake up. Wake up."

"I need another hour." Landon pulled the covers over his head, and I promptly removed the quilt.

"We already missed one practice. We can't be late for this one."

He placed the pillow over his head. "They don't want me there."

"One fight, Landon," I reminded him.

"We don't fight," he grumbled.

I pulled on his arm, trying to lift him. "You're heavy."

He rolled on his back and quietly admitted, "I can't keep fighting Cedrick over you."

Sensing he was finally ready to talk, I propped my head up on my hand. "What actually happened yesterday?"

"When I told him I wanted to push back the schedule, he told me I could have sex with you later and that he wasn't changing anything for bullshit. And I pushed him against the bus, and we were about to fight. Brian intervened."

I was silent. Yesterday didn't have to happen like that. Cedrick hated me, and now the rest of the band probably hated me, too.

Landon opened his eyes slowly. "You're never silent. Say whatever you want to say."

I tugged on the sheet in between us. "Technically, he was right. We could've waited."

"You didn't hear how he sounded," he explained.

"I can picture his tone. I've dealt with Cedrick enough."

His brows dipped. "You don't seem bothered."

"I can't let Cedrick get to me whenever he makes one of his comments. I accept that he's jealous of our relationship, which may or may not change, because he's used to being number one in your life. But everything someone says or does that's disrespectful to me doesn't warrant violence."

"I was defending you," Landon protested.

"And before me, you didn't fight. Just because I love that you want to be my knight doesn't mean I *need* you to be my knight every time."

He sat up. "I can't sit back and allow people to disrespect you just because you're good with it."

"I'm never good with people disrespecting me." I shot up. "Including you."

"I didn't disrespect you. I would never do that to you," he retorted.

I hit his arm. "You just did when you said I was good with people disrespecting me."

"And you just punched the shit out of my arm!" he howled.

We glared at each other, neither of us wanting to back down. I was so mad at him. How dare he insult me? Didn't he get…

Get what? I knew I had a point. What were we arguing about?

He rubbed his arm, and as we stared at each other, the scowl on his face slowly transitioned into an impish smile. I tried needlessly to hold on to my anger out of stubbornness.

"Stop being so damn cute so I can stay mad." I reluctantly returned his grin.

"You know you want to laugh." Landon chuckled, pointing to my mouth.

"Did we have our first fight as a couple?" I asked through the giggles that bubbled up from within.

He nodded and touched my cheek. "Yep, and we'll probably have many more, since both of us have trouble putting filters on our mouths."

I grinned so hard my jaw ached. "I am so happy."

"Me too." He started pushing me back down on the mattress, and I shook my head.

"We have to make up with Cedrick." I jumped out of bed. "Then, after rehearsal, we can have sex all night long."

He groaned again and covered his head with his pillow. "You really mean all night, don't you?"

I smiled as I headed to the shower. If I were to take a snapshot of this moment, I would swear my life couldn't be more perfect. Landon Hayes was my new man.

When we walked into The Hollow Bones' studio ten minutes before rehearsal began off 125th in Harlem, Cedrick and Charles were beside each other in the control room. Brian wore headphones and waved from the booth. Santiago hadn't arrived yet.

Landon's body emanated tension from every pore. Beads of perspiration popped on his forehead. He hated confrontation, and from what I'd gathered, he and Cedrick had never had any conflict until me. A fact that bothered me, because I'd gained respect for all the men of The Hollow Bones, even Cedrick. They worked hard and didn't have the egotism I'd often seen in the industry. This group of men just wanted to make "damn good music," which was their mantra. I refused to allow Landon to make me the reason this band, who'd been together forever, fell apart.

Pulling my wide-brim hat, used to disguise my identity, lower, I marched into the studio. Landon dragged his feet behind me.

Charles rose and hugged me warmly. "Morning."

I smiled back. "Good morning."

Cedrick kept his head down, focusing on his cell like he didn't see me, and I punched his shoulder. "Can you stop? Just stop."

He rubbed his shoulder and barked, "Landon, get your woman."

An amused Landon folded his arms, allowing me the floor to speak my mind.

"Exactly. That's what I am to him. I want you to be friends again. I don't have any, and that's the loneliest thing in the world. And I'm not the type of woman who wants to ruin friendships… at least not anymore. I already know what your smart ass was about to say." I held my hand up when Cedrick started to protest. "We're together, and things will change for him and for me. Just like whenever you get a woman or children, things will change. You all can't be these boys forever." I quirked a brow and glared at the four men, who all seemed to be listening. "The film crew will be here later today because I didn't want them to disturb our initial flow. That was a feat in itself, because I really don't have the power to tell them what to record or not record without an argument."

I took a deep breath. "Right now, I'll get myself something to eat and enjoy the city while you work out whatever you need to work out. Text me when you need me back here."

Landon's eyes were appreciative, and I squeezed his hand as I moved past him to the door.

"Janae?" Charles called. I looked over my shoulder, and his shy grin erased time from his thirty-three years. "You have friends now."

My heart fluttered as I gave him a little wave and exited the studio. I'd done my part to restore goodwill. The rest was up to Landon.

I'd never been invited to eat by another woman unless it was for business, and I couldn't help the smile that crept across my face when I spotted Frankie at the back of the restaurant. I bent to hug her before I settled across from her.

She gestured to the carafe. "I ordered already. You want a mimosa?"

I shook my head. "I don't drink anymore."

Frankie snapped her fingers. "That's right. You and Landon are the clean ones. Is he against you drinking?"

"I don't like how I am when I drink. He loves that I don't anymore, but he isn't the reason," I explained. "I've never been that chick, to do what a man told me to do, unless it was some sort of sexual game."

She sipped on her drink. "I hear that."

"What's going on? Where's Jeri?"

"Who knows? She's a party girl, living it up. I've never been one, and I'm past that stage now anyway. I'm chill in my room, reading or watching TV. Trying to keep up with Cedrick has been tiring. He still loves the club."

"Probably always will. Music and loud energy are in his blood. Just like the rest. Landon is the only one who prefers quiet."

"You lucked out with him. A handsome and rich musician who doesn't have a roaming eye is a blessing. The way that man defends you and is all about you is so sexy. Had Cedrick and the guys all quiet and numb after you left, trying to figure out what just happened."

"I hope they're working it out. I don't want to be the cause of any rift in the band. I told Cedrick and the guys to grow up because they're not used to Landon doing something just for himself. He's always been about the band, and they could do whatever they wanted, and now he has me. And I want him to have me and Hollow Bones. Cedrick has to accept I'm not going anywhere, like I accept he isn't either."

"I like you more and more each day," Frankie said.

"I feel the same about you. When we get back to Los Angeles, we have to do brunch and get manis and pedis and all that girl stuff," I said, hopeful that my lonely days were over even if, by chance, Landon and I didn't make it.

"Always down for brunch and a good spa day." Frankie held her glass up.

The waitress approached. "Do you need more… Wait, are you MILA?"

Frankie firmly corrected her, "Warner. She's Janae Warner now."

I smiled at Frankie's defense of me and then at the waitress. "I like to be called by my birth name."

The waitress nodded. "I apologize."

"No need. I want egg whites scrambled with spinach, any cheese but cheddar or American, and any mixture of fruit. Perrier water with a side of lemon." Another reason I didn't like taking meds. I couldn't mix any type of citrus fruit with my meds, which made my daily routine of drinking water infused with lemon and lime challenging.

The waitress walked away.

Frankie took a sip of her mimosa. "How has it been dating Landon?"

"It is a blessing, and I'm glad we found each other. Sometimes I do wish he liked to be outside. I'm more like Cedrick and the guys. I love a good party or two."

"Does he care if you hang out?"

I smiled. "No, he doesn't. He accepts that we're different and wants me to be me. I'm not always sure if he's truly the man he's supposed to be. The Landon I see is fun and makes me laugh. Loves all music and can rap and dance his ass off. But he doesn't show that side to anyone else. Maybe the guys… but I wonder if his reservedness is him, or if he's like the tortoise who ducks in his shell whenever he remotely feels threatened."

"You just got with him. You're still learning each other."

"He's always been like this puzzle. Amazing talent and unassuming. Quiet until he plays that guitar." I could feel myself being sucked into Landon Hayes obsession mode, so I waved my hand. "Enough about him. What's going on with you and Cedrick?"

She smiled, displaying one deep dimple. "Learning each other too. I don't have these lofty aspirations to be like you and Landon. Still, I wouldn't mind spending more time with him." Frankie rolled her eyes slightly. "I know. I know that he's not the type to be in a relationship, and he's made that clear. I just like him, you know?"

"I do. Be careful with your heart and have fun. You have his attention now, and you might keep it later. Just keep your options open. There are plenty of men, and you're a snatched woman from head to toe." I snapped my fingers in front of her face. "Thank you very much."

Frankie pursed her lips and dipped her head. "Facts." She picked up her cell and swiped until she found something, then flashed the image before me. "Your brother is delicious. What's his deal?"

"Eww," I squealed, though the picture she showed was a good one of Rashad. "He is so thirst-trapping in this pic. I need to call him."

"Can you do it in front of me? I would so holla."

"The Rashad I know is bad news. He loves women way too much and has three children and two baby mothers." I tilted my head, assessing my new friend. "But he might have matured in relationships, because he's been a good dad."

Her eyes twinkled. "Call him. It's all in fun."

I inhaled and blew out my breath. She didn't know that the only communication we'd had in four years was the text message I sent more than a week ago. "It's a Monday morning. He might be working."

"I bet he'll pick up for his baby sis."

I nodded and searched for his number.

He answered promptly with his usual: "What's up, buttercup?"

My eyes watered. "Same ol' same," I replied the way I'd used to.

"I can't believe you called," he said.

Aware that his booming voice carried, I tucked the phone closer to my ear. "Listen, I promise to call you later tonight or tomorrow, but I have one question."

"Shoot."

"How many women are you talking to right now?"

He chuckled. "Naw... not about to be tricked."

"You just told me it was more than one." I laughed, and Frankie shook her head ruefully.

"Why?"

"One of my girls saw your pic and asked about you. I warned her, but she insisted."

"Mm... is she hot?"

"Boy... bye." I snorted.

"Wait... wait... Is she?"

Frankie grabbed my phone. "I'm the one who asked about you. The next time you visit your sister, come holla at me too."

"Tell him he can visit any time after next month," I suggested, wanting him to know that I welcomed him.

I eased back in my chair, watching my friend talk to my brother. After all the craziness of the past two months since the rodeo in Houston, my life had already changed in ways I'd never imagined.

CHAPTER TWENTY-FOUR
landon

THE FOUR OF US WERE quiet after Janae made her grand entrance and exit. The tension I'd felt when I first walked in had been replaced by anticipatory energy about who would break the ice first so we could return to the easy camaraderie The Hollow Bones had always shared.

Charles sat back. "We're a band, and we can't let anyone get in the way of it."

I protested, "Janae isn't going to get in the way."

"I'm not talking about Janae. So far, she's been good for us. Each night, we're getting better and better. Off stage, she loves to have fun and hasn't been a diva. She cooks and takes care of us like a sister. From what I can tell, she doesn't try to take you away from us."

"Then what do you mean?" I leaned against the wall. Cedrick and I had yet to look at each other.

"I'm talking about the two of you," Charles said. "Handle your business like the best friends you've been and not with this macho bullshit."

I folded my arms. "He started it."

Cedrick pointed at me. "I tried to talk to you one on one, and you didn't hear me."

"Did you talk to me or warn me like I'm some child?" I hit my palm with the back of my other hand. "Whether you like her or not, you have to respect her because she's with me, and I care about her. She's not a groupie or some random."

"I do like her," he muttered.

"What?" Charles asked, though I knew we'd both heard.

Cedrick blew a raspberry. "Janae's cool. She's grown a lot since the last time we worked with her."

"Then why are you tripping?" I dropped down in the chair beside him.

Cedrick glanced at me before staring ahead. "You've been the constant in my life for fifteen years. The sun will rise and set every day because Landon Hayes is there to make sure it happens. I guess I never thought the day would come when that *didn't* happen."

"It was one day, Ced. I'm here now, and we can be here all night if we need to."

His jaw tightened. "Yesterday was the start of everything changing."

I quietly said, "That might be true because music was all we needed. You just never believed it would be me who would change first."

Cedrick twisted his lips and then slowly nodded.

"You helped me get this far, allowing me space and pushing me when I needed to use my voice. I'll always appreciate what you've done for me, and because you've been there when my parents didn't bother." I held my fist out. "I hope we'll continue to be brothers, no matter what the future holds. The Hollow Bones, forever."

The sounds of a violin drifted over us, and I looked back to see Brian playing inside the booth. "Figured you needed music to back up this cry-fest."

Cedrick tapped my fist. "Fuck you, Brian."

Charles laughed. "And we're back. Now, can we please get it together? Nineteen days, and we're on the road."

"No more disappearing acts, I promise." I smiled as I walked into the booth and picked up the guitar I kept at the studio. "I need to hear what you worked on yesterday. Where's Santi?"

"Running late, as usual. But we can show you what we did. I even wrote your part." Cedrick joined us in the booth. "Let's try to hammer down more while we're here. We'll get Janae's done by tomorrow and I figured we could get her crew to film us making the record. Pay them to edit it and drop the video and audio by the weekend. After that, we sit back and do what we do best."

We all said, "Make damn good music."

"When do you want Janae to come back? I need to tell her an hour earlier than we want her to be here," I joked. Janae still didn't seem to understand the concept of time. "On time" for her was at least fifteen minutes later than expected.

Brian chuckled. "Facts."

Cedrick said, "Tell her to come back in time for lunch and bring us something to eat. She doesn't have to get me anything vegan this time."

Charles shook his head. "Bro, give it up already. You love cheese too much."

"Yep. Stop following the trend." I started tuning my guitar.

Brian hit the drums in agreement.

"Fuck every last one of you," Cedrick growled. "Can't you see I'm trying to adopt a healthy lifestyle?"

We all stared at him for a long second before howling in laughter.

Cedrick bit back his grin. "Fine… fine… I'm done with pretending. I do love cheese way too much."

I picked up my cell and texted Janae.

She responded,

I'm bringing back turkey burgers and fries for everyone. I'll be back in time, before lunch. We have too much work to do.

"She's already on it," I informed them. "Now, let's run it."

"Brian, play that violin again." Cedrick squinted.

I smiled. "I know that look. You hear something."

"For Janae's song. We start with the violin."

"I see it… then Santi comes with the trumpet. I can also blow the sax with him if we want more of a chorus sound," I said.

Brian raised his hand in victory. "Number one."

Cedrick beamed. "Nothing less."

MAY 5

Del's jaw would be sore by the end of the night. He'd grinned from the beginning of "Fallen Star" to the end. We replayed it five times at his request in the studio. Janae sat next to him, her leg shaking sporadically as we waited for his opinion of the song we'd stayed up all night to finish. We were so into the music that the cameras didn't seem to faze the group and they didn't bother me.

Janae asked anxiously, "What do you think?"

He clapped. "It's a hit. You made the right decision to release independently again."

Janae hugged Del while Cedrick and I dapped each other.

"The guys will drop the video and audio tomorrow. We already posted a hint on our social media," Cedrick announced.

Del leaned back in his chair and looked at all of us. "Once this song hits, people are going to be asking for more appearances. Are you ready? Austin wants you. Next year, Jazz Fest in New Orleans is considering The Hollow Bones and Janae as a headliner."

"We're not a band," Janae interjected. "This was just a way to get me back out there."

"Well, it's working." Del shrugged.

Cedrick glanced at me before speaking. "Are you still selling us separately or as a combined band? Our album won't feature Janae, and she'll start working on her own stuff again soon, right?"

Del rubbed his hands. "Listen, I am trying to book you separately. Right now, everyone wants you both. We can spin it how we want. We can have a tour where we switch the headliners every night. One night, Janae closes. The next, The Hollow Bones."

I sighed. "Except Hollow Bones will be on stage the whole time. No one wants to see Janae with any other band but us backing her."

"Before everyone gets bent out of shape, let the song hit and tour more as a team. Grow your fanbase, and next year, you can tour separately. By then, Hollow Bones will have dropped album number two, and Janae will be signed with a label and done or almost done with album number four." Del searched our faces again. "It's a win-win, and it seems like you gel well. Am I wrong?"

Cedrick answered first. "We gel. Just don't want our brand to change where we're Janae and The Hollow Bones."

"I don't want that either, and I mean that respectfully." Janae squeezed the hand of Brian, who stood nearest her.

I shrugged. "Then we don't let it happen. Now, can we go eat or something?"

Everyone started moving around, and Del said near my ear, "Can you and Janae stay back?"

Cedrick narrowed his eyes, and I waved him on. "We'll catch up. We won't take long."

The crew started putting away their equipment, and soon the studio was empty except for the three of us, sitting in a small circle.

"I've arranged a few promo stops for you outside of the band. We want to get a photoshoot, so we have some publicity photos featuring the two of you. The photographer wants to capture you in love in New York."

"No, Del," I replied.

Janae picked up my hand. "Hear him out."

Del leaned forward. "The shoot can be intimate. Just you and the photographer. Your relationship is the buzz. You've been spotted out and about during the tour. Everyone wants to know more about you. Whatever happened between you and Cedrick the day you arrived in New York was captured, and the world is in a frenzy. *Is there trouble in paradise already?* We have to jump on it and make sure that the narrative stays positive."

"I don't want to use our relationship to sell records." My chest started to tighten.

Janae rubbed my hand. "We're not. We're selling Black love in all its beauty. I want the world to know how crazy I am about you." She implored me with her eyes. "Baby, we can keep you comfortable. Your hat can partially block your face, and you can have your guitar. We can request that we do it in a studio and not outside. If the photographer wants it to be around New York, he or she can edit it later."

I shook my head. "I don't want to do a shoot without them. These photos might seem like the first step to a solo career."

She gazed up at me. "Trust me. This gets you out of the shadows. People need to see the genius you really are and that real men are more than the alphas of the world. Think of the boy you were and how you can inspire those who are still the way you were. This isn't about breaking away from the group. This is you showing us who Landon Hayes really is."

I inhaled and slowly exhaled. "Okay."

I never knew love would make me expand my comfort zone, and maybe that was what Cedrick was really jealous of. Janae could convince me to do things for the sake of my career that he never could.

CHAPTER TWENTY-FIVE

janae

MAY 8

"WE CAN'T USE ANY OF these," I said as I reviewed the photographer's computer screen in Landon's office at his brownstone. Although he and I had made an attractive pair in various romantic and passionate poses from our shoot earlier that day, Landon had never fully relaxed, and it showed in the photos.

His hands were fists beside me. "I told you I didn't want to do this."

"And it shows. You look like you hated every minute."

The photographer said, "I can edit some things to make the pics work."

Landon stared at his hands, his jaw and mouth tight. He'd wanted to make me happy by agreeing to the shoot, but I'd done nothing to make him comfortable beyond suggesting his home as the shoot location. He was himself in this space more than he was in any space I'd seen him. We could do better in the photos, and we would.

I asked the photographer, "Can you come back in maybe an hour, two tops?"

The chic woman, whose hair remained stiff no matter how often she moved, looked around at her lighting equipment and the young male assistant. We'd been at it for hours. Hours I knew that worried Landon after he'd told the band he wouldn't miss any more rehearsals. "We can take a break."

I walked them to the front door. "I have an idea. Once you get back, you can tell me if it works."

Landon stood at the window in the office, staring out at the quiet Harlem community. "Sorry."

I propped my phone up on his desk, facing the window, and placed it on a timer to take multiple shots. I walked up to him, wrapped my arms around his taut waist, and rested my head against his back. "I'm sorry for expecting you to be anyone other than yourself. The woman was a stranger."

He looked back over his shoulder and smiled.

"God, I hope my phone caught that."

Landon's brow furrowed, and he glanced at the desk.

"Don't be mad." I got on tiptoes to kiss his lips. "I think we should take each other's pictures."

He tilted his head while I left him to pick up my phone and show him.

I grinned as we looked at what the phone had captured. Landon's stoicism, which seemed indifferent on the photographer's lens, presented as pride and strength in mine. The way I held on to him was like a woman who knew who she was and what she had in him.

"This is love."

Landon's breath caught. "Beautiful."

"Exactly." I held my phone up. "Think we up to it?"

He picked me up and tossed me over his shoulder. "After we have sex."

We laughed, and I snapped pics of us as he carried me to the kitchen. He placed me on the island and settled in between my legs. Landon took my phone out of my hand and snapped a couple of shots. "We label this one a woman about to be eaten out good and then sexed in the kitchen."

I laughed, taking off his hat and bandana, running my hands through his wild hair, and wrapping my arms around his neck as he eased my panties down my legs. He jerked me to the edge of the island, kneeled before me, wrapped his arms around my thighs, and indulged in my clit for lunch. My head flung back, I caressed my rigid nipples through my dress as his tongue played sensual music with the most intimate part of me. Being sexual loosened Landon up.

After a steamy romp in the kitchen, we took turns capturing on camera who we were and our growing love in various states of undress. When the photographer returned, she clapped in delight at the deliciously sensual photos we'd taken of each other. "I won't have to do that much to get these ready. And you just used your phones?"

Landon hugged me from behind, and we both nodded.

She smiled, lifted her camera, and snapped. "Perfect. Del wants to see the photos. Are you giving him permission to use any of these shots? I can probably sell some of them to other mags, but they'll want an interview."

I rubbed his forearm. "Not quite ready for an interview. As long as I can post one of my favs on IG and you give us proper credit, you and Del can use any of the photos the way you see fit."

"This isn't The Hollow Bones," Landon reminded us. "This is me and Janae."

The woman nodded with the biggest smile, and her bob finally moved. "That's clear on these photos."

MAY 9

The following night, I stared at the sky through the glass ceiling long after Landon had drifted off to sleep. I couldn't see the stars with the clarity I could down south, though the sky was just as vast and awe-inspiring.

My mind hadn't been quiet since New Orleans more than a month ago. None of the relaxation and meditation practices I'd learned in the last three years seemed to help. Or maybe my mind couldn't relax between this new relationship, the buzz with this tour, and navigating the balance between the guys and Landon. I missed Dr. K and her reassuring and comforting advice. Like a true professional, she'd emailed me a list of coping strategies and wished me well two days after I'd ended our therapeutic relationship.

Landon shifted on his side, facing me. I wanted to smooth the lines on his forehead without waking him. Landon didn't sleep well, either. He was restless and moved constantly, though his breathing remained slow and deep. Maybe it was because he wasn't used to having a warm body in his bed every night. Or maybe he couldn't rest because we had a single dropping tomorrow, and photos of us that would be plastered across the internet for all to see. Or maybe he didn't fully relax because his unconscious self held on to the nervousness he attempted to hide with his hat and his music.

Returning my attention to the universe, I fluffed my pillow and rested my head on it. When would be a good time to tell him about my history and all of my present? What would Landon say when he found out that I'd used alcohol and drugs to help with my moods and not just to perform? Or that as much as I hated it, I may need medications to function somewhat normally? Would he still accept me once he knew that I'd been diagnosed with bipolar after my suicide attempt that my old manager and ex had kept from the press?

I hadn't just disappeared from the music world. I'd wanted to disappear, period. I might not battle cravings for drugs anymore, but I fought against my darkness and irritability whenever people around me moved slowly while I moved fast. I worried that the beautiful man lying next to me, who contemplated everything he did, wouldn't understand my need to operate on instinct and impulse.

"When's the last time you really slept?" His eyes were closed, though his finger traced my neck and shoulder.

"Don't worry about me."

"No choice but to worry about you." A small smile graced his lips. "When, Janae?"

"Remember? I can go days without sleep."

His eyes slowly opened. "There are times I've seen you sleep. Is it just the ebbs and flows of your condition?"

Now would be the perfect time to tell him everything. Would *everything* include what happened when I was a teenager?

"Yep," I answered instead. I was becoming the poster child for bipolar but was still afraid to be completely honest with the man in my bed every night.

"You need to sleep," Landon insisted. "I noticed you're more jittery than you normally are these past few days."

Shit. "I'm good."

"You've been snappy," he said quietly.

"When? I thought I handled the photoshoot well."

"It's the in-between times. Like you make decisions for us because you don't have the patience to wait for me. You decide what we eat and where we go. Give me a chance to respond."

I resisted saying something that I couldn't take back.

He smiled. "Right now, you want to curse me out."

"I really do." I popped his shoulder playfully.

"Tell me."

I turned on my side and laid my head on the crook of my arm. "You're careful in every decision you make. It really is okay to just do it."

"It's also okay to take a moment." Landon stopped tracing circles on my skin.

"A moment or an hour?" I gripped his wrist when he removed the hand touching me. "Don't get mad. You know I'm telling the truth."

"Not mad. Trying to figure out how we can have a middle ground. I don't want you to feel like you have to answer for me. I allowed Cedrick to do that for me way too long. It's why he's having trouble accepting that you are the one I turn to now."

I raised my head slightly. "Hmm… I just realized you act on impulse when you believe I need protecting."

He chuckled. "According to Cedrick, I'm Captain Save-a-Ho."

I frowned.

Landon quickly pulled me into his arms and rubbed my back. "I didn't mean it like it sounded, or that he's ever called you out of your name. One of the first women I was with had been needy, and because I was excited to finally be in a relationship, I ignored the signs that she only wanted me because she saw my moneymaking potential."

"I do need you. I'm that needy woman who wants to be with you all the time."

He kissed my forehead. "I need you too, but you're not needy. You have a mind of your own, and you're determined to get what you want whether you have a man or not."

"My ex wouldn't agree with you."

"Well, I'm not him." His heart beat faster against my cheek.

"Landon, he doesn't mean anything to me anymore. He hasn't in a long time. It was a toxic relationship, and he was just smart enough to leave me first."

"Is that why you wanted to take those photos? To show him that you can move on, too? To compete with his pics with his new woman?"

I wryly commented, "Looks like we're never going to sleep. Might as well get up."

"I'm still tired. We can talk later."

I twirled one of his curls around my finger. "I want to braid your hair while we talk."

Lines appeared on his forehead again. "Right now?"

"Yep." I walked to his closet and donned one of his T-shirts. I then went into the bathroom and grabbed a large tooth and rattail comb and oil from my bag. I sat on the bench. "Grab a couple of pillows and sit between my legs." At his hesitation, I said crossly, "Boy, I'll wash the pillows. Get down here."

"Okay, Snappy Susie." He grabbed the pillow and slid from the bed, easing onto the floor between my legs. Naked.

"You won't get cold?"

"Naw." He kissed the inside of my thigh sending warmth through me. "I must love you to let you touch my hair."

My heart skipped at least five beats at his offhand announcement of loving me. Did he really mean it? Of course he did. Landon was intentional in anything he ever did or said.

I took a calming breath before I casually asked, "When's the last time you went to a barber?"

He exhaled, relaxing into my touch. "I cut my own hair when it gets too long."

"Didn't answer my question." I sounded like Dr. K, so I softened my tone. "Why don't you want anyone touching your hair?"

"I don't know. Just never liked it. I remember crying whenever my father brought me to a barber. He got so tired of fighting with me and punishing me that he stopped when I was about nine. I allowed my mother to clip the ends or cut when my hair grew too long. I rocked the post-COVID Trevor Noah look before it was popular."

I smiled, rubbing my hands together to warm the oil before threading my fingers through his thick curls. "I love your hair. Just think it needs some TLC."

He let out a low, contented moan. "That feels good, Nae."

I chuckled. "Is that your nickname for me?"

"I've been trying to find the right one."

"See what I mean? All that thinking when you can say what you feel when you feel it."

He leaned back tilting his head to meet my gaze and smiled. "I just did. It popped in my head and I said it."

"Oh…"

"Like I just told you that I loved you because it felt right."

Suddenly, my tongue was thick with expectation.

His eyes danced as he stared up at me. "It's all good with me if you want to take your time before you tell me you love me back." He added, "You look funny at this angle."

"What am I going to do with you?" I laughed, lowering my head to kiss him.

When I started to pull back, he gently cradled my neck, holding me in place. "Just accept me."

I nodded, my fingers tightening in his hair before he released me.

Taking the rattail comb, I started parting his hair gently through the tangles. "I wanted to take those photos for the reason I told you. I want to show the world what love looks like. To show the world how much I love you. The old me would have wanted to post pictures to be petty and show Adam that I'm good. Who I am now wants to show the world that I'm good and have a good man."

"I love how you slid that you love me in the midst of explaining why you wanted the photos."

"You think I'm afraid to tell you straight up how I feel?"

"Nope. You have no problem expressing yourself. I'm the one who struggles."

I kissed the newly exposed part of his scalp. "Not with me. I'm so glad you're getting used to my being in your space, because I plan to be around for a long time."

Landon's shoulders relaxed, and he let his head rest against my thigh. I combed his curls, gently working through the tangles.

I had never known this kind of peace before.

CHAPTER
TWENTY-SIX
landon

MAY 14

IN MY ESTIMATION, THE BEGINNING of the end started just four days after "Fallen Star" dropped. On Friday, we released the single. By Tuesday, the video and audio of us creating it were everywhere. Success should've felt like a victory. Instead, it sounded like a ticking clock.

The guys and I were in the studio working hard on our album when Brian shouted, "The fuck?"

I looked up from my guitar. "What?"

"Janae is being hammered by fans. She and the ladies are at Junior's in Brooklyn. Jeri is doing a Live right now. This is unbelievable."

Everyone else pulled their phones out, and I looked over Brian's shoulder, searching for Janae in the crowd and praying she was okay.

Jeri shouted, "Janae and The Hollow Bones just went number one with no publicity. They just dropped it the other day, and boom!" She laughed. "I see you, Brian, Ced. Y'all need to do a Live right now."

The guys started shouting, and all I wanted to do was find Janae.

"Do you see her?" I asked Brian.

He pointed. "She's standing on the table."

The crowd started chanting her name, and I could hear "Fallen Star" faintly playing in the background. Janae started singing to the restaurant, and I watched, mesmerized.

"Yeah, Del, we just heard. I knew it would be a hit… Am I dreaming?" Cedrick kept shaking his head, completely stunned.

Tears ran down Brian's face. Santiago and Charles were hugging each other.

Cedrick passed me the phone. "Del wants to speak to you."

I eased out of the booth while they alternated between celebrating and singing along with Janae.

"Hey, Del."

"I tried to call you on your phone. You should be smiling. If it wasn't for you, I don't know if Janae could handle all of this."

I nodded numbly. I was the one who wasn't sure I could handle what was about to happen, and I had no idea what exactly that was.

"Listen, I'm sending you a couple of suggestions for the cover we should go with for the single. The temporary cover circulating won't do. The photos of you and Janae were the chef's kiss."

"Why send the photos to just me?"

"Listen, I know you love the guys, but people are asking for you."

I looked back at my smiling brothers. "Del, we are a band. All equal."

"You've always been more than them. You could go solo right now, and the labels would offer you crazy money. No one has heard the guitar as you play it since Hendrix."

"I'm not leaving them."

"I don't want you to. Just making you aware of your power."

I looked at the two pics, and my heart sank.

The first one was simply two hats. My trademark porkpie hat and the fedora she'd been wearing to hide her identity, which she'd worn most recently on stage. I couldn't deny the appeal of its simplicity. The other one was a shirtless pic of me, though all I could see was the top of my chest and shoulders. Janae's hand was visible as she twirled the locs of my hair that peeked from underneath my hat around her finger. I was in the bed on my side, gazing at her, though it appeared I was looking directly at the camera.

The photographer had changed the pic to black-and-white, which made my eyes pop more. I looked like a certifiable star.

"Landon, are you still there?"

"Yeah," I weakly responded, holding on to the control desk.

"What do you think?"

"We can't use either one. I can't exclude them."

"They love you. They'll listen to you."

"Can't we make it a celestial scene or something to represent the title? Anything but what you just sent."

"I'll to send it to them, too. Decide as a group."

"No." I gripped the desk harder.

"If I don't, then you're making a decision without them."

"Fuck you, Del," I barked, and looked back at the band. From what I could tell, they were now doing a Live. The booth was soundproof, so we couldn't hear each other.

Del calmly said, "I'm not trying to hurt you or the band. This is business. If the group says no, I'll send more examples."

"Then not now. They're enjoying finding out we have an instant-hit record."

"You don't understand. You're making history. You went number one on an independent song, not backed by any major label. We can't wait for an undeniable cover. I thought we had time. Thought we would get buzz. Not this… not this."

I closed my eyes, trying to slow my beating heart and push breath through my constricted lungs.

"It's going to be okay, Landon. Decide as a group and tell me what you want to do with the cover, okay?"

"And the photos?"

"Regardless of if we use them for the cover or not, the pics will start circulating tomorrow."

"Shit."

"They're amazing, Landon."

I hung up. Del would never understand why I'd responded with the exact opposite of what he'd probably expected.

I sat at the desk and watched as each saw the text after finishing the Live. All except Cedrick jumped up and down and hugged. He met my concerned gaze. Their loud celebration broke the quiet when they piled out of the booth.

Brian pulled me up to hug me.

Charles teased, "When did you get hot?"

Cedrick stopped at the door and folded his arms. "Now what?"

"I say go with the sexy pic. The women want to see Landon like this." Santiago grinned wide.

"I actually like the hats," Brian said as he flopped in the chair behind me.

I stared at Cedrick. "I don't want any covers to imply I'm separate from The Hollow Bones."

"This single won't go on her album or ours. I'm good with either one," Brian said.

"I like that it looks like you're coming out of your shell," Charles added, choosing the sofa across from the engineering board.

"I don't want any cover that separates me from The Hollow Bones," I repeated.

Cedrick looked at his phone again. "Do you feel that way because you're afraid, or is this a business decision?"

I frowned. "What do you mean? Since when do we make decisions that are purely business?"

His head snapped up. "Since we agreed to work with Janae. We did it because it was a good move for The Hollow Bones, and right now, she's the best decision we've *ever* made. If you're afraid of the attention, that's not enough reason. What have we been doing for the last fifteen years if we're not going to see how far we can go? Huh? We created a song that we all agreed was a hit. And based on the response from the world, we were right."

"All that cover will do is lead to the public seeing me as the leader of The Hollow Bones," I countered.

He hit his fist. "Which you are. You're the only one who refuses to see what we all see. We don't do anything without you. That's why we were lost when we had to practice without you. You *are* The Hollow Bones. You came up with our sound and our name." Cedrick stepped closer to me. "Why did you want to call us The Hollow Bones?"

"Birds soar high because of their hollow bones," I dully stated.

"Isn't that what we're doing right now? We have the number one record in the country, and we don't have to share the money with anybody but Janae. You're my brother, and I will walk through a fire for you, but we can't walk in fear anymore." He picked up his cell and started talking. "We decided we're going with the shirtless pic… Yep, we're all on board, even Landon." He chuckled. "Yep, best decision. Thank you for having the vision for putting us with Janae."

The guys stared at me, clearly waiting for my response.

I rose from my chair and went back into the booth. I picked up my guitar and placed the strap over my head.

Through the intercom, Brian asked, "What are you doing?"

"Trying to avoid our being Icarus."

Brian frowned.

Cedrick responded, "In Greek mythology, Icarus had man-made wings to escape from his captor. He started believing he was invincible and ignored his father's warnings not to fly too high because the wax used to create the wings would melt. He soared too close to the sun, and the wax melted, and he tumbled into the sea." He shook his head. "The lesson in that story was to be humble while you take risks and not start believing your own hype."

Charles jumped up. "That man all deep and profound, and doesn't think he's the leader."

Santiago followed Charles into the booth.

"Wait, so we're not going to celebrate?" Brian held his hands out.

"We still have an album to work on," Cedrick said. "We'll celebrate after we work, like we always do."

Brian rolled his eyes to the ceiling as he stomped into the booth.

"Run it," I commanded, finally feeling my feet again.

CHAPTER TWENTY-SEVEN

janae

WHEN WE WALKED OUTSIDE JUNIOR'S to pandemonium, the adoring crowd energized me instead of scaring me. My driver served as security as he helped me get on the roof of the Lincoln Navigator. I partied with my fans longer as the music blasted from a nearby bodega. Jeri held her camera up, capturing the controlled chaos live. I was at the top of the mountain. This natural high was what I'd always wanted. I was grateful that I was sober and that I didn't use any medication. Whatever I felt was real and not manufactured or altered. Janae Warner had finally done it. I was at the top and hadn't self-destructed.

After I had danced to three popular songs by other artists, Frankie eased up on the hood through the crowd as I sang and danced. "Your fans are in the streets now and causing traffic jams. It could get dangerous. Police will be here soon."

Annoyed, I batted her away with my hand like she were a pesky mosquito. "Let them come. This is my moment. Ain't shit going to happen but good times."

"You're about to ruin your moment if it gets any more out of hand. Look around. We don't have the manpower to protect you if it gets worse."

Instead of heeding her advice, I started rapping to the next record that played, much to the growing crowd's satisfaction. She climbed down as I yelled, "I just brought H-Town to the Big A."

The people cheered loudly for their fallen star that had risen again like the phoenix from the ashes.

The heat of the May night and my unstoppable energy plastered my hair to my head, and sweat trickled down my face, wetting the vintage *Jason's Lyric* t-shirt I wore. My red Jordans gripped the top of the SUV's roof as I danced, the perfect shoes for a night like this.

Arms raised, I hyped my fans more by getting them to chant along with me. Most shouted my name. Others just screamed.

Then, a sudden tug on the bottom of my jeans sent me off balance. My breath caught as my foot slipped.

The world tilted, and I barely caught myself before falling, my heart hammering as my limbs fought for control. But that tiny misstep changed everything.

The energy shifted and the crowd surged forward.

A ripple of grasping hands and desperate faces. Adoration twisting into something else. Something more urgent. More dangerous. I searched for Frankie and Jeri.

Nowhere.

Panic coiled around my ribs. I shouted, "Calm down! There's too many of you!"

But the street was already packed tight with bodies, feverish and wild. The roar of voices blurred into chaos. It felt less like a celebration and more like a concert spiraling out of control.

What have you done, Janae?

A fan lunged onto the back of the truck, fingers grazing my calf.

My breath hitched. My foot slid against the SUV's roof. This time, I couldn't catch myself and the world lurched. I crashed onto my side, my head barely missing the metal roof.

The crowd gasped. Voices twisted with panic. I squeezed my eyes shut, fighting against the scream clawing up my throat. My hands scrambled for balance, but the surface was too slick, and I couldn't regain my footing. Goosebumps prickled down my arms.

Fuck. Fuck.

The walls were closing in. My breaths came short and sharp, my pulse a frantic beat.

I couldn't look. I couldn't face the danger I had thrown myself into. I needed to get inside the car. *Now.* But how?

My mind spiraled toward one thought. One person. I needed Landon. He would save me.

I opened my eyes and searched frantically through the crowd. Where was he? My pulse thumped wildly as I scanned the sea of faces. He had to know. He had to know I needed him. Why wasn't he here?

"Ms. Warner," a stern voice cut through the noise. "We have to leave now, or you may be arrested for inciting a disturbance. Police have been called."

I tore my gaze away from the crowd. The driver and a security guard had their arms raised, ready to help me down. Two more men held back the pressing fans, creating enough space for me to escape.

My body trembled as they lowered me to the ground. My sneakers hit the pavement, but my knees buckled. Before I could fall, they guided me into the SUV where Frankie and Jeri were already waiting.

Their wide eyes locked on the mayhem outside. The tinted windows shielded us, but it didn't matter. The energy still pulsed, the fans still knocked, their faces a blur of hands and shouts. The driver laid on the horn, but the crowd barely moved.

He wiped sweat from his brow. "We might need police assistance."

"No." I shook my head violently. "No. The media will twist this."

Frankie let out a sharp breath. "You don't hear the sirens? I told you to get down."

I clenched my fists. "And I have the number one song in the country after three years of silence. That was me celebrating." My voice was hoarse, edged with something even I couldn't identify. The rush, the fear, the desperation. My heart pounded like it would explode.

Tears streamed down my face as I jabbed a finger at the driver. "I pay him well to drive, and that's exactly what he's about to do."

Frankie's nostrils flared. "I can't with you."

"Can't do what?" My voice rose, cracking. I glanced out the window, watching the fans slap their hands against the glass as the SUV inched forward.

She waved a hand, dismissing me completely, as I slid into the row behind them.

"Can't do what?" My chest heaved. "Huh?"

Jeri leaned closer to the driver, her voice low but firm. "Keep inching forward. Keep honking. No one wants to get hit."

I twisted toward Frankie, my hands curled into fists against my thighs. "Can't do what?"

Frankie whirled on me, eyes flashing. "Can't deal with you when you're high."

A sharp laugh tore from my throat. "Then you can't deal with me ever, because I haven't used anything since Houston. This is me, Frankie. This is me, high on life."

Frankie's expression flickered. Shock, doubt, maybe even regret.

I nodded furiously. "Yeah. Yeah, I'm serious." But my voice wavered, the tears coming faster. "All I wanted was to have fun." My body curled in on itself, my arms wrapped around my knees as I rocked. "That's all."

Jeri reached out hesitantly. "It's okay. The car is moving."

"It doesn't matter." My throat tightened. "I messed up. Again. I'm that crazy bitch. It wasn't enough for me to celebrate in the restaurant. No, I had to cause a scene. On the street. In front of everybody."

My eyes darted around the SUV. I needed my phone. I needed Landon.

"Did he call?" My voice shook.

Jeri hesitated. "They're at the studio."

I clenched my jaw. "I know where they are. I asked if he called."

Frankie slammed her fist into her palm. "Keep talking to us like we're nothing, and we're getting out of this car."

"Go right ahead," I snapped. The moment the words left my lips, I hated them. God, why was I like this? I wanted to reach for her, to apologize, but I couldn't seem to move.

Frankie exhaled sharply. "I swear I'm done with you. You almost got us killed because you don't listen. You think money solves everything? Throwing your card at a manager to pay for the whole restaurant without asking for a receipt? You should be glad I made sure you got it back." She tossed my credit card onto the seat next to me.

I swiped at my wet face. "That's hilarious. I know money doesn't solve anything. If it did, I wouldn't be a mess." My voice wobbled, but I pushed forward. "You're not the first to be done with me. Probably not the last."

Jeri put her hands up. "Please. Please stop shouting. We're moving. It's over. No one got hurt. Tonight was supposed to be a good night."

Frankie crossed her arms and turned toward the window, shutting me out completely.

That did it. I curled into myself, my sobs breaking free. Somewhere between gasping breaths and bone-deep exhaustion, I sank into sleep, too drained to fight anymore.

A door creaked open, followed by the soft rustle of movement and a shift in the air. Warmth settled near me, familiar even through the haze of half-consciousness.

The cushion dipped beside me, and the scent of cedar surrounded me, steady and grounding. A low voice, calm and sure, cut through the fog.

"Nae, it's okay."

My breath caught, and without thinking, I curled toward the warmth before my eyes even opened.

Landon.

"My life jacket." My voice broke, the tears threatening again.

Landon moved closer, wrapping his arms around me, his grip grounding me in a way nothing else ever could. "Always."

I clung to him as we drove away, my heart still racing, my mind still spinning, but the storm inside me started to settle.

"How did you get here?" I whispered. "Where are we?"

"Frankie called me." He rested his chin on my head. "She didn't think you wanted the guys to know."

She was right. I had been able to hide this for so long by pouring my energy into sex, rehearsals, performing, and cooking. But tonight, my mask had slipped.

Frankie and Jeri sat across from us. Frankie's arms were still crossed, but her face had softened, just slightly.

I turned to her, voice raw. "I'm sorry. You were only looking out for me."

She gave a small nod but said nothing.

Landon kissed the top of my head. "It's all good. No one got hurt. No police trouble. The fans still love you."

Jeri smirked. "She's over here crying her eyes out with the number one record and a sexy man on her arm. Raise your head, you drama queen."

A watery laugh slipped from my lips. "I deserve that."

Jeri grinned. "Damn right you do." She turned to Landon. "You better get used to the attention. Del needs to hire security for the rest of the tour. You just became the sexiest man alive."

Landon frowned. "What happened?"

Jeri shoved her phone toward me. My breath caught. It was the photo. Landon. Shirtless. Sheets tangled around his waist. Eyes locked on me, dark and intense. My favorite shot of him.

My voice barely made a sound. "How did you get that?"

"Brian sent it. Said this was the cover of your single."

Landon shifted uncomfortably.

I swallowed hard. "You cool with it?"

He mumbled, "The group decided."

But his jaw was tight. His hands flexed against his thighs. And for the first time, I realized. He wasn't okay with it.

And neither was I.

MAY 15

I was naked in his bed, waiting anxiously to talk to him. I'd been out most of the day and night shopping and taking in a Broadway show, making amends with Frankie and Jeri while he was holed up in the studio. I loved that Landon had nothing to hide. He'd given me his code to his brownstone and cell without asking, as if we already shared his home. He may have had the money to have a separate residence for his women and multiple phones like previous men in my life, but he didn't play games.

However, he did have his ways. He preferred order in his home and liked things just so. I could not move things around without asking first, though he was always open to my suggestions. Sometimes he drifted off mid-conversation, his mind pulled toward music or astronomy. Other times he made a comment that stung without meaning to.

But none of it ever felt like a flaw, just part of who he was. More than anyone I had ever known, he listened when I spoke, adjusted when I needed him to, and cared in ways that went beyond words. That was why I knew he would hear me now. I needed his help to change the cover, and if anyone could make it happen, it was him.

The sounds of the code being entered through the system built into his headboard signaled that Landon was home, and I was both excited and irritated to see him. It was after two in the morning, and we hadn't spoken since he'd returned to the studio at the break of dawn.

He smiled when he saw me. "After an exhausting day, I'm so glad you stayed here with me. I love coming home to you in my bed."

"It feels like home already to me," I admitted.

"Good." He leaned over and kissed me, and I gripped his hand before he moved away. "You know I need to shower before I get in bed."

"I've been waiting to talk to you for hours."

He replied warily, "I was in the studio."

"I know where you were. You didn't call me."

"I would have, but Cedrick said you and your squad were going to see a musical."

"Hours ago, Landon."

He stood up to his full height. "Okay, I'm here now. What did you want to talk about?"

"Oh, I don't know. Maybe the song we just did together that went number one and the cover that doesn't include me. I texted you that I needed to talk."

"You told me that you were good with the cover. What else is there for us to talk about?" He took off his hat and tossed it on the bench.

"So, you only reach out when you think something's wrong?"

His shirt joined his hat. "Don't start that when you know I am here for you."

"Your phone went to voicemail."

Landon frowned, dropped his cell on the table beside the bed, and headed to the bathroom. "Shower and then talk."

"No." I hit the mattress.

He sighed loudly. "Why? Maybe I want to get clean, relax, and then talk. You can wait a few more minutes."

"It won't kill you to strip and get in the bed now." I patted the space next to me.

"Stop trying to make me do something just to see if you can," he shot back, then stalked off to the bathroom and locked the door.

I fumed until he finished his shower and walked out nude. No matter how many times I saw him, I still hadn't gotten used to the way he looked, and some of my anger fizzled. He slid into bed without a word and pulled me against his warm, clean body.

Landon always smelled good, his scent comforting as I snuggled into his side. It was always better when it was just us. He carried himself tensely in the world, always on guard when there was no music to anchor him. But here, in his home, with me, he was at ease. He had once flinched at my touch, needing time to adjust, but now he sought it out, pulling me closer like he needed the contact.

We'd made progress. I didn't want to ruin it with my temper.

"Now, what do you want to yell at me about?" he asked with a straight face. I still couldn't tell when he was teasing me.

"We accomplished something great. Why is this the first time we've talked about it? We should've gotten together to celebrate. Had dinner or something. Or had a night of fun with everyone. I only stayed out late with Jeri and Frankie because you didn't text or call me. Watching the guys communicate with Frankie and Jeri was frustrating, and I received nothing from you."

Until that very moment, I hadn't been able to articulate my troubling emotions. I'd thought my sadness was about the cover, and it partially was, but my hurt hit deeper. I'd assumed that since Landon had been my protector and my defender thus far, on the biggest moment of my life, he would be my supporter, too.

The rumble of his voice near my ear soothed my irritability. "So much happened. We were working on new music, and during a short break, we found out about hitting number one from Jeri when she went live with you at Junior's. I looked for you, praying you were not overwhelmed, and I was happy to see that you weren't.

"I was still shocked and in disbelief about our song. I was trying to process seeing you sing at the restaurant and the guys celebrating, and then Del sent me two pics as possible covers. He insisted I choose immediately and that we had to act fast. I didn't like either one because it didn't represent Hollow Bones. Del sent them to the rest of the band. The band disagreed and chose one of the photos we took. I didn't like being forced to choose between the two and started working on the album again. Then Frankie called me about you. I promised the guys I would return as soon as possible, and I've been grinding in the studio ever since. We are *this* close to finishing the album." Landon looked at me. "I wasn't ignoring you… or at least not in the way you think."

His heart beat steadily as he awaited my response.

"Can I see the choices?" I said, sighing.

He picked up his phone and showed me the two photos.

"What's wrong with the two hats? It's you and me."

Landon nodded. "I did like that one better, too. Except it didn't rep the group."

"And this one does?"

"I feel like you do, but I was outnumbered."

"Did you even bring up that I wasn't a part of the picture of you?"

"You can tell it's your hand because of the butterfly tattoo on your wrist."

I tapped the pic of him. "My face, Landon. Why isn't my *face* on the cover?"

His chest rose and fell. "Del chose the pics. Not me."

"This is where I need you to defend me."

"I didn't choose either one."

"You also said nothing is decided if the group doesn't all agree."

"You took the pictures, and this is a single not going on either of our albums. Why are you bothered?"

I waved my hands wildly around me. "I have a number one song, and my face isn't on the cover? Does that make sense to you?"

"We're not going to argue about this. Last night you said you were fine with it. It's your voice, Janae. In the video, we see you more than anyone else. Let my photo stand. Please."

"You're not even comfortable with the picture."

"So? You keep telling me to open up and be freer. This is how I'm doing it. End of discussion. I'm exhausted."

I hit him with my pillow. "You won't shut me up. The discussion is over when I say it is."

He put his hands under his head and looked at the ceiling. "Talk."

"You said you didn't want to use our relationship to sell records."

Landon slanted his gaze at me. "I don't. No one else cares about that except us. You heard what Frankie said. Del and the guys see us as good business, too, and I cannot deny that people like us together. I *love* us together and hope we're always together. Remember, I didn't want to do the shoot. I only went along with it because I wanted to please you. Don't bust my balls because the picture chosen doesn't have your face."

Turning over on my stomach, I tried to explain in another way. "I feel like the Black artist who's erased from the album because the label chose white faces."

"I don't know why you feel like that when the world recognizes you more than us. You were the one swarmed at Junior's. When we go places, people ask for you and not us. If you have an issue, take it up with Del. I didn't want to show the pics to the guys anyway. I suggested the galaxy or a one representing a star without any faces. I didn't think we should have our faces on the cover. He sent the images to the guys against my wishes because he said I couldn't decide for the band."

"You weren't trying to protect me. You were trying to protect The Hollow Bones." Old, familiar hurts burned through me. "Not even my manager looked out for me."

"My job is to protect you as my woman. Regarding the business, I can't be on your side *and* The Hollow Bones'. It's unfair of you to ask that of me or make me feel guilty." He continued to study the sky. "Are you done talking?"

I wanted to scream that I wasn't. All that would do was aggravate him when he'd clearly made up his mind. I was in this alone, as I'd always been. I moved away from him and turned over to face the wall.

Landon sighed loudly and turned on his side away from me.

I cried without making a noise, which I'd learned to do when I was a girl.

CHAPTER TWENTY-EIGHT

landon

MY EYES WERE CLOSED. MY breathing was slow and rhythmic.

My mind… My mind was another matter. I'd disappointed Janae, and I didn't know quite how I had. It had appeared she was having the time of her life. I thought everything with Janae was good. She'd had a moment, and it passed. She'd even seemed cool with the photo in the car last night. I'd thought she would've loved either photo as a cover because she'd taken them. I didn't think to defend her because I'd never had to consider someone else's feelings outside of mine and the band's. I also didn't want to approach the band on her behalf again. I needed to keep the two separate.

Her stillness as time passed concerned me. Janae moved almost constantly, even when we were in bed together. We both needed to rest. I got up, walked to my closet, and chose two of my hoodies. I pulled leggings from the suitcase she had yet to unpack, though I'd told her she could consider my closet as hers, and pulled on basketball shorts.

I walked back out and kneeled beside her. Tears streaked her beautiful cheeks, and my heart clenched. She opened her eyes, and I said, "Come be quiet with me."

She nodded. I stood and passed her the clothes. When she'd dressed, I held my arm out for her to hold, and we left my home. She leaned on me, and we walked in the early morning darkness. The sun had yet to rise.

Harlem was strangely silent, and we were like the only inhabitants of the city. We walked down the concrete steps and hopped on a train. I wrapped my arm around her, and she rested her head on my shoulder. I kissed the top of her head, and soon, she drifted to sleep.

I'd made her cry, and that pained me. I didn't think I was capable of handling such an emotion from a woman. I understood anger, irritation, indifference, and annoyance. Sadness was different. She'd been smiling this entire time, even when she wasn't happy. She'd never expressed sadness until last night. We both should've been ecstatic, because our song had done something songs just didn't *do*. Instead, we were on the train, exhausted and sad.

The sun warmed my skin, and other people got on the train on their morning commutes before I gently shook her shoulders. She squinted in the sun, looked up at me, and gave me the most glorious smile. "Landon, you're not wearing your hat."

Self-consciously, I rubbed the neat cornrows she'd made of my hair. "I forgot."

"You never forget."

"Lately, I have. Guess my concern for you outweighed my need to wear it." I focused on her beautiful face. The freckles across her nose and cheeks were more prominent in the sun.

She giggled. "I bet you're fighting hard not to pull your hoodie over your head now."

I admired her. "Naw… looking at you is enough."

Her eyes watered. "Did you sleep?"

I shook my head. "Someone had to make sure Candyman didn't come get us."

She laughed. "Candyman is in Chicago."

I pulled out my phone, pressed my head to hers, and took a selfie. "This is us after the biggest day of our careers. Exhausted, happy, and in love."

Janae glanced at me and then at the photo. "We *are* in love, aren't we?"

"I hope so, because I don't want to be out here alone anymore."

She blinked back tears. "How do you know to say exactly what I need you to say?"

"No idea." I slunk down in my seat. "I just know I don't want to be the one who makes you cry. I'm sorry."

"You don't know why you're sorry."

"That may be, but I apologize for not getting how I hurt you."

She shifted and leaned against the window as she looked at me. "That part."

"What?"

"I can't explain everything to you."

"Why not? We're still getting to know each other. From what I can tell about people, especially women, we will always be learning each other. Remember the day at the airport in New Orleans? I said I didn't know how I could do this. I meant to keep the lines drawn between you and Hollow Bones. I want to be with you, and I want to support your career, but I can't take sides against my band. Not even for you."

She nodded. "I get that. It's hard sometimes to be with a man who gets so into his music that nothing and no one else matters. Your phone is off or on silent for hours."

"And once you really start grinding on your next album, you'll be the same way."

"Umm… not quite. I'm more like the guys. In breaks, they're on the phone, talking and texting, taking a moment for themselves. I see how you're singularly focused."

"Kind of hard not to be when I had nothing but music for years. I'm not like the others. I don't have family or women checking for me. The guys are my friends and my family."

"I'm both now, too."

I tapped her nose. "Yep. And now you. I'll do better about communicating when I'm in the studio."

"And I'll do better about explaining myself and not expecting you just to get it."

"Thank you." I raised my brows. "Are we done talking now?"

She shook her head ruefully before pulling her phone from her hoodie's front pocket. "I need to talk to Del and ask him why he didn't consult with me about the cover."

I whistled softly. "I'm staying out of it, okay? That's between you and him."

"Understood." Janae smiled before focusing on her cell.

"Excuse me?" We looked up to a group of teens dressed in uniforms crowding the space around us. "Aren't you Janae and Landon?

Janae chuckled. "Landon Hayes of The Hollow Bones and Janae Warner."

"Yes… I thought that was Landon without his hat," said the girl who spoke for the group. "Can we take a picture?"

I inhaled and exhaled. Before I could do it, Janae pulled my hood on top of my head and said, "Yes."

By the time we made it back to my stop, we'd attracted a crowd of fans taking pics with us. I smiled and waved and allowed Janae to do most of the talking. She pulled on her hoodie, and we hurried out of the train station and back to my house, laughing all the way.

Once we slammed the door to my home, all that energy turned into sexual hunger. Our clothes were discarded within seconds, and I had her pressed up against the wall. My mouth and hands were everywhere, rough and tugging at her hair and her breasts while I tongued her down. Although she wanted to throw caution to the wind, I grabbed a condom from a kitchen drawer while she toyed with herself.

As soon as I protected us, I thrust deep inside of her with a fierceness and power she relished, if her loud moans were any indication. Janae held on tight as I pounded and pounded. Her ass knocked violently against the wall.

When I began to twist from the inside out, overcome with sexual tension in desperate need of release, without breaking contact or my rhythm, I lowered us to the floor, and we made love as if our lives depended on it in the foyer of my brownstone. Only the carpeted runner shielded us from the rigid and cold marble floors as we celebrated our success with our undeniable passion.

After we showered, I collapsed in bed for a couple of hours before returning to the studio. I chuckled as I fell asleep to Janae cursing out Del on the phone.

When I woke up, the room was dim except for the soft glow of a lamp she had moved closer to the floor. Janae sat on the carpet, a torn-open box in front of her, carefully pulling out plastic bags filled with small pieces.

I rubbed my eyes and sat up. "What are you doing?"

She glanced up with a smirk. "Setting up a project."

As I swung my legs over the side of the bed, I got a better look at the LEGO Millennium Falcon box. Several instruction booklets lay beside her, and unopened bags of bricks were scattered around her.

"That's not just a project. That's an undertaking."

She shrugged. "I saw it while I was out and figured, why not? I used to do puzzles to clear my head, but this seemed more fun. I know you like *Star Wars*, so I thought we could work on it together."

I moved off the bed and onto the floor beside her, rubbing my face as I blinked away the last traces of sleep. "You realize this thing can take days to build?"

Janae grinned and ripped open the first bag. "Good thing we don't have to rush."

I picked up a few pieces, rolling them between my fingers. "You ever build one of these before?"

She shook her head. "Nope. But I figure it's like anything else. One piece at a time."

I nodded and grabbed an instruction booklet. "You want to start with the frame?"

She exhaled, rubbing her hands together. "Let's do this."

We sorted through the pieces, scanning for the ones we needed first. She reached for a gray one at the same time I did, our fingers brushing for a second before she let me take it.

"We decided on two versions of the cover. One with you, and one with the pic you took of me looking at myself in the mirror. I take pictures of myself all the time, but that one of me… it hit different. Something about the way you captured me… I don't know why, but when I saw it, I didn't want to look away."

I clicked a piece onto the base of the Falcon and looked at her. "Maybe because, for once, you saw yourself the way I do."

Janae met my gaze for a moment before nudging the instruction booklet toward me. "Think you can keep up, or is this too advanced for a musician?"

I chuckled, scanning the next step. "We'll see."

We worked in companionable silence, sorting pieces, clicking them into place, and occasionally double-checking the instructions. The room felt warm, the soft rustle of shifting bricks and the quiet sound of our movements filling the space.

Janae stretched her legs out and sighed. "I like this. It's nice to build something that doesn't fight back."

I glanced at her, recognizing the weight behind her words. "Yeah. It is."

CHAPTER
TWENTY-NINE

janae

FEELING VICTORIOUS ABOUT THE COVER, I placed my headphones over my ears to listen to music, hoping to inspire myself enough to write. Del was in contact with a few different labels, trying to negotiate a new contract since "Fallen Star" had hit the airwaves. I wanted more decision-making ability on my next album than for my previous ones, and I had the power to do it this time. I'd been barely twenty-one when I signed my first deal. I'd learned about the good, the bad, and the ugly of the music business in the last seven years. I was determined to do better now that I knew better.

Landon's phone lit up on the bed while I bopped my head to H.E.R. and toyed with lyrics for a new song. Curiosity got the best of me. "Mom" flashed across the screen. I pushed the headphones off my ears and picked up the phone.

"Landon's phone. This is Janae Warner." I smiled, hoping his mother wanted to meet the new woman in her son's life. I pushed down any guilt about answering his phone without permission.

"Oh… oh, I see. Hello." Her diction was clipped and rather formal. "Is my son home?"

"He's in the shower… I mean, yes, he is." I hit my forehead with my hand. No mother wanted to know what her son may or may not have been doing to warrant a shower when she knew he was with a woman.

"Since you're answering his phone, I can only assume you are with him."

"I am." I prayed that Landon wouldn't kill me for telling his mother something that he hadn't yet told her.

"Then I would like to invite you both to dinner, or for dessert if your schedule permits, this evening to celebrate his new release."

"It's *our* release," I corrected her proudly.

She paused. "What's your name again?"

"Janae Warner."

"Yes, the singer on the song." Her voice inflection only changed a notch. "Then we can celebrate your success as well. We can meet at Sophia's for seven, which is in Harlem, so he can't use the excuse that he doesn't have time to travel to Brooklyn. Can you make sure he's there?"

"Yes, I can. Ma'am."

Even her laughter was haughty as she said, "I love people from the South. Look forward to meeting you."

"Me too." I hung up and waltzed into the bathroom, where he showered in the glass stall.

"I have to remember to lock the door when you're around." He smirked as he ducked his head, letting the water run over his hair and body. Landon wanted his hair loose again, and I'd promised to oil it once I unbraided it and he'd washed it.

"We leave on Sunday. Do you think we can enjoy the city together later today? Show me where you grew up. Maybe meet the parents," I said with a smile. If he didn't have to get to the studio, I would've joined him and convinced him with my mouth. I'd learned his body didn't know the meaning of "quickie."

"I doubt I have time. The show is tomorrow night, and once we get back into performance mode, we shift focus. The tour is over in another month. Just come back then, and I'll take you wherever you want to go."

"What about the parents?" I asked. He didn't talk about them like I didn't talk about mine. Still, I was intrigued. A beautiful couple who'd been married for years and raised a handsome son. They were music royalty. Maybe that would be Landon and me one day. A power couple rearing talented and amazing children. A strong family.

"What about them?"

"You said they live here. Can I meet them?" *Like tonight.*

"We're not that close."

"Okay, then maybe for dessert at a restaurant, since you're not that close."

He turned off the shower and toweled off. "Not a good idea. I haven't spoken to them since I got into it with my father."

"What happened?" *Shit.* I'd forgotten that he'd had words with his parents. That was probably why his mother had told me the plans instead of directly speaking with him. My face grew warm, and I hoped he couldn't pick up on my nervousness.

"The usual. They wanted to parade me around to their friends, and I wasn't in the mood. My father got angry and was in my face. My mama intervened, and he pushed her back with too much force, so I shoved him. Then I left." He shrugged like it didn't matter, though his tightened fists and the flash of anger in his eyes said it did.

"Was that the first time you put your hands on your father?" I took the towel and dried off his back.

"Yeah. It upset my mother, and the whole scene bothered me. I was about to have a panic attack when you texted me from the airport."

"Maybe it's time to make up. Your mother was trying to help. I learned a long time ago not to intervene when men get mad with each other. They forget what's around them. They're so hellbent on getting at the person they're upset with."

"I don't have time for family therapy right now. Too much on my plate. I'll deal with them after the tour." He passed me by and strode into the bedroom.

I followed him into his closet as he pulled on boxer briefs. "What about time for me later? Maybe dinner or at least dessert?"

He frowned. "We're about to go back on the road, and we'll be together all day again. I just told you that you can visit me after next month, and we can go anywhere."

I wrung my hands and shifted from one foot to the other. "Just for an hour… maybe two? Around seven tonight?"

Landon lowered his eyes to almost slits. "What did you do?"

"For someone who struggles with social cues, you seem pretty good at reading me," I joked, and rubbed the coin around my neck.

He glanced at the coin before folding his arms. "Janae."

"Umm… don't be mad."

Landon huffed. "You spoke to my parents."

"Your phone rang, and you were in the shower. I figured you would want me to answer your mother's call." I tried to open his arms. He didn't uncross them. "Your mother wants us to meet them at Sophia's for seven tonight. She even said it could be just for dessert."

He glared at me and had never seemed more like an alpha male than at that moment. Stubborn and unforgiving. My flirting wouldn't work this time.

"You're really pissed, aren't you?"

"The same way you would be if I told you I'd agreed to have dinner with *your* mother without telling you."

I protested, "That's different. My mother doesn't care about me. She doesn't call or try to get in touch. I told you we haven't spoken in four years."

Landon angrily pulled on a white T-shirt neatly folded on his shelf. "Bullshit. Del told me she wants to see one of our shows, but you refuse to invite or talk to her."

I stepped back. "You talked to Del about my mother?"

"Del spoke with me, hoping I could get you to reconsider. Told him it wasn't my place." He shook his head while grabbing cargo pants off a hanger. "You were about to go off on me about *just* talking about your mother with Del, but you wanted me to be cool when you answered my phone and *then* accepted an invitation with my mother without asking me first."

"No matter what you went through with your parents, it pales in comparison to what I went through with my mother," I insisted.

"How do you know that? We haven't discussed our families at all. Just because I didn't grow up in the hood doesn't mean your adolescence was worse than mine." He sat on the bench and grabbed his socks and Adidas.

"Says the rich kid. The threat of hunger trumps whatever you went through."

"Try being homeless until Cedrick and his family took me in when I was sixteen because I refused to deal with my father, who hated me, and a mother who rarely stood up for me anymore." He rose, jammed his hat on his head, and stormed past me.

"I didn't know." I rushed after him.

"No one knows but my parents and Cedrick. I might have grown up with money, but once I ran away, I had to build my own. This house isn't here because Mommy and Daddy paid for it." He jogged down the stairs. "I'm not meeting them for dinner *or* dessert."

"You can't just stand them up." I struggled to keep up with him.

"I'll text that we can't make it."

I managed to get in front of him and block the door while he picked up his guitar case. "Baby, listen. What if one magical day, we get married and have children? They need at least one set of grandparents."

His brows dipped, and his mouth twitched. "If I do this, then I'm telling Del to book your mother a flight to Los Angeles."

"Deal," I agreed, though my stomach lurched at the mention of seeing my mother. Brushing that negative thought away, I cooed, "Ooh… you want to marry me someday."

"It's just dinner with my folks."

I wrapped my arms around his neck and sang, "Janae and Landon, sittin' in the tree…"

He groaned while his cheeks flushed red. "Stop."

"Okay… okay. You're so cute." I dragged my hand down his nape.

"Not a puppy." He tugged me flush against his hard body.

I gazed into his eyes. "I promise dinner will be fine. I'm here now."

"And if they say or do anything to piss me off, I'm out," he warned before he pecked my lips hard and headed toward the door.

After I closed it after him, I collapsed against the door in relief.

A small crowd gathered by the sleek luxury sedan once it parked before Sophia's. We were coordinated as we stepped out of the door that the driver held for us. I'd bought Landon a dark blue hat and casual suit that fit his athletic frame, and I wore a strapless blue summer dress, ponytail, and makeup by Frankie. We looked like a glamorous power couple going to a famous Black-owned restaurant to meet his fabulous musician parents.

Landon gripped my hand as security from the restaurant moved us through the lines of people waiting to sit. People called our names and snapped pictures. Women catcalled and whistled at Landon. I shook my head at them, warning them playfully. Landon's hand was clammy, and his jaw was tight as he looked straight ahead. I tried to buffer his cold appearance with a bright smile and explained loudly, "We're late meeting his parents."

Getting inside the busy restaurant wasn't much better. Patrons gasped and gawked as we were led to a small area that blocked us from sight. The Hayes stood when we approached. Landon was an impeccable blend of his attractive parents. His dad was similar to him with his light brown skin and height. His mother had more mocha in her skin than I did. He'd inherited his curls and eyes from his mother, which made her more striking than her son. Mrs. Hayes wore her gray hair natural and cropped short to her head. She was a well-kept woman whose aura suggested that five-star meals, lavish trips, and luxury spas were a necessary and expected part of life.

Landon hugged his mother and barely nodded at his father. "Brandon and Analise Hayes, this is Janae." He introduced me with pride that would have warmed me if it wasn't shadowed by the disapproval that screamed from his mother's tight smile when she shook my hand. His father seemed pleasant enough as he covered my hand when it was his turn.

After we sat, Mr. Hayes started, "Since you were late, I took the liberty of ordering appetizers."

Landon retorted, "Then that's all we'll have. We need to get back to the studio. We're late because, as usual, you asked me to drop everything at a moment's notice to meet with you."

I squeezed the hand he still held. "The studio is not that far from here. We can stay longer."

Landon pulled his hat down farther. "Appetizers are all I'll have. I'm not that hungry."

Mrs. Hayes pleaded, "Can we just have a nice meal together?"

Landon tilted his head. "I don't know. Can we?"

Two waitstaff stood nearby, and I whispered, "People are watching us."

"You sound like them," he scoffed.

Ignoring his barb, I tried to ease the tension. "This is hard for Landon, but I wanted to try to bring us together. Families are important."

"Are you engaged or something?" his mother asked with a slight lip curl.

"Not yet," Landon answered. "We've been deciding when would be a good time."

I nodded, though I wanted to give him the side-eye.

His father smiled. "The timing couldn't be more perfect. A hit record and an engagement."

"Of course that's all you care about," Landon practically snarled.

Whew. And I thought I was bad when I spoke with my mother.

"Do you *like* 'Fallen Star'?" Landon suddenly asked.

His father averted his gaze.

His mother smiled at me. "I can see the appeal. You have a beautiful voice. You have a range perfect for jazz, or even the blues."

"Thank you, I've been told that. I just prefer hip-hop and soul."

"A shame that we don't have more voices like yours in our world. We need the type of attention you'd bring. Imagine what you could do if you remixed one of your songs to make it more jazz." Her smile finally seemed genuine. She may not like me as her son's woman, but she respected my talent.

"I never really tried to sing like that," I admitted.

"Then you should come to one of my classes, and I can show you how you can play around with your voice. My students would be so excited." She nodded expectantly.

"I would love that. Having one of the greats teach me anything about music would be an honor," I replied sincerely. Maybe we could bond over music.

"Janae doesn't live here," Landon reminded her.

"I'm sure she knows how to catch a plane back here if she chose," Mrs. Hayes bit back as the waiter returned with chicken wings, fried salmon bites, mac and cheese, collard greens, and cornbread. "Yes... the food is here in the nick of time."

Landon would explode soon if I didn't get him out of there. I would protect him even if his parents didn't warrant his rude behavior. I touched his thigh reassuringly under the table. "Listen, let's just eat this delicious food, smile for the cameras and people trying to sneak and watch us, and we can talk about me visiting your classes later."

Mr. Hayes finally spoke again, "I think that's best." He picked up his glass, half full with an amber liquor.

"You're being quiet. That must be your first." Landon gestured at his glass.

His mother's hazel eyes shone brightly as she hissed, "Stop it now. You're our only son. We're trying. You have to try, too."

"What exactly are you trying? Dad hasn't even listened to the song. At least you did."

"I've been busy with my students. I planned to listen to it." Mr. Hayes waved his hand dismissively. "You don't care if I listen to it or not. What I say has never mattered to you."

Landon huffed again. "If you're really trying, then you would've listened and then actually said you were proud of me or something."

"I *am* proud of you." Mrs. Hayes placed her hand on her husband's wrist. "We both are."

Landon steepled his palms on the table. "He told me I was an embarrassment the last time I saw him. That I always embarrass him. Why would I want to come home when the people who are supposed to love me the most can't really see me? Janae's been in my life a second, and she gets me. Why can't you?"

Mr. Hayes threw back his alcohol and put the glass down not so gently. "Has she seen you freak out? Has she seen you become so paralyzed with fear that you've pissed on yourself? Huh? That you only open your mouth to fight with me and let everyone else, like Cedrick and probably this young lady right here, run over you?" He looked at me with pity in his eyes. "If he hasn't embarrassed you yet, he will. My son, as brilliant as he is, can't handle pressure. Then again, you probably make the perfect pair, since your own track record isn't the greatest."

A shroud of hurtful silence covered the table, and whatever tenuous relationship Landon had had with his father snapped and might never be repaired. I clasped my hands together and bit back my desire to hurl an insult at Mr. Hayes. Why hadn't I listened when Landon made it clear that he didn't want to see his parents?

Landon's face flushed with anger and shame, his breathing sharp, controlled only by sheer will. I wanted to say something, to stand up for him, for us, but my voice felt lodged in my throat.

"You can talk about me all you want, but you won't talk about Janae," Landon said, his voice a dangerous calm. He pushed back his chair, slow and deliberate. "I'm done with both of you. Don't call me again."

He stood, shoulders squared, fists clenched at his sides.

"Landon, please… please." Mrs. Hayes touched my wrist. "I'm so sorry. His father has been drinking and… and… he didn't mean…"

"Respectfully, I won't let anyone hurt him… not even you." My voice came out steady, though I was shaking inside. I reached for his hand and took it, gripping it tight. I refused to look at Mr. Hayes because if I did, I might curse him out and make headlines again.

We turned away with entwined hands, and I whispered, "Baby, it's all right. We're going to get in the car and go home."

He said quietly, "I need to go to the studio."

"Okay… whatever you want. We have to pretend that we're okay if you don't want people to talk about us and your parents." I smiled up at him, hoping the pained look on his face would ease up. "Please… breathe. It's just a few more steps."

Landon nodded and gave me a strained grin. His hand was still locked on mine, and we might have been fine if I'd called our driver earlier. When we stepped outside, a crowd waited for us.

Cameras flashed. People were everywhere. A maelstrom of emotions directed at us. Our car moved up the street, but overzealous fans blocked the way, trying to get a glimpse of us. Beads of perspiration dotted his forehead, though it was a cool May night.

I remained quiet as he pushed firmly, blocking me with his body, through the crowd. I didn't stop or bother to chat because the fans were too wild, and I knew Landon couldn't take much more of the people pushing against us. I had to be his calm in the middle of a storm if he was to survive getting in the car without having a full-blown panic attack in front of all these people.

The driver got close enough to jump out of the car and then made enough space to open the door for us to hop in.

Once we were in the back seat, Landon clawed at his throat, his fingers trembling as he struggled for air. His breath came in ragged gasps. Shallow. Choppy. Desperate.

Panic flooded his wide, unfocused eyes.

"What's wrong? Landon, talk to me! Please… what's wrong?" My voice quivered, but I reached for him, gripping his arm as if my touch alone could keep him from slipping away.

He yanked his jacket off, hands fumbling as he popped the top buttons of his shirt. His chest heaved like he was fighting for breath he couldn't find.

"So… hot," he gasped. "My chest…"

The driver kept glancing into the rearview mirror, his own concern bleeding through his tense expression. "Looks like he needs medical attention. The hospital is not far."

Landon shook his head violently. "No. Hate hospitals. Studio. Cedrick." His voice cracked as if the effort to speak was too much.

I gripped his clammy hand and turned to the driver. "Take us to the studio. Now."

As we sped through the streets, I grabbed my phone with shaky hands and dialed Cedrick. He answered on the second ring. "What's up? Did Landon leave his cell?" His tone was light, completely unaware of the storm ripping Landon apart.

I pushed through the panic gripping my own chest. "It's Landon. He's having a panic attack. He's asking for you. We're heading to the studio."

A beat of silence. Then, Cedrick's voice sharpened. "How far are you?"

I glanced outside, scanning the street signs, struggling to focus through my own rising terror. "Ten minutes. Should I take him to the hospital?"

"No," Landon choked out. His body shuddered against me.

"Put me on speaker," Cedrick said.

I did, squeezing Landon's damp hand tighter as his breathing grew more erratic. His face was too pale, too red, too lost all at once.

Tears spilled freely down his cheeks, his body curling inward like he was trying to disappear inside himself. His lips moved, whispering over and over, "I… okay… I'll be okay…" but his voice shook with a lie even he didn't believe.

Cedrick's voice dropped to something calm and steady. "It's all good, man. Janae is here. I'm here. I need you to look at her."

"I… can't…" His chest spasmed with uneven gasps. His body trembled. "I can't… I don't want her to see me… like this…"

My heart cracked.

I cupped his face, forcing him to meet my eyes. "Look at me, Landon. I am not embarrassed by you. I am not leaving you. I love you." My breath shook, but I inhaled deeply and exhaled so he could follow. "Breathe with me."

Cedrick echoed, "Slow and steady, brother. You got this."

Landon's panicked, unfocused eyes flickered to mine.

I inhaled.

He tried.

I exhaled.

He staggered through it, a desperate, wheezing breath, but it was something.

I kissed his damp forehead, whispering against his skin, "Baby, we're almost there. Just a few more minutes. You can play your new song for me, okay? You love playing for me."

His fingers curled weakly around mine. He shivered violently. "I'm… so cold."

I pulled him close, wrapping myself around him as if I could hold him together. "I've got you," I murmured, my fingers threading through his damp curls, rocking him gently, willing my touch to quiet whatever storm was raging inside him. By the time we pulled up to the studio, the driver barely had time to park before Cedrick flung the door open and climbed inside.

His sharp gaze took in everything. The way Landon clung to me. The sweat-soaked shirt. The pale exhaustion painting his features.

And then, with a smirk that only Cedrick could pull off in a moment like this, he said, "Damn, dude. All this just to get Janae's attention? You already got her, man."

Landon's body was still trembling, but his middle finger lifted weakly. "Fuck you."

Cedrick grinned and placed a steady hand on his shoulder. "In and out, just like before. Breathe, bro."

Landon's chest rose.

Fell.

Rose.

Fell.

Still shaky. Still unsteady. But slowing.

I wiped his forehead with his jacket, pressing a kiss against his hand. His fingers were still clammy, but his grip was stronger now.

His breathing, finally, evened out.

His lashes fluttered open, the fear slowly retreating from his eyes. "I… want to go in the studio."

Cedrick looked at me. "Why don't you take him home? A shower, some rest—"

Landon shook his head. "I need my guitar."

Cedrick sighed but nodded. "All right, man. Can you walk?"

Landon nodded again, this time firmer.

But when Cedrick reached to help him, Landon ignored his hand.

I bent down, picked up his fallen hat, and handed it to Cedrick. He took it, then wordlessly placed it back on Landon's head.

Landon didn't acknowledge either of us as he walked inside.

Pain slashed through me. I wilted against the leather seat. I couldn't comfort him when he needed me the most.

Cedrick lingered by the door. "You're not coming in?"

I wiped at my damp cheeks and whispered, "He doesn't want me here."

Cedrick studied me for a long moment. "If you leave now, he's going to think you can't handle this part of him."

I swallowed hard. "Is that why you warned me? You thought I wouldn't stay?"

"Partially." Cedrick shoved his hands into his pockets. "His parents?"

"And then fans swarmed us in front of the restaurant. He was trying to protect me from the crowd. He held it together until we got in the car. I feel so bad because I pushed him to see his mother when he was already under pressure with the album and getting used to this new attention."

"Don't feel bad. He wants a good relationship with his parents. Any time they call, he's there, even if it triggers him. He's been holding a lot in, too. The late-night TV circuit has been calling, and I've spoken for the band in the past. They want Landon to speak. He's torn because he doesn't want to hold us back."

I moved closer to the door. "Has he ever seen a therapist?"

"I don't know. These attacks don't happen that often."

"He needs to see someone. He gets too anxious." I hugged myself.

Cedrick insisted, "He's fine. His last episode was months ago."

"There isn't anything wrong with having a therapist. I had one for years."

"Well, now isn't the time to suggest it because he can't start seeing someone right at this moment. We have four cities left. Wait until after the tour, please. It's just one more month. With the film crew around, is it fair to shove him in front of a shrink's chair, too?" Cedrick gestured toward the door with his head. "Come inside. We've been out here too long. He'll know we're talking about him. He's still embarrassed you saw him like that. Prove to him it doesn't matter. Please."

Deep love and concern shone in his eyes.

I nodded. "I won't say anything about therapy until after Los Angeles and tonight doesn't change my feelings for him."

Despite my fear that Landon would reject me, I'd been him countless times, including two nights ago. Ashamed of my behavior, I'd often shunned people and pretended they didn't exist when all I wanted was for them to understand.

"Then let's go," Cedrick said.

I reached for his hand. "I'm also sorry that I ever misjudged you."

"You didn't. I'm every bit of the arrogant asshole you believe I am." He helped me get out of the car and released my hand as we walked inside. "Landon has been my brother since we were kids, and I ride for my family. Glad he now has you, too." He half grinned. "Told you I can admit when I'm wrong."

When we entered the studio, Landon was in the booth with his head lowered, strumming his guitar. The rest of the band didn't acknowledge me as they watched transfixed from outside. The hauntingly beautiful music evoked my melancholic soul and reminded me of my sorrow and pain. By the time he'd strummed his final, stirring chord, there were no dry eyes in the room.

I wiped my tears and opened the door to the booth. "Come on, baby. Let's go home."

Landon and I locked gazes. Shame and fear still coated his luminous eyes, but at least he was no longer afraid to look at me. He placed his guitar on the stand, and I wrapped my arm around his waist when he joined me at the door. We didn't say goodbye to the band as we left the building and headed to his place.

CHAPTER THIRTY

landon

MAY 18

MY EARLIEST MEMORY WAS OF sitting beside my mother when I was three, and she used my hands to play the piano. She smiled and praised me the entire time, though she guided me in hitting the right keys. I loved my mother. Analise Ann Hayes. Loved her as any son loved his mother. Loved her so much that I didn't allow my father to hug me until I was seven. I'd blown a perfect note in his horn, and my father, who'd been careful with me, grabbed me up and held me to him. Although I resisted and held my body stiffly, he embraced me until I hugged him back. After that day, falsely believing we'd bonded over music, he was determined to make me the next great horn player. And when I chose the guitar, he considered me his biggest failure.

My mother would steal me away from my father with cookies and milk to practice her beloved instrument. My parents playfully argued over me and my talent. They ignored the fact that I didn't spend time with other children on the rare occasions we went to the park. That my birthday parties were always filled with adults. That I wore a hoodie or a jacket even when there was a heatwave in Brooklyn. That I flinched from any unexpected touch. That I wouldn't eat anything mushy like peas or avocado or allow my food to touch on my plate.

They ignored that I only spoke in their presence until middle school. And that I spent hours in my room focused on music and astronomy instead of girls. Like music, school came easily to me, and I excelled academically though I flunked socially. When my sixth-grade teacher recommended therapy after she had to coax me from underneath the table because I'd become emotionally overwhelmed, my mother requested a new teacher. She didn't want anyone who couldn't understand my genius or idiosyncrasies to educate her son.

While my mother was overprotective of me, my father chastised behaviors he didn't understand, which were most of my actions. Admonishing me when I didn't want to play outside with other children or watch sports with him. His lip would curl with disgust when I cried because "real men don't cry." He demanded I open my mouth when words I longed to say were trapped in my throat. Although my father never hit me because my mother didn't condone corporal punishment, he found ways to shove or push me whenever my behavior angered or embarrassed him when he was drunk.

My father did show me love at times. When sober, he exhibited patience and kindness. When I was twelve, he begged my mother to seek help for me because I seemed so unhappy. She was a traditional wife who followed her husband blindly and usually did his bidding, right or wrong. I was her exception.

> *I'm coming to your show tonight alone. I don't care if you want to speak to me or not. I want to see my son perform.*

I reread my mother's text for the umpteenth time. The gnawing hunched me over in my chair while the rest of the band were getting in place for the second of our shows in New York. The crowd had been wild Friday night, louder than any other we'd had thus far. The boys were home, and "Fallen Star" was burning up the airwaves. My hat had been pulled down low, and I'd remained in blue light, managing to thank everyone and introduce myself and then Janae before we left the stage.

I'd kept myself busy with rehearsals and my guitar to avoid talking to Janae about my breakdown. Knowing about my panic attacks and seeing me in the throes of one were two very different things. She tried to be there for me without pressuring me or asking me to talk about the incident.

My phone wallpaper was the selfie we'd taken on the subway. Despite the weariness in both of our eyes, happiness shone through. Janae had sworn she wouldn't leave me and that she loved me the night of my panic attack. I believed she loved me, perhaps more than she'd ever loved another man. She'd told me once she was needy, but I hadn't seen that side since Houston. Even the other night, she'd bounced back as soon as she saw me. She didn't need to be saved or rescued by a knight. Janae could stand on her own two feet, and sooner or later, she would realize her strength and leave me.

Someone knocked on the door.

Janae.

"Come in."

"Baby… we need to be on stage." She strolled in wearing a sparkly, emerald-green pantsuit. She didn't wear a bra, and one button held the top of the suit together. Frankie had styled her hair in cornrows, and makeup enhanced her brown skin and almond-shaped eyes.

"I hate that the makeup covers your freckles."

She rolled her eyes. "How about you compliment me instead of telling me what you hate?"

"You don't need me to say how your beauty captured my heart and won't let go."

"I do need you to say that." She walked to me, taking my hat off to run her fingers through my loose hair. "I need to braid it again. I'll do it while we're on the road."

I popped open her sole button and pressed the side of my face to her warm breasts and her stomach. "My mother is coming to the show. Might already be out there."

"Is that why you're still in here?" she asked while caressing my hair.

"Yeah. Despite it all, I want to please her. I want her to be outside cheering me as loud as the strangers around her."

"If she's here, then that's what she wants too."

"Music is the only reason she loves me. I sometimes wonder if she would even bother if I hadn't been this prodigy." I wrapped my arms around Janae's waist and kissed the diamond in her belly.

She pulled my head back by my hair and gazed down at me. "It's not the only reason I love you."

Her heartfelt words lifted my dour mood, and I pulled her right nipple in my mouth and sucked briefly. "Mm… can't wait to get you home."

She tapped my head. "Stop getting me hot so we can get on that stage. We have a show to do."

I rebuttoned her suit, grateful that she'd sought me out. "This better not pop while we're performing. New York doesn't need to see all that's mine."

"Whatever. Come on." She hurried to the door.

"Janae?" I was three steps behind her.

She wrinkled her face. "Landon?"

"Wear that suit home." I slapped her round ass hard and rushed past her before she hit me back.

♥

Toward the end of yet another good show, when it was my turn to thank everyone and introduce myself, Janae asked for the houselights to come up.

"Before we leave the stage, on behalf of The Hollow Bones and me, I want to say a special thank you to the phenomenally talented Mrs. Analise Hayes. Spotlight. She's over there."

I searched the audience like most of the fans, looking for my mother.

"Landon's beautiful mother is a Juilliard-trained classical pianist who taught her son everything she knows."

The spotlight finally found my mother, who seemed misplaced in her silk shirt, slacks, and pearls around this jeans-and-shirts-and-tight-bodycon-dresses crowd. We locked gazes as she waved to the audience. Her face was puffy, and she dabbed her eyes with a white handkerchief. I clenched my jaw before smiling, almost forgetting that cameras and people watched us.

"Another round of applause. Without her, Landon wouldn't be here. And I, for one, am forever thankful she had him." Janae winked exaggeratedly, and the audience laughed. "We need to get out of here. New York, you owe us nothing." She placed her mic on the stand, bowed, and left the stage. We continued to play another two minutes before we exited one by one. Me, Cedrick, Charles, Santiago, then Brian.

Although I took photos and celebrated our last night in New York with Janae and The Hollow Bones, my mind drifted to the woman who'd given me life sitting in the audience, finally proud of me. I'd been so sure she would disappoint me that I hadn't bothered to look for her.

I rubbed the guitar pick in my pocket as I smiled through the gnawing in my stomach. What did it mean that she was here and appeared to have been crying during my performance? Should I care? For so many years, I'd wanted my mother to stand up to my father. I'd needed that more than her random check-in texts and calls. Wasn't this what she'd just done by sitting in the audience… making sure her son was okay after his father fucked him up?

I exhaled and pulled my hand out of my pocket. She would have to do more than attend one of my shows to prove she loved me for me. I returned my attention to Janae and the fellas as we toasted to our continued success.

After another hour had passed, the activity behind the stage began to settle and quiet. Janae squeezed my bicep and whispered, "Your mother is in my dressing room. Please go see her for me."

My stomach lurched, and I opened my mouth to refuse until I looked into her hopeful face. I pecked her lips. "Okay."

"Frankie and Jeri already cleared out. I'll wait for you in the car."

The glam squad, our road crew, and the guys wanted to party on their last night in New York. Janae and I wanted to be alone.

I knocked on the door out of habit and then entered, holding my pick in my hand.

My mother seemed so small, wringing her hands in the middle of the small dressing room. "Thank you for seeing me. I didn't know how to approach you, but Janae sent someone to bring me back here." She tsked. "She's something else, on that stage and off. She asked me not to hurt you anymore. I see why you fell in love."

"She is, and I do love her."

We stood across from each other, a mother and her only son uncertain how to act toward one another when there should be no question.

She glanced down for a second before she spoke. "I wanted you to be the first to know that I've asked your father for a divorce."

"What?" I hadn't expected *that* announcement. She and my father were an institution. Unbreakable. Did the Earth just shift on its axis?

"You had an episode when you left the restaurant, didn't you?"

I nodded.

"I saw the signs, and I rose from my chair to follow you. Your father pulled me back down so I wouldn't make a scene because he knew you would reject me. I played the dutiful wife one last time and packed when we got home. I've been in a hotel for the past two nights."

"Ma, this isn't the first time you left him," I reminded her, and took a step closer.

"It's the last."

I searched her face and neck for any signs. "Did he hit you?"

She looked away. "No. I put up with him for too long. I left the drunk bastard so I can be myself. So I can love my son, and my son can love me again."

Impressed with this side of her, I smiled. "Nice to meet you, Analise."

She arched a sardonic brow. "Ma, Mama, or Mother to you."

"Duly noted." I shifted from one foot to another. "Why now?"

Her nostrils flared and her hazel eyes sparkled. "Because your father will never change, and you've grown into the man I always envisioned. Independent. Talented. A successful career and with a woman who's thriving, too. I keep picturing your wedding and babies, and I'm not part of that. I want to get to know you as a man. I want us to be close. Not because I want to show you off or brag about your accomplishments, but because I carried you inside me for nine months." She stepped closer. "You are my baby. Can we move forward?"

How long had I wanted to hear those exact words coming from her mouth? And she'd finally told me as I was becoming famous.

I gritted my teeth. "It's been too many years. That can't happen overnight."

She nodded. "You always had to have something to touch or in your hand when you were upset. I didn't want to accept that you needed that more than me." My mother hesitantly reached out and touched my cheek. "I used to be so mad that you didn't choose the piano or the trumpet. I'm sorry I never gave the guitar a chance. I've never heard anyone make a guitar sound like that. Simply amazing."

"Thank you," I said quietly.

She smiled at me with a mother's pride, the way she'd looked at me when I first learned to play the piano. The way she'd looked at me when she read stories to me at night. The gnawing stopped.

"When are you returning to New York? Maybe we can have lunch or dinner, just the two of us." She clasped her hands in front of her.

"In a month. We leave tomorrow morning for Minneapolis."

Her eyes lost their luster. She would be alone. All she'd had was my father. Between her career and his demands, she didn't have genuine friendships. My grandparents and aunt lived in Pittsburgh. She'd start teaching at the university in the summer, so she couldn't even visit them for a few weeks.

"You can stay in my brownstone if you need to while I'm gone. I'll check on you."

Her lips curved. "I would love that."

"How did you get here?"

"A car. I can call for another one."

"No, Janae and I can take you to your hotel."

When I turned around to the door, she hugged me from behind. I sighed and patted her arms. For now, I had my mother back. Time would tell if I had her forever.

CONFESSIONAL

janae

I SET THE PHONE'S CAMERA to landscape mode and set it on the nightstand, as the producer had suggested, since I didn't want any crew in Landon's bedroom, where I sat propped up against the headboard. I kissed the coin around my neck, waved at the camera, and took a deep breath.

"In my head, I call myself crazy at least once a day. It may not be politically correct, or I might get canceled once this show drops, because I believe that I'm a crazy bitch most days." I studied my manicured nails. "I looked up the word, and it said 'wildly incoherent or irrational,' and it also said 'overly excited or enthusiastic.'"

I refocused on my phone. "Another definition of 'crazy' is appearing 'absurdly out of place.' If those terms don't fit me, then I don't know what other word would. I ask for forgiveness instead of permission for those who take offense, but I choose to embrace that side of me, especially with how I've been acting these last few days.

"We're leaving New York in a couple of hours. Minneapolis and Chicago, I see you. These last three weeks have been nothing short of amazing. Recording and dropping a hit single, fans rushing us wherever we go, getting even closer to my glam squad, the fellas, and my Landon." I chuckled. "Ya'll better stop with all those nasty DMs to The Hollow Bones account. Landon doesn't have social media and never checks the band's account. And be nice when you see him in public. Despite how hot he looks, he's really chill and low key. Hates all the attention not directed to his music."

I pulled my knees to my chest. "The pressures of my success have been a lot, and I go from feeling like the luckiest woman on the planet to a pile of shit underneath someone's shoe. It has been hard to balance my moods or impulsivity with my hectic schedule. The other night in Brooklyn with my fans could have been disastrous, and it would have been all my fault. Luckily, everything is everything. Shoutout to the staff of Junior's and my fans who celebrated with me that night. It got a little scary, but I know it was because you rock with me, and I never want to take you for granted."

Tucking my chin on my knees, I sighed. "I'm at a crossroads because my career has already risen higher than ever before with the release of 'Fallen Star.' I can either continue to fly high or crash as I did three years ago. Except the stakes are much higher if I fail again. I'm surrounded by people who care, and I can't risk losing them."

Landon's breakdown had frightened me and forced me to hold a mirror up to my erratic or manic episodes. It wasn't fair to expect anyone to deal with my attitudes and behavior because of how *I* chose to cope.

"Because you've been on this journey from the beginning, I thought it was only fair to share this with you. Much as I wanted to fight my battle with sheer will, coping skills, and faith, I needed more to function at my best. Medicine may not be the optimal treatment for everyone with bipolar, but I hope it is for me." I picked up the orangish-brown pill bottle, opened it, and popped a pink capsule in my mouth. I chased it with my Perrier water. "I'm officially back on lithium."

I then stopped recording before I erased the video.

CHAPTER THIRTY-ONE

janae

LOS ANGELES
JUNE 9

IF WE'D THOUGHT NEW YORK exhausted us, the rest of the tour had drained us creatively and emotionally. Between photoshoots, interviews, and quick flights in between shows for live appearances on talk shows, I didn't know if I was coming or going. Sometimes I forgot to take my meds, and I knew that fucked with my moods, nerves, and sleep. I probably needed to set an alarm as a reminder, but then, I didn't *want* reminders. It didn't help that Landon rolled with the punches, no matter my irritability or how fast I moved. He truly seemed to accept my flaws and would rub my back or feet whenever he had a chance to remind me that I needed quiet, too.

The Hollow Bones stayed behind while Landon traveled with me, his presence lingering just enough to satisfy the curiosity of those obsessed with us. His silence only deepened his mystique, and before he knew it, his star was rising higher than he or the band had ever imagined. His unmatched talent on the guitar, the public's thirst for glimpses of our relationship, his quiet confidence, and the weight of his family's legacy combined to make him one of the most sought-after men in the country.

Now, his signature look was set. Shades, his ever-present hat, a guitar slung over his back, and his pick in hand. He never had to say much. Just a wave, a brief greeting, and the deep timbre of his voice were enough to send his admirers into a frenzy.

Sharing these moments with him, knowing his struggles, kept me from focusing on my own shifting energy. I admired how he handled his discomfort and anxiousness without substances as his vise. I didn't want to admit that my nonstop movement was slowly taking a toll, and I longed for the euphoria of the peaceful existence that only came from alcohol or drugs. Still, I reassured Landon that I was capable of handling the thrust back into the spotlight and all that it meant.

Old photos of my wild days of sex and partying with men who weren't mine resurfaced. I almost didn't recognize *that* Janae. I pretended to have thick skin whenever I saw or heard something about the old me while I worried incessantly that Landon, the band, or the ladies would remember that I had been that mean, spiteful woman. I'd learned from Dr. K that hurt people hurt, and I'd been through trauma that I'd taken out on anyone in my path. Getting back on meds despite the cotton mouth, dizziness, and dullness was an uneasy compromise to my healing. I wouldn't let my past dictate my bright future.

Landon and I had spent the last two months together every day, and the thought of not seeing his face, or feeling his strong arms around me, or inhaling his clean soap smell pained me. We would spend five days in Los Angeles, and our tour would officially be over until we reconvened for Austin City Limits in October. Landon and I hadn't discussed or made plans for our life after the tour, as if we were worried that what we had was only for this time, though we spent almost every waking moment together harmoniously.

We remained in bed on the bus when we weren't performing, rehearsing, or going on short promotional trips. We only communicated our needs and left unsaid anything troubling or deep about our past or future. I knew his mother had separated from his father and was staying in his brownstone. That was all he said on the subject, and I didn't ask or expect more. He would tell me about his family on his own time, mainly because I was reluctant to talk about my own mother, who would be at the concert in Los Angeles. Landon had invited her and my brother when I hadn't been able to bear to myself. Rashad and I had spoken a couple of times with promises to connect after the tour, yet neither of us had broached the topic of our mother.

My dark mood attacked me left and right. I used our isolation and our unspoken willingness to deny any real issues that could impact our relationship to our advantage. No serious talking meant less of a chance of snapping at or cursing out Landon because my negative thoughts and irritability were rampant due to the inconsistent use of my meds, along with all my stressors hitting me at once. I knew the darkness would pass, and I didn't want to risk my relationship because of my caustic words.

Landon Hayes was my one. I just couldn't allow the dark side of me to ruin something so beautiful, so wonderfully complex, and so meant for me. His vulnerability only tethered me to him stronger, and I wanted to help him if he needed it. Watching his daily struggles to be open to others and the world hurt and inspired me. Landon needed treatment so he could truly flourish and not have to suffer. Once we finished the tour, I would insist that he seek counseling, as I intended to do again myself.

On the night we arrived in Los Angeles, the bus rode around the city at my instruction. I wanted my people to feel the vibe. Los Angeles might be more known for the film industry, but it was a haven of all music genres. Songwriters and hopeful musicians moved there from all over the country for a chance at stardom.

After seven years, I'd grown to love this city even if it hadn't always loved me back. When people recognized our buses, they jumped up and down and shouted my name, clearly excited for my return, and my heart flooded with love.

Landon wrapped his arm around my waist and announced, "Welcome home, Janae Warner."

Los Angeles was indeed my home, and I would show up and show out for the gig on Saturday. I would prove that their belief in my talent the first time around wasn't a fluke. I was better and stronger and was there to stay. Hopefully, the man beside me, with pride and love in his voice, was here to stay, too.

◆

JUNE 11

After a busy day of pictures and filming our group at famous sites, Landon and I were cuddled up in my bed at my condo. We'd showered together and made love. He was on his side, facing me with closed eyes, humming a tune from their upcoming album.

"What if we leave Los Angeles and go to Austin for a few days? My house is there. I think it would be a good place for us to unwind and talk. Get to know each other outside of this tour."

He chuckled. "Guess you can afford to keep it now."

I popped his taut belly. "Even if I didn't, you could afford to keep my house for me."

His eyes lazily opened. "So, I'm your sugar daddy now?"

"Yep. Though I'd prefer you to be my husband." I eased up higher on him to kiss him.

"Mm… shouldn't I be the one to propose?" He kissed me back.

"I already know if I don't force the issue, we'll be one of those couples who are together forever without marrying. I don't want that for my life."

"Force the issue a year from now if I haven't asked you." He flipped on his back and flung his arm over his eyes.

I traced circles on his chest, trying not to be affected that he hadn't yet answered me about going to Austin, or by his nonchalance about marriage. "When we were in Houston, you said you weren't getting married or having a family. Has that changed?"

"I don't know."

"What do you mean you don't know?" I raised my voice. "You practically told your mother we were engaged when she asked at dinner, and now you don't know? Don't play with my heart, Landon."

"I'm not playing with you. I thought we were waiting to talk after the tour." The teasing undertone in his voice had shifted.

"It's a simple question."

He glanced at me before he sighed. "Nothing with you is simple. However, answering your question will lead to a drawn-out discussion, which would be better after the tour."

I pushed against the mattress to sit up. "You say you're different from other men, but you're just like them. You want to fuck me and get serious about the next woman."

"I'm not your ex or the married men you slept with, so stop comparing me to your past."

The curt reminder of how I once rolled felt like a dagger, and I shoved his chest. "Then act like it."

Landon turned onto his side and yanked the pillow over his head. Frustrated that he was shutting me out, I swatted at his back.

His voice came low and firm. "Janae, don't. I would never put my hands on you. Give me the same respect."

I folded my arms, glaring at the back of his head. "Then don't ignore me."

He exhaled slowly, tension rolling through his body. "You have a bad concept of time. The show in Houston was in March. It's only June, and you're mad because I'm not talking about marriage when all I do is show you that I want to be with only you. All this promotion is hard on me, and I do it because I love you."

I snorted. "Whatever. You do it for The Hollow Bones."

"They don't want me to do anything I don't want to do. Miss me on that."

He was right about everything. He made me feel loved and wanted. He pushed himself beyond his comfort zone to please me. If only I could get my mind to also register that he was right and not let my insecurities and negativity run amok. "Can we do Austin or not?"

Landon softened his tone. "I need to check on my mother. Come back with me, and I'll show you more of the city."

His answer didn't satisfy me. Something in me wouldn't let it rest. "Stop making excuses. You text her every day. She's fine. Admit you don't feel comfortable in any space that's not yours."

Landon pulled the pillow tighter over his head. "I can't talk to you right now. You're hellbent on fighting with me. It's not happening, so we might as well go to sleep."

I screamed loudly in frustration and jumped out of bed, nude. He sat up, frowning in disgust, an expression men gave me when they were tired of dealing with my moodiness and irrationality. Hurt fueled my anger. I had to end it before he did. "I can't do this anymore. I can't do this."

"Can't do what?"

"This relationship. It's not going to last anyway." Acid burned inside of me. I started rubbing my wrists and arms. "We don't have to see each other after Saturday night. We haven't been together long. We'll get over it."

"I won't get over it." His voice was steady. Certain. "I don't care how much time passes or how many years go by, I won't get over you."

Tears blurred my vision. "You don't know that."

Landon scooted to the edge of the bed, tugging me toward him. "I know I was low-key obsessed with any photo or video I could get of you when we contemplated whether to work with you or not. I know that since the night of the gala, I haven't stopped staring at you, thinking I'm one lucky man. I know being with you gives me hope that one day I will be married and have children. I'm thirty-one years old, and trust me when I say no one on this fucking Earth will ever make me feel like you do. I do know that."

Refusing to yield to his comfort, to his strength, to his warmth, I kept my body stiff. I couldn't give in to the fantasy of him. He was too logical, too careful, and I was a loose cannon. He couldn't handle me. No one could.

Tears fell. I hated that I desperately wanted to believe a lasting love with this man was possible.

"Is this your way of ending us because the tour is over, and you don't need me anymore? If it is, you don't need to pick a fight with me. Just tell me it's over, and it's over." Landon brushed back my hair.

"Just like that, we're over?" I asked, pushing away from him. "No fighting or yelling? You'd just let me go like I mean nothing to you."

He gripped my waist. "I don't know if I'm missing something or if it's you who doesn't know what she wants. But I don't know what's happening. You say you can't be with me, and then you're mad when I tell you we don't have to fight for us to end. What do you want from me?"

I struggled against him. "Let me go."

"Janae. Stop running. What do you want from me?" he repeated slowly. His lips brushed over my knuckles.

I exhaled sharply, my resolve breaking, and pressed my lips against his. "To never leave me," I softly admitted.

"Then I'm yours." Landon captured my lips in the sweetest kiss. I hugged his neck as his mouth drifted from my lips to my neck, sucking and licking. I arched my back, wanting to feel his tongue on my nipples. When he nibbled and tugged on my stiffened buds, my body spiraled into a rapturous descent. I crooned and pleaded for him to make love to me. Instead, he lifted my thigh and lowered his head to kiss and suck on my essence. Wanting… no, *needing* to feel him raw, I pressed him on his back and hovered over his erection, desperate for him to take away the doubt and the pain.

When I dropped down on his throbbing shaft uncovered, we moaned at the rawness of our bodies' joining. His eyes closed in pure pleasure. This time, he allowed me control as I rode us into a blissful oblivion.

CONFESSIONAL

janae

JUNE 12

"*I CAN'T BELIEVE I'M BACK* in Los Angeles, about to perform at the Forum. *Our biggest venue to date. And we are sold out. Completely sold out.*" I shook my head, letting the weight of the moment settle in. "*That is wild, right?*"

"*I know some of you are probably wondering how a hip-hop soul artist ended up in L.A. instead of New York, Philly, or ATL. Honestly, I did too. When I moved here, I thought L.A. was just Hollywood, Rodeo Drive, Compton, Issa Rae, and Kendrick Lamar. And yeah, it is all those things, but it is also something deeper. This city celebrates the richness and beauty of differences. It is a place where dreamers chase what feels impossible. A big city without the nonstop hustle of New York. A creative haven, if you can survive the traffic.*"

I shifted, pulling my *When I Get Home* sweatshirt over my knees as I curled deeper into the chair at Del's recording studio. The fabric was soft, grounding. Solange made that album about returning to herself, and tonight, that was exactly what this show felt like for me.

"*L.A. has been my home for the past seven years. For most of those years, I loved it. Even after my scandal, I did not feel too judged here. People in this city are too busy chasing their own dreams to worry about the fall of mine.*"

I exhaled, tilting my head back.

"*Ending the tour here feels like coming full circle. My career as MILA started in Houston and burned out here. My rebirth as just Janae has been more than I ever imagined. Every city on this tour has welcomed me with open arms. I know there are still some haters out there, but at this point, if you are still mad?*"

You are just jelly. Jealous that I am finally at peace with who I am. Or at least, I am getting there."

I tapped my nails against the mic, letting the moment breathe between us. *"Do not get it twisted, though. I am nervous as hell. Every day, I am praying that I step onto that stage and give y'all the show of a lifetime."*

I waved my hand, forcing a smirk. *"But, you know… no pressure."*

The producer's voice came from behind the camera. "What about you and Landon Hayes?"

I hugged myself, smiling at the thought of him. "Never thought I'd meet someone like him. No shade to my last relationship, but Landon is what I needed, even when I didn't know I needed someone like him. I love me some him!"

The producer shifted gears. "What does the success of 'Fallen Star' mean to you?"

I exhaled, still taking it in. "The success of 'Fallen Star' still astounds me, like I just found out yesterday. We wrote that song in a day. Just vibing, getting lost in the music, and trusting each other. We knew it was special. We just didn't expect a debut at number one."

I let out a breathy laugh, shaking my head. "The video of me standing on the tables at Junior's when I found out? Still surreal. One minute, I'm enjoying burgers and fries. The next, the whole place is screaming my name."

My throat tightened, emotions creeping in. "I cry too damn much. This tour has turned me into a puddle. First, performing again in Houston. Then, telling the world I have bipolar. And now, finding love? Yeah, I've been a mess."

I inhaled, steadying myself before raising my arms in victory. "Three years and counting in therapy. No booze, no drugs, and back on my meds. Taking care of myself, for real this time."

Looking straight into the camera, I let the words settle. "So, what does having a hit record mean? It means it's okay to fall. It's okay to crash and burn. Because if you fight for yourself, if you believe in yourself, you can rise again."

I paused, letting the weight of that truth land.

"And to co-write this song with The Hollow Bones? That's the highlight of my career. Hands down." My chest ached at the thought of the tour ending. "I don't know what I'll do without my brothers. L.A. is our last show. After that, we go our separate ways. They're heading back East, and I'm staying out here on the West Coast."

I blinked through the sudden sting in my eyes, forcing a smile. "The Hollow Bones have become my family. And I love them to death."

A knock on the door interrupted my talk

"I'm in the middle of my confessional," I yelled, and looked at the producer.

"It's on you."

Before I could decide if I wanted my time to be interrupted, the door opened, and The Hollow Bones, sans Landon, piled into the studio where I'd been recording one of my new songs in anticipation of a label deal. I pointed to the camera and the producer. "I'm kinda busy."

"We want to jump in." Brian pulled up a chair next to me. "We left your man playing the guitar. Once he gets started, you know he won't stop for nothing."

Cedrick and Charles stood behind me, fighting over who would do bunny ears over my head. Santiago kneeled on the other side of me to squeeze in.

I laughed at their antics. "I'm going to miss these men so much. They hated me at first."

"Not me. I've always rooted for you." Brian looped his arm around my neck and kissed my cheek.

"Stop kissing her ass." Cedrick popped the back of his head, and Brian punched Cedrick's leg without looking back.

"Okay, not Brian." I grinned. "But everyone else hated me. I messed with their money and they didn't want to fuck with me."

"Such a potty mouth, and she still owes us seventy-three dollars and five cents." Charles winked at the camera.

I rolled my eyes. "Whatever. I just made y'all a lot of money these past two months."

Cedrick tapped the back of my head playfully. "We're going to miss you too, big head."

I rubbed the spot he'd tapped and looked behind me. "My head is nowhere as big as yours."

Santiago and Brian laughed loudly while Charles said, "Now that's true."

I smiled at Cedrick, and he frowned back, though I saw the twinkle in his eyes. We had come so far.

Brian pushed his locs behind his ear as he stared into the camera. "We won't miss her that long. We wanted the fans to know that we love Janae Warner, and without her, we wouldn't have had the number one record in the country and sold-out shows. We also wouldn't have eaten such good food. This woman can cook her ass off. She needs to do a cookbook or open a restaurant." He rubbed his belly before leaning closer to the camera. "I don't know... Should we ask her to do a few more shows with us? Maybe cut another track or two in the fall?"

I searched their smiling faces. "Does Landon know?"

"Yep. We've been discussing it and told him not to say a word. We wanted it to be a surprise because it was our idea. Not his," Cedrick replied.

I jumped up and started dancing silly.

"Since there's no music playing, I guess that's a yes," Brian exclaimed, and they started dancing to the sweet sound of success and friendship. Cedrick grabbed my hand and twirled me around while Santiago pressed one of the control buttons.

"Stuck Between," the first release from their finished sophomore album, slated to be dropped later this year, sounded, and we danced even harder to Landon's song.

"Can you see why I love these men?" I shouted to the camera.

CHAPTER THIRTY-TWO
landon

JUNE 13

JANAE HAD BEEN PARTIALLY RIGHT about my reluctance to travel to Austin with her. It wasn't just about the city. Being in her space meant adjusting to a world that clashed with my own.

Her condo was stylish and modern, filled with personality. It was also overwhelming. She loved bright colors, bold art, and decorative pieces that seemed placed on a whim. My head spun just looking at it.

And she was messy. Not dirty, just disorganized. Clothes draped over furniture. Shoes scattered in places they shouldn't be. Half-full water bottles left behind like she had meant to finish them but got distracted. She insisted she had been too busy traveling to call her housekeeper, but I suspected otherwise.

Janae wasn't careless with money, but she managed three properties and had accumulated debt over the years. She never seemed worried about it, but I had a feeling she was not as comfortable as she let on. Sooner or later, we would need to have a real conversation about finances.

I paused at the thought. I had never gone this deep in a relationship before. Did I even have the right to ask about her money? Was offering financial advice overstepping? At what point did her problems become ours?

Part of me wanted to combine accounts and build something together like my parents had. Another part of me knew it was smarter to keep our finances separate, protecting both of us from any future conflict.

I sighed and rubbed my temples.

Janae was right about another thing. I hated change. But here I was, standing in the middle of her chaotic and colorful world, trying to figure out how to make space for both of us in it.

I strummed my guitar on her balcony, hoping I wasn't disturbing anyone. Four days in her space had left me feeling restless. In my own home, I played whenever I wanted, but here, I hesitated out of concern for her neighbors. The unease had been constant since we arrived in Los Angeles, except when she was in my arms.

I hated how much I needed her. The thought of losing her made it hard to breathe. That night, when I thought she was ending things, my heart felt like it had stopped. I stayed calm on the outside, but inside, the panic was suffocating. If she had walked away, I don't know how I would have handled it.

I rarely had episodes anymore because I had learned to manage them. Keeping my environment controlled helped me stay balanced. But my life had never included someone like Janae. She was unpredictable, impulsive, and constantly challenging the stability I relied on. I wasn't sure how much longer I could hold everything together.

The door behind me opened. I glanced back to see Cedrick step outside, smiling as he dropped into the chaise longue across from me.

"Frankie and Janae just left for the store to grab a few more things for dinner," he said.

I raised an eyebrow. "The store? Did she dress to blend in?"

Cedrick grinned. "Not at all. She wants all the love in Los Angeles."

"Glad I'm not with her. Her fans are vicious, and it's worse when we're together." I shook my head.

"How are you holding up?"

I shrugged. "Day by day."

"The attention is only going to get worse once our album drops. Are you up for it?"

"Do I have a choice?" I quirked a brow.

"Naw, bro. Get used to it." He smiled as he crossed his ankles.

"You seem happier now. You and Frankie a thing? Because I thought Janae just invited you over to eat dinner with us."

"We're not exclusive or anything. Trying her out for a while."

I chuckled. "She's not a car."

"I see the impact Janae has on you, and my parents have been in the marriage game forever, still loving each other. Maybe it's time for me to start getting serious, and Frankie is good people. She's not caught up in fame and works hard for her brand. She likes her independence, and I like that about her."

"I like her for you. She won't take your crap." I pushed his arm playfully.

"Just like Janae won't take yours. She pushes you better than I ever did." He gestured to my hair, which Janae had braided down again. "You used to wear the hat even in the house. You move around the stage more. You're taking pictures and smiling more. Traveling on planes just because she asks."

"I hadn't really noticed…" I started strumming my guitar again to avoid more conversation about me.

"Some things are still the same," he commented ruefully.

"What do you think about this chord sequence?" I asked.

Cedrick nodded. "I like it."

"Not sure if it's for me or Hollow."

His forehead puckered slightly. "Going solo on us?"

"No, not sure this music fits Hollow. Besides, I can't go on that stage by myself."

"You've been on stage with just Janae." She and I had performed "Fallen Star" at a late-night show in a small club in St. Louis.

"It wasn't easy. I'm most comfortable with Hollow Bones." I held my fist out. "I'm not going anywhere, Cedrick."

He bumped my fist. "You've been soaring above us for a minute now, and I'm here to tell you it's okay if you do. Whether you're with us or on your own, we're always your brothers."

I hugged my guitar to my chest. "I'm not leaving the band, and even if Del pushes for me to go solo, it's not going to happen."

Cedrick nodded slowly. "And it's okay if he does and you want to."

311

"Why do you keep insisting? I told you how I feel."

"You and Janae have been asked to open a special Grammy event in November. They had someone else in mind to do it, but they want you two now. Janae Warner, featuring Landon Hayes. Del told me first because he wanted to clarify that he wasn't trying to break up the band and asked me to talk to you."

"No," I answered without thought, and started playing again.

Cedrick was silent for a long time before saying, "You're going to lose her if you don't get help."

"Help? What do I need help for?" Painful discomfort rose inside me, and I couldn't temper my tone.

"You once told me that your parents didn't really see you. They tried to make you something you're not." He met my glare with determined eyes. "I've been doing the same thing since we met. I adjusted to you and how you needed things to be a certain way, and the band followed because we love you. Acceptance also means being honest when you're hurting others. Every time you have a panic attack, or whatever you want to call it, it hurts me, bro. It feels like you're dying in front of me. It takes me a while to recover to see you like that. I walk on eggshells, hoping not to set you off. That's not living for me or for you."

I gritted my teeth. "I'm sorry I wasn't lucky enough to have two parents who loved me unconditionally, sorry that my father hit my mother when he couldn't control her and only seemed to love me when I did what he wanted. I'm sorry if that fucks with me."

Cedrick dragged his hands over his face. "Stop blaming everything on your parents. You haven't lived with them since you were sixteen. You can't keep living carefully because you're afraid to break. I can't keep being there for you when you won't help yourself."

I slammed my guitar down on the balcony. "You don't have to do shit for me."

Cedrick swung his legs to the side of the chair and sat up. "Naw... naw, fuck you. You don't get to tell me that I don't have to do shit for you. I've been protecting you, looking out for you, and refusing to take projects because I knew you couldn't handle it, or at least you believed you couldn't handle it.

You want my help when you're struggling but reject it when I say something you don't like. You walk around like this honorable man who doesn't lie, smoke, drink, or fuck around, judging the rest of the world. But the truth? You're scared to live, scared to truly get help, hiding behind your phenomenal talent. That's a bad look, Landon."

I glanced toward the door and back at him. This wasn't Cedrick. "Be honest, it wasn't Del. Janae put you up to this. Is that why she invited you to dinner… to have some sort of intervention for poor Landon?"

"No. This is all me. Janae made me realize how I didn't push you to be better. She made me believe that change is possible." He gestured to the door. "That woman was out there bad three years ago wilding out, cursing out people, breaking contracts, and fucking around on a man who seemed to love her. Now all she sees is you. She kept her word to us and to you. She's shown up every single time. It hasn't been easy when she's snappy with us, Frankie, and Jeri, but she's trying. Reaching out to her therapist and distancing herself from us when she needs to. Both of you are soaring right now, and if you don't check yourself, she's only going to fly higher and leave you to crash and burn."

"You don't think I know that?" I spat. "She needs me now, and one day she won't. I'll deal with that day when it happens."

Cedrick narrowed his eyes. "You really prefer her helpless and needy and not strong and independent? Wow. You don't want her to get better so *you* don't have to change."

My chest heaved up and down, and I wanted to protest, though my words were lodged deep in my throat.

He stood. "I've always looked up to you, even with your ways. Proud to call you my best friend and brother. Right now… at this very moment, I can't say that because you're nothing but a coward. Give my apologies to Janae. I lost my appetite."

He walked back inside, and I slumped down in my chair.

CHAPTER THIRTY-THREE

janae

JUNE 14

I SHOULDN'T HAVE BEEN THERE. This space wasn't mine. It belonged to them. At least while we were in L.A. Still, I told myself I'd come to grab a jacket I left in Del's studio, but that excuse fell apart the moment I stepped inside. The jacket could wait. What I wanted, what I needed, was to *feel* something, to let the energy of this room reach me in a way nothing else had lately. Anything would do. As the days drew nearer to the biggest performance of my life and the reunion of me and my mother, my moods shifted rapidly. I was easily rattled, and sleep became a distant memory. I had to release. I needed a reprieve from the constant ball of emotion that threatened to consume me.

The room was unnervingly quiet. I'd expected to find the guys here, rehearsing or cracking up over one of their never-ending inside jokes, their noise filling every corner of the room.

I started messing with the equipment nearby, a simple setup hooked to a laptop. The guys had been working on something, and as I tapped a few buttons, the sounds filled the space. I isolated Landon's electric guitar riff first, steady and haunting. It sounded reflective and deliberate, full of unspoken depth, just like him. Then came Santiago's acoustic guitar. Its warmth and carefree rhythm usually grounded the band, but tonight it felt fleeting as I

315

silenced it. Charles's saxophone followed. Its smooth elegance cut through the track like a voice trying to be heard above the clamor. Finally, I pulled Brian's drums. The layered percussion unraveled as I muted the kick, then the snare, and finally the high hat, leaving the rhythm bare. With everything else stripped away, Cedrick's piano was last. His chords vibrated with a quiet intensity, almost defiant, as though they didn't want to fade. But I needed silence. It was time for my voice to carry the weight alone.

With each layer peeled away, I hit a few buttons to bring in synthetized strings, curious to hear how they might blend with a hint of percussion. Then I brought the beat back, tapping the pad to create a rhythm with presence. I looped the track, letting the sound build in intensity, though it still needed something more to ground it. Returning to the track the guys had laid down, I added back Brian's drums, adjusting their pace and rebuilding the beat piece by piece. The steady thrum of the kick drum laid the foundation, the snare crackled with tension ready to snap, and the high hat added a sharp, driving edge. The pulse came alive, demanding more, propelling me forward.

The mic stood idle, its sleek silhouette outlined against the amber glow of the sunset filtering through the drapes. I stepped closer through the dimness, fingers brushing the cool metal, a steadying contrast to the turmoil bubbling within. My breath hitched. It had been ages since I allowed myself to let go. Not for applause. Not for Landon. Not for anyone. It was for me, free from the crushing weight of expectation.

The weight in my chest pressed harder. The arguments, the silence from Landon, the sideways glances from Cedrick, the burden of trying to prove I wasn't the mess everyone thought I was. My past. My present. It all swirled together until I felt like I was choking on it. My fingers adjusted the mic stand instinctively.

I grabbed a pair of headphones hanging from a hook and slid them on, closing my eyes as I stepped to the mic. I didn't turn it on. This wasn't about hearing myself or being heard. The headphones isolated me, wrapping me in the sound of the music I was building, amplifying each layer while shutting out the rest of the world. This moment was for me, unguarded and unfiltered, free from the heaviness of an audience. Words began to tumble out, my truths flowing in a way that felt unrestrained and unrelenting. The mic was purely there to comfort me, like an old friend catching every note and pause. With the loop building, I added a deeper layer. A drumbeat here and a hint of strings there, letting the music carry me to places I hadn't dared explore in years.

I started with a soft, rising melody, my voice carrying a haunting hook that hovered in the stillness of the room. It wasn't loud or bold. It was just a gentle plea, each note trembling as it found its place. Then the words began to form, laced with the kind of pain that only grows with time.

"Don't be afraid, little girl, stand tall. They tried to clip your wings, make you feel small. Age ain't nothing but a number, they said. But who saw the cracks where innocence bled?"

My voice cracked. A tear slid down my cheek, but I didn't stop.

"Mama had dreams, but the rent came first. Left me searching for love in a world that's cursed. They called me a name, put shame on my skin. But I'm breaking the chains, let the healing begin."

A quiet presence in the room startled me, and I opened my eyes. Cedrick stood near the edge of the space before moving toward the piano, his gaze unreadable. My first instinct was to stop, to shut down, but he didn't say a word while settling on the bench.

His first notes were quiet, hesitant, as if he were seeking my permission. When I didn't stop, he leaned into the keys, playing with a rhythm that danced between smooth and jagged. His chords wove into my delivery, lifting the words as though pulling something visceral and aching from both of us.

"I fought in the dark, made a home in the fight. Built my own fire, now I carry the light. They laugh at the scars, they don't see the war. But I'm standing here, I'm worth fighting for. Took all the pain, wrote it into my veins. Turned the hurt into notes, now I'm changing the game.

"They tried to break my soul. But I'm still standing here. They tried to take my name. But my voice is clear. They tried to break my soul. But I'm stronger than fear. They tried to take my name. But I'm still standing here."

Cedrick's fingers flowed over the keys with an urgency I'd never heard from him before. Each note bled like a confession, raw and unfiltered, as if he were wrestling with something unspoken, emptying his own battles into the music. This wasn't the polished precision he usually brought to The Hollow

Bones. It was something deeper, more untamed. Every chord trembled with vulnerability, like my release had unlocked something in him.

Together, we weren't just making music. We were unraveling, shedding the weight we carried in silence.

The lyrics spilled out in a cadence that felt somewhere between singing and speaking, like truth wrapped in poetry. Some lines hit like a whispered prayer; others cut like declarations, raw and unrelenting. The tears came, but I didn't stop. This wasn't for anyone else. This was for the girl buried beneath the wreckage of her past, the dreams she once abandoned, the voice she'd been forced to silence.

As I allowed it to flow, Cedrick's playing pulled me forward, bridging the space between pain and healing, daring me to confront truths I'd never had the courage to face.

"Fame's a mirror, it shows all your flaws. But I built my own crown from the things I lost. They wrote me off, but I wrote my song. And this is for the girl who's been strong all along. Don't let the world tell you what you can't do. Even roses find roots in the hardest of truths."

The last note hung in the air, trembling. My chest heaved as I pulled the headphones off and let them dangle around my neck. Cedrick's piano carried a final, lingering note before the silence returned. He looked up at me, his expression softer than I'd ever seen it. He didn't say a word, just stood and walked over, squeezing my shoulder lightly. His nod said everything. Respect. Understanding.

As he walked out, my gaze followed him until something caught my attention. Landon stood in the doorway, arms crossed, his expression stern before it softened into something warm and loving.

He remained in the doorway, giving me the space to process this fragile moment, his presence both grounding and freeing. My fingers tightened around the mic stand as I turned back to the quiet room. My heart felt lighter, the weight less suffocating. I adjusted the mic again. There was more I needed to let out.

And this time, I wasn't afraid to.

CHAPTER THIRTY-FOUR

landon

JUNE 15

I STARED IN THE MIRROR of my dressing room. The guys were joking and teasing each other behind me, the usual antics to get rid of nervous energy before a show. If they'd noticed that Cedrick and I were distant, they didn't say. We hadn't addressed our conversation on Janae's balcony or the cathartic cleansing in Del's studio yesterday, subconsciously deciding to be cordial and respectful for the band's sake.

I stared at my attire for the show. My Alexander McQueen harness black shirt and black pants had been designed and tailored at Janae's request. The Hollow Bones were all wearing variations of red and black. Janae would rock a white suit with a custom red-and-black hat. This was a big night for her. She'd been restless since we arrived in town, and nothing I did soothed her.

Or maybe there *was* something I could do. Cedrick's words reverberated through my mind.

I removed my hat and ran my hands over my cornrows, then inhaled and started taking out one braid.

I caught Cedrick's widened eyes in the mirror, and he stepped closer. "You need help?"

I nodded.

He started on the other side. "We better hurry."

Santiago rubbed his hands together. "I've been dying to touch this dude's hair."

The room went silent, and we all looked at him with raised brows.

"Come on, don't act like I'm the only one. He has pretty hair," Santiago reasoned.

We all shook our heads in laughter, and I smiled at the reflection as Cedrick and Santiago started undoing my braids. "Someone needs to take a shot of this. I don't know when I'll go on stage without my hat again."

Cedrick frowned. "Fuck no. Don't want my alpha male card taken away."

"Oh, that happened. Already posted to our IG." Brian laughed from behind us.

"Charles, get him," Cedrick demanded.

"Why? I'm not in the picture." Charles started blowing his trumpet.

A rapid knock on the door interrupted our teasing camaraderie.

Brian opened it to an upset Jeri, who sobbed, "It's Janae. She's a mess. She won't get up off the floor."

My heart dropped to my stomach and I left the room without thought to my appearance, needing to get to her. When I hurried down the hall past staff and guests to her dressing room, her cameramen were outside filming, and I yelled, "Shut them off now."

I rushed into the room, and she was balled up in the corner, rocking, tears destroying her makeup. She was in her bra and panties. Her vulnerability sliced through me like a blade. Frankie, also crying, clutched her hands together helplessly.

"Give me her robe," I demanded, my voice hoarse.

With shaky hands, Frankie tossed me the satin robe, and I wrapped it around Janae, sinking onto the floor beside her. "Nae, come on, baby. It's okay. I'm here."

She didn't move, didn't acknowledge me. The blankness in her eyes gutted me. She wasn't here. She'd checked out.

"Did you take anything?" I asked, gripping her face gently.

Frankie shook her head. "No, she was already nervous. Her eyes were jumpy, and her hands trembled so much that I told her to hold them together.

Then her mother visited her, and when we came back into the room, she was like this."

Her mother. Of course.

I grabbed her face and shook it slightly until her eyes focused on me. "I'm here now. Remember, I'm your life jacket. Grab on and don't let go."

Fresh tears flowed down her face. She wiped her runny, reddened nose with the back of her hand. "I'm sorry. Please don't hate me."

"Shh… shh… You don't need to apologize." I wiped her tears with my thumbs. "We can walk out that door and go home, okay? If you can't perform, it's okay. I'll pay whatever we owe."

She shook her head violently. "Nooo… Then they'll hate me again. I have to… I have to…" Janae shook in my arms. "I need something, Landon. Please. I need something. Just this one time."

"No. You don't." I held up her coin around her neck. "You don't need anything but your talent and me. I can hold your hand and stand next to you. Whatever you need. If you want to go on that stage, we'll go." I pulled at my hair. "I wanted to surprise you and wear my hair like you love. Please, it will be okay. It's just a show."

Janae's eyes were wild and fearful as she weakly smiled and touched my wild strands. "Beautiful."

"I love you, and I can be strong for the both of us. Okay? Come on. You don't need drugs," I begged her, wiping impatiently at my annoying tears.

Cedrick said from behind me, "We're due on stage in fifteen minutes. We can delay if we have to, but we got to get her ready to go on."

Without breaking my gaze from hers, I grunted. "Forget this show. I'm taking her home."

"We can't cancel this close to showtime." He kneeled beside me. "Listen, Janae, can you sit on a stool and sing? We can say that you're feeling under the weather. We can do this."

"I need something. I… can't go on that stage… like this… and… they already hate me… I have to prove my mother wrong. Why does she hate me so much?" she wailed, and began scratching her wrists and forearms.

I gripped her face tighter. "Doesn't matter how she feels about you. Everyone in this room loves you. We are your family now. Look at me. I want you to be my wife and the mother of my children. You don't have to prove anything to anyone anymore, do you hear me?"

"I do... baby, I do..." She patted her face, then looked at Cedrick. "Can you give me something... just in case I can't pull it together?"

My blood ran cold at how she'd dismissed my undying love and replaced me with Cedrick. I dropped my hands from her face to grab my chest and protect it from the raging pain. I sagged against the wall, forcing my stomach not to empty its contents.

Cedrick glanced at me and then back to her. "I can't, Janae."

"Yes, you can. I've seen you pop pills before we performed in Chicago." She grabbed his lapel like a desperate addict, and I slowly rose on shaky legs, unable to see her like this.

"I don't have anything," he insisted. "We can sit here with you no matter how long it takes, until you can get on that stage as the Janae we've come to know and love."

"Wait... Landon." She hugged my leg and used my body to stand. "See? I'm already better. Don't leave me, baby. You'll see it's going to be all right. Give me thirty minutes, and I'll be ready. I won't take anything. I just wanted to have something in case I couldn't pull it together. That's it."

"The last time you had something 'just in case,' you took it," I wearily reminded her.

Janae smiled brightly, though her darting eyes were still heartbreakingly dull. "The last time I didn't have you. You're right. I can do this." Her eyes focused on something behind me.

Before I could turn my head to see what had grabbed her attention, Brian squeezed my shoulder. "Jeri will help you with your hair. Give us a minute with Janae. She's too close to you, and both of you need the space. It's going to be fine. If she isn't ready to go on stage, we won't go, okay? Now, take some deep breaths before you can't hit the stage, either. I have a feeling we're about to turn it out. She's just nervous because she's home."

I looked around the room at Frankie's, Cedrick's, and Brian's concerned gazes. We were a family, and they would help Janae remember that she could handle whatever came her way. Maybe I was placing too much pressure on her, too, and she could receive their comforting words better than mine.

Frankie straightened her shoulders and smiled at Janae. "We'll hook this makeup right back up and throw a wig under that hat. Landon is going to get that hair right, and we'll stay up all night after the show celebrating."

Janae nodded and blew me a kiss. "Love you."

"Love you more." I tapped my heart with two fingers and walked out of her dressing room to a worried Del, Santiago, and Charles.

Del hurried beside me and whispered, "What's going on?"

I said nothing until we returned to the dressing room while Jeri worked on my hair. "I don't know if Janae will be okay, though she says she will be. Apparently, her mother said something, and it shook her. I don't know what went down."

"Have you met her mother?" Del asked.

"We were supposed to officially meet after the show."

"Her mother is a piece of work. It probably wasn't a good idea to allow her to see Janae before the show."

Charles snorted. "No shit."

Santiago looked at me in the mirror. "What's our plan B if she can't make it?"

"Janae is hitting the stage," I reassured him. "Just might be sitting on a stool or maybe leaning against the keyboard or something until she gets her confidence back. We can start off with our songs, giving her time to relax. Maybe give them 'Stuck Between' from our second album. She'll remember who she is once the crowd screams for her and the music hits."

My cell rang. I picked it up from the vanity without looking at the caller.

"She's ready," Brian said, loud enough for everyone to hear my phone's speaker.

Del slowly exhaled while the men grinned at each other. I smiled at my reflection. My hair was finally wild and free.

Like Janae.

CHAPTER THIRTY-FIVE

janae

AN HOUR EARLIER

"JANAE, WHY ARE YOU SO cold? Your teeth are chattering," Frankie said as she started prepping my face for makeup.

"I can't seem to relax. Been trying all day. Landon has tried everything. Warm bath, music, a massage." Although I hadn't been taking my meds consistently, I'd tried to reach Dr. Brownson to see if I could take extra pills or get something else to take the edge off, to no avail. Even my time in Del's studio with Cedrick and Landon, which had initially worked like a salve, seemed like a far-off memory.

"Sex." Jeri giggled from the wardrobe rack. "If he gave you a bath and a massage, sex had to follow."

Despite my bad nerves, I managed to smile. "Yeah, we did."

Frankie pressed concealer around my eyes as she added, "It's just another show. Besides, it looks like you have more love here than anywhere else."

"I also have more haters here, too."

"Is that woman, who we will never name, still harassing you? Get over it. It's been years. She's the stupid one, staying married to him. You're not the only one he's been caught with. He's for the streets," Jeri retorted.

"He is for the streets, but L.A. is her city, too." I pushed out my breath, trying to regulate my nerves.

Frankie looked at me in the mirror. "Have you heard from your ex since you've been home?"

"No." I slowly met her eyes. "Landon would be upset if he knew I still wanted acknowledgment from my ex. Adam doesn't mean anything to me. I just thought that since I'm back in Los Angeles, he would've sent me a note or something saying he's proud of me. Performing at the Forum was a goal I shared with Adam that never happened."

"Why does it matter?" Frankie asked.

"Then I would know he truly forgives me for everything. I hurt him the most. He lost serious money bailing me out of my mistakes, and I caused drama in his family because he stuck by me."

Jeri's brows dipped. "It sounds like he was good to you despite everything you put him through. Are you sure you still don't have feelings for him?"

I chuckled. "Oh, he wasn't a saint either. We were taking turns cheating on each other. He just recognized before I did that we were toxic for each other, and because he cared, he didn't desert me like everyone else. Well, he didn't until he fell in love. He's a different man now. Guess my ego was hurt that I wasn't enough to change him."

Frankie laughed. "Girl, you can't change a man unless he wants to be changed. Maybe he grew into a better person, just like you did. He just happened to find love again first. Let that nonsense go, because Landon loves the air you breathe. All the women trying to get at him everywhere we go, and he doesn't even flinch."

I turned around on my stool to face them. "This real-love shit is crazy. Like this man barely raises his voice at me even though I deserve it half the time. He likes the quiet me and even the parts of me that are loud and need constant attention. He's not walking around jealous if I smile or hug another man. He trusts me, though he's fully aware of my past with men. I clung to Adam because I didn't have anyone else and not because I couldn't be without him. We were together for four years.

"It's only been three months with Landon. Yet if we broke up, I don't know how I would be able to function without him. I've never felt like this about anyone." Overcome with conflicting emotions about the worthiness of love meant for me, I covered my face, and they huddled around me.

Frankie said, "You're messing up my makeup."

"We have time to fix it," Jeri replied. "She's having a moment, and we're going to let her have it."

I lowered my hands and looked at them both. "Is this what it means to have female friends?"

"Yep. We're here for each other." Frankie started applying my makeup again. "If it wasn't for your taking a chance on me, my business wouldn't be growing, and I wouldn't have met Cedrick." She blushed. "He needs a lot more work than Landon, but I'm good kicking it with him."

Jeri sniffed. "I'm happy you're my friends, but I'm not trying to find love. I'm too young to settle down."

I wagged my finger at her. "Brian is sweet on you, so don't break my brother's heart."

"He'll live. We're messing around and he knows it." She backed away from me. "Now, let's get ready for this show so we can party all night."

Frankie turned me around to face the mirror. "Let's get it."

I exhaled, pushing out the darkness, feeling more like the light I needed to smash my performance. I touched my face. "My hand is warming up."

Someone knocked at my dressing room door, and Jeri answered, "Hey, Del."

Del stuck his head in and said in a low voice, "Your mother is right behind me, and she's dying to see you."

I snarled, "I thought I told you after the show."

He held his hand up. "I know. Give us a few minutes," he told the ladies.

I waited until they'd left. "Del, there's a reason I wanted to wait until after the show."

"She has flowers and wanted to at least speak to you. I can tell her you only have a minute, and she can join us at the after-party."

I pulled at my T-shirt and leggings. "Yeah, I still have to get dressed."

"The cameras are outside, too."

"Del, this isn't the time nor place."

"I'll talk to the producer about cutting this part if we need to. It's going to be fine."

I rolled my eyes. "You and Landon owe me. He insisted I invite her here too."

Del's chubby cheeks glowed with excitement. "Comeback is a success, a new man, and reconciliation with family. Reality TV gold."

I took a deep breath. *Relax. It's just your mother. A few minutes of torture, and then she's gone. Or she might surprise you and be nice.*

I unclenched and clenched my hands twice. "Send her in."

Del opened the door, and my mother walked in, beautiful as ever. Tall, curvy, with twinkling brown eyes, a button nose, and a luminous smile that hid the cruelty that lurked underneath. Like a fine wine, she'd aged well, appearing far younger than her forty-eight years. Cameras followed her as she opened her arms wide. "My Honey-Nae."

Tears rimmed my eyes at her nickname for me from our rare bonding times. "Mama."

She hugged me, smelling like I remembered. Dove soap and Pear Glace from Victoria's Secret. She pulled back. "You look amazing. Where's that fine man of yours? I thought no one could compare to Adam. I guess I was wrong. One thing I can say you know how to pick a man. Learned from the best."

"You'll meet him after the show." I ignored the dig. "I have to get ready. You have VIP at the show and at the after-party. We can catch up later."

"I have a surprise."

I looked past her for my older brother and only saw the film crew. "Where's Rashad?"

She wrinkled her nose. "Why would I bring my son to a city like Los Angeles when I have a man?"

"Of course," I said, pasting on a phony smile to hide my disappointment. I wanted to see him. Although he'd told me he couldn't take time off work, I'd still hoped he would surprise me. I didn't have beef with my brother. He was always stuck in the middle of me and my mother, and I was determined for that to change.

She returned to the door and pulled someone inside by their arm, and I had to bite my cheek to stop the gasp, since the cameras were trained on my face. "Antwon and I got back together a year ago. I'm sure you remember him. He wanted to speak to you, too. Make sure we can get over the past."

My heart raced, and I swore if I could have thrown up, it would have shot out of me like in *The Exorcist*. I couldn't speak as he grinned wide and hugged me. "Hey, Janae. Long time no see."

Avoiding eye contact, I nodded and backed away quickly. His touch made my skin crawl, and I looked at Del. "I need to get ready."

He took the hint and hurried them out of the room, along with the crew. I went to my wardrobe rack, trying to bring back the peace I'd been finally starting to feel before my mother and *him*.

I squeezed my eyes shut to stop the flood of memories. I hit the side of my head, trying to shake the horror that I felt then and now. The thoughts wouldn't stop, and my body started to burn from the inside.

I scrambled to find something in my bag or Frankie's to cut myself to stop the excruciating sensation. I found scissors and sat on the stool, trying to find a spot on my body that no one would notice. No matter how I cut myself, I would have to explain to Landon, who knew me from head to toe, how it happened. It had to be the tiniest sliver. Then maybe I could focus on my show and get rid of those thoughts of what happened with that horrid man when I was fourteen.

How could she do that to me? What kind of mother taunts you with your abuser?

I yelled to release the clawing pain that covered every inch of my body and slid to the floor, holding on to the scissors, wielding them like a weapon. Frankie rushed back in, followed by Jeri, and on instinct, I held the scissors up to defend myself.

Frankie placed her hands in the air. "It's me… It's me."

Jeri said, "I'll get Landon."

"No," I shouted, holding the scissors flat against my chest. He knew nothing of my childhood or teenage years. What would he do if he knew? He wouldn't want this fucked-up girl. No one would. I shook my head. "No… no. He won't understand."

Frankie inched closer to me. "Then give me the scissors, please."

"I'm so messed up. Why can't I be normal?" I screeched and dropped the scissors as I slid off the stool to the cold floor.

She urged Jeri, "Go, now."

When Jeri rushed out of the room, I crawled to the corner and curled up into a fetal position. My mind yearned desperately to forget, and my body craved release that wouldn't come naturally, no matter how much I wished it would. The metal coin resting between my cleavage couldn't help me. Landon couldn't help me forget.

I covered my head and sobbed at the fork in the road presented to me. Neither path seemed acceptable.

Once Landon had left the dressing room to finish getting ready, I looked at Cedrick. "You know why I need something. You know that it won't hurt me the way that Landon believes it will. I swear I'm not an addict, but I can't get on that stage. I can't."

Cedrick kept shaking his head. "He's my best friend."

I took his hands. "He doesn't have to know. Landon believes all drugs are wrong. My mother came all this way to fuck with me, and I can't function. Before you came in here, the pain and nervousness were so bad that I was going to cut myself with scissors. Please. Just a little something. Not enough to get me wasted."

Frankie sobbed, "Janae, no. You can't do this to him."

I kept my gaze trained on Cedrick. "I'm not doing anything. He knows, like I know, a little something takes the edge off, and that's all I need. I promise not to drink. I've been without anything for three months, and three years before that. I have to get on that stage. I have to kill it, or the world will hate me all over again, and Cedrick knows it's true. Everything we've built these last few weeks will be gone because I can't get on that stage."

Cedrick's eyes became glossy, and he opened his mouth and promptly shut it.

Brian pressed pills in my hand. "Take it."

Cedrick shut his eyes, and Frankie turned away. I popped the pills in my mouth and swallowed them dry. Refusing to feel any guilt for what I'd just done, I sat back down in front of the mirror, wiping my tears. I inhaled and exhaled, waiting for the familiar waves of peace to float through me.

In five, four, three… I will be as light as a feather, flying high above my worries and darkness.

The heaviness started to lift, and my chest relaxed.

I twisted my neck from side to side. "Tell Landon that I'm ready. Let's start with 'Lonely Woman' first and then give them a hint of 'Fallen Star' and then close with it."

Brian rushed out of the room, and Cedrick walked out much slower.

Frankie stared at me in the mirror, huffing and shaking her head, clearly disappointed.

"Don't you dare judge me. You don't have a clue what my mother just did to me. You want to be in this game, then you roll with the waves or get off the boat. Now, fix my face. We have a show to do," I barked.

She blew out her breath slowly and did as she was told.

My love for him raged as I watched Landon play his guitar near me. When his eyes were closed and he bit his bottom lip, nothing or no one else mattered. I envied his rare ability to transform a simple minor chord into a symphonic creation with unimaginable ease and humbleness. I also envied his steadfastness to his craft, to his band, and to me. I prayed his belief in me wouldn't falter once he realized that I'd broken my promise.

On my cue, his lips curved, and he tugged on his thick, wild curls. Landon had left behind his hat for me, and I wouldn't lose this beautiful man. I wouldn't.

I pulled my hat down lower on my head and sauntered on stage as the Los Angeles crowd yelled and screamed. I could do no wrong in their eyes. And I wanted to stay as long as possible on this stage viewed through their rose-colored lenses.

As I moved to the center, I signaled to Landon to quiet the music. I allowed my pain, my hurt, my anger, and my trauma to flow from out of me into an a cappella version of "A Lonely Woman."

I bowed deeply at the last note, and The Hollow Bones started chanting my name. Their harmonized sound traveled through the arena until the entire audience shouted, "Janae." Unburdened of the baggage I'd carried on the stage, I rose and spread my arms wide. Landon had been right, and if I trusted myself, the music would have been enough to unleash my troubles. As I stood there, I knew from the depths of my soul that I would never take another pill or drink alcohol. God had given me a gift to exorcise my demons, and I wouldn't take it for granted again.

I gestured to The Hollow Bones and encouraged the audience to scream louder for them. I blew a kiss at Landon, whose hazel eyes gleamed green as he beamed, and the noise grew louder at the evidence of our love.

"Los Angeles, are you ready?" I asked into the mic.

It was truly an unforgettable night at the Forum.

CHAPTER
THIRTY-SIX
landon

LIKE THE NIGHT OF THE rodeo show, I observed Janae flirt and laugh as she moved through The Deluxe Club as we celebrated the end of the tour. I sipped water, and those around me drank wine and champagne and were merry. Numbly, I watched her as she hugged Cedrick and then Frankie. I sat alone at the bar table for two for most of the night. It was a private party, so I wasn't bothered by zealous fans, though a few people from the restaurant and guests of the venue staff wanted selfies, and I obliged.

Janae weaved in and out of the tables set for our special night, held against the backdrop of the greatest African-American musicians in history. Michael Jackson, Beyoncé, Chuck Berry, B.B. King, and other greats graced the walls. Janae Camille Warner would be on those walls one day, and I would be proud to say that she'd once loved me and that I'd loved her. I picked up my cell and ran my finger over the selfie of us on the train.

I wasn't enough for her. I hadn't been able to help her when she needed me the most because what I could give, she didn't want, and I could never give her what she wanted. I'd been elated when she walked on the stage, strong, fierce, and beautiful. I'd thought her able to command a stage of that magnitude clean and sober. When we'd left the stage, and she avoided me, I'd known otherwise.

Even at this party, she refused to be in my presence for longer than a second. I continued to sit and observe as I contemplated my next move. Staying with her had become almost impossible after I realized what she'd done and that Cedrick had given her what she'd asked for. They'd convinced me to leave so he could feed the habit I thought she'd beaten. My stomach churned with hurt and disappointment that two people I trusted had tricked me.

"My daughter should never leave you alone. Way too handsome to be sitting here waiting for her." A pretty woman approached me with an outstretched hand. "I'm Ebony Tanner, Janae's mother."

I took her hand and smiled politely. "I see the resemblance."

Ebony touched her chest. "You were amazing. I don't think I cared about the guitar until you played it."

I sipped on my water and looked past her shoulder for Janae. She caught my gaze from across the museum and shook her head slightly. She wasn't going to come near us.

"What did you say to Janae earlier?"

Ebony's sculpted eyebrows met. "I didn't say anything." Then she smiled. "Oh, she's probably upset because she never liked my man, and we've recently gotten back together."

"Which man?" I scanned the room and noticed an older man standing awkwardly in the corner.

"Antwon." She turned around and beckoned to the same guy. He hurried to us and grinned like he was excited to be invited to an exclusive party.

I didn't smile and looked back toward Janae, who'd turned away and was talking to Jeri and Frankie.

"Antwon." The man held his hand out, and I emptied my glass, ignoring him. Embarrassed, he dropped his arm and tried again. "Thank you for everything. Del told us you and Janae arranged for the trip. First class all the way. Your concert was the best I've ever been to."

I nodded. I wouldn't be polite or friendly until Janae told me what had happened between her and her mother and this man.

"Call Janae over here," Ebony demanded with a tight smile. "I've been trying to track her down all night, but she's always busy with this person or that. She needs to speak to her mother."

"Janae doesn't need to do anything. You upset her, and I can't let you mess up her night any more."

"Whatever she told you is a lie."

I calmly replied, "She didn't tell me anything. She's never told me anything about you. Janae cares about family, and I insisted you be here tonight for her sake. I should've realized there was a reason she didn't want you around."

An observant Del passed nearby, and I called his name. He approached the table solemnly. "You need anything?"

"Yes. I need you to escort these two out of here. If they don't make a scene, they can keep their first-class tickets home and their nice suite. If they make a scene, they'll have to figure out where to stay and how to get home. After you escort them out, stop back here, please."

Del nodded and addressed the couple. "Come this way. Our driver can take you anywhere you want."

Ebony looked in Janae's direction as if she were about to ask for help, but Janae had moved somewhere out of sight in the large club. Antwon urged Ebony out of the place, angrily whispering something to her. I cracked my neck to release the tension as I watched them leave. I was wound up like a jack-in-a-box, ready to pop, and we still had cake and the champagne toast to end our tour.

When Del returned to my table, I said, "I'm ready to leave. Can we go ahead and cut the cake?"

He studied my face. "Are you okay? I don't think Janae's mother will cause any more problems."

I rubbed my guitar pick in my pocket. "Do you really care if I'm okay or not?"

Del eased into the chair opposite me. "Don't accuse me of not caring about you. The band hired me to manage its business side, and that's what I do. I think I've done a good job. It's not just you, as you keep reminding me." He opened his arms wide. "This is your night, and you're sitting here brooding. No one is coming over here because we can feel your vibe. You don't want to be bothered because you don't like these parties, but can you at least pretend to enjoy this one for your brothers?"

I snorted. "I'm upset with some of my brothers and finding it hard to fake it."

"What happened?"

"I'd rather not go into it. I can smile for the cameras. Can you just get everyone together?"

Del tightened his jaw and walked away.

Within ten minutes, we were all gathered by a massive red, black, and white cake. Janae stood beside me, and I held a possessive hand on her lower back. She was mine for now, and I would play my role. I smiled and laughed as I listened to the toasts of my friends and crew.

When it was Janae's turn, she looked at me. "I first want to thank Landon. He's been a trooper this whole tour, doing whatever we needed him to do when all he wants to do is play that guitar." Everyone cheered. "I love you to absolute pieces and don't know how I would've made it through these last few weeks without you." She stood on tiptoe and angled her face toward mine.

I pressed my lips against hers and whispered, "Love you more."

Janae smiled at me, her eyes tearing with relief. She turned back to the group and thanked some other people. I had no idea what else was said because the gnawing started impeding my hearing and vision. I declined the cake and champagne.

I kissed her forehead as the toast ended. "Enjoy. I need to go. See you at your place."

She tugged on the bottom of my shirt. "What happened with my mother?"

"I got rid of her. I won't let anyone hurt you as long as I'm around."

"Thank you, baby. I'm glad you got the hint that I didn't want to see her. I planned to avoid her all night. I'll tell you later what happened between her and me." Janae hugged me. "I love you so much. If you go to sleep, I'm waking you up once I get home."

"I'll be up," I promised. I caught a glimpse of Cedrick walking toward the restroom. "I need to use the bathroom and then I'm out."

Janae walked in the opposite direction as I headed toward him. When I walked in, I checked the stalls from the door. No one was in there except Cedrick and me.

"What did you give Janae so she could perform?"

Cedrick zipped up his pants and walked to the sink to wash his hands. "Is that why you've been sitting alone all night? She's fine. She's not intoxicated. We had a good show. Move on."

"Since when did we become the band who'll do anything to perform?"

"Since we have the number one song in the country and the expectations for us are at an all-time high. Janae would've never forgiven herself, and neither would the world if she didn't get on that stage. You can hide in the corners and pull your head down when your nerves get the best of you. She's front and center." He hit his hand. "She can't do what you do. You've always turned a blind eye when any one of us used to get on the stage. We've all popped pills and gotten wasted. There were times I needed something to perform to take up your slack." He backed up and raised his hands. "And guess what? We're fine."

"She's not you. This is a slippery slope for her. Can't you see that?"

"You sleep with her. Is she fiending every night for drugs? Is she sneaking out trying to find the nearest dealer?"

I shook my head. "She was like an addict before the show. You were there. I've never seen you or the guys act like that."

"Because we always have something just in case. I don't know what her mother said to her, but it did her in, right before the biggest night of her life." He moved closer to me. "Please, let it go. We just finished the tour to rave reviews, and our album is the next big thing. Can you just chill for once and not overthink this?"

"The Hollow Bones will never sell out. The Hollow Bones will always put its members above any money or opportunity. The Hollow Bones never make a decision unless we all agree." I stared into the eyes of my best friend. "You said you would never allow Janae to destroy the band. Well, guess what? You just did by giving her drugs. I'm out."

"Landon." He grabbed my arm, and I shook him off.

"Soar as high as you fucking want, and you can keep the name. The Hollow Bones isn't my band anymore."

I pushed the door and walked past everyone as I strode out to the waiting car. I kept my head tucked between my legs to keep the panic away on the ride to her place.

JUNE 16

I waited up for Janae so we could talk. She finally dragged herself home and crashed into bed with me, too tired to do anything but strip and sleep. I held her close, unable to drift off. I then packed my stuff, which didn't take long, since I kept my belongings neat and tidy. I had a flight back to New York in a few hours, and I had no intention of missing it.

It was after three in the afternoon and I'd just moved my belongings to her living room when she walked in wearing one of my shirts, wiping sleep from her eyes. I was fully dressed and wearing shoes. She frowned. "What are you doing? Our flight to New York isn't until tomorrow."

"I waited all night to talk to you, but you were too sleepy. I didn't want to just up and go without a word. You deserve more than my ghosting you, so I've been waiting for you to wake up."

"You're leaving?" she squeaked.

"Yeah. I need some space." I folded my arms. "What did you use last night?"

"I... I..." Her hands fell by her side. "I won't use anything again. This isn't a line or a plea. On that stage, I had an epiphany that the music was enough. That having you was enough to cope with whatever strikes. It's the truth."

"And the last time wasn't the truth?"

She moved to me. "Last night was so different."

"Yes, it was. You involved my friends. You asked Cedrick to give you drugs like I wasn't there. Then you lied to my face. Everyone did. I thought you managed to do the show without anything until the after-party, when I could tell you took something. You were too mellow and avoided me. What did you take?" Something compelled me to ask, though I didn't know if it would affect my decision to leave or not.

Janae touched my arms, and my resistance wavered. "Xanax. Just a stronger dose than what doctors prescribe. You know I haven't been able to sleep. I was determined not to use anything. I finally had control over my nerves until my mother messed me up all over again." Her voice broke. "I wanted to hurt myself…"

She sat on the sofa, lifting the hem of the oversized T-shirt she loved to sleep in. Spreading her legs slightly, she pointed to her inner thigh. "These are my old scars, the ones I covered with my sunburst tattoo."

My breath caught as she traced the ink with her fingers, her expression distant, lost in a place I couldn't reach.

"Yesterday, I grabbed scissors." Her voice was barely above a whisper. "I wanted to cut myself." She inhaled sharply. "I didn't… because I knew you'd ask about it. I knew you'd notice." Her eyes met mine, glassy with unshed tears. "Almost all of my tattoos hide scars."

The confession hit me like a blow to the chest.

"The pain was so bad after my mother left my dressing room," she continued. "I thought I needed something to get on that stage."

Her words hung between us, heavy and raw. I clenched my fists, overwhelmed by the depth of what she had just admitted, by the pain she had carried alone.

As I tried to digest all that, she moved to me and said, "Go check on your mother and meet me in Austin next week, please. Dr. K warned me that I would need a break after the tour… that I needed nature. Just come see me and let me love on you, and I can explain the ugly of me."

I shook my head. "You already showed me your ugly side. I poured my heart out to you in front of everyone, and you shattered it in pieces like I didn't matter. My parents made me feel that way. Other people have made me feel that way. I hate myself for forgetting what I already knew, that you wouldn't need me sooner or later. I hate myself for getting caught up in your web. I believed you would never make me feel that way."

Her head snapped back. "My web? I didn't trap you."

I hit my chest. "I meant *I* knew better. I knew how much I was attracted to you and how much I wanted you to pay attention to me. And when you did, I thought I won the lottery, and whatever doubts I had about you faded whenever you looked at me or kissed me."

"So you think I tricked you… that my love for you isn't real?"

"I believe you love me, and I'll always love you."

She unfolded my arms and slid under them. "Then let's just work it out."

I closed my eyes briefly. "Love isn't always enough. I'm not the man for you. Performing is in your blood, and as much as I think it's too much for you, I can't expect you to give up your dream. You might not use anything again for a long time, and then something will trigger you. I can't watch you go through that again because I'm always going to deny what you think you need. I can't."

Janae gripped my wrists, but my hands remained fists. "I'm not going to go through that again."

"Until something else triggers you."

"Do you know how it felt to see you melt down in front of me? I actually thought you might die for a second, and I'd never been more frightened in my life. You rejected me that night, embarrassed for me to see you like that, and I never once thought about leaving you. Not once. Because I took some stupid pills that your friends take too, you can't forgive me, and we're done?"

"Exactly why I said I'm not the man for you. You asked me to be your moral compass for a reason. You need someone like Cedrick, or any other man who can handle their emotions better than I can, or who doesn't care if you use drugs, because to men like them, it's not a big deal. And for me, it's a deal-breaker."

"I don't want another man. I want you," she implored me. "I'm sorry... I'm sorry."

I pulled her into me, holding her. "Knowing you could hurt yourself makes me want to stay and fix it, but that's not up to me. You told me you didn't need a knight, and you really don't." I kissed her neck one last time. "I need to go before I miss my flight."

She pushed back from me. "You need everything on your terms. You decided when we made love for the first time and when we became a couple. I asked you about a future, and you refused to say anything until yesterday, when you dangled it like a carrot to get me to do what you wanted." Her voice wavered, but the fire in her eyes didn't. "Now you're upset because last night, you couldn't steer things the way you wanted. And instead of talking to me, you just *walk away?*"

Janae threw her arm toward the bedroom, her breath coming fast. "I almost ended this *days ago* because I knew, sooner or later, I'd do something you couldn't forgive. And you—" her voice cracked before she forced herself to go on, "—you made me feel like that was impossible. Like you would *always* love me."

She let out a humorless laugh, swiping at her face. "I was a fool. You never loved me. You wanted me until you didn't."

Every word was a stab through the heart, and if I contradicted anything she said, my actions right then would negate them. There was nothing left to say. I stood.

"Get the hell out of my house." Janae stalked to the door and opened it. Photographers stood just beyond the gate, cameras lifted, fingers clicking away as reporters spoke urgently into their mics. The sight of them had her slamming the door shut and falling against it. "Nope. You can't go out there."

My stomach lurched. "How many are out there?"

She marched to me and jabbed my chest hard. "You're going to pretend we're good. Do you hear me? If the world knows we broke up the day after the last stop, then they'll believe we tricked them to boost ticket sales and our song. They'll hate me but still love you. We don't have to talk, but you better rebook your flight, because your ass isn't going anywhere right now. Especially when your face shows every emotion of what just happened between us."

I turned to the window and peeked through the blinds. A swarm of paparazzi and fans crowded outside the complex's gate, cameras ready, waiting for us to step outside. When I looked back, Janae stood with her arms crossed, her foot tapping in rapid succession. Her glare reminded me of a wife who'd had enough of her husband's shit.

I looked up at the ceiling and then back at her. Help me. I wanted to be that husband.

Before I could talk myself out of it, I blurted, "Let's go to Austin."

Her foot stilled. "What?"

"Throw some pants on, take a quick shower, and let's go. I'll buy whatever else you need. We'll take your car. Not up for crowds at the airport."

She narrowed her eyes. "You're serious? Now you want to be impulsive?"

"I don't want to be accused of always calling the shots. So, if you don't want to go because I suggested it, then we don't have to."

Her gaze turned ice cold. "I don't want to go anywhere with you. I'm done with this relationship."

A slow, deep gnawing spread through my chest. I shoved my hands into my pockets, resisting the urge to reach for her. "Okay. I'll sit on the balcony, play my guitar, and catch a flight late tonight."

Janae's lip curled in disgust, and she turned on her heel, stomping into her bedroom and slamming the door so hard the walls shuddered.

I exhaled, peeking out the window again. The crowd outside had doubled. Cameras flashed. Reporters clutched their mics, already practicing whatever story they'd spin from the first sight of us. Could I just walk out, wave like a politician, slip into some car, and disappear?

Probably.

But I had a feeling Janae would murder me in my sleep if I left without playing along.

The sound of running water filled the apartment.

I blinked, momentarily surprised.

She was actually going.

A few minutes later, the door swung open.

Janae wore leggings and a fitted hoodie, sleek and effortless, the kind of look that let her move through the world unnoticed when she wanted to. Her damp curls peeked out from under the cap she slid on as she yanked open the closet, pulling out sneakers.

"It's a twenty-three-hour drive, and I'm not touching the wheel." She still wouldn't look at me as she grabbed her purse. "And I'm going on the most expensive shopping spree in Austin that your wallet can afford."

I arched a brow. "Anything else?"

"Yeah. Don't say one word to me until we get to my house."

Why did this woman vex me so?

We weren't good for each other. Or maybe we were perfect.

I'd spent all night convincing myself to leave. Now, we were about to spend almost an entire day together, locked in a car with nothing but silence and miles of open road.

My head spun from the emotional whiplash. My body ached from exhaustion and nerves. My heart?

My heart was damn near soaring.

Janae must have caught my expression because she scowled. "Get that smile off your face. You don't get to be happy after ruining my morning with your bullshit." She stormed past me toward the stairs.

I bit my lip, fighting the grin I hadn't even realized I was wearing. Grabbing my bags, I followed her downstairs to the garage where she kept her pewter G-Wagon.

As soon as we pulled out, the paparazzi surged forward. Janae flashed them a dazzling smile, waving like nothing in the world was wrong. I followed her lead, raising my hand in a half-wave, my own grin practiced but effortless.

And just like that, we hit the road.

Our real journey had begun.

CHAPTER THIRTY-SEVEN

janae

AUSTIN
JUNE 17

"TURN THIS CORNER AND GO up the hill. My house is on the end," I directed Landon. The beautiful hills and winding roads trickled calmness over my still-angry heart. We'd been in this car together for a little over twenty-seven hours, with traffic, restroom, food, and gas stops. We'd driven without a night in a hotel.

"I finally get to hear your voice again." He smiled.

I poked his cheek. "Bet you didn't like the quiet this time."

"I didn't. I've grown accustomed to your noises and your mouth." He squinted. "Is that your house?"

I nodded, suddenly self-conscious. Landon came from money, and my ranch-style home was nestled in the woods of Austin. I was proud of this house that a poor Black girl from the Third Ward had chosen on her own. No one had seen it but me and the management team, who'd kept it up in my absence.

"This is nice," he said as he pulled into the driveway. "Can't wait to see inside."

"You like it?" I asked, pleased with his smile. "Never know with a city boy like you."

He tilted his head. "I should've agreed to come here with you when you first asked. I feel the peace already. I needed this, too."

The house had been aired out and fully stocked after I placed a call on the way here. The front door opened to a large living space, and from the entrance, you could see the courtyard and the woods beyond. Landon seemed immediately drawn to the twilight sky, walking across the room and out to the courtyard, where he stared at the stars.

"I can even see Mercury." He pointed in the distance behind the peeking full moon, sounding like an excited boy. "Austin was the first city I remembered seeing a sparkling sky in where I could also identify planets with the naked eye."

Watching him admire the galaxy, I wanted to jump up and down. Austin had been the right decision for us. I joined him in the courtyard. It had been designed with a fireplace in the corner for cold nights and was partially blocked from the sun on hot days. "This is my favorite part of the house and the reason I bought it."

He wrapped his arms around me and tucked his head near my ear. "You did good. I would've definitely helped you keep this if you couldn't afford to anymore."

I bumped my head slightly against his chest. "You can't talk like we this couple... just to take it back tomorrow because something I do upsets you. I'm human, and I'll make mistakes, just like you will."

Landon's arms tightened around me. "Then let's use this time to decide if we can be together or not. There are no cameras, no band, no tour staff, and no fans. Just you. Just me."

I tilted my head to see his handsome face. "That's all I ever wanted, a chance to show you all I am, because I can only be me."

"And I've come to the realization I can be a better me." Landon suddenly picked me up and tossed me over his shoulder. I squealed in surprise as he carried me back inside. "Where's your bedroom? We need to shower and then sleep. I'm exhausted."

"I'm still mad at you. Put me down." I actually loved the way he handled me, though I pretended to be bothered. "I'm not tired. I don't want to go to bed."

"Then watch me sleep." He pushed open the double doors to the primary bedroom and placed me on my feet in the bathroom. "Is your shower voice controlled?"

"No. It's just like my shower in my condo, Mr. Bougie."

Landon flipped the nozzles on, and the four showerheads sprayed water. He tugged me to him by my wrist. "Take your anger out on me in the shower."

Unwilling to give in to him, though my body yearned for his, I quirked a brow and touched his hair.

He grinned before he pulled off his shirt, reminding me why he'd become known as one of the hottest men in the country.

"I'm still trying to understand why you've been hiding all this." I reached for the button on his pants.

He leaned down and captured my lips. His tongue snaked inside my mouth, and we deeply kissed as he pushed down my leggings. Landon broke the kiss and replied, "Because it's only for you."

"Perfect answer." I removed my shoes and leggings and attempted to flee to my bedroom, but his strong arm pulled me back.

"Take off all your clothes right here," he demanded.

"What if I say no?"

He responded by leaning against the doorjamb, staring into my eyes. I couldn't look away, so I did exactly what he instructed. His dark gaze heated every inch of my body as I slowly lifted my hoodie over my body and tossed it on the floor.

"And those," he said, staring at my panties.

I stepped out of them seductively, longing for whatever he had in store for me.

"Beautiful." Landon dropped his pants and boxer briefs to the floor, and I smiled back at him.

I whistled. "Sexy as fuck."

He chuckled as he backed into the hot and steamy shower, taking me with him. The water warmed my body, and the tension in my muscles lessened. Sighing, I curved my arms around his neck, pressing my breasts against his chest, loving the feel of my soft fullness on his hardness. Landon lowered his head and brushed his lips over mine, opening my mouth using his tongue. I relished his sweet taste and the roughness of his stubble on my cheeks. Then he turned me around, pushed me up on the marble wall, and lifted my leg. He thrust deep inside as I placed my cheek on the marble, screaming with pleasure as he pounded into me over and over. No one had been able to excite me like this man.

The shower rained over us as he thrust in and out, and just as I was about to reach the pinnacle of my existence, Landon stopped moving. "Had enough? Still mad?"

I hit the tiles. The games he played with my body. "Have *you* had enough? Cuz I can do this all night, and you better keep up."

"I know." He grinned devilishly. He began to pump slowly. "Still mad?"

"Hmm... mmm."

"Show me." He kissed under my ear while still moving in and out of me.

I pushed Landon down on the bench in the shower to climb on top of him and slide down his thick pole.

And I took every bit of my anger out on him.

JUNE 18

The following afternoon, I awakened before Landon and turned on my phone. I had several missed texts and calls from the guys and Frankie. I eased out of bed, careful to not wake Landon, and sat on my sofa in the living area. My head throbbed as I scrolled through the texts.

I called Frankie. "Hey... is Cedrick with you?"

"No."

"Good, because I didn't want to talk to him before I've talked to Landon. Did Landon just up and quit Hollow Bones? Brian sent me a text begging Landon to call him."

"From what I understand, Landon quit the band because he believes Cedrick gave you drugs. And he disappeared and hasn't answered his phone since. I assume Landon is with you, or we would've heard from you by now."

"He is. We're in Austin, and he didn't tell me he left the band."

"Of course he didn't. Landon is so afraid to lose you that he'd rather take out his anger on everyone but the one person he should be mad at. Cedrick is pissed and not talking to me. The rest of the guys don't know what to do because they were supposed to head back to Harlem and finish the album. But hey, as long as you and Landon are all hugged up while all hell has broken everywhere else, do you."

My temples pounded viciously. "Not that I owe you an explanation, but Landon was planning to leave me too, and he would've had the paparazzi not been in front of my door. We came here to get away from it all and work through all of this. I'll figure something out to get them back together. He can't break up the band because of me. The Hollow Bones is his heart."

"Cedrick couldn't sleep, worried about Landon and trying to find out where you and he had gone. He's hurting, and he didn't do anything to deserve Landon's anger. I told you not to put Cedrick in the middle. But you had to have what you wanted and didn't care how Landon or anyone else felt."

Her tone grated on my nerves and added to my migraine. "I don't need to hear this. I told you until you know what I've been through, you don't have the right to judge me."

"Then tell me what made you act like that. Huh? We're supposed to be friends. What did your mother say to you, and why did Del escort her out?"

"We are friends, but I need to tell Landon before I tell anyone else. Be mad, or don't. I'll explain to you later. Just tell Cedrick I'm sorry, and I'll fix it." I hung up and rocked in place. I had to find a way to make things right for Landon and The Hollow Bones.

I pushed up from the sofa and decided to cook a late breakfast to keep my mind and hands occupied. We needed a hearty meal anyway. Landon wanted to hike around the nearby trail and Lake Travis, and I would use that time to talk about the band.

I had just finished setting the table with poached eggs, cheese grits, bacon, and toast when a shirtless Landon walked in. He glanced at the spread with hesitation before patting my ass. "Smells good." He went to the refrigerator. "Orange juice?"

"On the table. Don't worry, I'm boiling a couple of eggs for you."

He nodded and pulled me away from the stove. "Sit. You're still restless. Probably only slept a couple of hours."

"I'm good." *Three.* I'd slept three. We had more important things to discuss than my sleeping habits.

"Humor me." Landon cocked a brow and pulled out the chair for me, then waited until I sat. He sat beside me and picked up the platter of grits. "I'll wash the dishes."

"Thank you."

"No, thank you for the breakfast." He reached for my plate and added grits. His fresh scent wafted over the table.

"How often do you shower a day when I'm not around?"

"Several times when I'm at home." He shrugged and picked up a piece of bacon.

"If you can't, does that bug you out?"

"It was worse when I was younger. Now I can handle it. As long as I can take a shower before I sleep, I can deal. I use soap and oils that don't dry out my skin. Does it bother you?"

Though I had no appetite, I forced myself to take a bite of grits. "A good-smelling man will never bother me. Does it bother you that I usually take one shower and two on days when I have time?"

"No. I love your natural scent." He frowned. "Okay, I do want you to take a shower after you've been out all day and before you get in bed with me."

"I do take a shower when I get home."

"If you're out real late, you don't, and then want to be up under me." He wrinkled his nose.

I slapped his shoulder. "Why didn't you tell me that bothers you?"

"You're mean when you're sleepy and can't rest. I'm trying to stay alive." He snickered.

"I'm sleepy a lot."

Landon got up to retrieve his eggs and put them on his plate. "I know."

"Is that why you want me to be quiet with you, so I won't be mean to you?"

His eyes met mine. "No. I do that to take care of you. I want to take care of you. I want to be enough."

"You *are* enough."

"I wasn't Saturday night," he retorted.

I picked up my cell. "Is that why you left Hollow Bones? Everyone has been blowing up my cell because you refuse to answer yours."

He finished chewing. "It's not your business."

"You left because of me. It *is* my business."

Landon wiped his mouth with a napkin. "I left the band because Cedrick's decision was more than about you. He cared more about the show than you and me. He knows me better than anyone else, knows how I feel about you and drugs. He should've walked away from you, no matter how much you begged him."

"Brian gave me the Xanax. Not Cedrick," I admitted. "Cedrick didn't make the decision."

Landon's eyes widened, and then he nodded slowly. "Oh, I should've figured Brian couldn't resist you. He's been crushing on you this whole time. He wanted to swoop in and rescue you. Well, it's a good thing I quit the band and not just Cedrick."

Placing my hand on top of his, I reassured him, "Brian doesn't like me like that. He wanted to help."

Landon glared at me so hard I removed my hand.

He picked up his fork. "Finish your food so we can get out of here. Please."

"Landon, they're your brothers. You have to fix it with them."

"This trip is about you and me. I don't want to talk about Hollow Bones or anything else but our relationship."

"Why do you even want to try with me when you can't forgive them?"

Some of the indignant anger in his eyes slipped. "You told me you wanted to share everything with me, and I want to do the same because no one has ever made me feel safe enough to do that. I'm glad those people were camped outside, or I would have made the biggest mistake of my life. I believe you're worth losing everything, and I need to see if I'm right." He pushed my plate closer to me. "Please eat so we can explore without you passing out because of exhaustion. We have plenty of time to hash out anything we need to."

The hope in his expression settled my migraine and stirred my appetite.

CHAPTER
THIRTY-EIGHT
landon

JUNE 25

DURING THE WEEK THAT WE spent together in Texas, we were mostly silent together, an unspoken agreement to allow the last three months to fade into the background. Austin became our reset, a place to relax, regroup, and recalibrate before treading on the parts of us that could destroy what we both wanted — a true and forever love.

We'd been hiking in the heat for the last three hours. Today's walk had been tough yet exhilarating at the same time. I needed nature to help me breathe. To help me see the road ahead. Would the road be a lonely one, or would it be full of love, laughter, and happiness?

I held Janae's hand for most of the hike. She tripped and stumbled several times, clearly unused to walking across rugged land. I'd expected her to complain or refuse at some point, but she'd suggested doing short hikes every day. I'd told her I often took solo trips to nearby cities and states to hike and bike-ride to decompress. We both agreed nature made everything simple again.

Whenever I thought of Cedrick and Brian, I had a burst of energy to continue walking and dragged Janae behind me. I needed to work through my hurt and explain myself to her. The last thing I wanted was for her to add guilt that she'd broken up The Hollow Bones to whatever else she carried on her shoulders.

"I kept trying to figure out how your body looks like it does. I should've realized you rode bikes and walked. Funny how I used to see you. It's so not like you are," she said, panting as she rested against a tree trunk.

I scanned the path ahead and then looked at her. "Funny… like I'm someone you used to make fun of?"

Janae frowned. "What? I would never and have never made fun of you, even when I only saw you as a nerdy guitar player. Why would you say that?"

"Because girls like you in high school used to make fun of me." I started walking again, moving low-hanging branches out of her way as she followed. A colorful butterfly flitted around us.

"Woah." I recoiled and backed up against Janae, who started laughing.

"Don't tell me Mr. Love and One with Nature is scared of butterflies?" She snickered.

"I'm not scared. They're just gross." I scanned the area for the insect that appeared to float above a bush.

"How are they gross?" she asked, still smirking.

"Keep walking, please, since it doesn't look like it plans to move anytime soon." I pulled her by her wrist, and she resisted.

"I love butterflies. They are so majestic and beautiful."

"Yet still a gross caterpillar in the middle. That's all I can see."

Janae shook her head. "If you can only see how she started and not where she ended, you're missing the whole point." She moved closer to the bush to inspect the butterfly. "This is a tiger swallowtail. See the blue on the ends?"

"When you told me you loved butterflies, I thought it was on some poetic, flowy dress type of vibe. You really study this."

"I wouldn't say study. I just believe their existence is proof that we are meant to change and transform." She glanced over her shoulder at me. This Janae was still and focused. "It's why I have butterfly tattoos. Their growth from something ugly and gross to beautiful and mystical fascinates me. It means something special when they fly around you."

"Okay. Why did that butterfly fly around us?" I nudged her shoulder.

"Butterflies can reflect your inner self." She placed her hands on her hips and squinted at me. "You've been walking around all these years with all of this hurt inside of you, hiding who you are from the world. Maybe you're finally ready to show me, the type of girl you swore wouldn't give you the time of day, who you are."

I scoffed, shaking my head. "Trust me, you wouldn't have looked twice. No one really did except my teachers, who loved me. I could disappear in my music and spend my lunch in the band room learning how to play any instrument my teacher allowed me to touch."

"Why the guitar?"

I exhaled, letting my fingers graze the pick in my pocket. "My parents wanted me to learn the instruments they loved so bad. I was naturally drawn to the guitar. I could control how I wanted it to sound more than any other instrument. I felt seen whenever I played, whether anyone was watching or not."

Janae tugged on the hem of my shirt and made me look down at her. "You're so striking, though. I can't imagine no one noticed you then."

My gaze followed her hand, and I let out a short laugh. "I've gained muscle and paid enough attention to hide my geekiness, as you were so happy to point out at the gala. You remember, the one where you didn't even remember my name?" I tilted my head, studying her. "Would you have noticed me if you didn't try to run away that night? Would you be more into Cedrick or Brian or the other guys if you hadn't bumped into me?"

She hugged my waist. "How can I possibly answer that? Once we locked eyes that night, no one else in The Hollow Bones, or any other man, mattered. I noticed your staring at me because I kept staring at you, wondering why I never really *saw* you." She rested her chin against my chest and gazed up at me. "We're here now because, call it fate or serendipity, we noticed each other when we were ready for each other."

Her soft smile warmed my heart. "That weekend, I didn't care that you froze up whenever I touched you unexpectedly or that you have to position yourself on the same side of the stage. That you wore your hat all the time, or you have to hold on to that pick when you become uncomfortable, which seems to be every single day whenever it's not just you and me or the guys. It doesn't even scare me away that you have panic attacks and that eye contact is a challenge for you unless you're looking at me. I want to be with you, Landon. I love you."

I grinned pulling her closer. "I swear you make me feel like the month of October. All chill and cozy."

Janae laughed as she tapped my chest. "Yet you were ready to leave me."

"Just because I was going to leave you didn't mean I wanted to. It took all my power to not break down in front of you. I was afraid I wouldn't return to New York in one piece. As soon as you slammed the door and said I couldn't leave, I was so blissfully happy." I held her face in my hands, my thumbs caressing the softness of her cheek. "You can't use ever again. This isn't my trying to control your life or tell you what to do. I can't be with a woman who uses drugs or alcohol. I grew up with a drunk and physically abusive man and watched my mother get hit. My father has accomplished more than most musicians will ever do, and all I can see is wasted talent. I can't be my mother to you."

Her eyes teared up. "An apology can never be enough for what I put you through in L.A."

"Guess this is where I really talk about me." I pulled off my backpack and took out two bottles of water and a blanket to spread on the grass. I rested my back on the trunk of a large tree and patted the space between my legs for Janae to sit. We faced the serene Lake Travis, only a few feet away. The shade of the large tree kept the sun bearable.

"My earliest memory of my mother is a happy one. I was three, and she held my hand to help me play the piano. What I first remember about my father was his slapping her when I was five. They were arguing about me. I don't know why. I just remember that he smacked her across the face, and she picked me up and ran to my bedroom and locked us in there. He banged on the door, furious at first, and then he started apologizing. He didn't hit her often. I can only recall three times, but there was always that threat when he started drinking. My father used to promise us that he could handle his alcohol. I didn't allow him to hug me until I was seven. Maybe because I only trusted my mother's touch, or maybe because I was afraid of him." I focused on the way her fingers traced slow patterns on her knees.

"Did he hit you, too?" Janae asked quietly.

"More like slam me against the wall when I was sixteen." The words came easier than I expected. Maybe it was this place, this moment, that made it bearable to say out loud. "I think he believed I was too fragile to hit, and my mother might have killed him if he had. I didn't speak unless I was around the two of them, and I cried whenever my mother left me for too long. I remember crawling under the table at school when children teased me or when there was too much going on around me. My mother refused to get me any help because her son was perfect. My father was simply ashamed of me and let her deal with me."

I spoke about my childhood like it wasn't my own. This space in the middle of the woods in Austin had allowed me to detach from my emotions. Maybe it was the butterfly.

Janae laced our fingers together. "What happened when you were sixteen?"

I let out a slow breath. "I worked hard to finish school by my junior year to focus on my music. I never fit in at school, so prom, graduation, parties, and all the other rites of passage every teenager wanted, I didn't. I landed an audition at Juilliard. I was proud that I was good enough to even be considered. I practiced my guitar night and day, preparing for my big moment. Two nights before my audition, my parents informed me that they'd used their connections to change up my audition to play either the piano or the trumpet."

"Wait… you hadn't even practiced on those instruments, and they expected you to succeed?"

"Not a brag. I'm so good with the trumpet and the piano that I didn't need to spend hours practicing. My parents knew that." I swallowed hard. "To spite them, I purposely missed notes on the trumpet. I didn't know my father had access to my audition tapes. When he came home from work, he barged into my room and pinned me to the wall with his fists. He yelled how he was ashamed that I was his son, and he wanted me out of his house. My father called me a sick fuck."

Janae let out a soft gasp and squeezed my hand. "The smell of alcohol was on his breath, and he kept knocking me against the wall as he shouted that I'd purposely ruined the audition. The walls started closing in, and I couldn't breathe. I must have blacked out, because the next thing I remember is my mother crying and turning on the shower in my bathroom, telling me I needed to clean myself."

I felt her press her face into my shoulder, breathing unsteadily.

"My father was more of an emotional abuser than a physical one, but when he lost control, he always felt guilty afterward. He'd promise me and my mother the world, swearing things would be different. That whole cycle of domestic violence is real." I pressed the side of my head to hers, grounding myself in her presence. "After he put his hands on me that night, he stood outside my door, apologizing over and over, saying he'd make it up to me. But I didn't believe him. I couldn't. I knew I couldn't stay."

"So you left." Janae's voice was quiet, but her grip on my hand tightened.

"I packed a few clothes, grabbed my guitar, and used what little savings I had from my allowance and the music contests I'd won to survive. Cheap hotels and hostels at first, then abandoned buildings and homeless shelters when the money ran low. I played my guitar in subway stations and on the streets of Times Square for food. I recorded myself on my phone, hoping YouTube would be my way out. I told myself I'd apply to other music programs, but I had to make it through each day first."

I exhaled, staring out at the lake. "The irony? Running away forced me to become everything my parents never thought I could be. I had to communicate more, make decisions, perform in front of strangers. I had no one but myself to rely on."

Janae traced circles on my forearm, waiting for me to continue.

"I was on the streets for about two months before Cedrick saw my videos. He sought me out. He was the first person who only saw my talent. Nothing else. No baggage, no bullshit. Just my music. He convinced his parents to let me stay with them, and the only condition was that I had to tell my parents where I was. I did, and they were just relieved I was alive. For once, they stopped trying to mold me into something I wasn't."

I swallowed, finally looking back at Janae. "I never lived with my parents again. I kept in touch, visited when they asked, but I never let them into my space. Until now, I hadn't even invited them to my brownstone. Not once."

Her thumb brushed against my knuckles. "That's a lot to carry on your own, baby."

I nodded, pressing a kiss to her temple. "Maybe I don't have to anymore."

A weeping Janae pulled back, studying my face through blurry eyes. "All I wanted was to meet them because I pictured them as this power couple, deeply in love, raising their immensely talented son. It was this perfect vision I had for us."

I exhaled slowly. "You asked if my thoughts on marriage and family had changed, and I told you I didn't know. And I didn't. Before you, I never let myself imagine a life with someone long-term. I had one girlfriend before you, if you could even call her that. Dating was fine. Sex was easy. But letting someone all the way in?" I shook my head. "I never thought it was something I'd be capable of."

Her fingers traced over my wrist, waiting.

"Then you came along. Relentless. Stubborn as hell. A gnat that wouldn't leave me alone until I had no choice but to love you."

Janae's scowl was instant. "A gnat? Really? Of all things, you compare me to a tiny, annoying bug?"

I chuckled, pulling her against me and pressing a kiss to her cheek. "I also thought you were an elusive butterfly. Too wild and free for me to ever really catch."

Her lips curled into a slow smile. "Much better." She cupped my face. "I want to love you through it all."

I let out a breath, my forehead pressing against hers. "I believe you. That's why I'm willing to risk everything for you."

She sighed. "You don't have to risk anything, Landon."

Not ready to talk about The Hollow Bones, I held up a hand. "Just us, right now. While we're here."

She blew a raspberry. "Since we're talking about just us, have you ever been to therapy? Ever been diagnosed?"

I stiffened slightly, the easy moment shifting into something heavier. "No."

Janae wasn't deterred. "You've always just guessed at what you might be dealing with?"

I ran a hand through my hair. "I figured I had anxiety because of the panic attacks. Thought maybe I was autistic at one point, but I don't fit that category either. At least not now. I have outgrown some of the things I used to do."

Her voice softened. "Maybe it is time to stop guessing and actually get answers. You grew up in a violent home, Landon."

A muscle in my jaw ticked. "I'm good."

She studied me for a moment, searching my face, but I wasn't ready for that conversation. Not yet.

I stood abruptly, reaching for her hand. "It's a long walk back, and I want to try that Mexican place on the other side of the lake."

"We're done talking?" Janae frowned.

"For now. I have no plans except to be here with you for the next few days. We have time to talk about everything."

My words seemed to satisfy her, because she allowed me to take her hand and lead her out of the woods.

JULY 3

"I swear your pettiness knows no bounds," I grumbled as I steered the pontoon boat, built for twelve, toward the middle of Lake Travis. Janae had insisted we spend the day on the water, swimming and making music just for fun. My guitar rested across two cushioned seats, and the lunch she had packed sat beside her. "Why are we driving this ourselves when we could've rented a yacht with a captain? I told you before the tour started that I don't do water."

"Again, how do you love nature and not vibe with water?"

"I'm from Brooklyn," I replied flatly.

"Can you even swim?"

"Of course," I said, insulted at the question.

She smirked. "I wanted you to steer the boat so I could have access to your body the whole time."

I chuckled, prying her hands from my arm and moving them higher. "I want to enjoy this day before you wear me out. Let me steer this boat while I still have energy."

"I can drive too." She reached for the wheel, and I popped her hand lightly.

"Hey, that hurt," she protested.

"You have many talents. Driving isn't one of them, and I'd like to survive this day."

She rolled her eyes. "How about you take us near that sandbar so we can chill for a bit?" She pointed toward a small patch of land near the edge of the greenish-blue lake. We were mostly alone in this section of the lake, with only two boats floating in the distance. "Then you can tell me about that conversation with your mother this morning… if you actually heard anything."

"You knew exactly what you were doing when you changed in front of me, and then you took your sweet time cooking and packing while wearing that."

"Who, me? In this old thing?" She gestured to the bright pink bikini peeking through her matching mesh cover-up. I had never seen her in a bikini before, and when she pranced around the house this morning, my focus had been shot to hell.

I turned the wheel toward the spot she'd pointed out. "My mother wants me to help her talk to my father about the divorce. I don't see it going well. He has never listened to me, and he still thinks of her as his property."

"Maybe this is her way of trying to get you two to talk," she suggested, lowering her sunglasses and leaning back against the seat, soaking in the sun.

"Maybe." The sounds of the lake and distant chatter settled me, easing me into a conversation I probably wouldn't have had under any other circumstance. "I like it out here. My mind races, but my body is always churning, twisting, gnawing. Since we've been in Austin, I've felt… calm. Until now, I couldn't talk about my family, let alone how their marriage affected me. Even my guitar couldn't make that easier."

"Or maybe you never had anyone you felt safe enough to talk to about them."

I nodded, a small smile tugging at my lips. "I never thought I'd meet someone like you."

She stretched lazily. "Apparently, since we were only supposed to be here a few days, and I heard you tell your mother we're staying until mid-month."

"I'm not ready to deal with everything yet. And I'm also not ready for us to be in separate cities. I've gotten used to you up under me, making it impossible for me to breathe every night."

She smirked. "So what do we do about that?"

I hated that I couldn't see her eyes behind the shades. We had spent all this time together, yet she still hadn't opened up about her mother or what really happened in Los Angeles. I refused to pressure her, but I also knew we couldn't move forward if we didn't confront it.

"I don't know yet," I admitted. "We can start by visiting each other when we go back home and take it from there."

She hesitated. "I think you need time to deal with your parents before I visit."

I met her gaze. "I think you need that same time to deal with your mother and your brother."

Her mouth tightened. "My brother and I will be fine. I don't want to deal with my mother. Maybe not ever."

"Seems like you should," I started, but she immediately whipped off her shades.

"That's not your business, just like Hollow Bones isn't mine."

I raised my hands in surrender. "You're right."

It had been almost three weeks since Los Angeles, and I still hadn't spoken to Del or anyone in the band. Our album was dropping at the end of August, and we were supposed to start promotional shows in two weeks.

"I've been thinking about getting another tattoo while we're here," she said, changing the subject.

"Why? I thought you only got them to cover scars." I quietly assessed her. Was she struggling again and not telling me?

"That's how it started, but it's not the only reason. I actually like how they look on my skin." She rose, running a hand across my chest. "You'd look so good with one. The ink would so eat on your skin. Ever thought about it?"

"Not really. I try to avoid needles at all costs."

She giggled. "Another thing you're scared of."

"Plenty of people hate needles," I muttered.

"Okay, but if you had to get one, what would it be?"

"Hmm… maybe a crescent moon. Something representing the universe."

She grinned. "It would look so sexy on your chest."

I shook my head. "Inside of my wrist. Somewhere I can see it easily. A tattoo on my chest would be for other people to admire."

She wrinkled her nose. "Good point."

"Would you get another butterfly?"

"I don't know. I want something that represents where I am now. Something that represents us."

I nodded. "I like that. You might be the only person who could make me ignore my fear of needles."

She cooed. "So sweet. Love you." She brushed her lips against mine before pulling off her cover-up and diving into the lake.

I stopped the boat, dropping the anchor, and watched her arms move powerfully through the water. She was a strong swimmer. Strong in ways I hadn't even fully understood.

I had judged her for disappearing years ago, for running away from her responsibilities. But I was doing the same thing now. I had broken my word. Not just to The Hollow Bones and Del, but to the people expecting us to show up. I had already missed three engagements. I had turned a blind eye to my band's drinking and drug use but had criticized Janae for the same.

A loud scream snapped me out of my thoughts.

"The fuck?" I ran to the edge, ready to dive in. "What's wrong?"

"Ugh, all these fish are surrounding me!"

"Do they bite?"

"I don't think so. It just feels weird." She swam quickly back to the boat. As soon as she reached it, I grabbed her hand and pulled her in, stepping back as she climbed aboard. Water dripped from her skin, and I peered down at the lake, watching the small, brightly colored fish darting just below the surface.

"Yeah… that's unsettling. Much prefer butterflies." I grabbed a towel and wrapped it around her, resisting the urge to hold her close.

Janae clung to the towel and narrowed her eyes at me as I took another step back. "Seriously, Landon?"

"I mean… those fish were all over you. I'm glad you made fried chicken instead of fish for lunch." I guided her to a seat. "Sorry, Nae, no sex for you out here. You need to get clean first."

She huffed dramatically, flopping into the seat with her arms crossed. "Wow."

I chuckled, grabbing my guitar. "Not until you shower." I started strumming. "Before you get stuck in attitude mode, tell me what song this is."

She shot me a glare. "I'm not playing."

"Suit yourself." I strummed the strings. "People forget that Prince was an otherworldly musician. That Bruno Mars and H.E.R. can kill a guitar just as well as they sing."

Janae leaned forward. "No reason to be jealous of anyone. Your talent is unmatched."

She looked around at the vastness of the lake. "No one knows us out here. Be the you that no one sees. Just play."

For the first time in a long time, I let go.

CHAPTER THIRTY-NINE

janae

JULY 20

WE WERE NEARING THE END of our time in Austin, and soon we would have to decide what came next. For us. For him as a solo artist. For me and my music. Del had been calling, wondering when we would resurface. I had to go back to Los Angeles. Landon needed to figure out what his future looked like.

Most nights, I could not sleep, knowing that before we left here, before we returned to the real world, I had to bare everything to him the way he had to me. No more half-truths. No more hiding.

I watched him sleep. His long lashes curled against his cheeks, and his chest rose and fell in a slow, even rhythm. He was finally getting the rest he needed. Finally at peace after years of warring within himself.

I had never been so drawn to someone. I could spend every second with him and never grow tired of it. For five weeks, we had lived like tourists, trying new restaurants, shopping, and driving around this green oasis of a city in a state known for dry, flat land. We debated everything from politics, TV shows to the top five entertainers of all time and whether New York really was the best city in the U.S. We hid behind shades and hats when we wanted to go unnoticed and took quick selfies with fans when we could not. We even did a pop-up performance of *Baby I'm a Star,* me singing while he killed the guitar.

We made a good team. Onstage. Offstage.

Being together and away from everything had been healing. I slept more. He relaxed more. If we had known every day would feel like this, we probably would have eloped.

Still, I owed him more. He had given me his whole truth, and I had expected him to move past my mistakes without doing the same. He had stood in front of the people who mattered and declared his love for me, and I had dismissed him like a crack addict chasing my next fix.

I could hear Dr. K's voice in my head, sharp and unwavering. *Stop playing the victim. Own your choices. Own the consequences.*

As dawn painted the sky in muted pastels, my mind felt clearer. I stretched, slipped a robe over my naked body, and stepped outside to the courtyard.

I had been so proud when I bought this house. I pictured it filled with friends and family, hosting long dinners, lazy Sunday mornings, and laughter echoing through every room. And yet, I had barely spent any time here. No one had ever visited. The vision I had for this place never came to life.

For a long time, I regretted that Adam never saw this house. Now, I was glad. The only man I would ever have memories of here was Landon.

Austin felt right for him. He blended into the city's pulse effortlessly. Even in public, when fans approached, he never seemed rattled. I wondered if he had ever truly been at home anywhere before this.

I stepped to the edge of the courtyard, surrounded by lush greenery, closed my eyes, and lifted my arms, palms facing the sky. I let my senses take over, just as Landon had taught me on our quiet train rides.

I heard the world move. The chirping of birds. The rustling of leaves. The distant hum of crickets.

I inhaled.

I took in all the things that made me who I was.

My voice. My creativity. The people who truly saw me, The Hollow Bones, my girls, the ones who stayed. My passion. My fight. My love for Landon.

Then I exhaled.

I let go of everything that had tried to break me.

My family's dysfunction. My mother's abuse. The darkness inside me. My self-inflicted wounds. The men who mistreated me. The drugs. The self-doubt.

I did it again. And again.

Each breath stripped away something heavy, peeling back the weight I had carried for too long. For the first time in forever, I felt free.

Better than any high I had ever chased.

"Don't move. A butterfly landed on your hand." Landon's quiet, awed voice broke the silence. I slowly opened my eyes and squinted at my hand.

An orange-and-black butterfly rested on my palm. I whispered, "It's a monarch or a painted lady." I studied the colorful wings longer. "A monarch's color is richer. Thinking this is a monarch."

"I love that you know that." He stepped beside me wearing only boxer briefs.

"Do you know how long I've wanted one to land on me?" I said softly, not wanting to disturb the tiny miracle happening.

"I can't believe it's just sitting there like you're some sort of plant."

"She's reminding me that it's a time of transformation, to do what makes me happy and to follow my passions." Joyful tears trickled down my face. Everything I'd ever been through had led to this very moment with the man standing behind me. "That I am deserving of the life and love that I crave so desperately."

"I hope with me, because I've never seen anything more beautiful in my life."

I nodded. "Right? This one has to go on my next album cover." I lightly touched one of the wings, and the butterfly fluttered away.

His hands curved to my waist as we watched the magical creature return to nature. "I meant you. I have never known anything or anyone more beautiful than you."

Chuckling through my tears, I relaxed against his warm, bare chest. "You insist on making it hard for me to hate you."

"Until I insult you or judge you. Hating me becomes pretty easy then," he teased, and kissed my neck.

"I could never hate you. I love you too much for that." I squeezed his arms and took a deep, readying breath. "I also want you to understand why I fell apart the night of the show in Los Angeles. I appreciate your patience with me and not forcing or demanding for me to talk. I can't let you walk away from me before you know everything." I turned around in his arms and rested my head on his chest.

"I'm here."

Holding on to him, I finally admitted, "The man that my mother brought with her to our show sexually abused me for months, and would've raped me when I was fourteen if my mother hadn't come home early from work. I hadn't seen him again until he walked into my dressing room."

Landon's body stiffened, and his heart beat rapidly beneath my ear. "The man who tried to shake my hand and smiled in my face did that to you?"

I nodded. Regardless of Landon's reaction, I would tell my truth.

He dropped his arms and demanded, "Get in the car. Houston is two hours from here."

"Woah… wait."

"Naw. He did that to you and can't get away with it. There was a reason I kicked him and your mother out of the party."

I laughed and flung my head back.

"Why are you laughing?" He gripped my shoulders.

"I'm just so happy that you believe me without thought. No interrogation or explanation. You just believe me."

"Why wouldn't I?"

"Exactly." I captured his scowling face with my hands. "Look at me. You're not going to jail for that lowlife. I hate him with everything inside of me. He hugged me and smiled backstage like he had amnesia. My skin crawled, and if I could've scrubbed off the layers of skin that he touched, I would've. As much as I would love to see you stomp his ass, I need you here with me, not locked up or broke because he sued you."

Landon's eyes were wild, and he seemed unable to refocus on me as he kept shaking his head. "You haven't seen your mother in years, and she brought him as her date? Does she know what he did to you?"

I let out a bitter laugh. "She knows something happened. She just thinks it was my fault. That I seduced a grown man." I shook my head. "That same tired, disgusting excuse that keeps happening to girls while their mothers refuse to admit that they chose monsters."

Landon cursed loudly and hugged me tightly. "I'm sorry that your mother would do that to you. I don't blame you if you never speak to her again. I just know I better not see that son of a bitch again." He turned his head and spit on the ground. "Sorry. My blood is boiling right now at how she could flaunt that piece of shit around you, and on my dime."

I shut my eyes. His thudding heartbeat and the faint sounds of chirping birds in the nearby woods lulled me into a peaceful existence despite the painful recalling of my past.

"I always knew my mother was a piece of work, but I underestimated just how cruel she could be. I gave her credit for leaving him back then, but when she caught him trying to rush out of my room, she didn't protect me. She attacked us both. She kept hitting me, screaming that I stole everything from her, and my brother had to pull her off me. She ended things with him but never forgave me. From that moment on, she hated me."

I swallowed, forcing myself to keep going. "I started smoking weed and doing whatever drugs I could find just to numb the pain of living in that house. She already preferred my brother over me… I was always too hyper, too mouthy, too much. After what happened, it got worse. Every chance she had, she tore me down. Made me feel like I was nothing. And it didn't matter that I kept my grades up. I went from an A student to barely passing because I stopped showing up to school by senior year."

I let out a soft, bitter chuckle. "I've been through so much just to be standing here with you."

Landon pressed his lips to my forehead and rubbed my back, his touch steadying me. "I'm listening."

I inhaled deeply, grounding myself. "After graduation, I did whatever I had to do to survive. I put up with the worst men just to have a place to sleep. Worked odd jobs, stayed in cheap motels, and prayed that my talent would be enough to save me. When I got discovered at that club in Houston and my career took off at twenty-one, I hadn't dealt with any of it. The trauma. The pain. The fear. I went from being a broke girl from the Third Ward to having everything I ever thought I wanted. But I didn't know how to handle it. I didn't know how to accept love or if I was even worth it. I thought men were shit, but I still didn't know how to be alone."

I lifted my gaze to Landon's, his red-rimmed eyes searching mine. "That's why a part of me struggles to believe you love me. Because you were so quick to leave."

His grip on me tightened, his voice raw. "I get it. How could you believe I love you when I made you feel disposable?" He pulled me into his arms, holding me so tightly I almost couldn't breathe. "I'm sorry, baby. I'm so damn sorry for how I treated you."

"That's not all I need to say." I pulled away from his embrace.

Landon didn't let me go far. He took my hand and pulled me onto his lap on the patio sofa. "Talk."

I hesitated, then met his gaze. "I don't want you here with me if it's because you see me as some helpless, broken woman who needs saving."

His head snapped back. "I don't see you as broken."

"If we're going to be real, I need you to be honest. You love rescuing me. It's like my problems give you something to focus on so you don't have to deal with your own."

Landon exhaled sharply, running a hand through my hair. "I am being honest. I see you as this vibrant, strong woman who doesn't always realize her own strength. Taking care of you isn't about rescuing you. It's who I am. I would slay dragons for you, and I've never been a fighter." His voice dropped. "Cedrick accused me of wanting you to stay helpless so I wouldn't have to face my own issues. Until that night in Los Angeles, I thought he might be right. Seeing you like that…" He shook his head. "It broke me. But I knew I had to be strong enough for the both of us."

I resisted the urge to groan. "That's my point, Landon. That night… that was me. The woman who begged for help because I felt like I was drowning. I'm fierce, I'm a badass, but I also have doubts. I have insecurities. I get stronger every day, but my dark side doesn't just go away."

I took a steadying breath and ripped the Band-Aid off. "I started taking my meds again and didn't tell you at first, because you kept saying how much you love seeing me raw. But the raw me? She abused drugs for years because she didn't understand she had a chemical imbalance. The raw me has been self-destructive in ways I'm still trying to come to terms with."

Landon's jaw tightened, but he stayed quiet as I continued.

"You know I've cut myself, but what you don't know is that I actually attempted suicide when I was twenty-five. I disappeared to get treatment because I was barely hanging on."

Silence stretched between us. Landon sank back into the sofa, his eyes shadowed, his expression unreadable. The weight of my confession settled between us, thick and heavy.

I studied the lines in his forehead, the way his fingers curled against his thighs. Was this too much for a man already carrying his own battles? My issues weren't temporary. They weren't something I could promise would never come back. No butterfly, no amount of love, could erase them entirely.

I shivered, though I wasn't sure if it was the morning air or the fear that I was about to lose him.

"Say something."

His hands warmed my arms as he slowly answered, "I heard rumors about suicide, but your team shut them down. I didn't believe it because… you didn't seem like the type to give up."

"Anyone can give up. Anyone," I said firmly. "I lost everything because of my arrogance and entitlement. No one else was to blame, not my mother, not my ex, not even the industry. I made the choice to have an affair with a powerful man married to an equally powerful woman. My album, the one that was supposed to send me into superstardom, tanked because of their power. My label dropped me. Adam left. Everything crumbled."

I swallowed, pushing through. "That night, when I wanted to end it all, I reached out to my mother and realized she had blocked me. Adam was the only one left. When he didn't pick up, I sent a text. Something vague but final. He got to me before the pills and alcohol did. He saved me but made it clear that after that, we were done in every way except friendship. He helped me get into treatment, and he was there for me until he couldn't be anymore. I'll always have love for him because he supported me when I had nothing. But we weren't a love match. I didn't fully get that until the gala, until I bumped into you and felt something I had never felt before."

Landon absorbed my words, his breathing steadying. He rubbed my arms, his touch grounding me.

His voice was gentle and careful. "Have you felt like that since?"

"No. I have felt low. I have wanted to hurt myself, but not to end things. More as a way to release the pain. Back in Houston, after the rodeo. In New Orleans, after our fight. I was in your bathroom, holding your razor, ready to cut my thigh. But then I thought of you. I thought of how you see me, how you believe in me, even when I can't. And I put it down. In that moment, I knew I never wanted to go back to that place again." I met his gaze. "That is why I finally told the world I have bipolar. I was done hiding from it."

Landon exhaled, as if he had been holding something in. "So, why didn't you tell me you've been on meds? The real reason."

"I wanted to tell you, but I didn't know if you would still love me if you knew I needed meds to keep me from spinning out of control."

I sighed. "You knew about therapy, but therapy alone isn't enough for me. Therapy is like church. You go because you need the message again and again to stay whole. My treatment is the same. It keeps me stable. It keeps me from losing myself completely. Even still, I want to get off meds again one day."

Landon frowned. "I don't see that much of a difference in you."

"That is because you only see the outside. You see what I let you see. What you don't hear are the thoughts, how self-defeating and ugly they can be. It is like the worst things people have ever said about me are stuck on repeat, screaming at me until I can't hear my own voice."

I swallowed hard. "Then there is the wildness, the impulsivity. The meds quiet the noise in my head. They level me off. My highs aren't as high, my lows aren't as low. They keep me from spiraling when real life happens, like trolls, or my mother, or when you and I are at odds."

My shoulders drooped. "But I don't feel like myself when I'm on them. My mind is foggy. My voice doesn't sound as clear. I have to change my diet. No citrus, no certain routines that help my vocal cords."

Landon nodded, thoughtful. "I did notice you stopped putting lemon in your water. I thought it was just a small change since you're not performing right now."

"Citrus and lithium don't mix," I explained, swirling the water in my bottle. "The meds help, but they dull everything, not just the bad parts."

Landon's eyes sharpened. "Dull everything… like?"

I hesitated, then sighed. "Like my emotions. My creativity. My instincts. Even pleasure."

His gaze darkened with understanding. "So… your sex drive is lower?"

I smirked despite myself. "Of course, that's what you focus on."

He leaned in, voice dropping an octave. "I mean… you want sex even more than you do now?"

I shook my head, tucking my hair behind my ear. "It's not about wanting it more or less. I still want it. I still crave connection, intimacy. But before, I used sex like a drug. Some of the reason I cheated, the reason I used to sleep around, was because of my impulsivity. That, and not liking myself enough to say no."

Landon's expression darkened, his voice quieter but firmer. "So… if you weren't on meds, would you cheat on me?"

The directness of the question caught me off guard, but I didn't flinch. I curved my hands around his face, holding him steady. "No, baby. I'm telling you that I'm not that woman anymore. I haven't been for years. I've worked too hard to let my past define me. Meds or no meds, I don't want to be that person again."

I looked away, staring at the water like it held the rest of my confession. "On meds, that urgency, that hunger? It's muted. Like someone turned the volume down on a song I used to play on repeat."

Landon exhaled slowly, eyes never leaving mine. "So now, when you're with me… it's different?"

I nodded. "With you, it's not about silencing something. It's about feeling everything."

A beat of silence stretched between us, thick with something unspoken. He reached out, tracing his fingers along the inside of my wrist, where my pulse thrummed beneath his touch. "I don't want you muted, Nae. I want you real, even when it's hard."

I swallowed, my throat tight. "I know. That's why I'm telling you. I wasn't taking my meds properly until this past month, here in Austin. But I've seen the difference. You saw it too. Before, I could go three days without sleep. Here, I've been able to rest. When you made me be still, when you forced me to sit in the quiet, I finally let my body relax, even when I wasn't taking them."

He frowned. "I wouldn't say I forced you to relax."

"It felt forced sometimes," I admitted. "I'm like a kid who doesn't want to go to bed. I never know how I'll wake up. That's the hardest part… never knowing when the darkness is going to come for me. But being here with you, with everyone, it has made it easier."

I traced my fingers over his chest, grounding myself in the steady beat of his heart. "Can you love me like this? Knowing all of it?"

Landon scratched at his growing beard, studying me, his expression unreadable. "It's a lot… but so am I."

He let out a slow breath before he continued, "Here, in Austin, it feels like we could really make it. But I keep thinking about what happens when we go back. You love the spotlight. I hate it. You need people, crowds, energy. I would rather be in nature, playing my guitar where no one is watching. I just wonder if our differences are bigger than our similarities. If we make sense outside of this bubble."

"Are you at least going to consider getting help?" I pressed. "You deserve to shine too, Landon. You keep yourself in the shadows because it is safe, but you are the brightest thing I have ever seen. You are like the crescent moon you love so much. But the full moon?" I spread my arms wide. "That is when it is most beautiful."

His jaw tensed. "My panic attacks don't happen enough to be treated. Maybe I'm just not meant for what everyone else thinks success is."

I climbed into his lap, cupping his face. "That is a cop-out. Jimi Hendrix, Amy Winehouse, Janis Joplin… their struggles didn't define their greatness. The world saw them for who they were, even when they couldn't see themselves. And you? You have something special, something no one else does."

I met his eyes. "People love us together because they know two people like us finding each other is rare. It is like the butterfly, a mystical, fleeting thing. That is what we are."

His chest rose and fell as he stared past me into the woods.

I blocked his view, and he dragged his gaze to mine. "It's not just the panic attacks, Landon, although how your body shuts down on you is enough alone to seek treatment. It was scary to watch you go through it. Made me hold up a mirror to how I might appear to others when I'm spiraling. Watching you struggle when I'm not sure you have to is hard. Everything has to be a certain way for you to relax. Life has too many variables to be like that. You walk around with a hat, the guitar, holding on to your pick and who knows what else you do to make it through a regular day. You really don't like people touching you outside of me at this point. Why do you want to be uncomfortable from the second you step out the door?"

"You can ask anyone on the street if they're comfortable once they leave their homes," he replied. "Most would say no. People drink, smoke, use drugs, sleep around, are addicted to their phones or work, and whatever vices they have to cope. We all do *something*. I've come a long way from that kid my father talked about because I worked at it, and you're not going to set me back because your opinion of how I honor my talent is different."

"What's wrong with checking out therapy to see if there are other techniques that might work to help you be the Landon that I know and love to the world? You have to promise me if you have another panic attack, you're going to speak to someone."

He stared at me blankly.

I nipped his bottom lip. "I'm serious, Landon. I can't make all the concessions in this relationship. We both come from dysfunctional families, and we have our own issues. I want to break that destructive cycle for our future children."

"You want to have my babies, which means you can deal with me even when I do things that annoy the hell out of you." His eyes twinkled.

"I can as long as you agree to seek help *when* you have another panic attack."

"*If* it happens again, I'll get through it as I've always done. I'm fine, Janae. I don't need the world to see me. I just need you to see me. Besides, I don't mind performing. It's the promotional crap I don't like."

"Okay, then why haven't you answered Del about opening the Grammys show?"

He blinked several times before he answered, "Playing that won't make or break me."

"No, it won't. But you're scared to do it."

Landon studied my face for a long moment. "Honestly, I don't know if you can handle the pressure either."

"I can," I asserted.

"No, you can't if we're being real with each other. You are, in my opinion, the most dynamic performer I've ever seen, whether you're high or sober. You thrive in smaller venues and those intimate settings where you feel the connection. The two times you used were in larger venues." He cocked his head. "Before this tour, when was the last time you performed to a small audience?"

I reluctantly replied, "Before I was discovered."

"After that, you were always in these big arenas, intoxicated every single time. A lot of pressure to fill seats and more pressure to make sure you can entertain all those people." He paused. "You are a people person. The trauma you experienced as a child made you distrust, but when you feel safe you want to laugh, talk, and comfort others. How you've been around me and the guys is a person who cares about what happens to us. Hell, I'm not sure you have bipolar." He gripped my wrist before I protested. "I meant, you may have a lot of the symptoms, but you've experienced trauma like I did. Maybe our reactions to our childhoods are what made us like we are. Maybe I didn't allow anyone but my mother to touch me because even as a toddler or a young child I knew my father was capable of harm. Everything I did was about protecting my space, just like I do now. Maybe growing up in a household where you never felt loved or accepted and then suffered sexual abuse didn't result in a chemical imbalance, but it changed the way you see the world."

"What are you saying... that I shouldn't be treated for bipolar? I shouldn't perform in big arenas again?" I frowned.

"I don't know." He picked up my hand. "It's something to consider. Maybe the meds don't work for you because they're not treating what they're meant to treat. Or maybe the meds do the job and you're forcing yourself past your comfort zone unnecessarily. We both know you can handle the smaller venues. You barely break a sweat when you step on the stage. Why can't we do two or three shows a city in the small venues?"

I narrowed my eyes. "You and me, or me and The Hollow Bones?"

He averted his gaze. "Thinking maybe it's time for me to go solo."

I shook my head. "Not like this. They're your brothers."

"I don't know about that. They put a show above your welfare. The band I know would've canceled a gig if any of us couldn't perform."

"Why are you being so stubborn about this?"

"Because I'd take on the world for you. You're mine, and my friends should've never intervened." Landon's jaw was set. He was never sexier to me than when he put his foot down, even if I didn't agree. He wasn't budging, at least not right then.

"Okay, I'll leave it alone. Hollow Bones is something you have to work through." Turning to straddle him, I asked, "What about you and the Grammy show in November?"

Landon tightened his grip on me. "I need you to hear me and not take it personally or as a rejection, because I love you, and I'll never love a woman the way I love you."

My stomach dropped. "Speaking like that doesn't help."

His sigh held all the heartbreak I felt coming. What I thought I'd staved off during the weeks we'd been here.

"I think we need to see if we really want to be together through it all. I can deal with all you bring to the table except the drug use. You used drugs while taking your meds. That fact concerns me, Janae. You could've killed yourself mixing drugs like that."

"Well, I didn't, and I won't do it again. I knew on that stage it was the last time, and I know even more after being here in Austin with you. I needed to reset and regain perspective."

Landon stared past the trees, his body rigid, his silence thick with words he would not say. The longer he avoided looking at me, the harder my heart pounded, each second stretching unbearably. My stomach coiled tight, bracing for the inevitable. I slid off his lap, sitting beside him on the sofa, gripping the edge like it was the only thing keeping me upright.

"Just say it," I murmured, my voice steadier than I felt. "Stop dragging it out. Stop pretending there is another ending to this."

His eyes closed, and for a moment, I thought he would not answer. Then, slowly, tears slipped from beneath his lashes, carving paths down his face.

"Remember that night at House of Blues?" His voice was raw, barely above a whisper. "When I asked you to wear that flower?"

I nodded, my throat tightening. "You said you wanted me to wear it so you would know that, for one night, I wanted you too."

His lips parted, but he hesitated, like he was forcing himself to say something he did not want to. Finally, he exhaled sharply. "You are a bright star, Janae. And I never want to be the shadow that dims your light." His gaze found mine, filled with something deeper than sadness, something like surrender. "You are going to rise from here. I know that. And I also know that when the pressure builds, when the stage is too big, you might convince yourself you need something to get through it. And maybe you will. Maybe you will not. But who am I to tell you that you should not when I see people do it every day and come out just fine?"

The words cut through me, sharp and deliberate.

I sat up straighter, hands curling into fists. "You are a coward."

Landon flinched, but I did not stop.

"I told you I would not use again, but that is not enough for you. You are so afraid of taking a risk on me, on us, that you would rather push me away than see if we can make it."

His jaw clenched, eyes flashing. "Every time I step on that stage, I take a risk."

"No," I shot back, shaking my head. "Playing music is not a risk for you. It is a language you have spoken since you were three. You do not even have to think about it. Try talking to people. Try standing in the center instead of hiding at the edge of the stage. Try putting yourself out there in a way that makes you vulnerable, and then tell me you know what real risk is." My voice wavered, but I held his gaze. "You are okay with us as long as you control the terms. But you cannot control me, so you would rather let me go than take the chance that I will prove you wrong."

Landon pushed to his feet, his movements stiff with frustration. "Look around, Janae. We have built something real here. This is not about control. This is about peace." He gestured toward the trees, the lake, the world we had created in Austin. "Here, we work. Here, you are safe. You are taking your meds, you are sleeping, and you are not reaching for anything to numb yourself. We could wake up every morning and hike. We could buy a boat, have slow Sundays on the water. You could cook those ridiculous meals you love making for me, and we could create music together on our terms, not theirs." His voice caught, and he took a step closer, kneeling in front of me, his hands closing around mine.

"We could have that mad kind of love. The kind that never fades, never burns out. You say you want forever. This could be it. All you have to do is choose it. Choose me. No stages, no spotlights, no expectations. Just us." His grip tightened, his eyes pleading. "Tell me you want to stay here with me, away from all of it, and mean it. Do that, and I am yours. No Hollow Bones. No career that demands more from me than I am willing to give. Just you and me. No regrets."

I stared into his adoring eyes, seeing the life he was offering me. The safety, the certainty, the unwavering love he would give me without hesitation. I knew, without a doubt, that he meant it. That if I said yes, he would pour everything he had into making me happy, into protecting me from the world and from myself.

But love was not about protection. It was not about making a world small enough to control.

And that was why we both knew what my answer had to be.

"No."

CHAPTER FORTY
landon

NEW YORK
JULY 23

TO SAY I WAS HEARTBROKEN would be an understatement. I was heart *shattered*. Or maybe heart exploded. Every part of me hurt when I moved and breathed. My lungs didn't want to expand fully. As much as I ached to even exist, I had not one regret from loving Janae Warner. I would always root for her and her success.

When she dropped me off at the Austin airport, we both fought back tears, knowing that it would be so much easier to just forget the conversation that had ended us. To forget the truth and be together until we couldn't bear to live the lives we'd decided to live because we were afraid to be apart. I stuck a hibiscus flower in her hair, kissed her softly, and didn't look back once I got out. If I did, I wouldn't be able to leave my heart. My soul.

We resolved that if I decided to get back with The Hollow Bones, we could be cordial and friendly enough to do a couple of shows together. I told her that if that happened, Del would touch base with her. I also gave her permission to perform with them if I never returned. The Hollow Bones weren't just me. My brothers were all talented in their own right.

In the airport, I hurried to my gate. My shoulders were hunched, and a cap and dark glasses covered my hair and eyes instead of my porkpie. I'd become too recognizable as our relationship had continued to blaze through the entertainment world, especially when we'd been spotted out and about in

Austin. We'd also decided that we wouldn't make any public statements and would allow the buzz to die down when we appeared separately in public.

When I landed in New York, the excitement I usually felt didn't happen. The world would be gray for now.

The driver pulled up to my brownstone and I grabbed my bag and guitar. The last time I'd stood right here, I'd been in love with Janae and was showing her my home. I trudged up the stairs, missing her and dreading the inevitable drama of my parents.

My mother had been so excited that I was on my way home. She couldn't wait to see me and talk. She'd asked about Janae, and I'd simply told her that Janae needed to handle some business in Los Angeles. My mother had begun to like Janae, and they would chat when she called for me.

I would ask my mother for a night of rest, and then tomorrow we could begin to pick up the pieces of *her* life and find a new way for them to fit together.

As soon as I opened the door, a broken vase and turned-over chairs greeted me. The refrigerator was open. My heart sank to the floor. I dropped my bag and clutched my guitar. What the hell? Had someone broken in? Did a crazed fan find out where I lived?

My eyes landed on the coffee table Janae picked out, flipped to its side. The LEGO Millenium Falcon that we had started building together sat in ruins, shattered across the floor. My chest clenched. We had never finished it. We said we had time, believing we could always come back to it. Now, it was destroyed before it was ever completed. Just like us.

A choked noise pushed past my lips. I squeezed my eyes shut, pressing the heels of my hands into them. *Not now. Not here. Focus.*

I forced my feet to move, my heartbeat erratic. *Find her.*

"Mama!" My voice ricocheted through the space, too loud, too raw. Silence.

I spun around, scanning the destruction. Her purse was missing. Her shoes were gone. She could still be at work.

Or… something else.

A muffled scream.

My blood turned to ice.

I ran. Bolted up the stairs. Two at a time.

Then I heard him.

"You think you can ignore me?"

A man's voice. Slurred. Sharp with anger.

The walls shrank in around me. My body froze.

That voice. That tone.

The past crashed into me, full force.

Hiding in closets. My mother's hand clamped over my mouth. The sound of glass breaking. Footsteps too heavy, too fast. The crash of furniture toppling over.

My father's temper. His rage. The destruction that followed.

This was not a memory. It was happening again.

My chest seized.

But I was not that helpless kid anymore.

I barreled forward and slammed my shoulder into the door. It burst open.

And I saw red.

My mother stood backed into the corner, her lip split, her eye swollen. But not broken. Even now, even like this, she was still fighting.

My father loomed over her, his hand raised.

No.

Not this time.

Something inside me snapped.

Without thinking, I lifted my guitar and swung.

The impact shook my arms. My father staggered forward, roaring. He turned, bloodshot eyes wild with confusion.

Then he saw me.

Recognition flickered.

Then rage.

He lunged.

I met him halfway.

We hit the ground, fists flying.

I did not stop. Every punch was years of rage.

For my mother.

For me.

For every time he looked at me like I was nothing.

For every time he made her cry.

For all the years he left us alone.

I kept hitting him, my knuckles splitting, my chest heaving, my body shaking with something wild and primal.

"Landon, stop!"

My mother's scream tore through the haze.

I froze, breath coming in jagged bursts. The world tilted.

My father groaned beneath me, his lip split, his eye swelling.

My hands trembled. Bloody.

I stumbled backward, stomach twisting. The room swayed.

"Mama," I whispered, but my voice was wrong. Thin. Distant.

Her sobs sounded far away. Everything did.

The walls closed in.

The air thickened.

My throat sealed shut.

I gasped.

Nothing.

Clawed at my neck. My chest locked tight.

No air.

No air.

Black spots bloomed in my vision.

I tried to stand. My knees buckled.

"No, no, no," I muttered, over and over, hands twitching, grasping for something solid.

But nothing was real. Everything was slipping.

I rocked slightly, fingers twitching, curling into my palms.

"Please, no, no, no," I whispered frantically, breath shallow, uneven, desperate.

I needed help.

I needed Cedrick.

I needed Janae.

But they were not here.

I was alone.

Tears burned my eyes as I fumbled for my phone, my hands shaking too hard. The room blurred.

My body was not listening.

My head spun.

"Make it stop," I murmured, barely audible. "Please, I don't want to be here."

My lips trembled. The pain was too much. It clawed inside me, sinking its teeth in deep, ripping me apart from the inside.

"I don't want to feel this anymore," I muttered again, my voice barely above a breath.

I collapsed onto my side, gasping.

Darkness crept in.

The last thing I felt was my phone slipping from my fingers.

Then…

Nothing.

JULY 24

The steady beeping of a monitor pulled me from sleep.

No dreams. Just emptiness.

I tried to move. Something held me down. Frowning, I blinked against the dim light, my body sluggish. A dull ache sat heavy behind my eyes, pressing at my skull. I tugged again. Still restrained.

Leather straps. Both wrists.

Unease crawled over me, slow and suffocating. I turned my head, scanning the room. Pale yellow walls. No windows. No clock.

A hospital. Maybe.

I flexed my fingers. The skin at the crease of my elbow stung. A red-dotted bandage covered my vein. Blood had been drawn, but there was no IV. No tubes.

My chest tightened.

Why was I tied down?

I shifted my wrists, testing the hold of the restraints. Tight, but not painful. Not handcuffs. If I had been arrested, wouldn't they have cuffed me?

The thought made my stomach twist. My heart picked up speed, not racing but uneasy, like it knew something I had not figured out yet.

Had I killed him?

I swallowed hard and pressed my head back into the stiff pillow. The memories began to unfurl, hazy at first, then clearer. The house. The fight. My father's face, bloody and contorted with rage. My mother screaming. My own fists, bloody. Shaking.

I forced my breath to stay even, but my body felt weighted, like I was sinking beneath something too heavy to fight.

How did I end up here?

Had my parents called the cops? Lied? Said I attacked him unprovoked?

I closed my eyes briefly, trying to pull the pieces together, but everything was just out of reach.

The restroom door creaked.

I turned my head.

My mother stepped out, wearing sunglasses.

Her face was unreadable.

"Mama?" I squeaked out.

Fresh tears rolled down her already-stained cheeks as she rushed to my bedside.

"Why am I like this? Where am I?"

She brushed my hair back like she used to when I was a boy. "It's almost five in the afternoon. You've been in the hospital since yesterday. They sedated you because you wouldn't calm down enough to breathe when the medics arrived."

"Why am I tied up?"

Her lips curved slightly. "Shh... it's okay. You're under observation."

I glanced around the room again. "Is this the psych ward?"

"Yes. I asked for a private suite."

"Does anyone know I'm here?" My voice came out rough, like I had swallowed glass.

The last thing I needed was headlines screaming about Landon Hayes being locked in a psych ward, especially with our second album about to drop. Even though I had quit the band, I didn't want anything to hurt them.

A dull pounding started in my temples. The media would twist this. They would somehow blame Janae. They always did.

"No one knows but hospital personnel," my mother said. "Our lawyers put together an ironclad NDA. I am not even supposed to be in here for the first twenty-four to seventy-two hours, but I had to use my power and money for something."

For once, her obsession with our family's image had worked in my favor.

Still, I didn't want anyone to ever know I had been confined to this bed. Except Janae. The need to hear her voice hit me like a fist. She had been my life jacket.

"I just passed out," I muttered. "Why are they treating me like I'm a threat? Is it because I hit him?"

I could not even bring myself to say *father*.

My mother's breath caught. She hesitated. "You blacked out in your mind, but in reality, you went into a rage. You started yelling over and over again that you wanted to die. That you had nothing to live for." Her voice cracked. "You kept screaming until you were hoarse. I had to call an ambulance because you were curled up on the floor, barely breathing."

She sniffed. Her fingers twisted together in her lap.

"Your eyes were… gone. My baby didn't exist anymore, and I had to call for help. When they came, you were still muttering to yourself. And when we finally arrived here, you were like this." She gestured at the restraints. "The doctor was afraid you would hurt yourself because you kept saying 'death.'"

"What? I really couldn't breathe, and it hurt so bad that I wanted to die. But I didn't really *want* to die."

She shook her head. "Baby, it was much more than that. I should've gotten you help when you were a boy. I should've realized you needed more than me. I thought you were dying. I couldn't get you to come back to me. Maybe now you can get help, son."

"Stop saying that. I'm fine." The words came out sharp, too quick. I needed to believe them. "I just got upset because he was hurting you, and I couldn't let him do that anymore. That's all. I'm fine. I'm fine."

I kept repeating it, but each time, it felt more like a lie.

"Where is he?"

My mother's nostrils flared. Her hands curled into fists at her sides. "I don't know, and I no longer care."

Her voice was ice.

"He could barely stand, but I threatened to kill him if he didn't leave. The only reason I didn't call the police, the only reason he's still breathing, is because I didn't want you to be accused of his death." She exhaled sharply. "Your father no longer exists. He is dead to me. *You* are the only one who matters."

Her hands trembled as she ripped off her sunglasses.

I sucked in a breath.

Both of her eyes were swollen, blackened with deep purple bruises.

"I'm the fool for believing in him," she spat. "For thinking, over and over, that he'd stop drinking. That he'd finally be a better father. He fooled me for years. He cut down, made me believe we had gotten past the ugliest side of him. Until I chose you. Until I left."

She shook her head, eyes burning with fury.

"Never. Fucking. Again."

The hate that she'd just expelled struck me to my core. In that moment, I almost felt sorry for my father. He'd forever lost the woman who'd stood by him through thick and thin. He'd lost the woman he'd loved more than life itself because he couldn't overcome his demons and had been the devil himself in how he treated my mother.

I opened my hand to hers and held tight when she gripped it. "I'm not going anywhere. My place is huge. Just move in permanently with me, okay? I'll protect you. I won't ever let him hurt you again."

She smiled weakly. "I need to be there to care for you, as well as make sure you're taking your meds and doing whatever the doctor recommends."

"I am fine, Mama." The words felt heavy, but I forced them out. "I'm not going to have another episode. I'll take whatever they discharge me with, but I'm not refilling anything."

She searched my face, her eyes wary, but I pressed on.

"I admit that I have to live with anxiety, and I know I have a need to control my environment. But it is up to me how I want to cope with it. Not anyone else."

As soon as I said it, Janae's voice echoed in my head.

Her promise. The way she swore she would never use again. The conviction in her voice. And how I had not believed her.

Now, standing in this moment, saying my own words out loud, I wondered if this was how she felt. Did she believe, deep down, that she could do everything in her power to keep that vow? That she could choose to fight it, just like I was choosing now?

Mama nodded, then suddenly collapsed against my chest, sobs wracking through her body. I wanted to hold her, but the restraints hindered me. I also had no more tears to shed.

I was done breaking. I was done being helpless. Not as a boy. Not as a man. Not ever again.

JULY 26

I stared blankly ahead as the social worker drilled me about my mental health. My mother and I had met with the doctor and requested that the restraints be removed, and that had happened shortly after I regained consciousness yesterday. The residual grogginess from the sedative had faded and I wanted to be discharged. Two days of this hospital was more than enough. The social worker asked for privacy, and my mother had gone to the cafeteria.

After spending the last hour asking me question after question about my physical and mental symptoms and family history again, she finally asked me, "When's the last time you wanted to kill yourself?"

"I've never wanted to kill myself," I replied. "I keep telling you all that, and I'm still in here. I got into a fight with my father, and it upset me. I just ended a relationship, and there was a lot going on. The anxiety hurt so bad that I begged to die. But I don't and never have had plans to take myself out. Please discharge me."

She rose. "It's up to the doctor. He's diagnosed you as being on the autism spectrum. You landed in the hospital because you had a severe panic attack with psychotic features, and he has a treatment plan he wants to review before he discharges you. I can do it with you if you prefer."

"I told him already that I disagreed. I have anxiety sometimes, but that's it. I am not psychotic or crazy." I clasped my hands, refusing to allow anyone to label me.

"Mr. Hayes, anyone can break from reality when everything is happening at once. Psychosis is the result of that, where you aren't sure anymore of who or where you are. You lost touch with the present because your mind wanted to protect itself. You said you were going through a breakup, and then the fight with your father might have been too much for your mind to handle. We just want to offer you ways to cope."

"And I told you that I'm good. That doctor can't keep me here because I disagree with the diagnosis. You tell the doctor that I'll sue for mistreatment and discrimination, because I'm not supposed to even be in here. My mother didn't know what to do when I was having an episode. I would've been fine without medicines or the hospital." I slammed the bed with my fist. "Get me the fuck out of here."

The social worker grew flustered and rushed out of the room.

"I always knew you had it in you." My father's chuckle outside the door iced my blood. I was still weak and had no way to protect myself.

Despite my vulnerability, anger and not fear ruled my emotions. "Get out, you horrible piece of shit. I don't want to hear anything you have to say."

He walked fully into the room, with a slight limp, also in shades and with a bandage across his nose. It was really laughable how we, as a family, even under the direst of circumstances, wanted to uphold the Hayes name and legacy.

"I wouldn't want to talk to me either." He shrugged and jammed his hands in his pockets. "Keeping them there so you know I won't touch you."

"Mama will be back soon, and I don't want her to know you were here."

My father exhaled and pulled off his glasses. His eyes were almost swollen shut, and his light skin was mottled red and blue around his cheeks and temples. His lip had a cut. "I've been staring in the mirror for hours at the damage I've done to this family. At what I've become. And I thought... for a long time, I thought the best thing I could do was disappear. But leaving this world wouldn't fix anything. It would only bring more pain to you and your mother."

"All you ever cared about was image. Now you're saying you have to stay because it would make the Hayes name look bad," I scoffed.

"No. No, this isn't about me. This is about you and your name. The world is your oyster right now. The public wants you, and I can't allow my actions to pull you down anymore. I won't contest the divorce. She can take whatever she wants, and I'll leave you and her alone. I'm not here for forgiveness because I know that won't and shouldn't come, though I am sorry for everything."

"I've heard this before. You'll change, and you're sorry. All lies to me. The next time you want to send a message, send it through your lawyer." I could feel my chest tightening, and I couldn't allow my father to bring me to that lonely, awful place ever again.

"I know you hate me. You always did." He spoke so softly that I had to strain to hear him. "Do you know how hard it was to have you as a son? From the beginning, you didn't like me. You would scream at the top of your lungs whenever I touched you or tried to pick you up. I used to be so frustrated. Me and your mother had waited ten years to have you, and when we did, you couldn't stand me. Then, when I noticed you loved to hum as an infant and moved your head to my music, hope came back that we could bond the way I'd always wanted."

"So what? You can't love me because I'm not the son you envisioned? You can't see the man I've grown up to be and be proud?"

His head snapped back. "I am proud. *Been* proud."

I shook my head. "No. You're not. I don't always recognize social cues, but I know when you're being genuine with me. All I see is jealousy. And I don't know why. What do I have that you haven't already achieved?"

My father stared at me a long time before he finally replied, "Your freedom. Being different allowed you to float under the radar, to move how you wanted. You didn't have to be social and weren't expected to be anything but what you dreamed. You rose to the top even when I couldn't push you because you would break—"

"Well, guess what? You did push me, and I did break. Why else would I run away from home at sixteen? Sixteen, and I'm on the street trying to figure it out. Can't go to either grandparent because they live across the country, and I knew my dream was here in New York. But that was the best thing you could've ever done to me. It forced me to ignore my need to hide. I had to overcome being shut in a room, playing my music. I had to survive. I had to open my mouth. I had to figure out how to be normal, and sometimes I still fail. But I've come a long way with the help of Cedrick and the guys who loved me for who I was, I am, and will ever be."

His jaw tightened, and he rolled his neck. "I recognized your struggles before your mother did, and maybe I was hard on you because I didn't want you to be me. Ironically, now I can't stand that you're *not* like me. You learned how to exist without using a damn thing. You know why I drink myself into a stupor every other night?" He laughed loudly. "It's to fight off my own panic attacks and depression. You are the me I was too afraid to be. All these years, and your mother never knew that every time I grabbed a bottle it was to fight off that gnawing and scared feeling that I was losing control… that I didn't fit in, no matter how hard I tried."

I gasped, though he didn't appear to notice. His description of the constant nervousness and feeling like an outsider was the same as mine.

He studied his feet before he stared back at me. "This is the last piece of advice I will ever give you. You're in here because you still need help. Don't be a fool like me and lose everything and everybody you love. Get the help you need and see how much further you will fly. You didn't name your band The Hollow Bones for nothing."

Long after he left, I stared at the door he'd exited through.

JULY 29

Three days later, wearing my porkpie hat again, I pulled open the doors to the studio, knowing I would find Cedrick working alone in the wee hours of the morning. He loved the piano and keyboard as much as he loved sound engineering. When I walked in the room he looked up, barely nodded, and

THE SIDE OF BEAUTIFUL

continued playing around with the bass in one of our songs. It'd been six weeks since we'd last spoken, and before that, we'd never gone more than a day without words in the fifteen years we'd known each other. My electric guitar was still in the booth. I entered, picked it up, strapped it around my neck, and started playing new music inspired by the last few weeks. Cedrick eased back in his chair and nodded with a pleased smile.

When I hit the last lingering note, making the guitar shrill, Cedrick whistled his approval through the intercom.

"I called that one 'Landon's Promise,'" I huskily said. My emotions were spent after the last few days, and I needed the sanctity of the booth to help me confront the first person who'd chosen to love me for me.

"For you or for The Hollow Bones?"

We locked eyes through the glass. When he'd posed the same question weeks earlier, I thought it impossible to go solo.

"Depends." I shrugged.

Cedrick folded his arms. "Say whatever you need to say."

"Why didn't you tell me Brian was the one who gave Janae the drugs?"

"Because if I had some, I would've given them to her myself," he answered.

I ducked my head, trying to make sense of what he was telling me. "You know me. You know I would never agree to giving her anything. I left that room thinking I could trust you to do what's right."

His nostrils flared. "*Your* definition of right."

"The fuck? She wears a sobriety coin around her neck. In what world was that okay? Enlighten me, Ced."

"Our world. We don't live a normal life." He tapped the board with conviction. "When you love someone, you don't want to see them hurting. Janae brought light into your life. Into all of ours. That day in Del's studio, I'll never forget it. The way she let us in, the way she let me in... her vulnerability cracked something inside of me that I am still trying to understand. Janae became my sister. And even now, if she calls and says she needs me, I am there. We all are."

I shook my head. "She doesn't need that kind of help."

"That night, after you left, she begged me." His voice softened, but the intensity in his eyes never wavered. "She was hurting, Landon. And she knew you couldn't give her any drug to numb it, because you don't understand that kind of need. The need to just not feel a motherfucking thing."

He exhaled sharply, his expression tight with emotion. "Janae wasn't fiending. That was not what I saw in her eyes. She was drowning. Wounded. Trying to claw her way out of something too deep and too dark. She did not have enough time to find the surface before the show. Before the biggest moment of her career. And why? Because her own mother, her own flesh and blood, decided to rip it away from her."

Cedrick pushed back from the desk. "I have seen that look in your eyes when you are struggling, and I would do anything to help you. Anything to pull you out of that place. I know what it is like to need something, anything, to take the edge off. To find a way to push through when your mind and body are working against you. I have had my own crutches, my own ways of coping. I am not saying it is the right way, but I also cannot sit here and judge her. Or Brian. I cannot apologize for his decision, but I understand why he made it."

His chest heaved up and down, mirroring mine.

He crossed one fist over his chest. "But I am sorry, man, for overstepping my bounds because she is your woman, and for doing anything that would make you believe that you don't mean more to me than this band. I call you my brother because that's who you are to me. Whether you want to be in Hollow Bones again or go solo, you are and will always be my brother."

I regarded the man who'd truly been there for me. "In that case, 'Landon's Promise' is for The Hollow Bones."

Cedrick broke out into a grin as I walked out of the booth. We grasped hands and pulled each other in for a brotherly hug.

CHAPTER FORTY-ONE

HOUSTON
JULY 23

WHEN LANDON KISSED ME AT the airport and exited the car, I wanted to chase him down and make him stay. I wanted to hold on tight and never let go of him. To know I would never feel his lips on me, play in his hair, or wake up in his embrace again shattered my soul. We were both so vulnerable that he would've turned around and gotten back in the car if I'd asked. He'd become my friend, lover, and rock. My life jacket. We'd been preparing to jam together for the rest of our lives. We'd been growing into that forever love that we sang about, and now we would never be again.

I had already packed up the car so I wouldn't have to return to my Austin home, that would forever be associated with Landon and the love I'd never thought I would have. I honestly didn't know if I could return to that house without him. Five weeks of uninterrupted time in which we'd loved freely. Until we hadn't.

In spite of the heartache and pain, I'd been proud of myself when I dropped him off and headed to Houston to see my family. Landon had given me a choice to be with him, and I'd chosen what was best for me. I couldn't and had never lived in fear. Every step I'd taken once I left my mother's home had brought me to where I was today. If I'd lived in fear, I would've never left Houston. If I'd lived in fear, I wouldn't have moved to Los Angeles. If I'd lived in fear, I would still be still hung up on my ex, who'd moved on with no intention of looking back. If I'd lived in fear, I wouldn't have gotten into treatment and stayed. If I'd lived in fear, I wouldn't have attempted to get my career back. If I'd lived in fear, I wouldn't have announced to the world that I had bipolar. If I'd lived in fear, I wouldn't have allowed myself to fall in love with Landon, and that would have been the biggest travesty of all.

I'd already called ahead and told my brother I was on the way to talk to him and my mother. He said he would support whatever I had to tell her because he had his own issues with Mama deciding to date a man who'd sexually abused his sister. He told me that it was just her at home today. Antwon wasn't there.

I pulled in behind a silver Lexus SUV in the driveway. It must have been Rashad's car. He'd worked himself up to manager at a local oil change shop and had been doing well. He'd told me that his seven-year-old son, whom he'd been raising on his own for the last three years, would be with him. I hadn't seen my nephew since he was a toddler, and I couldn't wait to know him a little again.

I nibbled on my nails while I sat in the driveway until I remembered I'd stopped biting my nails once I left my mother's house. She'd had way too much impact on me, making me regress to that teenager who bit her nails. No more. I couldn't and wouldn't give that woman any more energy after today.

The front door opened, and my brother walked out with an excited smile. I hopped out of the car, and he lifted me off my feet into a bear hug. He hugged me so tightly that I felt all the love he'd ever had for me in his embrace.

He pulled back to look at me and then dragged me back into his arms. I tapped his back. "Okay… okay… I got it. You missed me."

Rashad laughed and dropped his arms. "Still my baby sis."

We both looked toward the house and sighed loudly.

He looked down at me. "You ready?"

I stared at the modest four-bedroom home in the southwest area of Houston, a far cry from the rental we'd once had in the Third Ward. "The

THE SIDE OF BEAUTIFUL

first thing I bought with my advance was this house, and you know what she said… that she would've preferred the money." I chuckled, though the sound had no humor.

"We don't have to go inside. We can get Mexican or barbecue and pretend like we're ordinary people, and we can hang out at your hotel," he offered. "When she got back with dude, I moved out. I wasn't subjecting my children to a fucking molester. I only visit her now so she can see her grandchildren. I can't be around her negativity anymore. Toxic is toxic. It doesn't matter if it's our mother."

I half smiled. "You sound like my old psychologist. No, I need to see her. The more I'm able to fight real demons, the less likely I'll fail again at the false ones."

We stood side by side as I rang the bell, like we were selling internet services and not visiting our mother.

A round-faced boy with the biggest cheeks dressed in a polo shirt and slacks opened the door, looked at his father, and then at me. "Are you Auntie Nae Nae?"

Oh, how he looked like my brother at that age. I stooped to kiss his cheek. "In the flesh."

"Me and my daddy listen to your songs all the time." He hugged my neck warmly and smiled up at his father "You told me I would like her, and I do."

My eyes welled up at the innocence that a creep like Antwon could steal if he were given a chance. "I already like you too, and after we leave here today, you're going to come to stay with me and your daddy at my hotel tonight. Is that cool?"

He looked up at me. "Do you play the drums?"

"No, but I do have a tambourine."

"Can you teach me?" he asked, his face brightening.

"I can. When you visit me in Austin or Los Angeles, I'll have some drums for you to play."

Rashad grabbed his son in a headlock. "Boy, leave your auntie alone. She already told you we're hanging out with her tonight. We'll order room service and everything."

He hugged his father around the waist and looked up at my brother with love.

I nudged Rashad. "Look at you being Daddy."

"I'm trying. I know I'm a better dad than that deadbeat of ours. At least I show up for my children," he said firmly.

"How many times have I told you to come get me before opening the door, RJ?" Our mother appeared. "Janae? You didn't tell me she was coming," she said to Rashad.

"I asked him not to say, and I won't stay long," I promised, not wanting to be in her presence longer than I needed.

"Stay as long as you like. Even if your boyfriend kicked me out of your little party."

"For good reason," I retorted, already regretting coming.

Rashad only nodded.

"Have you forgotten how to talk?" she asked him impatiently.

"Oh, you talking to me now? A few minutes ago, you had nothing to say to me. Just wanted to spend time with RJ," Rashad snapped.

"It's cool." I hugged my brother to me. "We've been catching up and making up for lost time. We realized that we allowed you to get in the middle of us. He and I don't have any beef with each other, yet we haven't spoken in years until a few months ago, and that's not going to happen again."

Our mother tilted her head. "I never kept you apart."

I wagged my finger. "It's the doubt you put in our heads. That Rashad must not care about me. Or 'your sister don't call you anymore because she too busy for you.' You know, those doubts that we don't love each other that you kept stirring up in our minds."

Before Mama could respond, RJ pulled her and me by our hands into the foyer. "Grandma, we're going to her hotel after this so she can teach me the tambourine."

"Oh, is that the plan?" She looked up at me and Rashad.

Rashad responded, "Just RJ and me. We'll get the girls from their mother to stay with us tomorrow."

Her nostrils flared. "Why are you here?"

"Are you still with Antwon?" I asked.

She lifted her chin. "I broke up with Twon, and if you're here to start trouble, you might as well leave."

I cracked my neck to try to release my tension. "I can either say what I have to say to you in front of RJ, or we can talk privately. Either way, I'm not leaving until I say what I need to say to you."

Mama cut her gaze to my brother. "Is he going to hear whatever you have to say too?"

We both nodded. "Yep."

"If it was me, I wouldn't give you another chance, bringing that bastard around Janae," he added.

"Another chance?" She frowned.

I bent down. "RJ, if you go to one of the bedrooms and don't come out until we say so, we'll have cookies-and-cream milkshakes at the hotel, okay?"

The boy's eyes rounded, and he rushed out of the foyer.

Mama folded her arms. "What do you have to say to me?"

"Why?" The simple question rang loud and clear.

She waved her hand. "I shouldn't have brought Twon to Los Angeles. I didn't think how it would affect you. It's been years, and you've had men since him. I didn't think it mattered."

"The man tried to rape her and you think that wouldn't affect her?" Rashad thundered.

"I told you, she went after Antwon to spite me and then lied to you when she got caught. You believe anything your sister tells you."

"You sound straight crazy. I'm going to the car. I can't do this. I don't want to disrespect you, Mama. I ain't got time for this." He walked deeper into the house and yelled, "RJ? Let's go."

Wearing a confused frown, RJ rushed back into the foyer. "Yes, Daddy?"

"We're going."

I added, "You did good. We'll have the milkshakes, promise."

RJ hugged his grandmother around the waist, and she patted his back while still glaring at her children.

Rashad held his son's hand. "When you finish, we'll be outside in the car waiting for you."

I touched my brother's arm and smiled, grateful that he'd been there for me thus far. Now, everything else was on me.

Once the door closed behind him, I turned to my mother, my voice trembling under the weight of years of pain. "Why do you hate me?" My chest tightened as I forced myself to keep steady. "What did I ever do to make you hate the air I breathed, when all I ever did was live for you? All I ever wanted was to make you proud."

My throat burned, but I pressed on. "Three years ago, I tried to end my life because I had no one." I held out my wrists. "These tattoos cover the scars from the razors I dragged across my skin. How twisted is that? I had to cause more pain just to stop the pain of believing I was alone. That no one in this world loved me. Especially you."

Tears blurred my vision, but I refused to stop. "I haven't spoken to you in four years, and yet, I still pay every bill in this house. Because despite everything, I love you." My voice cracked, raw and open. "And you've never even had the decency to say thank you. And after all that, after everything, you had the nerve to show up at the most important concert of my career with the man who abused me."

A broken sob tore through my chest, years of agony rising from the depths of me like a storm. "That man had been grabbing my breasts and my ass since the day you brought him into our lives. I did everything I could to avoid him. I wore baggy clothes, stayed out of the house whenever he was around. I sacrificed my own peace just so you could be happy, just so you could finally have a boyfriend."

I sucked in a sharp breath and let the words spill from the place I had buried them. "And then, that day… he almost raped me." I locked my gaze onto hers, daring her to look away. "He cornered me in my room, covered my mouth. I couldn't scream. I couldn't fight him off. He was too strong. And then I heard your keys in the door, and I thought… finally, she will see. Finally, she will know the truth.

"But you didn't protect me." My voice dropped to a whisper. "You beat me. Like I had stolen your child-molesting boyfriend from you."

I took a slow step forward. She took one back. Her eyes shimmered, but I had long since stopped hoping for tears that meant anything.

"What happened to you to make you this way?" My voice was quieter now, but no less fierce. "Did someone hurt you? Did Grandma treat you like this? What did I do to deserve this, Mama?" I hit my chest, the ache unbearable. "I used to be so proud to be your daughter. I used to perform every single show like you were watching, even though you never came to one. Not one."

I swallowed hard. "And the only time you did show up, you came to destroy me."

I let the silence stretch between us, let the weight of my words settle into the cracks of a foundation that had been broken for as long as I could remember. Then, finally, I breathed.

"But not anymore." My voice steadied. "I am worthy of so much more than how you treated me. I am worthy of love. Real love. From a good man. From a real family."

I exhaled long and deep, stepping back. "This is the last time I will ever speak to you, and I am at peace with that." I wiped my face with the back of my hand, as if physically clearing away the years of grief. "This house? It's in Rashad's name now. Whether he keeps it or sells it, that's his decision. But I won't let you come between us anymore. I want to know my nieces and nephew. I want to be the aunt they deserve."

And just like that, the weight lifted.

I threw my hands in the air, my chest rising with a feeling I had never known before... freedom. I jumped once, then again, letting out a shout so full, so uninhibited, I could have sworn I felt the presence of something greater than myself. This. This was what it meant to be free.

Mama stood frozen like a statue, as if she were unable to say anything.

"Bye, Mama." I didn't wait for a response and strode out of the house with my head held high.

When I stopped at my brother's open window, our mother wordlessly watched us.

Rashad glanced between me and her. "Are you okay?"

"I will be fine." The residual hurt of not having a good relationship with my mother would still be there. I would just have to focus on those who loved me, like my brother.

"Did she answer your questions?"

"I never expected her to."

Rashad shook his head and started his car. I walked to mine, and soon we left the home while she stared after us.

LOS ANGELES
AUGUST 19

Loneliness loomed whenever I thought too hard about what I'd given up. Then there were days when I wasn't sure I *had* given up. Landon had seemed so certain he wasn't the man for me and couldn't handle my big career. It made fighting for him seem futile. Some days, I raged at him. Other days, I only wanted to crawl into bed with him. My meds were keeping the edge off and allowing me to sleep. Or maybe because my emotions were entwined with relief from confronting my mother and joy at being the aunt I'd always wanted to be, initially, I didn't feel the doom and gloom of losing Landon, the wounded ache of a breakup with a man with whom I could see forever.

When August rolled around, I started falling apart after no contact from him. I had been sure he would call and check on me as a friend or as my life jacket. I had crying spells and negative thoughts about my ability to have a lasting relationship. I didn't crave drugs, only Landon. Del or my brother called me every day to check in. I told Del I needed until September to move forward. He argued that the sooner I returned to work, the sooner I could function again. I had to continue striking while the iron was hot. Del tried to goad me by telling me that Landon had rejoined The Hollow Bones and was preparing to promote their new album, and that I needed to show him I was good, too. All that did was remind me of being with him and what we'd lost.

I was in bed watching episodes of *Insecure* for the twentieth time, empathizing with Issa's longing for Lawrence, when someone knocked on my door. Fear coursed through my veins, and I could hear Landon's voice admonishing me for not hiring security, since, somehow, people knew where I lived.

I checked the camera on my bedside table and released a sigh of relief. Frankie.

Rising out of bed, I threw a silk robe over my pajamas and opened the door without speaking, then dropped down on my sofa and patted the space beside me. Frankie shook her head and held her arms out. "I hug when I haven't seen friends in a long time."

Joy loosened some of the persistent tightness in my chest as I eagerly rose to hug her tight. "I wanted to reach out and apologize a trillion times. I just didn't know how. Never had girlfriends before."

"Picking up the phone works wonders." Frankie pulled back from the embrace and studied me. "This hair is a mess, and you look like crap. One friend to another."

"Thank you," I shot back sarcastically. "I told Del to give me until September."

"That's two more weeks. It's time to get back to living. Rashad asked if I seen you since you returned from Houston, and when I told him no, he begged me to see you."

"Rashad?" I sat back down on the sofa, and she joined me. "He didn't tell me you were talking. What happened with Cedrick?"

She propped her legs on my coffee table. "Hope you don't mind."

I waved my hand. "No."

"We ended things the day after the L.A. show, before they returned to New York. He said he didn't do long distance and was too upset about Landon leaving the group to focus on my feelings. I didn't like how we ended, but it would've happened sooner or later because we wanted different things. Your brother and I have been talking, and he wants to hang out when he visits you for Labor Day."

"I should call him right now and ask why he didn't tell me," I teased.

"I wasn't ready for you to know. I didn't want you to think I used your brother to get over Cedrick."

"I want you to be happy, whether it's with Ced, my brother, or some other dude." I tapped the cushion between us. "I'm glad you're here so I can apologize in person for what I put you and the guys through. I promise you that it won't happen again. I'm back on meds and spending quiet time with myself. I need you in my life more than I need any drug or song."

Frankie smiled wide. "All's forgiven. And when you're ready to tell me what happened with your mother, I'm here."

"Thank you, and I will over a long brunch with limitless waffles, since I can't drink." I hugged her around the neck. "I already made peace with Brian and Cedrick over the phone. They accepted my apology, and we're cool again." I sighed. "Just need to get over Landon."

She tsked. "Please don't let him stop your flow when he seems to be doing fine."

"How do you know?"

She pulled out her phone. "They were all hanging out in New York at this club two nights ago to celebrate their album, and you know he doesn't hang out."

On their IG page, Landon rocked a Jimi Hendrix T-shirt, cargo pants, and a porkpie hat, allowing his curls to show. He'd pushed up his sleeve, inadvertently showing off his toned bicep as he laughed, his eyes locked with Charles. Women were all around, clearly waiting to pounce. This Landon didn't seem like *my* Landon. He seemed exactly the type to take home one of the women who clamored for his attention, and my stomach flipped and burned. I'd upgraded this striking yet reserved geek into a certifiable hottie. No wonder he hadn't called or texted me. Petty anger fueled my energy.

Giving Frankie's phone back to her, I hopped up. "Think it's time I move on too. Can you hook a sister up? I want to hit up a few spots and remind people who I am."

She cocked a brow. "Only if I'm doing it for a friend."

"Only if that friend who prefers to be at home reading comes with me," I said, pulling her with both hands toward my bedroom.

And just like that… my life started yet again.

CHAPTER FORTY-TWO

landon

NEW YORK
SEPTEMBER 7

MY MOTHER MOVED INTO MY place in August after selling our family home within a week of it coming on the market, though she had yet to announce their separation and pending divorce formally. She hosted an estate sale of the furniture, décor, and paintings in the home. The only things she kept were photos and memorabilia of my childhood. She wanted nothing to do with my father.

We hadn't heard from him and had no desire to. My mother had started therapy to heal from years of emotional and physical abuse. She encouraged me to join her, but I wasn't ready to delve into our past tumultuous relationship. I wanted to focus on going forward, and so far, she and I were forming a new bond. We were getting to know each other as individuals and fellow musicians. I'd always be grateful for Janae because she helped me grow accustomed to someone else being in my space, and after a few weeks of living together, I liked coming home to my mother, who still cooked the best Cornish hen and carrot soufflé.

Shortly after Mama moved in, Del sent hours of recordings featuring The Hollow Bones and wanted me to review it so that the producers of the reality show wouldn't air anything that I was against. We were given veto power over any footage involving only our band, since we originally weren't supposed to be featured in the show. I was the last to look at it. They left it up to me to decide what to cut. My mother insisted that we watch it together, because she wanted to know more about my life as a musician.

As we were reviewing some of the footage that brought back fun and bittersweet memories of our time on the road, she said, "It's obvious you love each other. Is it because of me and your father that you don't believe you can be together?"

I paused the video and shifted on the oversized, comfy sofa Janae had ordered before leaving. It'd been delivered shortly after I was discharged from the hospital. I'd been sleeping on that sofa instead of my bed ever since.

"Janae used to have a substance abuse problem and has bipolar, as you've heard. I love her like you used to love my father. I love all of her, and I was afraid I would enable her the way you did him. Give in when I knew I shouldn't or because I wanted to please her. Then I feared my need to protect her would ultimately clip her wings. I didn't want to do that to her."

Mama tucked one leg under the other and poked my forehead. "I made a lot of mistakes as a mother and a wife, and they affected you. But me and your father? We are not you and Janae."

She grabbed the remote and pointed it at the TV. The video started again. It was us, working on her song. Janae stood beside me while I played a few chords, searching for the right one. I had been so focused on my guitar that I hadn't noticed the way she was looking at me. Her smile was huge and goofy, filled with something so tender it made my heart skip two beats.

Mama's voice was soft but sure. "Almost every time the camera catches the two of you in the same space, you are either staring at her or she is staring at you. It is magic, Landon. Pure magic. That is why fans could not get enough of you as a couple. Because what you had, what you have, felt real. Genuine. Something we all want."

She patted my knee. "You keep saying you are afraid when you talk about Janae. What are you afraid of, son?"

I did not answer. I was not sure I could.

She did not push. Just kept going, her voice thoughtful. "I stayed too long with a man who was bad for me because I was afraid of what was on the other side. But I cannot tell you how much I have enjoyed these last few weeks with you. With you and my therapist, I am finding peace again. And that? That is priceless."

She squeezed my knee. "Whatever decision you make in this life, do not make it out of fear, okay?"

I smiled weakly. "If only it were that easy."

"It can be if you let it to be." Mama rose from the sofa. "I'm going to get ice cream out of the refrigerator. You want anything?"

I shook my head as I watched her walk into the kitchen. She did seem happier than I could ever remember. "Hey, Ma. I love you."

She stopped and turned to me. Her face softened, and she clasped her hands across her heart. "I love you too."

Settling back on the sofa, with thoughts of Janae swirling around my head, I picked up my phone and called Del.

When he answered, I told him, "The Hollow Bones isn't cutting anything. Whatever Janae wants to keep and air, she should. This is her story. Not ours."

"I think she will appreciate that," he replied. "Is there anything else you want me to tell her? You do have Austin in October, and I need to make sure you two are cool, since neither one of you has gone public about breaking up. We don't need drama with your second album doing so well." Our second album had avoided the sophomore jinx and debuted at number three on the pop charts and number one on the R&B charts, and we were the darlings of the critics.

"Naw… there won't be drama. Tell her that I'm working on being that full moon."

"Excuse me?" Del sounded skeptical.

I chuckled. "She'll know what that means."

I hung up. Maybe, just maybe, Janae and I would find our way back to each other.

SEPTEMBER 30

As our Austin City Limits performance neared, the gnawing that had been almost nonexistent after being hospitalized started again. The band and I were back to our regular schedule, although Brian and I hadn't spoken about what happened with Janae. Memories of that night still evoked sadness and disappointment at the fact that I couldn't help her and that Brian could. A man who'd been my closest friend besides Cedrick, who seemed to understand and know when to give me space. Maybe that was why he'd kept his distance outside of the studio since I'd been back. Our easy rapport had become stilted. Professionally, we remained harmonious and reconnected without missing a beat. However, knowing that The Hollow Bones would soon be reunited with Janae worried me. Knowing that Brian and Janae would see each other again gnawed at my soul, though I pretended otherwise.

Four days before we were to fly to Austin, I wasn't quite ready to go home after a long day of recording. Playing at the studio kept me from obsessing over Janae or cyberstalking her. She seemed to be thriving as she continued promoting "Fallen Star" on her own and advocating for people living with bipolar. I still ached for her, and all my newfound attention from women didn't faze me. I wanted only one woman, and I had no idea if that was even a possibility anymore. Yet I subconsciously saved myself for her.

I was so focused on playing that I hadn't realized Brian had stayed back, watching me from the board in the control room. He pushed up his sleeves and took the rubber band off his wrist to tie up his locs. A sure sign he wanted to talk.

I placed my guitar on the stand, exited the booth, and plopped on the sofa. He swiveled the chair around to face me, and I maintained eye contact, though I wanted to look away to stop the gnawing.

"Um…" Brian rubbed his hands together. "I don't know where to start, but I don't want to go to Austin with this big-ass elephant blocking us from being the friends and bandmates we were."

"Which one? The fact that you wanted Janae for yourself or that you gave her drugs when you knew how I felt?" I retorted.

Brian's eyes widened. "I guess I deserve that."

"We really don't have to talk. Whether we're friends outside of the band hasn't impacted our music."

"So only Cedrick matters?"

"Cedrick didn't give her the drugs." I cocked my head, daring him to give me another reason why we should be friends again.

"Landon… that night, she was hurting. Maybe you can't understand it, but sometimes life gets you, and you just want it all to go away. And I was scared that the longer she stayed like that, the more likely it would only get worse."

"I do understand it. Without her, the pain hurts so bad some days I would do anything to not feel, but I don't." I didn't want to mention that my last episode had landed me strapped to a bed, or how I'd wanted relief so badly. "I hated that you gave her Xanax, but it's more because you did it behind my back. I trusted you, and trust has never been easy for me."

He closed his eyes briefly and pushed out his breath. "Can we get past this?"

"I don't know. I'm not mad or bitter. Just numb when it comes to you. That night changed everything for me and Janae. She is and was the love of my life."

"She still could be." He leaned forward. "I did crush hard on her. Why wouldn't I? Bruh, most men love Janae Warner. But that woman could only see Landon Hayes. When we were on the streetcar that night, she barely said a word to me. Her mind was elsewhere. But when she saw you on the stairs, playing the guitar and pouting, the energy shifted, and she suddenly started laughing when she hadn't even giggled at anything I'd said on the streetcar."

I chuckled at the memory and how jealous I'd been.

"I knew then that this woman would never give me a shot. Do you know how many men would kill to be with Janae? You're so afraid you can't hold on to her that you let go of the best thing that ever happened to you."

I shook my head. "You don't know shit about our relationship."

"But I know *you*." He pointed at me. "Love is a risk, and no matter how much you want to predict the ending, you can't. Most people don't get together thinking they'll break up, and guess what? Some relationships do end, and some last forever. No one knows what category they'll be in until it happens. All I know is if that woman was with me, I wouldn't be going nowhere. She would have to fuck about twenty men and then ghost me, and I would still be waiting by my phone, hoping she'll call."

My laughter escaped before I could stop it. "Why are you so stupid?"

Brian snatched up his cell phone and pressed it to his ear. "*Ringggg…* Hello? Janae? Baby, is this you? *Hello???*" He grinned, returning his phone to the console. "Shiit… I'm being real. You better get your girl before she remembers she can have any man she wants."

"As long as that man isn't you," I said, half teasing.

"Say less." Brian put his fist out. "I'm sorry, bro. I won't jeopardize our friendship and the band ever again. If it's any consolation, I haven't taken anything since that night out of respect for you and Janae."

I bumped his fist.

"So, we good?"

"We will be," I grudgingly replied. "Now get out of here. I need to focus."

"I'm out." Brian rose and exited the room.

I slunk down on the sofa, pulled my phone out of my pocket, and called her number before I lost my courage. Just when I thought it was going to voicemail, she picked up, sounding breathless.

"Landon, is everything okay?"

I replied more nonchalantly than the nerves ringing my ears would suggest I could. "Yeah. Why wouldn't it be?"

"You haven't texted or called in three months."

"You haven't reached out to me either," I reminded her.

"Why are you calling?" Her voice sounded cold.

"Checking to make sure we're cool with each other when we meet up in Austin," I said feebly.

"I'm a professional. We'll do a sound check and run the same show we did in New York, and then we won't have to see each other again for months." She paused. "If that's all…"

She was slipping from me once more, and I had to say something. "Did Del tell you what I said?"

"He did. But based on how this conversation is going, it doesn't really seem like you're different."

"Janae, I'm trying."

"*This* is you trying? Calling me after three months and then not saying much?"

I gripped my phone. "I've been through a lot since we last spoke."

"So what? I have, too. If you'd bothered to check, you would know."

"Can you lose the attitude?" I grumbled. "I forgot this mean side of you."

420

"You used to love all of me… No, wait, you only loved the parts of me that you could control."

I laughed. "You and I both know I couldn't control a thing about you."

"Which is why you broke up with me?"

"What? Is that the false narrative in your head?"

"Landon, I swear if you sit up here and say that you didn't break up with me, I ain't saying shit to you in Austin."

"I didn't. I told you that we could get married and have a family if you wanted to have a low-key life, but you don't want that type of future, and I respected that."

"And I'm respecting you enough to tell you I'm getting off the phone instead of just hanging up. Bye, Landon."

"Wait—"

"No." The call disconnected.

I threw my cell, and it crashed against the wall. Even in my frustration and anger, I couldn't help the smile that spread across my face.

In four days, I would breathe her again.

CHAPTER FORTY-THREE

janae

AUSTIN
OCTOBER 4

I'D NEVER BEEN SO RELIEVED to end a show. As the final note faded, I bowed and then swept my hands toward The Hollow Bones, introducing the members one by one and saving Landon for last to thunderous applause. He'd clearly been elevated to leader status whether he claimed it or not. He blushed, waved, and guided me off the stage with his hand possessively on my lower back. I had to pretend with the broadest smile that his hand didn't burn where his palm lingered. Being this close to him had me damn near swooning. He'd already had a quiet confidence about his talent, but during sound check and on the stage, he'd come more and more out of his shell. Meanwhile, I'd sounded off key and played it off by saying that I was a little rusty at singing live. But it was the meds, and I hated it.

Being in front of a live audience always infused me with vibrant reds and pinks, and now the colors were subdued pastel blues and greens. Trying to stay hydrated and avoid cotton mouth kept me running to the bathroom every hour, disrupting my rehearsals and focus in the studio. I woke up at the crack of dawn to jot down lyrics as my body geared up for more prescription drugs and less creativity. I was finally working on my fourth album, and I wanted it to be my best. But how could it be my best when I wasn't the best representation of myself, the woman who'd attracted a butterfly one summer morning?

This was my first time performing at an outdoor show with such a large crowd, and in my opinion, I'd sucked. Austin City Limits was a three-day festival that invited more than one hundred acts playing various genres of music, and we'd been honored with high billing. We took photos and signed autographs behind the stage and then were ushered toward the SUV that would take us to 6th Street, a popular touristy area in Austin reminiscent of Bourbon Street without the strip clubs where we would make an appearance at a bar. I clowned and joked with the guys while Landon watched as he'd always done in the past. And, like in the past, knowing he watched me thrilled me.

After being at the bar for an hour, I leaned closer to Cedrick, who stood behind me. I couldn't take much more of hanging around Landon and not being able to touch him. "I'll get the car to bring me home. I'm tired."

He narrowed his eyes. "You okay?"

"Yeah… you know." I glanced in Landon's direction where he played guitar on stage while Charles and Brian hyped him up.

Cedrick's jaw clenched. "I do."

I hugged him. "Y'all smashed, as always. Until next time. Tell the guys I'm sorry I had to run."

His eyes were sad. "Yeah. Take care, Janae." He signaled to security to walk me through the crowds. Once I reached the car through screaming fans, grateful for the tinted windows, I bunched my legs up to my knees and buried my face there.

A few minutes passed, and we hadn't moved. I peeked around me. "Any reason we haven't gone anywhere?"

The driver said, "I was instructed not to leave yet."

"I'm tired. I don't live far from here. You can be back within thirty minutes, forty tops."

"I've been given orders."

"From who? I'm the boss, too."

The driver shook his head without turning around.

I pulled out a phone and thought of catching an Uber. But in Austin, during this festival, I would get mobbed. "Ugh."

I flopped my head back as the door opened. I glanced to my right, and Landon eased in the car. "What are you doing?"

"Just drive." Landon looked at me. "Where?"

"This was your idea."

"Your house?"

I folded my arms. "No. I have someone waiting for me." It was Frankie, who'd traveled with me more for support than for my makeup and hair. But he didn't need to know that.

He frowned. "You moved on already?"

"Haven't you?"

"No. I told you that I would never get over you." His hazel eyes blazed as he instructed the driver, "My hotel."

Instant desire slicked my panties. "That's not a good idea."

Landon smirked. "Because of your man or because you're scared?"

I jerked my head back. "Since when you get so cocky?"

"A lot has changed."

"Tell me."

Landon glanced at the driver and then at me. "We need privacy. My suite has a separate sitting area." He smiled. "It's your fault we can't walk around or sit in a lounge and talk like normal people."

"I'm not going to your hotel. It's too much."

"Is that why your performance was off tonight?"

"Fuck you. I don't need you to tell me I sucked." I bristled. Of course *he* would have noticed.

He sighed, reached into his pocket, and pulled out two crisp hundred-dollar bills. "Carlos, I need the car."

"Got ya." The driver pulled to the side of a not-so-crowded street and smiled at us as he took the money, got out, and walked away.

Landon took off his hat. "Move to the front from within the car, and I'll get out."

I maneuvered myself to the front passenger seat as he jumped in the front, unrecognized.

He started talking while he drove. "I wasn't trying to insult you, and I don't think you were using. You didn't suck at all. The audience loved us, so you did your job. I'm asking what's wrong."

The concern in his tone broke my resolve. "It's the meds. I've been on them consistently since Austin. It makes my mouth dry, and no matter how much water I drink, it affects the quality of my voice. Then my energy is flat. Good thing is that my mood has evened off, and I've been sleeping more."

Landon smiled. "You just cursed me... You sure your mood is balanced?"

I punched him. "Where are we headed?"

"The nearest place we can park and talk." He looked at the cell in my hand. "Need to call him?"

"No," I answered. I wasn't letting Landon off the hook yet. I'd seen The Hollow Bones' IG posts, and he was definitely hanging out more, even at the bar. He hadn't resisted when a couple of women who ran the club asked him to come on stage and play. Landon was all man, and though he may not be over me, that didn't mean he hadn't been sexual with another woman or women.

"What can you do about the meds affecting you?"

I shrugged. "Talk to my psychiatrist. I'm not going to jeopardize my mental health again. Just need to tweak more. I need to be hopeful, because I have to sing."

"You will." He slid the car into a grassy area and opened the roof. "Put your seat back."

We both leaned as far back as the seats could go and stared at the twinkling sky. The smile on his face as he gazed upward brought tears to my eyes. This was what I loved about Landon. All of his layers. All of his sides. All of him.

In the quiet, I started to speak. "I talked with my mother and told her pretty much everything I ever wanted to say. It wasn't pretty, but I said it. She didn't really respond because I doubt she could refute anything. Hard to accept that the person who brought you into the world doesn't love you. Or maybe she does and just doesn't like me. We haven't spoken since I confronted her. At least my brother and I are cool again, and it's been fun getting to know him as an adult and be an aunt to his children." I tapped Landon's thigh. "He's with Frankie now."

He turned his head and looked at me. "Told Cedrick he lost a good one. Just like I did."

"Damn it. Stop kissing my ass." I tapped his nose.

Landon's eyes suddenly watered, though he chuckled. "Guess what?"

I didn't answer, sensing that whatever he'd say next would be monumental.

"Umm… besides my parents…" He took a breath. "Besides my parents, no one knows I was locked up in a psych ward. They used their influence and money to keep my hospitalization a secret."

I gasped and covered my mouth. "Oh, Landon."

"My talk with my parents wasn't a talk at all. I walked inside my house fresh off the plane from Austin, full of heartbreak, and my father was hitting my mother. I smashed my guitar over his back and beat him until my mother intervened. I didn't know if she was protecting me or him. I lost it out. I started believing I had no one. No you, no Cedrick, no Hollow Bones, and no mother. From what I can remember and what I was told, I wanted to die. Not that I planned to kill myself. It just hurt that bad. Supposedly, I lost touch with reality, and I had to be sedated to get in the ambulance. I woke up with restraints because I was on suicide watch." He averted his gaze. "I was diagnosed with autism and anxiety and had a brief psychotic episode."

"Why didn't you call me? I would've been there for you." I picked up his hand, which rested on the console. "Life jacket, remember?"

"I wanted to. God knows how I fought not to call you. I was embarrassed about what happened between my parents and that I couldn't handle it. Then I got locked up like I was an animal." His jaw tightened.

"Now what?"

"I vowed that I wouldn't let myself be defined by another episode or label. I've never been certain if I fit on the autism spectrum, but I do know I'm neurodivergent. I process the world differently, and I'm learning to embrace that just like you're finding your way with bipolar. My mother sold our family home and lives with me now. We've been enjoying each other, and we talk about music for hours. I haven't seen my father since the hospital, and I've made peace with that, too."

I kissed the back of his hand to comfort him and just as quickly wiped it. "Sorry, force of habit."

Landon's hand swept up my nape, and his gaze caressed my face. "I want to kiss you, and I don't think I can stop if I do."

My breath caught in my chest. "You don't have to stop."

The right corner of his lips lifted. "I think I do. I don't cheat."

Confused, I asked breathlessly, "Cheat? You have someone?"

He raised one brow. "No. You do."

"No, I…" I groaned when his smile grew. "I hate you."

"I hate you too," he whispered, and returned his focus to the sky.

We held hands while we were quiet together and stayed like that all night. As the sun began to rise over the horizon, Landon pulled into my driveway. He jumped out of the car and helped me out, then walked me to my front door. We held each other for a long time, reluctant to part, though all we'd done for the past six hours was talk more and hold hands.

I rested my chin against his chest and gazed at his handsome face. "I enjoyed tonight."

He smiled. "Me too."

I wanted him to ask me out again, make plans, or something. Instead, he gave me the sweetest forehead kiss and backed away.

I clasped my hands together over my heart. "When will I see you again?"

Landon promised. "I'll find you."

He said it with such certainty that I had no choice but to believe.

LOS ANGELES
OCTOBER 13

Dr. K ushered me into her office, and I promptly removed my shoes, pulled my legs up, and sat with them crossed in her large, comfy chair. "It's been a while. I'm glad you recognized that I would be here if you ever needed."

"My emotions were so jumbled the last time we spoke," I said. "I have more clarity and I need you to be a part of my treatment. I'm back on meds. My bloodwork is up to date. Overall, I'm well. Still doing good, and alcohol and drug free since June. I'll explain that part later. Became official with Landon and had the best and shortest relationship with him because I wanted more than to have a trauma bond partner. I confronted my mother about the past and I'm completely okay if I never speak to her again. I saw Landon again while we were in Austin last week, and we behaved as friends. Me and my brother are tight. The Hollow Bones broke up briefly because of my decision to use but got back together, and I'm still friends with Frankie and Jeri. Just had dinner with them last night." I clapped my hands.

Dr. K laughed. "That's got to be the fastest catchup I've ever heard."

"Yep. Because what I need to discuss today is important, and I didn't want to get caught up in the details of everything that has happened in the last five months. I wanted to meet with you to make sure my current treatment is the best fit for me."

She tilted her head. "You've been taking your meds as prescribed, and for how long?"

"Started back in May and been consistent since July. I've been sleeping okay. The mood swings are manageable, and I'm not impulsive."

"Sounds good."

I slightly rocked. "I'm too mellow, and I can't get the flow I used to have. Because of my dry mouth, no matter how much water I drink, my voice is not as clear as it used to be. I know I need some sort of treatment. I just don't think this is the right one. I'm working on my fourth album, about to go on tour in a few months. I have to get this right."

"Have you spoken with Dr. Brownson?"

"I will. I wanted to talk to you first. When I was in Austin with Landon, he brought up a good point. He asked how we know for sure I have a chemical imbalance. Maybe my childhood trauma impacted me the way his trauma impacted him, and that's why I am what I am. Then trying to balance the chemicals in my brain with medicines may not make sense. Think about how diagnoses change with the cultural norms. At one point, homosexuality was considered a mental health diagnosis that needed to be treated. Then they had that insane diagnosis that said a slave that tried to run away had a disorder."

"I'm fully aware of drapetomania." Dr. K sighed. "Maybe you were born with an imbalance that some people can handle, and if you didn't have the trauma, you could have handled it. Are you trying to say you don't have bipolar?"

"All I'm saying is that, yes, I meet the criteria for bipolar disorder, and I take treatment seriously. But that's not all I am. I refuse to deny my reality or dismiss the struggles of others by pretending it doesn't exist. That would be reckless and unfair. I've spoken at high schools about my journey with mental health and substance abuse, and I've had students tell me my story gave them hope. That matters.

But I am not just a diagnosis. I am not just a survivor. I am not just the girl with bipolar. I am Janae Warner. A woman. An artist. A person with dreams, love, and ambition beyond a label. That's what I need people to see. Do you understand?"

She nodded with a smile.

"And I want to keep at it until I find the right mix of treatment for me and live the life I want to have."

"Janae, you surprise me every time."

"Well, you're really going to be surprised when I tell you that I plan to get back out there and date."

She asked, with an arched brow, "Are you over Landon?"

"I'll never get over him. He showed me love, respect, and true acceptance, and the sex was always hot. We had the most wonderful time looking at the stars and catching up in Austin. He's been through a lot with his family and his mental health, and yet he seemed happier than I ever recall. But I haven't heard from him since a week ago, so I need to move on." I'd resigned myself to the fact that I couldn't keep my life on hold for him.

"Is there someone else you're interested in?"

I shook my head. "Not yet. I'm just open."

"Then why not reach back out to Landon?"

"I didn't really go into details about our breakup. Simply put, Landon needed healing as much as I did, but he wasn't ready to face it the way I was.

Until he could truly live in his own skin, free and unburdened, we wouldn't make it in the long run. He was recently diagnosed as being on the spectrum and with anxiety, and he is determined to manage it without therapy or medication. That is his choice, but I cannot keep moving forward while he stays where he is. We cannot keep clinging to each other's pain and calling it love."

Dr. K clasped her hands together. "Are you sure you are not overanalyzing? That has always been one of your biggest hurdles. Either acting on impulse and making reckless decisions or letting doubt sabotage something before you give it a real chance. That was what I was trying to caution you about the last time we spoke. Love, especially new love, can feel intoxicating, euphoric. But without balance, without a real foundation, the crash can be devastating. I wanted you to be mindful of the highs and lows, not to strip you of love, but to help you find one that lasts. If I came across as judgmental, I regret that. My goal has always been to provide you with a space where you can be honest without fear."

I exhaled slowly, pushing down the emotions creeping up my throat. "I wouldn't be here if I didn't trust you. Maybe I did feel judged at the time, but I know you have always had my back. I need people around me who will tell me the truth, even when it is hard to hear."

Dr. K tossed her clipboard onto the desk beside her. "Then hear me now. I saw the reality show. You two weren't just together. You were in love. And from what I could see, he genuinely cared about you. Yes, there was trauma bonding, and that is undeniable. It may have drawn you to each other. But love is not just about how it starts. It is about whether it can grow.

"How you choose to heal is yours to decide, just as how he chooses to cope is his. Maybe acknowledging his diagnosis is enough for him. Maybe he needs more but is not ready to admit it. That is his journey. The real question is whether you are shutting the door out of fear of repeating past mistakes or because you truly believe there is no future with him.

"Because if there is even a small chance, it is worth exploring before you walk away for good."

I laughed. "I can't believe you watched my show. You don't seem the type to watch reality TV."

"Oh, I watch them all. I even watch the one where the people are working on a yacht. My guilty pleasure." Dr. K chuckled.

"And I hear you about Landon. Maybe I will, or maybe I won't reach out. My priority now is getting the right treatment."

She smiled. "Understood, and I'll leave the subject of you and Landon alone for the time being."

"Thank you. I can obsess about him during our next session."

Dr. K said warmly, "Welcome back, Janae."

NEW YORK
NOVEMBER 8

Stretching my arms and legs, I bounced around the dressing room at Madison Square Garden, preparing to open a special Grammy night celebrating rhythm and blues. I already had my dress and makeup complete. Frankie and Jeri had already been escorted to their seats so they could see the show as guests of mine.

I moved about the small room, trying to keep my nerves in check. I'd been prescribed anxiety meds to use on an as-needed basis, and I'd been switched to a natural supplement by a pharmacist and herbalist to stabilize my moods. I was followed closely by my mental health team to make sure my current treatment fit me. My vocals were strong again. My energy was back. I was ready to storm the stage.

Tonight, I wore a purple jacket that cinched at my waist and heels. One button held it together, and if Landon were there, he would say that I'd better make sure it didn't pop so no one else would see what was his. Or he would pop it open and press his head against my breasts because I was his comfort. His life jacket.

"God, I miss that man." I traced the intricate tattoo of the moon right above my heart, visible through the top of my jacket. I'd gotten the ink after he sent me the recording of his song to honor him, to honor our love whether we found each other again or not.

My less-than-stellar performance and our brief time in Austin had forced me to rethink the long road ahead, especially if I couldn't find the right mix of treatment so I could do what I loved. Landon and I could have this easy life even with our complicated, beautiful minds.

I planned to call him and catch up, since I would be in New York for a few days. I could check on him and his mother. I would call him after the show, and maybe we could catch a late-night train so fans wouldn't harass us. Maybe we could talk again about being together. Or maybe we'd just be quiet.

I stared at my reflection. My eyes were bright, luminous, and full of life. A bouquet mixed in with other flowers from fans and other well-wishers caught my eye because of the card with handwriting I recognized. I picked it up.

I couldn't be prouder of you. Much success in your future.

Adam.

Now I believed he'd forgiven me for everything. Adam had finally sent the acknowledgment I'd wanted all along, but it only reminded me it was validation I no longer needed.

A knock on my door startled me.

"It's time," the voice on the other side called.

Butterflies swarmed in my stomach as I walked out and followed the stage manager to my mark. One of her assistants passed me a mic. I wouldn't be introduced. I would just stroll on stage and start performing a melody of hits, then transition into "Fallen Star."

My nervousness disappeared. I was doing exactly what I was meant to do. I hit the stage with bravado, displaying my lyrical skills first. Madison Square Garden rocked with me and rapped along to "Premier," and then I slowed it down with "A Lonely Woman." The crowd grew even louder.

As I hit the last note, the lights went out on me, and the spotlight shone on a lone guitarist near the back of the arena. His hat was pulled down low and he focused on his instrument. The crowd roared while my heart threatened to explode. Once he hit the first note and met my gaze, I finally released the breath I'd unknowingly held. I couldn't tear my eyes from him as he slowly made his way to me.

Every note haunted the Garden as he walked through the aisle with his trademark hat, his eyes trained on me. Everyone was on their feet, enthralled by the song I'd first heard when he played it for me on the boat.

Tears flowed down my face as I saw the certainty in his eyes and in his body language. He walked tall and certain. Fearless. To everyone else, he was a musician passing through the audience like so many before him. I knew differently. This was the ultimate sacrifice for him. This was Landon showing me he didn't want to live in fear. This was him being the full moon. This was him showing the world his instrument was just as expressive as any voice. This was him showing me he wanted to be with me. This was him showing me that he would not be afraid to soar as high with me as that elusive butterfly.

By the time he'd walked up the stairs to join me on stage, most of the audience had wet cheeks that matched mine. When he removed a tropical hibiscus from his jacket pocket, tucked it in my hair, and kissed my lips softly, I wanted to swoon. He whispered in my ear, "My forever life jacket."

"Always," I breathed.

He grinned wide and spoke into my mic. "Ladies and gentlemen, I'm Landon Hayes, and this is the phenomenally talented Janae Warner."

I wrapped my arms around his neck, holding on as if I could stop time, as if I could keep the tears at bay. His touch was light but reverent as he traced his finger over my new tattoo just above my chest, right beside my coin.

Wonder flickered across his face, his hazel eyes glowing under the stage lights. Then, with a knowing smirk, he stepped back, lifted his guitar, and struck the first electrifying chords of Prince's *"Baby I'm a Star."*

I laughed as the beat kicked in, feeling the energy surge through me. The audience clapped along, their voices rising in unison as I joined in, singing. Landon grinned, feeding off the crowd's excitement, before he signaled to me to segue into our song, "Fallen Star."

He and I had left our mark on music history that night in Madison Square Garden.

EPILOGUE

landon

NEW ORLEANS
EIGHT MONTHS LATER

BREATHE. IN. OUT. PAY ATTENTION *to the rise and fall of your chest. Remember, anxiety is only the fear of the worst thing happening.*

What is the worst thing that could happen?

I let out a short laugh. *If she rejects me, I'll be humiliated in front of everyone. But even then, I'm not going anywhere. And neither is she.*

I paced back and forth in our penthouse suite in New Orleans.

Janae was slated to open the Essence Music Festival, and The Hollow Bones were her special guests. We had recorded another hit together, the song that she and Cedrick started in Del's studio. Though not as massive as "Fallen Star," "Weightless" had hit number one after a month on the charts. Her fourth album had also gone to the top upon release.

She'd already left for makeup and wardrobe at the Superdome. I would leave the suite and join the guys in an hour. In the meantime, I had to get through this recording.

I dropped down on the sofa and practiced breathing as my therapist had taught me last year. After seeing the changes in my mother and Janae because of therapy, I'd decided to give it a try. I didn't want medicine, but I did want to see if there were alternative treatments to help with my paralyzing anxiety.

I hadn't wanted to tell Janae I'd started therapy when we saw each other in Austin. I hadn't been in it long enough to determine if it made sense for me to continue. But I liked my counselor, a Black man who was a social worker, a few years older than me. We'd seemed to gel from the beginning, and I could open up to him about anything. We worked closely together and tirelessly on managing my social anxiety when I told him I wanted to perform at the MSG show.

He'd told me to focus on Janae, and the rest would come. He'd been right. That night had become the start of my career as a solo artist, though I remained with The Hollow Bones. That night had also been the start of us as an unbreakable couple, determined to do what we needed to do to stay together. We'd decided Austin was the best place for us to live together, though we kept our homes in Harlem and L.A. My mother lived in my brownstone and had started creating a life where she performed more and re-established relationships with her family and old friends.

Like Janae's mother, my father kept his distance. I liked Rashad and enjoyed it when he and his children made the drive to visit us. We were all becoming a family. He and Frankie were still going strong, and she had intentions to move to Houston in the near future.

I'd even become a guest lecturer at Juilliard during the spring semester, a role I loved immensely. I taught young, impressionable students about piano and guitar. Whatever lingering issues I had with my parents, I still thanked them for pushing me as they had, because I wouldn't have gone as far as I had if they hadn't. And I wouldn't have met the love of my life.

Although I missed my brothers from The Hollow Bones whenever Janae and I were in Austin, we'd all accepted that the only constant in life was change, and if we were going to be as strong as we had always been, then we had to adapt. The band had committed to being alcohol and drug free to honor Janae and me. They'd also changed in other ways. Santiago was in a serious relationship, and Brian seemed ready to settle, too. Cedrick and Charles were self-affirmed bachelors, at least for the time being.

I exhaled, feeling the weight of how much had shifted in just a year.

A rustling sound pulled me from my thoughts. The producer of Janae's hit reality show adjusted the camera, checking the lighting and audio levels. He glanced up and asked, "Are you ready?"

I nodded and held my guitar as I spoke into the camera. "This is my confession."

janae

WE WERE ON FIRE AS we wrapped up opening night of the three-day Essence Festival. I loved that we were back in New Orleans and headlining a festival I'd admired and had performed at when I was MILA, which now seemed like a lifetime ago.

Right before our last song, "Fallen Star," the screen dropped down to show montages of each of us as children, teens, and adults. The crowd cheered for each of the guys of The Hollow Bones like they would any heartthrob group, whose sophomore album had been a popular and critical darling. My reality show had not only given the world a peek into my life on the road, it had also let fans get to know a little bit about all of them.

I'd learned that I couldn't do back-to-back performances, and touring didn't appear to be an option for me to maintain stability. An occasional performance or appearance seemed to fit the balanced life I sought. My regimen was an ever-shifting beast, but I could honestly say I had more good days than bad. Even on my bad days, my moods usually didn't last long because I fought the darkness, and Landon helped me be quiet. And when he became overwhelmed, I knew how to coax him back into relaxation. We truly were each other's life jackets.

I was dancing and yelling as the montage continued, and I howled the loudest when the screen displayed Landon at different stages of his life, ending at the photo that had started it all for us. The picture I'd snapped of him staring at me, in love.

A ripple ran across the screen, like a film strip caught in a projector. Then Landon appeared on the screen, holding his guitar, his hat cocked backward, allowing some of his hair to show. The crowd went wild as he strummed slightly before he laughed.

"Let me stop before I get into my music. This is my confession. I know most of you have seen Janae's reality show, and how she never hid how she felt for me. We were here in this very city as our friendship blossomed into love."

The crowd oohed and aahed.

I searched for Landon, who was no longer on stage, and then my heart thumped hard against my chest. *He wouldn't, would he?*

The guys from The Hollow Bones wouldn't make eye contact from their usual positions on the stage. They were either waving at the audience or looking at the screen. My mind raced with possibilities, and my hands started to tremble. I'd figured sooner or later we would discuss marriage. Or maybe this was him just telling the world what he'd been through.

Don't get ahead of yourself. This is not him. He wouldn't propose in front of all these people. He would do it quietly and privately in our home in Austin. Just the two of us. My breathing became a little easier.

"I struggled at first with how I felt about her. Not that I wasn't obsessed from the beginning, but I was scared that I couldn't hold on to this woman who loved to vex my soul." He strummed again, almost absent-mindedly. "I watched her be honest with you and with herself, and she inspired me to look in the mirror and face who I really was and who I wanted to be. And I am a better man for me and my brothers of The Hollow Bones… and for the woman I want to share the rest of my life with."

Landon's hazel eyes glistened as I stared at the big screen along with the tens of thousands of people in the audience.

"This is my confession. I never thought I would ever marry and have a family because I didn't believe any woman could love every part of me. My strengths, my struggles, my phases." His voice was steady, but the emotion in his eyes told a different story. My eyes moved to the tattoo on his wrist, identical to the one on my chest, as he continued. "But then I met a woman who saw me. A woman who embraced every side of me as deeply as I loved every side of her. A woman I want to marry. A woman I want to have all my babies with one day."

The audience screamed as Landon appeared on stage and stepped closer, moving with certainty, his focus locked on me. "I figured since our relationship started in the public eye, we would let them in one last time as I ask you, Janae Camille Warner, to be my forever life jacket and become my wife."

My heart swelled, my jaw ached from the unstoppable smile spreading across my face. I could float like the balloons we planned to release at the end of the show.

"Yes!" I shouted, throwing my arms up in victory.

Landon barely had time to react before I launched myself at him, wrapping my arms around his neck as he caught me. His lips crashed against mine, a kiss full of love, full of certainty, full of everything we had fought for. The world around us melted away. The roaring crowd, the flashing lights, the thousands of eyes on us. None of it mattered.

The Hollow Bones started playing "Fallen Star," and Cedrick led the audience in singing along. Landon and I simply held each other, swaying, breathing each other in, lost in the moment we had unknowingly been building toward all along.

We had come so far from that night at the gala. Me, standing outside, wondering if I belonged. Him, watching me, afraid that he never would.

But we had chosen each other. Over our fears. Over our pasts. Over the doubts that once tried to define us.

And I was forever grateful that we had fought through the most complicated parts of ourselves to create a love this beautiful.

This novel explores the depths of love, struggle, and the ongoing process of healing. While it delves into themes of trauma, addiction, and mental health, it is a work of fiction and not a substitute for professional guidance. Every journey is personal, and seeking support from trusted professionals, loved ones, and community resources can make all the difference.

Above all, this story is a testament to the power of connection. No one has to face their battles alone. If you or someone you know is struggling, help is available.

You are seen, you are valued, and your voice matters.

ACKNOWLEDGEMENTS

This beautiful story of irresistible love, unwavering resilience, redemption, and acceptance of all we are through the lens of people grappling with life challenges will forever hold a special place in my heart. I want to thank all of the helping professionals, the Dr. Ks of the world, who understand that mental health is every day and a part of us all. A special shout out to my editor, Lauren, who helped make this story the best it could be. To Keisha and the Honey Blossom Press Team, my publisher who loves to push my creative and writing boundaries, even when I'm stubbornly resistant. Thank you for inspiring me and sharing ideas and thoughts about these amazing characters to ensure their journey remained real and raw. A special appreciation to my betas, street team members, and sensitivity readers who gave honest and critical opinions to ensure readers would feel fairly represented and not triggered in harmful ways. To my amazingly talented family and friends who have supported me in any endeavor since DAY ONE. To the Janaes and Landons of the world, we see you and love you! Lastly, I want to thank my daughter, who has always created her own path and proven time and time again her inner warrior and her belief in the magic of the butterfly.

RESOURCES

The mental health resources listed in this book are provided for informational purposes only. The inclusion of any organization, website, or service does not constitute an endorsement, nor does it guarantee the quality or effectiveness of the services provided. Mental health care is highly personal, and readers should research and verify the credentials of any provider or organization before seeking support. If you are in immediate crisis, please reach out to a trusted professional or emergency services in your area.

United States-Based Resources

Psychology Today – *www.psychologytoday.com*
A nationwide directory of psychologists, therapists, and mental health specialists. The website also features articles on mental health, relationships, and self-improvement.

National Alliance on Mental Illness (NAMI) – *www.nami.org*
The largest grassroots mental health organization dedicated to education, advocacy, and support for individuals and families affected by mental illness.

Telehealth & Online Therapy Services
BetterHelp – *www.betterhelp.com*
Grow Therapy – *www.growtherapy.com*

These platforms offer virtual therapy and medication management from licensed professionals. Always verify the credentials of assigned therapists or providers before engaging in services.

Insurance & Local Services
If you have **Medicaid, Medicare, or private insurance**, you can request a list of covered mental health providers through your plan's website or customer service line.
Your **state or local Department of Health** can provide information on low-cost or no-cost mental health services for those without insurance.

Mental Health & Crisis Support Apps

Before using any mental health app, check user reviews, privacy policies, and verify that assigned providers are licensed professionals.

988 Suicide & Crisis Lifeline – *www.988lifeline.org*
A nationwide, 24/7 crisis line offering immediate support for individuals experiencing suicidal thoughts, emotional distress, or crisis situations.

Emergency & Law Enforcement Communication

If you or a loved one is experiencing a mental health crisis and need immediate assistance, call **911**.

Clearly state that it is a **mental health-related emergency** to request crisis-trained responders.

International Mental Health & Crisis Resources

United Kingdom
Mind UK – *www.mind.org.uk* – Provides mental health support, information, and advocacy.
Samaritans UK – *www.samaritans.org* – Free 24/7 support for anyone in emotional distress, call **116 123**.

Canada
Crisis Services Canada – *www.crisisservicescanada.ca* – Call or text **988** for mental health support and suicide prevention.
Government of Canada Mental Health Services – https://www.canada.ca/en/public-health/services/mental-health-services/mental-health-get-help – A directory of mental health services, crisis lines, and regional resources across Canada.

Australia
Lifeline Australia – *www.lifeline.org.au* – 24/7 crisis support, call **13 11 14**.
Beyond Blue – *www.beyondblue.org.au* – Mental health information and support.

New Zealand

Mental Health Foundation NZ – *www.mentalhealth.org.nz* – Provides resources and support services.

Lifeline NZ – *www.lifeline.org.nz* – Call **0800 543 354** for crisis support.

Europe (General)

Mental Health Europe (MHE) – *www.mhe-sme.org* – Advocacy and support across European countries.

International Suicide Prevention Helplines –www.suicidestop.com/call_a_hotline.html – A global directory of crisis helplines by country.

Asia

Samaritans of Singapore (SOS) – *www.sos.org.sg* – Call **1767** for emotional support.

iCall India – *www.icallhelpline.org* – Free counseling via phone and email.

Africa

South African Depression and Anxiety Group (SADAG) – *www.sadag.org* – Mental health resources and crisis helplines.

Nigeria Suicide Prevention Initiative – Call **0800 700 7000** for mental health support.

Latin America & the Caribbean

Argentina – Fundación INECO – *www.fundacionineco.org* – Provides mental health support.

Mexico – SAPTEL – *www.saptel.org.mx* – 24/7 helpline at **800 472 7835**.

Caribbean – Lifeline Jamaica – Call **888-991-4146** for mental health support.

Final Note

If you or someone you know is struggling with mental health challenges, please reach out. There are professionals, organizations, and resources ready to help. You are not alone.

DISCUSSION QUESTIONS

1. The importance of image is a recurring theme throughout the story. How do you think the pressure to uphold a certain image influenced the characters' reluctance to seek help?

2. Why do you think Landon struggled with being labeled or diagnosed as being on the autism spectrum?

3. At what point do you believe Janae fully embraced her bipolar diagnosis, and what led to that acceptance?

4. Janae has engaged in self-harm and attempted suicide in the past. How does the novel explore the emotional weight of these experiences? Do you think the story accurately portrays how overwhelming emotions can lead to these behaviors?

5. In Austin, Landon tells Janae that maybe her symptoms aren't due to bipolar disorder but rather a result of trauma. Do you agree or disagree with his perspective? Why?

6. In today's climate, words once commonly used can now be considered harmful. Janae often refers to herself as "crazy." How do you feel about the use of this term in relation to mental health? Does context affect its impact?

7. Was Janae a likable character? How did her struggles shape your perception of her, particularly in moments when she hurt others?

8. Do you think Janae and Landon could have a lasting, healthy relationship if they didn't acknowledge or treat their mental health conditions?

9. Do you believe Dr. K was a good psychologist for Janae, or did her approach feel judgmental at times?

10. Can a relationship built on shared trauma become a healthy one? Why or why not?

11. Another major theme in the story is the power of friendship. Do you think Landon or Janae were good friends to others? Why or why not?

12. Do you understand why Janae initially stopped seeing Dr. K? Do you think it was an impulsive decision, or was it part of her healing process?

13. Throughout the story, Landon worries that Janae might come between him and The Hollow Bones. Do you believe this was true? Why or why not?

14. Do you agree with Brian's decision to give Janae Xanax the night of the L.A. concert? How do you feel about the use of prescription medication versus other substances for coping?

15. Landon encourages Janae to keep wearing her sobriety necklace even after she relapsed. Do you believe that once someone has struggled with addiction, they are always considered in recovery? Why or why not?

16. Both Janae's mother and Landon's father express love for their children but struggle to show it. Why do you think they have difficulty expressing love in a healthy way?

17. Should Janae or Landon have fought harder to repair their relationships with their parents? Does maintaining boundaries with toxic family members mean leaving them behind entirely?

18. Analise Hayes remained in a tumultuous relationship for years despite her talent and ambition. What do you believe finally gave her the strength to leave?

19. Janae and Landon are drawn to symbols of change and transformation (butterflies and moon phases). How do these symbols reflect their journeys? Do you think their love helped them embrace their growth, or would they have eventually found their way without each other?

20. Why do you think Landon finally decided to seek help? Was there a turning point for him?

21. Who do you think ended the relationship in Austin? Janae or Landon? What were the key factors leading up to it?

22. Who was your favorite character, and why?

23. Who was your least favorite character? Do you think this character is redeemable?

24. Despite growing awareness, mental health issues still carry stigma. Why do you think that is, and how does this novel address those challenges?

Made in United States
North Haven, CT
12 July 2025

70610247R00266